Praise for Lucy Foley's

THE INVITATION

"Lucy Foley crafts a subtle, dramatic story of guilt, desire, and long-held secrets....Lushly described settings and Foley's keen but compassionate eye for her characters combine to make *The Invitation* a beautiful, bittersweet journey of loss and redemption."   —Katie Noah Gibson, *Shelf Awareness*

"*The Invitation* is a riveting, dazzling romance, set in the most beautiful places on earth. I wanted to go wherever Lucy Foley took me."

—Anton DiSclafani, author of *The Yonahlossee Riding Camp for Girls* and *The After Party*

"Pop this tale of love, secrets, and obsession right into your beach bag."   —*People*

"Richly atmospheric and emotionally resonant, *The Invitation* is a compelling love story that takes us far beyond the alluring Italian coast and the film festival at Cannes to a darker place, where the wounds of war are still fresh, and secrets hide just below the water's surface. Lucy Foley's lavish depictions both immerse and transport, inviting us to cruise along with this glamorous and enigmatic cast of unforgettable characters. A great read."

—Brunonia Barry, author of *The Lace Reader*

"The aura of Cinecittà glamour and the atmosphere-soaked voyage up Italy's Mediterranean coast make the trip worthwhile."

—Mary Ellen Quinn, *Booklist*

"A beautifully complex and vivid story, full of repressed longing and secrets. An absolutely enchanting tale."

—Lucinda Riley, author of *The Orchid House*

"Certain that they'll never meet again, journalist Hal and socialite Stella indulge in an illicit rendezvous. But when they're reunited on a yacht in Cannes a year later, temptation is everywhere."

—*Cosmopolitan*

"Fans of *The Villa* by Nora Roberts will enjoy the mystery, nostalgia, and atmosphere of Foley's novel set on a yacht gliding across the Mediterranean....A perfect summer read."

—Kathe Robin, *RT Book Reviews*

"Can I find words eloquent enough to describe this novel? Lucy Foley's *The Invitation* is so exquisite in its writing that it may take a place among the classics—but it was the combination of the glittering, glamorous setting and the magnetic characters that mesmerized me. This book is luminous."

—Elin Hilderbrand, author of *The Identicals*

"An utterly seductive story depicting forbidden love and loss in 1950s Italy. The perfect beach read this summer."

—Louise O'Neill, author of *Asking for It*

"Foley weaves a very satisfying love story, and readers will be especially taken by the luxurious Mediterranean setting."

—*Publishers Weekly*

"In 1950s Italy, a young journalist publicizing a film embarks on an affair with a rich man's wife. But while the privileged world of the Italian Riviera oozes glamour, it carries the scars of wars in Europe. Lush, romantic, and cleverly crafted—a brainy beach read to relish." —Deirdre O'Brien, *Daily Mirror* (UK)

"Glamorous and romantic and bittersweet all at once, this is a fabulous story with such wonderful, intelligent prose."

—Beatriz Williams, author of *A Hundred Summers*

THE
INVITATION

A Novel

Lucy Foley

Back Bay Books
Little, Brown and Company
New York   Boston   London

To my darling mother, Sue, and father,
Patrick: chief friend-maker and historian!

Also by Lucy Foley

The Book of Lost and Found

Back Bay Books
Little, Brown and Company
Hachette Book Group
1290 Avenue of the Americas, New York NY 10104
littlebrown.com

First published in the United States in hardcover by Little, Brown and Company, August 2016
Originally published in Great Britain by HarperCollins UK, July 2016
First Back Bay paperback edition, August 2017

Back Bay Books is an imprint of Little, Brown and Company, a division of Hachette Book Group, Inc. The Back Bay name and logo are trademarks of Hachette Book Group, Inc.

The publisher is not responsible for websites (or their content) that are not owned by the publisher.

The Hachette Speakers Bureau provides a wide range of authors for speaking events. To find out more, go to hachettespeakersbureau.com or call (866) 376-6591.

ISBN 978-0-316-27347-3 (hardcover) / 978-0-316-27290-2 (paperback)
LCCN 2016930096

Printing 5, 2022

LSC-C

Printed in the United States of America

THE
INVITATION

PROLOGUE

Essaouira, Morocco, 1955

Essaouira feels like the end of the world. It takes several hours in a bus or car from Marrakech, along a bone-jarring route that is more track than road. Once here the sweep of the Atlantic confronts you, buffeted by the omnipresent wind. Forbidding and grey as an old schoolmistress.

The town itself is governed by this sea: salt-sprayed and wind-blown, a straggling stretch of white and blue. From the roof terrace of my building you can see the wide boulevards that surround the souks. Then the smaller, serpentine passages within them, hedged on either side by riotous piles of wares. But the market here is a much less fractious place than that of Marrakech, where the stall-holders wheedle and heckle. Perhaps it is that the pace of life is slower than it is there – than it is, really, in any other place I have visited in my life. There are a few other Western expats here, like me. Most are exiles in some respect, though the causes are perhaps too diverse for generalization: McCarthyism, bankruptcy, broken marriages. The long shadow of the bomb.

On the other side of my terrace, the view is straight out across the Atlantic. I like to be up to watch the blue-hulled fishing boats setting out in the young hours and then, at dusk, heading home laden with the day's catch. It lends a rhythm to the day. I know the moods of the sea now almost as well as those fishermen, and there are many. I like to watch the weather travelling in from the outer reaches: the approach of the occasional storm.

Sometimes I find myself panicking, because I realize that I cannot remember her face. I feel that she is slipping from me. I have to wilfully summon her back, through those fragments of her that are most vivid. The scent of her skin warmed by the sun, a smell like ripened wheat. I remember the way her eyes looked when she told me of everything she had lost.

On the rare days of calm I used to imagine her emerging from the depths like Venus, carried towards me on the sea foam. Or not carried perhaps, that was not her way. Striding out of it, then, shaking seawater from her sleek head. But, of course, it is the wrong sea. Thank God for that. If I had spent these years gazing out upon that other sea, I think I would have gone mad.

I wonder sometimes if I *have* gone a little mad. The *majoun*, of which I have become partial, has no doubt not helped. Sometimes when I have taken it I experience hallucinations, in which I am absolutely convinced that the thing I am seeing is real. Sometimes these occur days, even a week, after my last fix of the stuff. At least it doesn't affect the writing. Perhaps it helps.

That spring was the start of everything, for me. Before then, I might have been half-asleep, drifting through life. Before then I had not known the true capacity of the human heart.

I remember it all with such peculiar clarity.

Though I know that now is the time to do this, or never at all, I cannot deny my dread of returning to that spring. Because what happened was my fault, you see.

PART ONE

1

Rome, November 1951

Now the city is at its loveliest. The crowds of summer and autumn have gone, the air has a new freshness, the light has that pale-gold quality unique to this time of year. There have been several weeks of this weather now, without a drop of rain.

When the city is like this, Hal does not mind being poor. To live in such a place is in itself a form of richness. He is self-sufficient. He has a job, he has no dependants, he has somewhere to sleep at night. A small bedsit in downmarket Trastevere, fine, but it is enough to call home. So different from the life he would have had in England that he might be living on another planet. This suits him perfectly.

Hal has been here for five years now. His father, he knows, thinks that he is treading water. If his son is going to do something as trifling as journalism he should at least have continued working for the English broadsheet. And here he is, a freelancer, writing whimsical pieces for a local paper. His mother is more supportive. Rome, after all, is the city of her birth. He learned his Italian from her. Half the stories she read to him as a child were in her mother tongue; the most beautiful language in the world. Now he uses it so regularly that it is beginning to feel like his first language; the English left behind, a part of his old life.

When he arrives at the place Fede is already waiting for him, drinking what appears to be his second espresso. He grins. 'Hal! I like this place. I can see why you come here. So many beautiful women.' He nods to the group in the corner. None of them can be much older than eighteen, but they are dressed in mimicry of the movie stars they no doubt admire: rouged cheeks, cinched waists. One draws on a cigarette self-consciously, blowing a thin plume of smoke over her shoulder in what must be a gesture borrowed from a picture. Her friend carefully outlines her mouth with red lipstick. They are the inheritors of the economic miracle, Hal thinks, modelling themselves on the film stars and fashion models in the pages of the new glossy magazines. They might be a different species altogether from the black-clad matrons glimpsed in Trastevere hanging out their washing, heading to church, looking exactly as they might have done in centuries past. This is Rome, is Italy, all over: the modern and the timeless coexisting in uneasy, spectacular conjunction.

'They're not women,' he says to Fede, watching as the trio explodes into sudden laughter. 'They're girls. They're schoolgirls playing truant.'

'That's how I like them.' Fede pinches the air between thumb and forefinger. 'Tender as the finest *vitello*. Look, she's making eyes at you.'

Hal glances back. Fede is right – one of them is looking

at him. Even this look of hers is modern in its boldness. She
is beautiful, in the way that green, unblemished things are.
Hal can at least see that, but he can't *feel* it. It is like this
with all beauty for him now. He looks away. 'You're vile,' he
says to Fede, teasing. 'I don't know why I bother with you.'

Fede raises an eyebrow. 'Because we help each other out.
That's why.'

Hal's espresso comes and he knocks it back. 'Well. Do you
have anything for me?'

Fede throws up his hands. 'Nothing at the moment, my
friend. It's slow at this time of year.'

The biggest and most interesting of Hal's interviews tend
to come through Fede, who works in the city's nascent insti-
tute for culture.

'Oh.' Hal finds it hard to disguise his disappointment.
There are slim pickings on the interview front all round. His
editor at *The Tiber* has made it quite clear that another
whimsical 'expat in the city' piece won't cut it – and he can't
afford to lose this job.

'*But . . .*' Fede says, thoughtfully, 'there is a party.'

'A party?'

'Yes. A contessa is throwing one for her rich friends.
Trying to attract investment for a film, I heard. I have an
invitation, but cannot go. It is next month – I must be in
Puglia by then, for Christmas.' He glances at Hal, sidewise.
'Unless you are returning to your family, too?' One evening,
when he'd had too much to drink, Hal made the mistake
of telling him about Suze, about the engagement. Ever since,
Fede has been unremittingly curious about Hal's former life
in England.

'No,' Hal says. 'I'll be staying here.' He knows his mother,
in particular, will be disappointed. But he doesn't want to

face her worry for him, his father's pointed questions about when he is going to make something of himself.

'OK then. Well, I thought you could go instead of me.'

It could be interesting, Hal thinks. 'How would I get in?'

'Well,' Fede says, patiently, 'you could pretend to be me. I think we do not look all that different.'

Hal chooses not to point out the obvious. Fede is half a foot shorter, with a broken nose and brown eyes where Hal's are blue. The only similarity is their dark hair.

Now Fede is expounding his idea. 'And think of all those rich women, looking for a little excitement.' He winks. 'Trust me, *amico*, it's the best Christmas present I could give you.'

He fishes a card from his bag. Hal takes it, turns it over in his hand, studies the embossed gold lettering. And he thinks: Why not? What, after all, does he have to lose?

December

He walks all the way from his apartment. He likes walking: there is always something new to see in this city. It seems to shift and grow, revealing glimpses of other lives, other times. There are layers of history here, times at which the barrier between the present and past appears tissue-thin. He might rip at it and reveal another age entirely: Roman, Medieval, Renaissance. This reminder that the present and his place in it are just as transient has a strong appeal. Beside so much history, one's own past becomes rather insignificant.

Of course, there is a more recent time that must be banished from conversation and thought. The war meant humiliation, tragedy. It meant hardship and poverty too. People want prosperity now, they want nice clothes, food on the table, *things.* It is the same in England. There was the jubilation over the victory, the hailing of the returned heroes. And then there was the great forgetting.

The address is a little way beyond the Roman Forum, and Hal skirts the edge of it. The stones at this time are in silhouette, backlit by the lights of the city. At this time they appear older yet: as though placed by the very first men.

The place turns out to be a red-brick medieval tower, soaring several storeys above the surrounding rooftops. He has seen it before and wondered about it. He had guessed an embassy, a department of state affairs, the temple of some strange sect, even. Never had he imagined that it might be a private residence.

Torches have been lit in brackets about the entrance, and Hal can see several gleaming motor cars circling like carp, disclosing guests in their evening finery. There are bow ties and tails, full-length gowns. He is not prepared for this. His suit is well-made but old and worn with use, faded at the elbows of the jacket and frayed at the pockets of the trousers. He has lost weight, too, since he last wore it, thanks to his poor diet of coffee and the occasional sandwich. He can't afford to eat properly. When he first wore it he had been much broader about the chest and shoulders. Now he feels almost like a boy borrowing his father's clothes.

All day it has been threatening rain, but there have been several grey days like this without a drop, so he hasn't bothered with an umbrella or raincoat. But only twenty yards or so from the entrance the heavens finally open, like a bad joke. There is no warning, only the sudden chaos of the downpour, rain smoking across the pavement towards him. Instantly his hair, shirt and suit are drenched. If he appeared bedraggled before he must seem now like something that has crawled its way out of the Tiber. He swears. A woman, emerging from one of the sleek cars, darts an alarmed glance in his direction and hurries in through the doorway.

At the entrance he feels the doorman's gaze irradiate his person, find him wanting. '*Cognome, per favore?*'

'Fiori.'

The man looks at his list, frowns. '*E nome?*'

'Federico.'

He knows even before the man looks back up at him that it has not worked. 'You are not he,' the doorman says, with evident pleasure. 'I know that man. He works for the Ministero. It is my job to remember faces. You are not he.'

Hal hesitates, wondering if there is any use in arguing with the man. After all, if he is confident that he knows Federico by sight . . . But it is worth a try. '*Ma, ho un invito . . .*' He fishes the card from his pocket.

The man is already shaking his head. Hal takes a step back. Only now that he is about to be turned away does he realize how much he has been looking forward to the evening. Not merely as a means to making new contacts, but as a taste of another side of life in the city – the sort glimpsed occasionally through the windows of cars, and the better sort of restaurant. It would have been an experience. The thought of his apartment, cold and dark, depresses him. The long walk back, through the wet streets. He should have known that Fede's scheme would be useless.

He tells himself that really, he wouldn't have wanted to go anyway. He doesn't need to experience that life: it isn't the one he has sought in coming to Rome. And yet there has always been a part of him – a part he isn't necessarily proud of – that has always been drawn towards the idea of a party. Perhaps it is because of his memories of the ones his mother used to throw in Sussex: the lawns thronged with guests and lights reflected in the dark waters of the harbour beyond. To be in the midst of this, with a glass of some watered-down punch in his hand, was to feel he had stepped into another, adult world. Funny, how one spent one's childhood half-longing to be out of it.

'What is the problem here?'

Hal glances up to see that a woman has appeared in the doorway alongside the man. She wears an emerald green gown, almost medieval in style, a silver stole about her neck. She is quite elderly, in her mid-seventies, perhaps, her face incredibly lined. But she has the bearing of a queen. Her hair is very dark, and if artifice is involved in keeping it this way it is well concealed.

The doorman turns to her, triumphant but obsequious. 'This man, my Contessa, he is not who he says he is.'

Hal feels her gaze on him. Her eyes are amazing, he realizes, like liquid bronze. She studies him for a time without speaking.

'Someone once told me,' she says then, 'that a party is only an event if there is at least one interesting gatecrasher in attendance.' She raises her eyebrows, continuing to study him. '*Are* you a gatecrasher?'

He hesitates, deciding what to say. Is it a trick? Should he persist with the lie, or admit the truth? He wavers.

'Well,' she says, suddenly, 'you certainly look interesting, all the same. Come, let us find you a drink.' She turns, and he sees now that the fur stole falls all the way to the ground behind.

He follows her up the curved staircase, illuminated by further lighted sconces. They pass numerous closed doors, as might confront the hero in the world of a fairytale. The gown, the centuries-old bricks, the flames of the torches: modern Rome suddenly feels a long way away. From above them come the sounds of a party, voices and music, but distorted as though heard through water.

She calls back to him. 'You are not Italian, are you?'

'No,' he says, 'I'm not.' Half-Italian – but he won't say that. The less you say, the fewer questions you invite. It is something to live by.

'Even more interesting. Do you know how I guessed? It is not because of your Italian, I should add – it is almost perfect.'

'No.'

'Because of your suit, of course. I never make mistakes about tailoring. It is English-made, I think?'

'Yes, it is.' His father had it made up for him by his tailor.

'Excellent. I like to be right. Now, tell me why you are here.'

'My friend had an invitation. He thought I might want to come instead of him.'

'No, *Caro*. I mean to ask why you are in Rome.'

'Oh. For work.'

'People do not come to Rome for work. There is always something more that drives them: love, escape, the hope of a new life. Which is it?'

Hal meets her eyes for as long as he is able, and then he has to look away. He felt for a second that she was seeing right into him, and that he was exposed. He understands, suddenly, that he won't be able to get in without answering her question. He is reminded of the myth of the Sphinx at Thebes, asking her riddles, devouring those who answer wrongly.

'Escape,' he says. And it is true, he realizes. He had told himself Rome would be a new start, but it had been more about leaving the old behind. England had been too full of ghosts. The man he had been before the war was one of them; the spectre of his former happiness. And of all those who hadn't come home – his friend, Morris, among them. Rome is full of ghosts, too – centuries of them. There is perhaps a stronger concentration of souls here than in any other place in the world: it is not the Eternal City for nothing. But the important thing is that they aren't *his* ghosts.

She nods, slowly. And he wonders if he has made the exchange, given the thing demanded in return for entry. But no, her questions haven't ended yet.

'And what do you do here?'

'I'm a journalist.' As soon as he says it he decides he should have lied. People in her sort of position can be obsessive about privacy. She doesn't seem disturbed by it, though.

'What's your name?'

'Hal Jacobs. I doubt that you will have—'

But she is squinting at him, as though trying to work something out. Finally, she seems to have it. 'Reviews,' she says, triumphantly, 'reviews of films.'

But no one read that column – that was the problem, as his editor at *The Tiber* had said.

'Well, yes, I did write them. A couple of years ago now.'

'They were brilliant,' she says. '*Molto molto acuto.*'

'Thank you,' he says, surprised.

'There was one you wrote of Giacomo Gaspari's film, *La Elegia*. And I thought to myself, there are all these Italian critics failing to see its purpose, asking why anyone would want to look back to the war, that time of shame. And then there was an Englishman – you – who understood it absolutely. You wrote with such power.'

Elegy. Hal remembers the film viscerally, as though it is in some way seared into him.

'After I read that,' she says, 'I thought: I must read everything this man has to write on film. You saw what others didn't. But you stopped!'

Hal shrugs. 'My editor thought my style was . . . too academic, not right for our readership.' It had been replaced with an agony aunt column: '*Gina Risponde* . . .' Roman housewives writing in to ask how to get their whites whiter, lonely men asking how to conceal a balding pate, young women eager to work in the capital asking whether it was really the immoral, dangerous place their parents spoke of.

The Contessa is shaking her head, as though over some great wrong. 'But why would you work somewhere like . . .' she seems to be searching for the name.

'*The Tiber*?'

'Yes. You should be writing for a national magazine.'

It must be nice, Hal thinks, to live in a world in which things are so easy. As though one might merely walk into the office of one of the bigger magazines and demand a job. There had been interviews. But nothing had come of it. And his work for *The Tiber* has – just about – allowed him to pay his rent, to feed himself.

'I work there because they'll have me.'

'I wonder if they know how lucky they are.' She looks at him thoughtfully. 'Perhaps when my film is made you can write a review of that. Only a good one, naturally.'

He remembers, now, Fede saying something about a film. 'When will it be made?'

'When I can afford it. It is why I am throwing this party – to try and persuade others they want to see it made too.'

'Ah.'

'I need to use all my powers of charm.' She smiles, suddenly. 'Do you think I can do it?'

He says, honestly, 'Yes, I do.' Because she does have it, a charisma beside which the charms of youth or beauty are so much blown thistledown.

She laughs. 'I am suddenly delighted to have you at my party, Hal Jacobs.' And then she beckons, with one beringed hand. 'Please, follow me.'

Now they are reaching the top of the staircase where the final door stands open to reveal a seething crowd. As Hal steps into the room, his first thought is that he is surrounded by people of extraordinary beauty. But as the illusion thins, he realizes that this is not the case. There is ugliness here. But the gorgeous clothes and jewels and the very air itself – performed with scent and wine and expensive cigarettes – do a clever job of hiding the flaws.

As the Contessa steps toward the crowd, the energies of the room extend themselves toward her. Heads turn and several guests begin to make their way in her direction, as though drawn on invisible wires. She looks back at Hal.

'I'm afraid that I am about to be busy,' she says to him.

'Of course. Please, go to your real guests.'

She smiles. 'Hal Jacobs,' she says. 'I *will* remember.' And then, before he can ask exactly what she means by this, she winks. 'Enjoy my party.' Then she walks into the crowd and is enveloped by it, lost from view.

Hal wanders through the throng, picking up a flute of spumante from a waiter and sipping it as he goes. One of the things that strikes him is the number of different nationalities in attendance. A few years ago, he was in the minority as an Englishman. Holidaymakers were only allowed to take £35 out of the country with them. Most stayed at home. Now, they are returning – and perhaps in greater numbers than before. He isn't sure how he feels about this.

The thing that unifies this crowd, across nationalities, is the same thing that gave that initial impression of beauty. They are all of a type.

He attempts to catch the eye of the guests that pass him, but every gaze slides over him and then on, in search of more important fare. Several times, he launches himself forward into a group, tries to enter the conversation. He just needs that one opening, then he feels certain he will be able to make things stick. And yet it does not come. Mostly he is ignored. It is something that happens in increments: a guest steps slightly in front of him, or a comment he attempts to make is ignored, or the circle simply disperses so that he is left standing on his own. At first Hal can't decide whether it is intentional or not. But on a couple of occasions he is quite actively frozen out. One man turns to give him a terrible stare, and Hal is so bemused by the impression of something like hatred, that he takes a step back. Apparently this set do not take well to newcomers. He is a cuckoo in the nest, and they know it. Usually, though it would be arrogance to admit it, Hal is used to being looked at by women. He has always been lucky in that respect. But here he is not given a second glance. Here something more than good looks is being searched out, something in which he is lacking. He is less than invisible.

Eventually, tired of the repeated humiliation and the noise and hot crush of bodies, he makes for the doors visible at the far end of the room, open onto a fire escape. He will finish his drink, he thinks, have a cigarette, and then go back in and make another attempt, buoyed by the alcohol. He will not leave here empty-handed; he merely needs a little time to regroup.

Outside he discovers a flight of stairs leading up, not down, to the roof of the tower itself. Curious, he climbs them. He is astonished to discover himself in the midst of a roof garden. Rome, in all its lamplit, undulating glory, is spread beneath him on all sides. He can see the dark blank of the Roman Forum, a few of the ancient stones made dimly visible by reflected lamplight; the marble bombast of the Altare della Patria with its winged riders like cut-outs against the starlit sky. Then, a little further away, the graceful cupola of St Peter's, and further domes and spires unknown to him. A network of lamplit streets, some teeming with ant-like forms, others quiet, sleeping. He has never seen Rome like this.

For a vertiginous moment, he feels that he is floating above it all. Then the ground reforms itself beneath him; he begins to look around. There are palms and shrubs, the smell of the earth after the rain. He gropes for the word for it: petrichor.

He hears running water and discovers a fountain in which a stone caryatid, palely nude, pours water from her jug. Nearby, a bird caws, and with a great flustered commotion takes wing into the night. He peers after the black shape, surprisingly large. A parrot? An eagle? A *phoenix*? Any of these seem possible, here.

He appears to be quite alone. Clearly the opportunities presented by the crush inside are too good for the other guests to miss. He looks toward Trastevere. Somewhere down there he has gone to sleep every night since his arrival in the city, utterly ignorant of the fact that such wonders existed only a few miles away.

'Hello.'

He turns towards the voice. It is as though the darkness itself has spoken. But when he looks closer he can make her out – the very pale blonde hair first, gleaming in what little light there is, then the shimmering stuff of her dress. Now he sees the fiery bud of a cigarette flare as she inhales. He is struck by the strange notion that she was not there before, that she has just alighted here like some magical winged creature.

'Sorry,' she says, and leans forward so her face is caught by the light spilling from the interior. His breath catches. He had somehow known from the voice that she would be beautiful, but had not been quite prepared for what has been revealed. And something strange: he feels the fact of it go through him like a sudden coldness.

She has sat back again now, and immediately he finds himself hoping for another look at her face. There is an intonation that he can't quite place. American, but something else to it, too. Perhaps, he thinks, it is the accent of one who has lived in this rarefied sphere for a lifetime.

'I'm Hal,' he says, to fill the silence.

'Hello, Hal,' she says. A slender white arm appears then, and he sees the wink of diamonds about the fine bones of the wrist. 'I'm Stella.'

He takes her hand, and finds it surprisingly warm in his.

She stands then, and comes to stand beside him at the rail. Now he can detect the scent of her: smoky, complex – a fragrance and something hers alone.

'Look at it,' she says. She is looking out at the city, leaning forward hungrily. 'Don't you wish,' she says, 'that you could dive in and swim in it?' She really looks as though she might, he thinks – plunge off the side and into the night, like a white feather falling through the blackness.

For a few moments they gaze down in silence. The sounds of the nighttime city float up to them: the blare of a car horn, a woman's laughter, a faraway trickle of music.

'Do you know the city?' he asks.

'We had a tour . . . the Colosseum, the Sistine Chapel, the Pantheon . . .'

He is so struck by her use of 'we' that he can't at first catch hold of what she is saying. She is still going, counting the sights off on her fingers: 'St Peter's, the Spanish Steps . . .'

'Well,' he says, 'you've done the tourist trail.'

She frowns. 'You don't think that's a good thing?'

'It isn't that,' he says. 'They're wonders in their own right. But there's more than that to this city.'

'You know it well?'

'I live here.'

'I suppose there is a side to the city that I won't ever see.' She says it with an odd kind of sadness, as though she feels this loss.

'Yes,' he says. 'I suppose so. You'd never find my favourite things in a guide.'

'Such as?'

'Well, such as the fact that the best time to see the Forum is at night, when there's no one else there. And I know a bar where they play the best jazz outside of New Orleans. But I suppose you're rather spoiled for choice, being an American.'

'No,' she says. 'I don't think I've ever listened to jazz before. Not live. What else?'

'A garden . . . almost completely hidden behind a high wall, a secret place. Unless you know how to find it.' He catches himself. He sounds like a braggart. It isn't like him.

'You would show me?' She says it in a rush, as if she has dared herself to ask it.

He is surprised. 'Yes, if you'd like.'

'Now?'

'Why not?'

He knows that it would be a bad idea. He should go back in there and make himself known to the great and important. This might be his only chance to mix with these people, to establish some sort of connection with them. And there is something about this situation that strikes him as perilous. He has spent the last few years keeping a careful guard upon himself, living within self-imposed limits. He should politely decline. Except he finds that he can't quite bring himself to do so.

'OK.'

'Good.'

She doesn't know anything about me, he thinks, and yet she is coming with me, a complete stranger, into the night of a foreign city.

'Do you need to tell anyone?' he asks her, remembering the *we*.

'No,' she says, 'I'm alone.'

They make their way back down the steps and into the warm fog of cigarette smoke, the press of bodies. She attracts admiring glances, he notices, from both the men and women.

Near the door, his eyes meet the Contessa's. He thinks he sees her look quickly to Stella and then back again. For a moment she frowns, as if working something out. And then she turns back to her companion.

*

Outside in the street her pale head and outfit glitter through the darkness as though summoning all of the light to them. She shields her face with one hand as the headlamps of a passing car strafe across her. The driver, a man, cranes for a view of her through the window. His look is greedy and Hal feels something close to hatred for him, this complete stranger.

She turns to him, awaiting his move. Suddenly he fears that nothing he can come up with will be enough.

They walk through the Forum, the dark stones standing sentinel. He points out the remains of the Temple of Saturn, of which only the ribs of the front portico remain. The Basilica Julia. He shows her – he is thankful for the moonlight that allows it – the detail that has always fascinated him more than anything else: the marks where the bored audiences of the trials held there had scratched games into the stone. She has seemed interested by it all, but suddenly he sees her shiver, pulling her wrap around herself.

'You're cold?'

'No.' She glances across at him. 'Do you mind if we go somewhere else?'

'Of course – why? Don't you like it?'

'Yes – no. I do, but this quiet . . . it does something to you.' She takes a cigarette from a tin in her little reticule, and her lighter, and he sees that her fingers are trembling as she tries to trip the flame into life.

'Here.' He takes it from her and does it himself.

'Thanks.'

'Where do you want to go?'

'I don't mind. Somewhere – different.'

He takes her to a bar he knows, in a certain secret square.

The place is full, even at this hour. She steps before him into the warmth of the place. As he follows he sees the glances of the other customers: lecherous, envious, reverential. With her outfit and her pale blonde hair she could be a movie star. But not a Monroe. There is something less immediate, more foreign about her appeal.

As soon as she has seated herself one of the waiters is hovering, ready to take her order.

'What are you having?' she asks.

'Oh, I thought I'd have a beer. But please, have anything you'd like.' If he has the cheap beer, he thinks, he can afford to buy her a couple of the more expensive offerings. But, to his surprise, she says: 'I'll have the same as you.'

In the corner, a small jazz trio – double bass, sax, trumpet – are playing a number so rough and fervent that one can feel the vibrations of it in one's chest. He watches her as she listens, her head on one side, her eyes half-closed.

When the beers arrive, the sight of her sipping hers, sitting in her finery, with that diamond bracelet about her wrist, is so incongruous that it makes him smile. She looks at him, venturing a smile of her own.

'What is it?'

'You look as though you should be drinking champagne.'

'I hate it,' she says. 'I never learned to like it.' She takes another sip. 'I like this, though.'

'Good. It's Italian. I always have it here.' He doesn't say: *because it is the only one I can afford.*

'How long have you lived in Rome? For a while?'

'Yes,' he says. 'For a few years.'

'And where were you before?'

'London.'

'Ah. And why did you come to Rome?'

What was it the Contessa had said? *There is always something more . . . love, escape, the hope of a new life.*

'I came here to write,' he says, and is immediately surprised at himself. He hasn't admitted this to anyone, not even Fede. Why did he say it, and to a stranger? But perhaps it is the very fact that she is a stranger.

'Write what?'

'A novel, I suppose.' Next he will have to admit that he hasn't written anything beyond the first paragraph. He must deflect attention from himself. 'And you,' he says quickly, 'you're here on holiday?'

'Yes.' He waits for an elaboration: how long she is visiting, where she is staying, who she is staying with – he remembers the 'we'. He has learned this – that if you wait long enough, the interviewee will feel uncomfortable or bored enough to fill the gap. But she says nothing. She is a little too good at this game, he thinks. All he knows of her is her first name, and her nationality. And there is a question over even that, because there is that accent, that slippage revealing some foreign note beneath.

'Where is home?' he asks.

'Home?' She looks thrown, for a second.

'Yes. Where do you come from?'

Funny, but the question seems to give her pause. It fits, he thinks, with his idea of some ethereal creature who comes from nowhere and might vanish back into the darkness in a moment. 'I live in New York,' she says.

'And is this your first visit to Europe?'

'Oh, no. But I haven't—' he sees her catch herself. Then, slowly, as if carefully choosing her words: 'I haven't travelled to Europe for a while.'

The war, he thinks, probably. It has taken a while for Americans to start coming back.

She takes another sip, and as she does he sees something he had not noticed before. It gives him a shock. On her left hand, two of the fingers are completely missing: the smallest and the ring. The trauma is clearly an old one, the skin healed over the knuckles, but ridged with scar tissue. It is a strange thing, this violent absence, because she seems to him so complete and unblemished. Without warning she puts down the bottle and catches him looking.

'An accident,' she says, 'when I was a child.'

'Did it hurt?'

'Do you know,' she says, 'I don't actually remember.'

She does, he thinks, watching her. And it did hurt a great deal. Now, as never before, he understands Fede's curiosity about his own background. The reticence is tantalizing.

Now she is checking her watch, and he guesses what is coming next. 'It's getting late,' she says.

'I haven't shown you the garden,' he says, before she can say that she needs to leave. He has no idea what he is going to show her, now. But this doesn't matter. The important thing is that she stays. That the evening, the strange enchantment of it, is prolonged. The thought of his apartment, dark and empty, is suddenly more than unappealing – it is something almost fearful.

To his relief, she agrees. He shows her the entrance to the garden, a slender door in an unremarkable wall of old brick. Fede told him about this place. No one knows who it belongs to, he explained, or who cares for it. So few people know of it that it is a true sanctuary.

There are clementine and orange trees growing here, now burdened with ripe fruit. Among them are statues:

putti, faceless goddesses wound about with ivy: some so enmeshed in it that they look half-consumed by it. And then on the wall behind them the really special thing. A gorgeous fresco of fruit trees, like a reflection of the garden itself, and pale nightingales and a sky of midnight blue. Only a few of the details are visible in the moonlight, but he hears her catch her breath at the sight. He thinks, suddenly, that he would like to take her here in the daytime, so that she can see the colours. The background is a blue that looks particularly antique, not of the modern world, a colour lost to time. Fede claims that the painting is a Roman original. It could be ancient, it looks it. But it could be a medieval imitation and still be older than the relics of many cities.

He gestures back towards the real clementine trees. 'Would you like one?'

'Yes please.'

When he passes the fruit to her their fingers touch for an instant, and the contact is like a heated brand. It causes everything to shift for him. He hasn't felt it, this specific kind of excitement, for such a long time. He had thought that he might not again. And now here . . . with her, with someone he has only just met. It makes no sense.

He watches as she removes the peel in a single strand. 'I've never managed to do that.'

For the first time, she smiles.

The flesh is cold from the air, and incredibly sweet. But what he would like, he thinks suddenly, watching her eat hers, is to taste the juice on her mouth. The thought is another flare of warmth. When he looks up at her she is watching him. And he thanks God that she has no way of knowing what he is thinking.

'Where are we?' she asks. 'I've lost my bearings.'

'The Aventine hill. It's one of my favourite places.' There's a stateliness to it, a solitude. 'The Forum is back that way,' he points. 'And across the river is where I live – Trastevere.'

'What's that like?'

'Some parts are rather grand – but I'm afraid I don't live in one of those. It has . . . character, I suppose. Sometimes the streets are so narrow you feel the walls might actually be moving in towards you. In a way, it's where real people live. The real Rome. I mean, for those that can't afford an Aventine villa, or an apartment near the Spanish Steps.' He catches again the gleam of diamonds and thinks she is probably from that small club of people who can.

'I'd like to see it.'

'Really?'

She nods.

He sees her take it in: the narrowness of the cobbled streets, the shuttered houses with the washing strung between, the cat that slinks its way through the shadows. The recent rain gleams underfoot like spilled ink.

'I like it.' She can't mean it. 'Where do you live?'

'Not far from here, actually.'

'Will you show me?'

Perhaps he is mistaking her meaning . . . and yet he doesn't think so. All he can think to say is, 'Are you sure?'

For a second, she appears to waver. But then she gathers herself. 'Yes.' He has the distinct impression that this is some dare she has set herself. He can't believe that it is normal for her. And yet the whole evening feels as though it is under some kind of enchantment – an evening in which 'normal' has been forgotten.

'It's very small,' he says. He doesn't take anyone back there: it is a hovel. 'Perhaps we could go somewhere else . . .' He is thinking. A hotel? Not her hotel, but perhaps another, anonymous . . .

'No,' she says. 'Take me there.'

He has another moment of doubt. She seems . . . how to put it? A little fraught. The confidence of her manner isn't fooling him. Perhaps the sensible, the gentlemanly thing, would be to suggest that he accompany her back to her hotel and leave her at the reception. But it is beyond him. He is filled with longing, half-blinded by it. That feeling part, so long anaesthetized, has come briefly to life.

They say nothing else to one another as he leads her through the few remaining streets, and they walk a couple of feet apart, as though some invisible force dictates it.

His apartment is in a worse state than he had remembered: the espresso pot has leaked a treacly stain onto the small table; the bed is barely made. He sees it through new eyes. How it is at once almost empty and yet disarrayed. The exposed light bulb, the meagre rail of clothes, the detritus of his life piled variously about. He has lived in it for years as one might live in a hotel room for a week.

But she is intrigued, rather than appalled. He sees her drift towards the makeshift desk with the portable Underwood. Holding, not a page from the novel, but the beginnings of an article for *The Tiber*, a horribly unfunny sketch about an Englishman coming to terms with the concept of risotto. *Imagine a rice pudding, only . . .*

She will see it, and know that the novel is a pipe dream. She will think him pitiable. He rushes into the space, to block her off.

'Do you want . . .' he looks at the espresso maker, wondering how quickly he can clean and heat it, '. . . a coffee, perhaps?'

'No, thank you. I wonder . . .'

'What?'

'Do you have something stronger?'

He has whisky, which she agrees to. He makes them up – explains that he doesn't have an icebox. She doesn't mind. He watches as she drinks hers steadily. She puts it down, emptied, and looks at him.

He looks on, hardly breathing, as her hands go to the buttons at her neck, and begin to unfasten them. Her movements appear assured, her expression fixed, but then he sees that her fingers are trembling so badly that each is a struggle. This makes him want her all the more.

'I haven't done this before,' she says, as though it needed saying.

'Neither have I.' It isn't strictly true – he has been to bed with women on the first night of knowing them. But not like this, somehow. Never has the whole of him been alive to it in this way.

She is shrugging the dress from her shoulders, and now she stands before him in her slip and underthings, nude to the waist. He sees how soft her skin looks; how some foreign sun has tanned it in places, and left it milk-white in others. He sees the small, taut indentation of her navel, the dusky nipples.

He is freeing himself from his clothes as quickly as he is able, and she moves back towards the rumpled bed, watching him, all the time.

He realizes, with something almost like amusement, that they have not kissed one another and yet here they are, two naked strangers. It would take so little to shatter this moment, to tip it over into absurdity. His mind is too full to make sense of all of it. And then she reaches her arm out to him, and he steps towards her, and feels her hands on him, her hands moving downward, and his mind empties of all thought.

Afterwards, he goes to pour them each another drink. She lies in the bed and watches him, the sheets pulled up about her. He brings the glasses back to her, and they drink in silence for a few minutes. He wonders if she, like him, has suddenly been reminded of the strangeness of the situation, of the fact that they know nothing about one another.

'Is that where you write?'

He follows her gaze to the makeshift desk, the typewriter, and realizes that what she must be seeing is a romantic image – a false one. He drains the glass, feels it burn through the centre of him. And perhaps it is the work of the whisky, perhaps it is his knowledge that they may never meet again, but he feels a sudden compelling need for honesty. 'I have a confession. I'm not a writer. I thought I was, once.' She has turned her head on the pillow to look at him. He coughs, continues. 'I had a collection of short stories published. Not in a big way, you know – but it was something.'

In 1938, just out of university. It was a very small press, and the print run had been a few hundred copies. And yet, nevertheless, here it was: him, a published author, at the age of twenty-one. The sole review had been good if not absolutely effusive. That was enough. There was time for improvement. He had his whole life ahead of him. His mother had been overjoyed. His father, a Brigadier, a hero of the Great War, had been . . . what? A little bemused. All well and good for Hal to have this hobby before doing the thing, the real job, that would mark him out as a man. Hal knew, though, that this was the thing he wanted to do for ever. He feared it, because he wanted it so badly.

'I've lost it now,' he says. 'I can't do it any longer.'

There is no answer at first, and he wonders if she might have fallen asleep. But then she says, 'What happened?'

'The war,' he says, because it is an accepted cliché these days – and also partially true.

It was something that had changed, in him. Every time he tried to write he felt the words coloured by this change, as though it infected everything. As though it could be read in every sentence: this man is a coward; is a fraud.

He won't see her again. 'Someone died,' he says, 'a friend. He wrote, too. After that, I haven't felt like I deserved to be doing it . . . not when he never will.' The liberation, of saying it aloud.

She doesn't ask for him to explain further, and he is relieved, because he feels only a hair's breadth away from telling her the whole thing, which he might regret.

'You won't have lost it. Once you're a writer, it's in you, somewhere.'

'What makes you say that?'

'My father was one.'

'Would I have heard of him?'

'No,' she says. 'No. I don't think so.'

'Tell me about him.' But no answer comes, and when he looks down at her, he sees that her eyes are closed.

2

That morning, watching her readying herself to leave, his body had been alive with remembered sensation. In the unforgiving early light he had seen with some surprise that she was a little older than he had thought: several years his senior, perhaps.

She was pale, anxious, altered. She had hardly looked at him, even when he spoke to her, asked her if he could get her anything, walk her to her hotel. When she had sat and rolled on her stockings she had ripped the heel of one in her haste to be dressed and gone.

The last thing she had said before she left was: 'You won't . . .'

'What?'

'You won't tell anyone about this?'

'No. Will you?'

'No.' She had said it with some force, and he had wondered if he should be offended.

Then she had left, and his apartment had become once

again the small, untidy, unremarkable place it had been before. He had lain in the tangled sheets, with the warmth of the new memory upon his skin.

She will be back in America now, no doubt. Undoubtedly she is no longer in Rome. But he keeps imagining he sees her. Through a café window, in the Borghese gardens, buying groceries at the Campo de' Fiori market.

Those few whispered sentences, in the moments before sleep, had been the frankest conversation he could remember having with anyone in a long time. Perhaps since before the war. That had been one of the problems, with Suze. Every time he had tried to talk she had seemed so uneasy, or, worse, bored – that he hadn't wanted to say any more. So he'd never managed to tell her about what he had done; about his guilt. Perhaps she had guessed that there was something she wouldn't want to know, and this was why she had been so resistant to being told. She had wanted to see him, as everyone did, as the returned hero. If you had returned alive, whole, you had had a Good War; you were heroic. This thing he wanted to tell her would not fit with that image.

Stella: he realizes he never even found out her last name. Yet he doubts that she would have told him, had he asked. It was all part of it, the sense that she was holding some vital part of herself back. It had intrigued him, this reticence, because he recognized it in himself. And then, in bed, she had briefly come apart, and he thought he had caught a glimpse of that hidden person.

He would like to talk to her again, to see her once more. But no doubt the peculiar magic of it had been due to them being strangers.

He can't even remember her face. Had she been so

beautiful as all that? Usually, he has a good recall of detail. He can recall what she had been wearing, but when he thinks of her face, the impression he is left with is like the after-effect of staring too long at a lamp.

There is one thing, though, one inarguable fact. For the first time in years – years of insomnia or fitful, disturbed sleep – he had a full night's rest, and did not dream.

He learns that the Contessa has got the funding for her picture. Fede tells him it is some American industrialist, keen to cloak himself in culture perhaps. Filming has apparently already begun, somewhere on the coast, and in a studio near Rome. Not Cinecittà, though, but a tiny set-up owned by the Contessa herself. An interesting name: *il Mondo Illuminato*. The Illuminated World.

On a whim, he takes a detour one morning past the building that had housed the party. But the whole place is shut up, looking almost as though it has remained thus for the last five hundred years. Perhaps he should not be surprised. The whole night had felt hardly real.

3

March 1953

An early spring day, almost warm. He walks to work along the river, squinting against the light that flashes off the water. The city looks as glorious as he has ever seen it, wreathed in gold, and yet as ever he feels as if he is looking at it through a pane of glass; one step removed. Perhaps it is time to move again, he thinks. Perhaps he should have gone further afield in the first place: out of Europe. America. Australia. Money, though: that is a problem. North Africa could be more feasible. Somewhere out of the way, where he might live on very little and make a last attempt at the wretched writing. The war novel: the one meant to make some sense of it all. The problem, he thinks, is that one has to have made sense of something in one's own mind before committing it to paper.

As soon as he enters the office, he is stopped by Arlo, the post boy.

'A woman called, and asked for you.'

'She did? What was her name?'

'Um.' Arlo checks the note. 'No name.' And then defensively, 'She said she was a friend – I didn't think to ask.'

'Where is she?'

'She's staying at a hotel . . .' Arlo searches for the name, raises his eyebrows when he finds it. 'The Hassler.'

He wonders. It *could* be her, he thinks. He cannot think of anyone else he knows who could afford to stay at the Hassler, after all. He feels a thrill of something like anticipation.

'This way, sir.'

Hal follows the man into the drawing room. His first thought is that it is precisely the sort of atmosphere his father, the Brigadier, would be drawn to. It reminds him powerfully, in fact, of the Cavalry and Guards club, where his father would stay while in London. From the windows the Spanish Steps are visible, thronged with life. The room is not crowded, but he searches in vain for a glimpse of blonde.

The waiter is leading him now toward a table in the opposite corner. When he sees its occupant, seated with her back to him, Hal is about to tell the man that he has made a mistake. This cannot be the person he is meeting. But then she turns.

'Ah,' she smiles, and raises one eyebrow. 'You came, I'm so pleased. I did not know if you would be interested in keeping an appointment you were actually invited to.'

'Contessa.' He takes the seat opposite her.

'I thought I would keep my invitation mysterious enough to intrigue you.'

'It certainly did.'

'You guessed that it came from me?'

'Ah – no, I did not.'

She peers at him, and smiles. 'You hoped that it was someone else?'

'Not at all.'

'Well,' she says. 'I have an offer of work for you.'

'You do?'

Her smile broadens. 'Ah, but you're interested now!'

'What is it, exactly?' As if he is in a position to turn down anything. But he did not live with his father for so many years without learning something of how to conduct business.

Before she can speak the waiter has appeared to take their order.

'Bring us some of that *gnocchi*,' she tells him. 'The one that Alessandro makes for me.'

The man nods, and disappears.

'So,' she says. 'To business.'

'Of course.'

'My film, *The Sea Captain*, is being released this spring.'

'Congratulations – I heard that you had funding for it. I didn't realize it was finished.'

'Thank you.'

The *gnocchi* arrives now. Hal has only eaten the dish *alla Romana* – doughy shapes submerged in sauce and baked. These are delicate morsels, scattered with oil and thin leaves of shaved truffle. They are delicious – and Hal notices that the Contessa, despite her extreme slenderness, is enjoying them with the same relish as he.

'Who directed the film?' Hal asks.

The Contessa smiles. 'Giacomo Gaspari.'

'Goodness.' Hal is impressed. 'It must be something.'

She nods and says, without preamble, 'It is. Quite brilliant – which I can say, because I'm not the one responsible for that. It will be screening at the festival, at Cannes.'

'That's wonderful.'

'I hoped that you might come with us.'

'To Cannes?'

'Yes – but on the journey there, too. I've planned a trip first. A tour, along the coast where it was filmed, to publicize it. And to make the people of Liguria feel that they are involved, that it is *their* film. It is what they do in Hollywood: why should we not do it here?' She smiles at Hal. 'I thought you could cover it.'

'For *The Tiber*?'

'No,' the Contessa says, with a note of triumph. 'For *Tempo*.'

Tempo is in the big league – Italy's answer to the American *Life*. 'But how? I don't know anyone there.'

'Ah, but I do. They asked me if I knew of a writer who would do it – and I suggested you.'

Hal can't help asking. 'Why?'

'I like the way you write.' Seeing his expression, she smiles. 'I told you I would not forget. Luckily, the editor at *Tempo* agrees with me that you are the right man for the job.'

'When?'

'The film festival is next month. But you would be needed for the two weeks before it, too.'

'Well,' Hal says, trying to process it all. 'I suppose it depends . . .'

'On the fee? I'm afraid the one they've offered is rather small.' She names the sum: it is still far more than *The Tiber* pay for an article. 'But I thought I would help. Because you would be doing me a personal favour, too.' She takes a fountain pen from her reticule and scribbles on the menu. She turns it towards him, and says, with genuine regret, 'I'm sorry it can't be higher. I have a budget, you know . . .'

Hal stares at it, absorbing the significance of the extra nought. With it, he could travel to one of the wild, liminal places he has been thinking of: certainly North Africa, Australia even.

'Yes,' he says. 'I could do it for that.' To do anything other than accept, considering the sum in question, would be idiocy.

'Excellent. I will put you in touch with the man I spoke to there.' She takes up her fountain pen again, and passes the menu back to him. There written next to the *primi piatti*, is an address: *Il Palazzo Mezzaluna, vicino a Tellaro, Liguria*. He has not been to Liguria: has only a vague idea of brightly coloured houses beside an equally luminous sea – glimpsed, perhaps, on a postcard.

'You will need to be there,' she says, 'in three weeks' time.'

'I shall,' he says, quickly. 'Thank you. Thank you so much.'

The smile she gives him is enigmatic. He feels a sudden trepidation. He has learned to distrust things that seem too good to be true.

4

Liguria, April 1953

His first impressions of Liguria are snatched through a smeared train window. These are visions at once exotic and banal: washing strewn from the windows of red-tiled, green-shuttered houses, road intersections revealing a chaos of vehicles. Palm trees, tawdry-looking railway hotels. The occasional teal promise of the sea. The sea. At the first glimpse of it he finds himself gripping the seat rest, hard. Sometimes it has this effect on him.

This whole mission still has about it an air of unreality. If he hadn't had that slightly stilted meeting with the editor at *Tempo* – who seemed as bemused as he did as to why he had been chosen – he might have reason to believe it was all the Contessa's little joke.

'Keep it light,' the man had said. 'What do the stars eat and drink, what do they wear? What is Giulietta Castiglione reading, ah, what does Earl Morgan do to relax? Stories of cocktails in Portofino, of sun on private beaches. Of . . . of a sea the colour of the sapphires our leading lady wears to supper.' Hal had tried not to smile. 'Nothing too worthy. Our readers want escapism. *Niente di troppo difficile. Capisci?*'

'*Si,*' Hal had said. 'I understand.'

La Spezia is no great beauty, though there is a muscular impressiveness to the place, the harbour flanked with merchant vessels and passenger ferries. Not so long ago there would have been warships marshalled here. To Hal they are almost conspicuous in their absence. The enemy's own destroyers and submarines, sliding beneath the surface black and deadly.

He catches the passenger ferry, and realizes that it is the first time he has been afloat in years. Again, he reminds himself, it is all different. The tilt and shift of the boat much more pronounced; so close to the water that he can feel the salt spray on his cheek. He concentrates on the sights. Here, finally, is the fabled beauty: the land rising smokily beyond the coast, the clouds banked white behind. A castle, rose-gold in the afternoon sun.

He looks at his fellow travellers. Poverty still pinches some faces tight, clothes are a decade or more out of date. Marshall Aid, it seems, has not lessened the struggle by much for them. In the relative prosperity of the capital it is easy to forget – to feel, sometimes, like a poor relation.

At Lerici, a little way down the coast, all the passengers disembark. Hal hasn't yet worked out this part of the journey, but according to the map the place should be only a few miles by water. Hal goes to the skipper, who lounges against the stern with a cigarette and scowls at him through the smoke.

'Il Palazzo Mezzaluna?'

The man takes a lazy drag, squinting as though he hasn't understood. Hal repeats himself. As comprehension dawns, his question is met with a short, derisive bark of a laugh, a shake of the head.

'No,' the man says. 'It isn't on my route. It is a private residence.'

'Yes,' Hal says. 'But for a little extra?'

'No, signor. I am finished for the day.' But as Hal turns to leave him he shouts something, gesturing to several small crafts heaped with fishing gear. A group of sunburned men sit near them, sharing an impromptu picnic of bread and shellfish, shucking them with their knives and sucking the morsels from the shells.

Hal approaches them and asks his question. One of the men shrugs and stands, brushing breadcrumbs from himself. He leads the way over to his boat and moves a few items around – nets, a can of oil, a box of bait and a rod – to make room for Hal and his bag. Hal clambers in, aware of the ambivalent gaze of the men who remain, eating their oysters. What do they make of him, this Englishman in his tired suit, climbing in beside the fishing tackle?

The man starts his engine and they putter out of the harbour, pitching dangerously as they cross the wake of a larger boat. Then back out into the navy blue of the open sea, rounding the nub of the headland. The little boat speeds across the water, sending up a fine salt spray. After only fifteen minutes or so the man points to the shore.

'*È là!*'

In the distance: a semicircular opening in the dark mass of trees, separated from the water by a silvery thread of sand. And nestling among the trees, dead centre, an enormous building. A grand hotel, one might presume, seeing it from afar. As they draw closer Hal is better able to make it out. A palace, in the Belle Époque style. The façade is a coral pink that anywhere else in the world would look ridiculous . . . and yet here, drenched in the evening sun, is something like magnificent. A white jetty stretches out like a piece of bleached driftwood into the blue depths. A figure waits, watching their approach.

Hal steps onto the jetty, heaving his bag after him. The waiting figure is a liveried member of staff who strides toward Hal, hand outstretched for his luggage. Against the spotless white of his uniform the leather case looks small and battered.

'Good evening, sir.'

Hal goes back to the fisherman, pays him, quickly. The man seems a little bemused, as though he had never expected his shabby passenger to be welcome in such a place. With a shake of his head, as though to clear it, he fires his engine and is gone.

It is evening now, Hal realizes, the light like blue glass. Before them rises a shallow stone staircase flanked by a line of pine trees. Each is topped by a fluid dark abstract of foliage, like a child's drawing of a cloud. Their resiny scent fills the warm air. The man leads the way, moving so briskly that Hal has to jog a little to keep up. They move past a series of gardens, each, Hal sees, is different from the last. 'The Japanese garden,' the man says, as they pass the first: and in the manmade pools Hal glimpses an iridescent carp, sliding fatly among trailing pondweed. There are ornamental bridges, gravel raked into intricate patterns about carefully shaped hillocks of moss. Then the Moroccan garden, filled with bright blooms that spill from urns painted a luminous blue. The Italian garden: a stately formal arrangement of dark shrubs and classical statues. As Hal and his guide pass, a flock of white doves take wing. It is itself like a film set, Hal thinks, hardly real.

Inside, the house is a cool space, reminiscent of an art gallery. A couple of line drawings that might be Picasso – his eye isn't good enough at this distance to be certain. A cuboid nude that could be Henry Moore.

The room that he is shown to is white, high-ceilinged.

'You can change here for the evening,' the man tells him. 'Drinks are at seven thirty.' Hal looks down at his travelling suit. Change into what, exactly? The suit is crumpled, but it is by far the smartest thing he owns. He wore it *because* it is the smartest thing he owns. And so he sits down on the bed, looks about himself. The window has a view out towards the back of the house, where a great stone terrace leads down into further manicured gardens, showing now as a dark emerald green. A space hewn by the twin forces of wealth and will out of the natural gorse. At the far end is a line of tall cypresses. In the weakening light they are black sentinels, funereal in aspect. Suddenly he catches a shimmer of gold, which resolves itself into the hair of a woman. She wears what appears to be a long black dress, camouflaged against the trees behind her so that only her face and arms can be made out. An unnameable excitement runs through him. He goes to turn out the light in the room, so he can make the scene out better, but when he looks back she has disappeared.

At eight o'clock the open window discloses the unmistakable sounds of musical instruments being tuned: the squawk of violins, the throb of a double bass. Hal showers in the gilded bathroom, sloughing off the crust of salt, and glances quickly in the mirror. His clothes are more creased than ever. But his face betrays little of his tiredness. He knows that he is lucky, to look like this. His face is his passport.

When he returns downstairs the gardens have been transformed: lit now by a host of lanterns and filled with guests. Some of the guests are from a similar crowd to the party in Rome; they have that same lustre of wealth, of lives lived on the grand scale. But he sees, too, children dressed as if for the beach, dark-haired girls in simple sundresses, men in casual trousers and unbuttoned shirts. Along one wall of the house a line of elderly men sit and talk with great intensity: all wear battered caps in various sun-faded hues, sandals on hoary feet. The women who Hal presumes are their wives look on censoriously from a few metres away and they, too, wear an unofficial uniform: floral-patterned smocks and woollen cardigans. Hal's suit no longer seems such a *faux pas*. But he is aware that he belongs to neither tribe: not that of the dinner jackets, or that of the summer slacks. He is an anomaly.

'Hal.'

He turns, and finds the Contessa. She is wearing a tangerine linen dress than could almost be a monk's tabard, with a large hood pulled up over her hair. It is one of the more eccentric outfits Hal has ever seen.

'I'm so pleased,' she says. 'I worried that you would change your mind.'

Hal thinks that she can have no concept of a journalist's living, if she imagined he might have been able to turn her offer down.

'I wanted to know something,' he says, because he has been wondering. 'How are we travelling to Cannes?'

'Ah,' she says, 'but you will find out tomorrow morning.'

'All these people are coming too?' He gestures toward the crowd.

She laughs. 'Oh, no. No. I have invited them all for the evening.' She counts off the different groups on her fingers. 'There are friends, the film crowd, your colleagues from the press' – she gestures towards a passing photographer – 'and some of the people from the village near here. They come often – especially the children and their parents – to swim off my jetty, and walk in the grounds. It is why I make such an effort with the gardens. And they appreciate a good party, like all sensible Italians. Wait until the dancing starts. But first I will introduce you to the other guests. Come.' She beckons with one hand.

The man she leads him to first is etiolated-looking, with blond hair so pale that it is almost white, receding on either side of the head severely. A thin face, with all of the bones visible beneath the skin. He is dressed in a wine-coloured suit – beautifully made, but with the unfortunate effect of making his complexion sallower still.

The Contessa moves into English. It is the first time Hal has heard her use it, and he is surprised by her fluency. 'Hal Jacobs, meet Aubrey Boyd, who will be taking the pictures to accompany your article. This man is the only true challenger to Beaton's crown, in my opinion. He is a simply splendid photographer – makes one look like a goddess. He has a way of making all one's little wrinkles disappear. How do you do it?' The Contessa is impressively wrinkled even for one of her advanced years. A life well-lived, Hal thinks, much of it in the full glare of the sun.

Aubrey Boyd raises one thin eyebrow. 'I cannot reveal my magic.' And then, quickly, 'Though none was needed in your case.'

'He did the most wonderful series on American heiresses, didn't you, Aubrey? Posing like so many Cleopatras and

Anne Boleyns. And let me tell you,' she says to Hal, conspiratorially, 'none of them will ever look like *that* again in their lives. I know that your pictures will look fabulous in *Tempo*.'

'Yes,' Aubrey says, a little dubiously. Hal has the impression that he sees the magazine as somewhat beneath him.

Next the Contessa is introducing him to Signor Gaspari, the director, hailed in recent years as a god of Italian cinema. The man cannot be taller than five foot five, the hunch of his shoulders robbing him of a couple of inches. Something about the way he stands suggests a body that has been put through more than its fair share of suffering.

'My dear friend,' the Contessa says, as she stoops to embrace him. 'Meet our young journalist, Hal.'

'I loved your last film,' Hal says.

'Thank you,' Gaspari says, solemnly, without any visible sign of pleasure.

Hal remembers it vividly. The war-torn city, beautiful in decay. And that protagonist, the solitary man, wandering through it. His aloneness all the more profound for the hubbub of crowds surrounding him. The atmosphere of the film, the exquisite sadness of it. He tells Gaspari this.

'You have understood my intention well,' Gaspari says.

'I wondered,' Hal says, 'whether you might have meant it as a lament for Rome – for the country? To what was lost in the war?'

Gaspari smiles – but it is a melancholy, downturned smile. He shakes his head. 'Nothing so lofty as that, I'm afraid,' he says. 'My intentions were . . . much more human. The loss was one of the heart.'

Hal senses there is a story here – one he is intrigued to hear.

'Another drink, Giacomo?' the Contessa asks, as a waiter passes by with a tray.

'Oh no,' Gaspari waves a hand. 'Thank you, but I must be returning to my room now. I wanted to come for a little while, but I am no good at parties. And Nina needs to go to bed.' He glances down, and Hal follows his gaze to where a tiny dachshund sits, quite still, the black beads of her eyes trained on her master. Then Gaspari nods to them both and moves away, the dog trotting at his heels.

'A wonderful man,' the Contessa says. 'A great friend, and a genius. Some, I know, think he is a little odd. But genius is often partnered with strangeness.'

'He looks . . .' Hal tries to think how to put it. 'Is he well?'

'He suffered greatly,' the Contessa says, 'during the war.'

Hal waits for her to continue, but she does not. She has turned towards another man, who is approaching them across the grass. He is elegant in fine, pale linen, with leonine hair swept back from his brow. A fingerprint of grey at each temple. He is not particularly tall, but there is something about him suggestive of stature. A trick of the eye, Hal thinks. A confidence trick. He smiles, revealing white teeth. Even Hal can see that he is handsome, in that American way. And somehow ageless – in spite of the grey.

'Mr Truss.' The Contessa's smile is not the same one she gave Signor Gaspari. It is the smile of a diplomat, measured out in a precise quantity.

'It's a wonderful party, Contessa. I must congratulate you.'

'Thank you. Hal, meet Frank Truss – who has been very supportive of the film. Frank Truss, meet Hal Jacobs, the journalist who will be joining us.'

'Hal,' Truss puts out a hand. Hal takes it, and feels the

coolness of the man's grasp, and also the strength of it. 'Who do you work for?'

Without knowing why, Hal feels put on his guard, as though the man has challenged him in some indefinable way. 'I don't work for anyone in particular,' he says. 'But this piece is for *Tempo* magazine.'

'Ah. Well.' He flashes his white smile. 'I don't know it. But, clearly, I will have to make sure to watch what I say.'

'I'm not that sort of journalist,' Hal says. It sounds more hostile than he had intended.

'Well, good. I'm sure you're the right man for the job. Great to have you on board.'

He speaks, thinks Hal, as though the whole trip were of his own devising. Odd, but there is something about him – his statesmanlike bearing perhaps, his air of entitled ease – that reminds Hal of his father. A man who expects deference. And if he is anything like Hal's father, it is an unpleasant experience for those that fail to show it.

As Truss moves away, the Contessa turns to him, confidentially.

'He's the money behind the film,' she says.

'Oh yes?'

'A powerful man.' She lowers her tone. 'He has other business in Italy – industry, I understand. And . . . It is also possible that he may have certain connections here one would rather not look too closely at. *I*, certainly, am not going to look too closely at them. Perhaps investing in the arts looks good for him. But he describes himself as a man of culture: so that is how I will view him. And I like his wife, which helps.'

'His wife?'

'Yes,' the Contessa searches the crowd. 'Though I can't see

her here. Never mind, there will be plenty of time for us all to get acquainted. But – ah – there is our leading lady!'

It is a face known to Hal because of the number of times he has seen it in newsprint and celluloid form. Giulietta Castiglione. Her outfit is surprisingly modest, a sprigged peasant dress, cut high at the neck. Her small feet are bare, more likely a careful choice than real bohemian artlessness. She has black hair, a great thick fall of it – the longest strands of which reach almost to her waist. There is a hum of interest about her. All the men – old and young – are transfixed. From the elderly women emanates a cloud of disapproval.

They say she has already turned down marriage proposals from some of the biggest names in Hollywood and in Cinecittà. And she was engaged, for a period of precisely one week, to her co-star in the film that made her name in America: *A Holiday of Sorts*.

Hal caught *A Holiday* in a Roman cinema, dubbed into Italian. It was a blowsy comedy: an American ambassador falls in love with a Neapolitan nun – played, with improbably ripe sensuality, by Giulietta. It should have been the sort of film one might watch to while away a rainy afternoon and then instantly forget. But there had been something about the actress: the combination of knowing and girlish naiveté, the curves of her body at odds with that virginally youthful face. She had been disturbing, unforgettable.

In the flesh, her charisma is more tangible, and more complex. Hal, watching her dip her head coyly in answer to a question from one man, and then throw her head back and laugh in answer to another, quickly begins to realize that she had not been playing a part so much as a dilute version of herself.

'Well,' the Contessa says, 'quite something, is she not?' And then, 'Wait until you see her in the film.'

Hal wonders how this sensual presence will translate itself into Gaspari's work. The two seem as contradictory as fire and water. But perhaps this will be what makes the combination work.

Despite himself, he is beginning to look forward to the trip. Before he had thought only about the money, how it would make everything easier for him. But he sees now that here is the promise of an experience out of the ordinary, one that will help him forget himself. And the chance to be in the presence of a great storyteller; for that is what Signor Gaspari is. To learn from him, perhaps.

At some point the Contessa is drawn into conversation with another guest, and Hal is free to roam on his own. The drinks keep coming and Hal, who for a long while hasn't been able to afford the luxury of getting drunk, takes advantage of them. By his fifth – every one so necessary at the time – the evening has melted into a syrup of sensation. He wanders through the grounds, meeting guests and forgetting them instantly.

Later, the dancing begins, and Hal finds himself thrust into the fray. The poor girl whose hand he has commandeered trips and squeals, to no avail, as he spins her around and around and around, and the lantern lights become a vortex of flame about them.

In the small hours he wanders down to the gardens. Peacocks strut about freely, disturbed from their sleep by the din of the party. He sits down upon a miniature stone house, blinking in an attempt to clear his head, and observes one of the males. The bird preens himself, his plumage gleaming in the lantern-light, tail feathers rustling importantly. And

yet for all the beauty of his feathers, Hal sees that the creature's feet are scaled and ugly, like a common chicken's. This
suddenly strikes him as philosophically significant.

'You think you're special,' he tells the bird, labouring over
the words, 'but you aren't. We're all just chickens, underneath
it all, however much effort we put into not revealing it.'

Later, he remembers the woman he saw in the gardens
behind the house, at dusk. Though it was several hours ago
he has some drunken idea that she will still be there; that he
only has to go and look for her. So he makes his way round
to the back of the house, and towards the dark line of
cypresses, his way illuminated now only by the silver light
of the moon. Of course, she is not there. Perhaps she was a
figment of his imagination.

As he turns to make his way back to the house – he must
go to bed, he knows, or wake up here covered in pine needles
– he sees something gleaming dully upon the ground. He
stoops, and finds an earring – a stud of some large, cut stone,
the colour indiscernible in the gloom. He puts it in his pocket.
So she was real, after all.

5

He wakes with a start, and stares about in confusion at the unfamiliar room. He knows that he is not in Rome, because there his view is of the tired brickwork of the building opposite. Here he can see only lancing blue. Everything hurts him: the strength of the light, the whiteness of the room . . . He shuts his eyes, and opens them again, hoping that the pain this time will have lessened, but there is no change. Shakily he climbs out of the bed and sways his way across to the bathroom. Now he is remembering, but in a series of dislocated images: a peacock, the Contessa's monk-like robe, that final drink. A man with white teeth bared in a smile.

His face in the mirror betrays little of the night's excess. 'It's strange,' Suze told him, once, 'but you somehow look even better when you're tired. It's almost unnerving.' But he does feel terrible. What would help, he feels, would be to bathe his head with cool water. He splashes his face with water from the tap, but he can't seem to get it cold enough. He thinks: the sea.

It is still early enough that most of the guests won't yet be about. Certainly, no one is visible as he makes his way downstairs and down through the gardens. And yet as he nears the end of the path he glimpses movement at the far end of the jetty, and stops. A golden head emerges, then the rest of her. She wears a black bathing suit, high at the neck but generously cut away at the shoulders. He watches her move up the jetty toward him and feels a nudge of recognition. A famous actress, perhaps. After all, anything is possible in this place.

She stoops and picks up her wrap, which lies strewn across the boards, and ties it with a quick, careless movement about her waist. Hal watches, standing completely still as if under some sort of spell.

She has nearly reached the path. For the first time he sees her face properly, and only now does he recognize her.

She looks different from the last time he saw her – still beautiful, of course, but before everything about her had seemed polished to a high sheen. Wet, her hair appears darker than before. Her legs are pale and bare.

He watches as she loops her wrap around the back of her head with her other hand – the left – to rub it dry. Then she glances up toward the house and sees him. He sees how she goes still, like an animal freezing before taking flight. He hurries his pace towards her, as though she might flee from him.

But she stays in her spot on the path, clutching the towel to herself.

'It's you,' he says, as he walks toward her.

'Yes,' she says, quietly, 'it's me.' He has somehow managed to forget the exact sound of her voice – the oddness hidden beneath the American accent, as though the latter has only been lacquered over the top.

She is not pleased to see him. He can see it in her face – the dismay, even something like fear. Her gaze moves up towards the house as though she is aware of an audience watching. Involuntarily he finds himself turning to look, but sees no one there.

'I assumed I wouldn't see you again,' he says.

'What are you doing here?' she asks, as though he hasn't spoken. Her voice is low, almost a whisper.

He stalls. 'I'm the journalist,' he adds, feeling suddenly put on the defensive. 'I'm writing a piece for *Tempo*.'

'Journalist? I thought you were a writer.'

'I am.' He tries not to sound too defensive. 'It's a form of writing, like any other.'

She doesn't reply. He is unnerved by the fixity of her gaze. She is studying him as though trying to convince herself he is really there. Then, remembering herself, she looks away, gives a shake of her head. And when she looks back at him her expression is a blank. Hal has the distinct impression of a blind being drawn hurriedly down.

'Well,' she says, running her hand through her damp hair, 'I see.' And then, with visible effort, 'And how have you been?' There is an impersonal civility to her tone. This is not the woman he remembers. Then she had been reticent, but not false.

'I didn't see you at the party last night,' he says.

'Oh. I wasn't feeling well.'

And then he thinks. 'It was you, wasn't it?'

'What was?'

'Last night. At the end of the garden, by the trees . . . wearing that black dress.'

Her face is a blank. 'No,' she says. 'I was in bed.'

He remembers now the emerald stud in his suit pocket. 'I found something – an earring.'

'Not mine,' she says, brusque. And then, politely, 'Did you enjoy it? The party?'

'I don't remember that much of it, to be honest.'

'Ah,' she nods. 'And who did you meet?'

'Aubrey Boyd, Signor Gaspari. Another man, an American – Truss, that was his name. Do you know—'

But she cuts him off. 'The water's cold,' she says, and draws the towel tighter about herself. 'I have to go and change into something warmer.' Still she avoids his gaze. 'I'll see you later, perhaps. At breakfast.'

'All right,' Hal says. 'I meant to ask—'

But she has already moved beyond him – carefully, so that a good couple of feet of air remain between them – and is striding purposefully toward the house. He watches her all the way up the path, the wrap snickering away from her in the breeze.

He walks down to the jetty, where her wet footprints form a trail on the bleached wood, yet to dry in the sun. He shrugs off his shorts and shirt and, without giving himself time to think about it, dives from the end. Only too late does he realize that he does not know how shallow it is, but he is lucky – when he rights himself his feet don't touch the bottom. And frigid; very much a spring sea, without weeks of warmth behind it. A sting against the flesh, but gradually becoming bearable. He has swum in the Solent in April; it is nothing compared to that. He has known greater cold, too, cold that steals the breath and binds fast and deadly to the flesh. But he will not think of that.

He lets it surround his aching head; rolls onto his back and kicks away from the shore. The water is still about him. It seems to cradle him, to buoy him up. This is the sea of his boyhood: of childhood trips to the Sussex coast.

They had gone to the beach together: Hal and his parents. East Head had been the favourite, a white spit of land crested with soft dunes. Water, warm in the summer shallows but cold where the bottom shelved into the main channel. It was where he learned to swim – a good place for it, because it was so benign. No, he thinks now. That's not quite right. Not all benign. The treachery of memory. At the far end of the spit the calm surface hid a secret current, straight out towards France. A woman had been swept into the open sea one summer. A child the next year – and her father had saved her, only to drown himself. He was never allowed to swim at that end of the beach, and there was a flag there, to warn of it. But every summer someone disregarded the warning.

Ah, but those long, drowsy, salty days on the beach eating sandwiches gritty with sand. His mother glamorous in her headscarf and wrapper, her toenails painted with dark varnish. His father still dapper, but running slightly to fat. Never quite her match.

What he would give to return to that place. Not childhood, precisely, but that place of simple pleasures, of unknowing-ness. That is the problem with home: it reminds him of what he was, what was lost. And the sea has been changed for him forever now.

He pushes harder, driving himself through the water, thinking of nothing but the movement, the labour of his muscles.

Pausing briefly to look back at the shore, he realizes that he has already come some way. He is almost as far from the jetty as he is from the finger of land that curves round in front of the bay. He might as well swim to it, see what is on the other side.

It is further than he had realized, and the sea becomes rougher further out. But finally he reaches and rounds the small spit of land. Revealed on the other side is a yacht, moored a little way off the coast at anchor. It is clear from the relative size of the men visible on deck that the boat is huge. There are two masts, each appearing as tall – perhaps taller – than the boat is long. The hull is dark blue. It seems designed for crossing oceans at great speed. Now Hal understands. This is how they will be making their way to Cannes.

Swimming back is a little harder. The jetty appears very small, a great distance away. His muscles ache. He isn't worried, but he is bored of it now, fatigued. Perhaps the tide is against him too, for it all feels more difficult. Does the Mediterranean have a tide? He isn't certain. His hangover intrudes as it did not on the outward leg, his head beginning to ache as though his brain has swollen too large for the skull.

The last forty metres or so are most difficult of all. It feels as though something has wrapped itself around his legs. There is some sort of current, he realizes, one that must have helped him on the way out. Now it is tugging at him, pulling him away from the shore. His muscles ache with the effort and occasionally he swallows a mouthful of briny water. You are meant to swim sideways with a current, he thinks – but if he were to do that he would be taken past the headland and into open sea. For the first time since he learned to swim, he feels something like alarm: a sense of real danger. He does not seem to be getting any closer to the shore, and yet the effort merely to stay in one spot is extraordinary. Will he call for help? Would there be any use in it? He squints up through the sweat and the water fogging his vision, and cannot see anyone in the garden. But just as he decides that he must do it, no matter the humiliation, his final effort propels him further than before. The current's hold on him seems to slacken, as though an invisible hand has instantly released him. His movements become easy again, he is moving forward. Though he feels his tiredness through his whole body it is difficult to believe now in the danger of a few seconds before.

When he finally pulls himself from the water, his arms are weak, his legs shake. Unable to think of anything else to do, unable to quite make sense of what has happened to him, he lies prone on the warm wood and waits for the sun to dry him.

Her

My hands are still trembling. It took great determination not to run from him: to remain for a few minutes, instead, and talk as civilly as I could manage. I knew that we might be seen from the house. For that reason, I had to act as normally as I could.

I cannot believe it is him. I worked hard afterwards, to put that night in Rome from my mind. Forgetting is something I am adept at. I had almost been able to convince myself that it hadn't really happened. Not because the memory of it was abhorrent. The opposite, in fact. This was what made it dangerous.

When I get back to the room, to my relief, Frank is in the dressing room, the door closed. He calls to me, through the door.

'Did you have a good swim?'

I stop. Is there something in his tone? Does he know? Could he somehow know about Rome, and have orchestrated this? . . . I am being absurd. If he had known, I would have found out long before now.

'Yes,' I say, 'yes. A little cold, but refreshing.'

'Good.'

I hadn't swum far. Enough to feel my muscles ache. Off at an angle, to avoid the current the Contessa had warned of: an undertow along this stretch of coast that has been known to sweep swimmers out to sea. The English poet, Shelley, drowned only a little way along the coast from here: it is not so benign as it appears.

I find myself moving, despite my better judgement, to the balcony. I am drawn there in the way one is often compelled to do the destructive thing: to press the bruise.

The view is out to sea and in the broad blue I can make him out. His dark head, the occasional glimpse of a limb, the churned water like a scar about him. It is difficult to tell at first in which direction he is swimming. And then I realize that he is trying for the shore, but is making no progress. Is he in trouble? Frank, I know, has a pair of binoculars. I go to the smallest of his travelling cases and open it. My pulse is thudding in my ears. Because how will I explain myself if he finds me, rooting through his luggage?

I find them in their leather pouch and return to the balcony. I can see, now, that he is in trouble. Some invisible force is preventing him from making any headway, and he appears to be tiring. I understand now: it is the current. I should have warned him. What can I do? If I were brave, I would run from the room, sound the alarm, no matter the attention it would draw to myself. I am a coward . . .

Such a coward that I am going to let him drown in front of me? I must do something.

But I see that something has changed. He is gaining on the jetty. He has forced himself through the current somehow. The relief leaves me weak.

'What's so interesting out there?'

I turn and find Frank framed in the doorway, watching me. He is the picture of relaxed elegance in his powder-blue suit. But he is never quite relaxed – it is the key to his success. If one knows what to look for, one can see the animal alertness beneath the languor.

'Oh,' I say, moving in towards him. 'I was trying to see across to Portovenere.'

'Can you?' He moves towards me, his hand outstretched for the binoculars.

'No,' I say. I'm not certain. I didn't even look. Rather than handing them to him, I place the binoculars on the dressing table and step toward him.

'Please,' I say. 'The clasp of my swimsuit – I can't seem to unfasten it.'

There is something that very few people understand about him. He has been described on numerous occasions as a man of unusual self-possession. But what isn't known is that he is also bound by certain potent appetites. I step out of the swimsuit, knowing that his eyes are on me. On the skin I have revealed, tightening in the spring breeze from the balcony. This is one of the few times in which I feel the balance shift towards me, in which I become powerful.

By the time he steps out onto the balcony, and I after him, there is no sign of the man I knew in Rome. I could almost bring myself to believe – *to hope* – that he had disappeared.

*

Hal

Showered and dressed, Hal is summoned to breakfast. The terrace in front of the house, which the night before had supported the band and the bar, is now set with a table bearing breakfast fare. A whole salmon glistens – rather raw and naked-looking in the strong light – beside dishes of charcuterie and cheese, a cornucopia of fruit: strawberries, oranges, grapes; a basket of burnished brioche loaves and other delicacies. There is champagne, but Hal gives this a wide berth. He loads his plate with food, feeling hollowed with hunger after his swim. As he lifts his fork to his mouth it shakes slightly; his body still electric with adrenaline.

Signor Gaspari is there, his little dog on his lap, and next to him sits the photographer, Aubrey Boyd. Hal gestures to the seat next to Aubrey.

'May I?'

'By all means.' Aubrey's plate, balanced on his lap, bears five segments of grapefruit, fanned out in a bloom-like pattern. He probes one with a fork, speculatively.

'Not hungry?'

'Oh, I can never take much in the morning – and I intend to wear a thirty-two until I die.' Aubrey appraises Hal. 'You certainly seemed to enjoy yourself last night.'

'Yes,' he says, queasily remembering the final drink. Something about a chicken.

Aubrey Boyd watches him, amused. 'I saw you disappear off into the gardens late on. So I think you missed Giulietta Castiglione dancing in little more than her bathing suit. Spontaneous, apparently. That little white dress simply happened to disappear at some point and then – *pouf* – there was a great deal more of Giulietta. I got some excellent shots.' He sips his water. 'You'll get to meet her properly on the trip, of course. I'll introduce you – I took the promotional shots for *A Holiday*.'

'Thank you,' Hal says. 'In fact,' he says, with careful disinterest, 'there was someone else, too. I met her this morning – though I didn't see her last night.' He decides not to mention the previous encounter. 'I wonder if you know her?'

'Describe her to me.'

'Her name's Stella. I don't know her surname. She's blonde . . .' he is about to say beautiful, but stops himself in time. 'Short hair,' he says, instead. 'American.'

Aubrey frowns. And then he seems to think of something. 'An odd accent, though?'

'Yes.'

'Oh yes,' Aubrey says, slowly – with something slightly cruel in his look. 'In that case I think you have met Mrs Truss.'

It takes several seconds for Hal to digest this. 'Mrs Truss? She's . . .'

'That American investor's wife? Yes, old chap.'

'You're sure?'

'I don't know her first name, but I rather think it must be her, from your account. Ever so glamorous. Hair the colour of money. She's quite something, is she not?'

Suddenly, certain elements fall into place. Her reticence in telling him anything about herself, her haste in leaving the following morning. Her horror at seeing him on the jetty.

'Oh,' Aubrey says. 'Why – there she is now.'

Hal looks up. There she is indeed, looking quite different to the person of a couple of hours earlier. A white shirtdress, heeled sandals, her hair combed. She is well suited to him, the elegant man appearing behind her in his blue suit. They are a matched pair, he realizes: they make more sense together than apart. His hand at her back – a caress, or possibly a steer.

So he was the one-time adventure, the penniless young man in his garret. He thinks of the smallness and shabbiness of the studio, and wonders if that was part of the thrill. He should have known, then, seeing the wealth she wore about her. Hair the colour of money, indeed.

He watches her, compelled in spite of himself. He thinks that his eyes would be drawn to her even if he did not know her: there is something innately watchable about her; the unique grace with which she moves. It does not appear affected. But who is he to tell? He knows even less of her than he thought.

He watches her husband too. He had decided he did not like the man, but perhaps he should pity him. Hal has made him that old-fashioned word: a cuckold. Except that he is not a figure that invites pity.

The Contessa has appeared now and is greeting them, offering them both champagne. Stella is shaking her head, but he – Truss – takes one for them both and hands her a glass. He is steering her towards the end of the table now, nearer to Hal. She glances up and catches sight of Hal watching her. Good: he rather wants her to see, to see that he understands now what she is. She looks quickly away.

She finds a seat at the furthest possible distance away, says something to her husband – *her husband* – and sits down. But Truss does not appear to be happy with her choice. He is gesturing to the patch of shade thrown by the parasol, only a few feet from Hal. She shakes her head. And Hal watches as the man takes her by the arm, and half-lifts her out of the seat. He isn't quite able to believe what he is seeing. To anyone glancing over, it would look as though he is merely helping her from her chair. But to Hal, who has watched the whole interaction, it is something different. He sees the firmness of the grip about her upper arm, the expression on her face: vacillating between humiliation and fear.

He feels in some way that she has let him down. Being married to a man like Truss, a rich man's wife, makes her ordinary. There are women like her on the Via Condotti every day, stepping from cars, trailed by their hapless spouses. Sweeping past the doorman at Bulgari, trying on, no doubt, the biggest, ugliest, costliest baubles they think they can get away with. And then to Caffè Greco, to compare these new spoils with the others of their species sitting about them. He has never paid these women, or their husbands, any heed before. They have been so far outside his own sphere, and his Rome, that they might as well have been from another planet. If he had thought of them, well, it might have been with something approaching contempt. He can see, now, reflected in the morning sun, the wink of gems at earlobes and wrist. He supposes that at least she has managed to find herself a wealthy man who is not fifty years her senior, balding and fat. Perhaps by the standards of such women she has landed a coup, even if he is a bully.

And yet . . . she didn't seem the sort, to be bought off with trinkets. He would have credited her with more intelligence, a greater sense of self-worth.

He catches himself. One evening – and a few brief moments this morning – that is the sum total of how long he has known her. He knows nothing about her. It is nothing but the work of that pernicious thing that once served him so well in his writing: the overactive imagination. She had told him so little about herself that he couldn't have known anything about her. And it is a relief that he has found out the truth. Now she will take up no more room in his thoughts.

6

Her

I am sure that when people see me, they see someone weak. And they would be right: I am. I wasn't always, though.

I hadn't thought about the girl I used to be for a long time. I hadn't spoken her language, the old language, or even thought in it. Maybe I dreamed in it sometimes, but if I did I tried to forget that as soon as I woke. And then, a year ago, something happened that made me remember her.

I suppose I need to go back to the beginning.

To Spain, 1936.

To a town, cradled in the lee of the surrounding hills. It has been there since medieval times, under the sun. Red roofs and cobblestones, green fountains and moss, scent of coffee and aniseed.

It is there that I think I left her, the girl that I was. Or perhaps somewhere on the road to Madrid.

The last good memory.

June. A very hot night, too hot to sleep indoors, though the farmhouse was built to keep the warmth out. So my father – Papa – makes a makeshift tent for us, of old canvas and furniture. A gauze net over the opening, to keep the bugs out. An oil lamp for light, blown out once we have bedded down. Papa, my little brother Tino and me. We lie there with the dark surrounding us.

I didn't know how alive the night could be before now. Deprived of all other senses, in our soft cocoon, it is cacophonous. We lie there listening, as my father names the sounds for us: the fluted exclamation of an owl, the frog music, low and guttural. Then, through the opening to the dark garden, the biggest miracle of all. Living pinpricks of light, much closer than the stars, but seeming for a moment to borrow their brilliance. *Las luciérnagas*. The fireflies.

They remind me a little of Papa. When you find yourself in the spotlight of his interest, there is no greater feeling. And then without warning, it will blink off – he will have made his way on to something else. He is a man of great passions, though most are fleeting. Our education was one. He removed us from school, claiming that our heads were being filled with religious dogma, announced that he would teach us himself. At first, he was wonderfully dedicated to it. He spent hours with us in his study, a generous – if sometimes impatient – tutor. As with his views about many things, his idea of what children should learn was a little eccentric. As a result, I got a good grounding in Greek philosophers, Spanish literature and German political theorists, speak English well and French passably, but know almost nothing in the way of basic arithmetic. Then, one day, the lessons stopped. He needed to focus on the second

book: he needed us out of the study, actually . . . out of
the house, making as little noise as possible. They never
resumed.

The garden was another. Papa didn't think of it, after a
while, though he had grand plans for it at one stage. Once,
when my aunt and uncle came to visit from Madrid, they
helped to clear the weeds that had grown over the vegetable
beds. They always seemed to enjoy spending time with Tino
and me – they have no children of their own. My uncle, Tío
Salvador, cut canes for beans and made bird-scarers for our
fig tree. Tía Aída showed us how far apart to plant the
potatoes, carrots, lettuces. All the while my father sat in his
study, hammering away so hard at his typewriter we could
hear the clack of the keys outside, above the chatter of the
crickets.

The passions that remain steadfast: his writing, his politics,
his country. He is a great man, Papa. His first book, about
the struggle for a modern Spain, made his a name to conjure
with. It has been read by the people that matter, as Uncle
Salvador said, even if wasn't a bestseller. Besides, the next
book – more ambitious, more polemic – will be the one to
make his name.

We love him helplessly. At times, desperately.

Often, he is away from home. He will go to Madrid to
give lectures. Or he will go on his crusades: to poor peasant
farmers in Estremadura, to industrial workers in the Basque
country, explaining the concept of Socialism. It is not so bad.
We always know he will return. I am fifteen now, nearly a
woman. Besides, even when Papa is here I do most of the
work about the house. He isn't lazy, he simply doesn't see
the need for such things. While he is working on his second
book – which he has nearly finished – he would quite happily

live on hunks of stale bread, and let the house fall down around us.

I have always looked after Tino, too. My mother died giving birth to him. She was English, and extremely clever: my father met her studying at Cambridge. She had been told that she probably wouldn't be able to have another child, after me. But she had been determined, as she was about many things. I thought I might never be able to forgive the baby for it, that I might hate him. But when I saw him for the first time – truly *saw* him, with his solemn dark eyes and pale silk of hair – it was as though he had reached out with his little fist and taken hold of my heart. From then on, it was his. I knew that I would fight like a lioness to keep him safe from harm.

Tino is a dreamer. He will spend hours drawing in his sketchbook, fantastical diagrams that seem to bear no relation to anything glimpsed in life. Except I asked him, once, what they were and he told me: 'the bees'. As I looked, I began to understand. He had watched them move from flower to flower, and had tried to replicate the various paths of their flight with his crayons: a different hue for each bee. So what looked like nothing more than a great tangle of colour was actually something strangely logical, and oddly beautiful. That is a fitting description of his character, I think.

While other six-year-old boys might be pulling the wings off flies, Tino is content to watch his bees for hours, learning their secrets. On any given day, if you were to look from the windows of the kitchen, you would be able to see the top of his head above the stone wall that separates the main part of the garden from the hives. There are six hives in total, producing far more honey than we would ever be able to eat ourselves. They were another fleeting interest of Papa's. Luckily, Tino's love for the bees has far outlasted his.

To my eyes the movements of the insects appear aimless. But Tino has explained to me that the bees are organized, incredibly so. There are patterns to their movements, varying from season to season, that he is learning to read. He has told me about the queen, the female workers, the male drones. How they build and clean their hive, how they make, dry and store the honey, how they could make a new queen, if they needed one, in a special cell in the honeycomb. The ordinary worker-bee larva becomes something extraordinary, becomes a mother. Just sometimes I think that if we could make ourselves a new mother – or if we could make me into a real adult – things might be easier for us.

That evening, when we camped in the garden, above all of the other nighttime sounds I remember that of Tino's breathing, fast with the wonder of it all. I felt his hand reach for mine, and I took it, and held it tight.

'Can you see them?' he asked.

'Yes.'

We watched them, the dancing points of light, for so long that even when I closed my eyes I could see them there, imprinted somewhere behind my eyelids.

That, then, is the last good memory. It has taken me a while to bring myself to remember past that point.

July 1936

It is a few weeks later, a July morning. I discover Papa listening to the radio. When I ask him if he wants me to make him a coffee – he drinks several cups a day, thick and black in the Turkish style – he makes a quieting motion with one hand. I listen with him, to see what it is that has him so excited.

There has been an incident, in Morocco, the announcer says. A young soldier has led some soldiers into an uprising there. They are trying to make their way to Spain. This is not the thing that frightens me; the man on the radio insists that it will be snuffed out within twenty-four hours – if that. The frightening thing is my father's face, when he turns to look at me.

'It's coming,' he says. 'I knew it would happen. I've been saying it for the last year. But they've become complacent.'

'But the man says—'

'He says what they think people want to hear.'

'Hear what?' We turn, and see Tino, trailed by his elderly cat, Señor Bombón.

My father is, I think, about to tell him – but I get there first. 'Nothing, Tino,' I say now. 'It's nothing.' For what is the point in a six-year-old worrying over something that does not concern him, that will be over before it has even begun? Especially a child who has terrible nightmares already: whose imagination is an overly fertile place. Even innocuous-sounding phrases – a chance mention by my father of 'the trees in the distance' turned those trees into one of his great fears. When he woke up screaming one night and I went to ask what the matter was, all he would say, as he clung to me, was: '*los árboles, los árboles*'. Sometimes, still, he wets the bed – a thing that we have to keep a secret from Papa, because Tino can't bear the shame of him finding out.

Now, when he looks unconvinced, I say: 'I've been wondering, something, Tino. About the bees. Perhaps you could explain it to me?'

It is a low trick, perhaps, but it works.

How long, though, will I be able to hide it from him? Because the thing is not crushed. Not in twenty-four hours, not in forty-eight. It spreads to the mainland. It moves through the country like a forest fire, snatching new fuel to feast upon. Seville, Cordoba, Saragossa, Papa tells me: all have fallen to these men they call the rebels. There are soldiers, trained marksmen, marching from their barracks to massacre unarmed townspeople. Besides the Spanish soldiers – known for their skill in the fine art of killing – there are the Moorish soldiers, known too for their talent, but also for their absolute lack of mercy.

Often, now, we hear the roar of aircraft above us. Tino will run out into the garden and watch them with a kind of wonder. And there is something awesome in them: in their speed and deadly grace. They are German, Papa says: Adolf Hitler is sending them to help the rebels. Mussolini, of Italy, is sending tanks and soldiers.

We are not their target, yet. Some other small town is, perhaps – or one of the big cities. How long before that changes?

Even as I understood the danger, there was a part of me that didn't believe it would come. Or that even if it did it would only sear us a little, it couldn't change us. The thing we had, our happiness, was too sacred. The arrogance of imagining that I was unchangeable. That what we had was stronger, somehow, than this thing that had engulfed the whole country. That was a hard lesson to learn.

PART TWO

7

Liguria, 1953

Appearing around the dark finger of land is a yacht: the same one Hal saw on his swim. Her navy blue hull gleams, the line of her prow is as sharp as a shark's tooth. There are gilt fittings all about, sheening in the sunlight like newly minted coins. The twin masts appear, from this perspective, to pierce the sky. Even Hal, who knows so little about boats, can recognize that she is a beautiful work of construction.

'She is quite something, is she not?'

He turns to find Frank Truss beside him. Hal nods.

'I own a schooner,' Truss says. 'She's in the States at present, of course. Southampton. Need to get her transferred over here some time. Sixty foot – a beautiful creature.'

'Goodness,' Hal says. 'I used to own a Firefly.'

Truss frowns. Hal has the distinct impression that he

doesn't like to admit ignorance on any point. Finally, he says: 'It's a yacht?'

'It's a small wooden dinghy,' Hal says, and steps away.

Aubrey Boyd wants to take a photograph. He gestures to Hal. 'You, dear fellow, if you wouldn't mind. Yes, you have exactly the look.'

'I don't think it would be right,' Hal says. 'I'm the journalist. Surely it should be Giulietta, or Gaspari . . .'

'Not for this one,' Aubrey Boyd tells him. 'Anyway, why so shy? Are you afraid that the camera will steal your soul? It's only a little fun.' As though the matter is decided, he attaches the flashbulb and frames the scene. Hal steps forward reluctantly and stands before the sea, the yacht behind him. The other guests observe – perhaps trying to understand the supposed perfection of the fit.

Then Aubrey finds his next subject. 'Mrs Truss, if you wouldn't mind.'

She smiles, politely, and tries to demur. Hal catches sight of Giulietta Castiglione, whose expression is unforgettable. She is not used to being passed over.

Aubrey is not to be deterred. 'Please, Mrs Truss. Your blonde hair, with his dark. You look so picturesque together. The perfect contrast . . .' He turns to Truss. 'If you wouldn't mind, of course.'

Truss nods his acquiescence.

Still, she does not step forward. Then Truss reaches over and takes her by the wrist. 'Come on, Kitten. Do as the man asks.' Like an errant child, she is guided to stand beside Hal. She stops a foot away, near enough that he can make out the fine gold hairs on her bare forearms, but far enough that there is no chance of any part of them touching.

Aubrey raises his camera. 'A little closer together, if you wouldn't mind.' He laughs. 'Anyone would think you two were the married couple.'

Giulietta's co-star – the man who plays the sea captain of the film's title – arrives moments before they set sail. Hal doesn't recognize him immediately. He knows from somewhere the great golden head, the exaggeratedly handsome features, but can't place them. Only when Aubrey Boyd whispers the name does he understand. Earl Morgan. He can't believe he didn't know him. But then there is a marked difference between the figure standing here and the heroic one he has viewed onscreen.

There is something off about the man, though Hal cannot quite work it out until he steps nearer. Up close, Morgan looks terrible. The boyishly handsome looks are marred, as though in a state of decay. There is a loose, febrile look to his skin. His eyes, his most famous feature, are still very blue, but the whites are pinkish-yellow, as though pickled.

He puts up a hand, smiling slowly as he looks about himself. Hal thinks that even now he appears to be playing a part: the star greeting his audience. 'Hi.' There is a resounding silence. 'Sorry I couldn't make it for the party,' he says. 'I had to catch up on some sleep, you know how it is.'

'Mr Morgan.' The Contessa smiles graciously at him. 'You look well rested.'

Morgan nods. 'Indeed I am. It seems this Italian air is the thing for me.'

Hal tries to decide whether he is imagining the slur to Morgan's speech. He turns to Aubrey, and whispers. 'He seems a little . . . well, drunk.'

'Dear chap,' Aubrey says, 'he's drunk all the time. It would be far more remarkable if he were sober. They say he's spent the last couple of years in a spa, trying to dry out – though it's clear he's still soused in the stuff. He's one of the Contessa's little projects. I suppose we all are, in a way.'

Before Hal can ask exactly what he means, Aubrey has made his way over to Morgan, to ask if he may take a photograph.

They set sail. It is a mere few kilometres across the Gulf of the Poets to Portovenere, their first stop, but the commotion with which their departure occurs would be better suited to a ship taking off on a great voyage. The Contessa's household staff come to see them off: some standing on the jetty, others amidst the terraces. The house soars behind, nestled in its dark bank of trees. But gradually it, too, is diminished – becomes a cottage, a child's doll's house.

Then there is only the water and the wind. The guests look at one another, unsure of what to do, whether to speak, like actors who have suddenly forgotten their lines. All except for Truss, who is reading the papers in one of the seats on the foredeck.

Hal glances at Stella. She stands a little distance from the group, and her gaze is turned from them. If they are all upon the stage, he thinks, she is the one waiting in the wings, hidden in its dark recesses. He remembers again how she had been in Rome. Quiet, but self-possessed. Her quietness has a different quality now; she is subdued. He looks away. He watches, instead, as Earl Morgan staggers over to the other chair and sits down. The actor turns toward the sea, until perhaps he thinks no one can see him. Then his smile – his whole face, in fact, appears to collapse in on itself. It is a horrible sight, as though the man is coming apart at the seams. Presently, loud snores are heard from his direction, and the hand that had been holding his drink slackens, allowing the empty glass to roll gently back towards them, the slice of lemon flopping onto the deck like a tiny, dead fish.

Portovenere

The water in the Gulf of the Poets is calm, protected from the violence of the sea without by a long sea barrier at the mouth. In the distance the shadows of vast ships cluster about La Spezia harbour, vessels of heavy industry and war.

'Not worth a visit, in my opinion,' Aubrey Boyd pronounces, looking back at it, 'unless you have a fetish for the industrial.'

'I was there yesterday,' Hal says. 'Briefly.'

'Oh, gracious.' Aubrey lifts his eyebrows. 'You *are* intrepid.'

All come up on deck for a better sighting of the town, even those who have seen it before.

'It is my favourite,' Signor Gaspari says, quietly. 'The Victorians flocked to the Cinque Terre, but Portovenere was the one they forgot.' He looks at Hal, and gives his down-turned smile. 'I hope people continue to forget.'

Hal can make out a vivid strip of houses, each painted a different colour: ochre, sepia, rust red, dusky pink and, occasionally, a slice of blue: the colours of earth and sky. They are like the bright spines of so many books crammed together onto a bookshelf; a quiet spectacle. Aubrey Boyd gives a soft cry of delight, and reaches for his camera.

Above the town is the great grey mass of an old castle: ruined and yet from this distance retaining something of majesty. For Genoese ships, Gaspari explains, it would have been a welcome sight: the first glimpse of home. On the other side is an uninhabited island, a steep green nub of land emerging from the water like the backbone of some sleeping sea creature.

As they motor towards the harbour a boat arrives with men clamouring to give their assistance. Roberto, the Contessa's skipper, solemnly tells their would-be guides that his men have everything under control. Reluctantly they manoeuvre further away. But when they catch sight of Giulietta in her black sundress there are whoops and cheers, ardent declarations. And suddenly two cameras appear with huge mounted flashbulbs. Giulietta tosses her head and turns away – but this has the effect, Hal notices, of displaying her profile to its best advantage.

Aubrey turns to Hal. 'Prepare yourself for a great deal more of this. They are like cockroaches, these men – they follow some scent only discernible to them. And nowhere breeds them in greater numbers than Italy.'

'Before supper,' the Contessa announces to the party, once they have moored, 'we will have a screening of the film. The audience at Cannes are getting a preview, but those on this boat will be the first to experience Signor Gaspari's creation.' She turns to the director, who inclines his head modestly.

As they are taken across on the tender, Hal turns to Gaspari. 'So no one has seen it yet, apart from you? Even the actors?'

He shakes his head. 'No. It keeps it purer, this way.' He lowers his voice. 'Free from ego, from meddling. Though there was some pressure, this time, to share the rushes.' And Hal is certain that his gaze moves momentarily toward Truss.

They are led through the marina to the ruins of the old Genoese fort. Flaming torches illuminate the arches and pilasters in all their ravaged grandeur. From within, the place no longer looks formidable, Hal thinks, but vulnerable: spreadeagled before the wind and rain that have for centuries been feasting upon it, picking the old bones clean. As they make their way up he glimpses a forlorn window in a fragment of wall, offering an unnecessary aperture onto the sea beyond. They are ushered into the still-intact part of the castle, where a projector and chairs have been set up. They wait as a young man threads the machine with nervous hands and Hal, watching him, wonders if it is the first time he has ever done it. But after a couple of false starts, the wall opposite flickers into life, where a piece of canvas has been stretched across it.

The first shot fills the screen and suddenly Hal understands the significance of where they are sitting. The view is from the battlements of the same fort, but by some artistry of set design the arches appear intact, restored to their former glory.

Earl Morgan appears on the screen, looking out to sea, costumed in a sixteenth-century naval commander's outfit. Hal wonders how much make-up it took to hide the decay of the man. He looks implausibly youthful and heroic. Cut to a view of him at the helm of a great galleon, then a battle scene with an Ottoman ship, which almost makes Hal smile, because it is so artful, so synchronized: rather like a ballroom dance. Even when men fall dying to the boards. Was there once a time when war would have looked like that? Unlikely. But the alternative would make unpalatable viewing.

The battle won, the galleon is making for home. Another shot of Morgan, picturesquely windblown, looking out to sea. The next shot is of the water. And there is a person in the water, flailing. Drowning. It has an unprecedented effect on Hal. Instantly, he feels as though he has been drenched in cold water. He stares at the image, trying to make sense of it. It is almost exactly as he has dreamed it, as though it has spilled onto the screen from his own mind. He stands. All he can think is that he has to get outside. He pushes past the knees that block his route. He isn't sure whether he manages to apologize aloud, or whether the words form only inside his head. He lunges through the open doorway. In the courtyard he breathes great lungfuls of the cooling air, and feels the tightness in his chest begin to dissipate.

For days and even weeks afterwards, though he knew it was impossible, he kept thinking he glimpsed something in the water. It was always, of course, a trick of light and shadow – and of his own imagination. But to lose someone that way – there was a lack of certainty about it.

'Are you all right, Mr Jacobs?'

Hal looks up and sees Signor Gaspari. All he can feel now is humiliation. The horror is passed, though he can still feel his heartbeat through his whole body. The speed with which it took hold of him, the power of it, was astounding.

'I'm fine,' he says. 'I drank too much last night. I thought I'd step outside for a moment to get some air.' It is unprofessional, but it is better than admitting anything of the truth.

'Ah,' Gaspari smiles his sad smile. 'I'm pleased to hear it wasn't my film that was so objectionable.'

'No. I'm so sorry. It must have looked very rude.'

As he stands his legs feel insubstantial, as though he is not quite in contact with the earth. It will pass, he thinks, with an effort of will. The important thing is to get back inside, and pretend none of it ever happened.

*

He is able to catch up quickly enough. He can only have been outside for a matter of minutes, though he felt that he re-entered the room a different man.

The figure in the water turns out to be a woman, who the captain has rescued and brought aboard the ship. She is played by Giulietta Castiglione: black-eyed, wild-haired, relentlessly seductive. Against his better judgement, the captain begins to fall for her. The atmosphere on board the galleon is powerfully evoked: the claustrophobic, gossipy watchfulness of the men. Hal recognizes it. It was exactly the same on board *Lionheart*. As Perkins, one of the other ratings, had put it, 'You can't break wind in this place without the news finding its way onto every deck.'

The superstition, too, is familiar. There had been rituals and old wives' tales and lucky charms – all the way up through the ranks. He'd seen a lieutenant-commander take a small piece of silver out of his pocket – a locket, perhaps – and run his thumb absent-mindedly over it before a strike. Morris, Hal's best friend on the cruiser, had one of the little white gloves his wife had worn on their wedding day. Somehow, despite all the grime one came into contact with on board, he had managed to keep it spotlessly clean. Suze had given Hal a silk scarf, which he would take out from time to time. Yet every time he looked at it he was reminded simply of how far away she was in every respect.

Upon return to Genoa, the captain defies the scandalized reaction of society – and his harridan of a fiancée – to follow his heart and marry his new love. Together, they embark upon a ship travelling to the newly discovered Americas.

The possibility of beginning again, somewhere new. As the credits roll, Hal realizes that he is sitting far forward in his seat, his face tilted up towards the screen as though he is literally trying to drink it in. He sits back. And watches, unable to look away, as Truss bends his head towards Stella and murmurs something into her ear. She nods, and Truss smiles. For a terrible second, Hal thinks that he is about to watch him kiss her. Just in time the Contessa begins to applaud, the rest of them following suit.

'Well,' she says, standing, and bidding Gaspari to take a bow. 'Is it not a triumph?'

It is. Somewhat more of a Hollywood offering than *Elegy*, but still with those elements that characterize Gaspari's work: scenes of a haunting, melancholy beauty, and the rawness of the performance demanded from the leads. Earl Morgan, Hal thinks, brings impressive credibility to the sea captain: a man wrung out by war, but trying to hold everything together for his men.

But there is optimism in it. *Elegy* had been a leave-taking. A mourning of something – or someone – lost. *The Sea Captain* is the opposite. Though it is a film set centuries ago, it is about the future, about hope. It will appeal, Hal thinks, to audiences everywhere who are tired of looking back.

He feels the curious glances of the others as they leave. To his relief no questions are asked about his sudden disappearance. He is still shaken by how quickly it all took hold of him. Nothing for so long and now this. His life in Rome, he realizes, was static, was safe.

They have dinner on the ramparts above the sea. A woman has been brought to serenade them, but the wind and the echoes upon the stones distort her voice. What should be exquisite melodies are transformed, at times, into the shrieks of a banshee.

All of the heat of the day was in the sun. Now, with the wind up, it is much cooler, and the singer shivers in her thin ballgown until Truss moves to place his jacket about her shoulders. She thanks him with a lingering smile and Hal cannot help but watch, fascinated. This, then, is the charm of the man at work.

He can hear the sea, far beneath them, sucking and gnawing against the stone. It is open water, that side, not the serene calm of the harbour. 'There is bad weather coming soon,' the skipper, Roberto, had told Hal, with a kind of morose pleasure. Already the waves sound louder, hungrier than they have yet.

They take their seats for supper, and Hal finds himself placed between Stella and Giulietta Castiglione.

He tries, first, to engage Giulietta in conversation, but she resists every attempt to be drawn out. Finally, when she begins to study her reflection in the back of the spoon, he gives up, and turns to his left.

'How are you?' he asks Stella, with faultless formality.

'Well, thank you.' She gives him a quick, polite smile. 'Good.'

Then she says, in a barely audible murmur, 'I'm sorry.'

He thinks he understands all that she means to encompass by it. But it is not enough, somehow. He wants to make her uncomfortable, he realizes, make her see that this is equally awkward for him. He wants to provoke her. 'I'm simply confused,' he murmurs, 'because it was you—'

'Mr Jacobs.' She looks up at him, and he sees something in her expression that unnerves him: fear. 'Please,' she says. And then, through her teeth, 'People are looking.'

He glances up and finds the Contessa's gaze on them, her

expression unreadable. Truss though, is turned away, speaking to the singer. His hand rests on the back of the chair, the picture of ease. But this doesn't mean anything. Hal has already decided that he is the sort of man who notices everything.

He looks for something innocuous to say. If Stella chose, he realizes, she could merely turn her head and start a conversation with Signor Gaspari on her other side, cutting him off. And though he decided only a few hours ago that he would avoid all but the most necessary interaction with her he finds that he wants to keep her attention. 'It's a fascinating place,' he says, gesturing around them. 'Don't you think?'

He expects her to simply agree but he can see her considering the question, turning it over. Then she says, 'I'm not sure that it is, actually. It feels full of . . . of death.'

'Well,' he says, curious, 'there's a great weight of history here. But surely that is part of its charm.'

She appears not to have heard him. 'These stones – they're like a skeleton that has been left out in the open, that has suffered the indignity of not being given the burial it deserves.' There is something like real pain in her voice. He stares at her. Now she is the one not playing by the rules.

'Stella,' he says, and then quickly corrects himself. 'Mrs Truss, this castle was built centuries ago. The people who once lived here have been dead – and buried – for hundreds of years. These are nothing more than stones.'

But she does not seem to be listening. 'How long do you think it takes,' she asks him, 'before the dead are forgotten entirely?' She sounds intent now, almost angry. He wonders briefly if she has had too much to drink – but her wine glass appears untouched.

'I'm not sure,' he says, cautiously. 'But probably as long as there is someone living to remember them.'

He looks at her, hoping that it is enough.

It isn't. 'But don't you think there are some things that should never be forgotten? Even as time softens the marks?'

I don't know what you want from me, he thinks.

'What can you two be talking about?' Hal looks up to find Truss regarding them across the table. At his words the other guests turn to look, too. He smiles at Hal. 'I'm sorry, Mr Jacobs – is my wife giving you a hard time already?' Now he looks at Stella, who has not raised her head. 'She gets carried away, sometimes – don't you, Kitten?'

Silence.

'Well, Kitten?'

She nods. Truss gives a little mock toast with his glass and turns back to Gloria. Stella takes a long sip of her wine. Then she turns to Hal. 'Forgive me,' she says – shortly, bitterly, as though it was he who chastised her in front of all present. Before he can think of something to say to her, she has turned away.

The evening seems to have fractured, after this. The guests sit in silence, the plates have been cleared away, the wine bottles emptied. The wind has picked up, and Aubrey Boyd shivers miserably in his thin blazer. A faint-hearted soul might call an end to the dinner now. But the Contessa is not that.

She speaks fearlessly into the silence. 'Some of you,' with a nod to Gaspari, 'already know this, but I thought it might be interesting for those who don't. The film is based on a strange legend in my family. My ancestor was the sea captain played so superbly by our leading man here,' she turns to Earl Morgan, but his eyes are glassy with drink, and he seems barely to register her comment. Undeterred, she takes something from the pocket of her jacket. Hal tries to get a closer look at it. A little pot, made from ivory – with some sort of design carved into it.

'This,' she holds it up, 'belonged to him.'

She passes it to Earl Morgan, who studies the pattern for a few seconds disinterestedly, and then hands it on. Now Stella has been passed the pot by Gaspari. Hal watches her examining it, with quiet focus. She turns it over and around in her hands. And then, with an audible pop, she prises the thing open.

'Ah,' the Contessa says, pleased, 'you have discovered its secret. I was wondering when someone was going to do that.'

The others crane to see. Stella holds it up, so that the inside is visible. A dial of some sort, with spokes of alternating red and green, encircled by a gold band.

'A compass,' Aubrey says, peering over her shoulder.

'Broken,' she says. 'The arrow . . .' she watches it for a few seconds, tilting it back and forth, 'it keeps going round and round.'

'Yes,' the Contessa says. 'A shame. But perhaps only to be expected, considering its great age.'

Finally, it has come to Hal, and he has a chance to study it himself. There had been a large bronze compass mounted on the captain's bridge of the battlecruiser, which he had got to see only after they had been decommissioned. Funny, how little the design has changed. It has a peculiar weight in his hand, and a surprising warmth that he assumes must come from the touch of the others before him. North, he presumes, is the point marked by a fleur-de-lys.

He turns it toward the Contessa, and points to the flower. 'Why this?'

'The three petals,' she says, 'represent religious faith, wisdom, and chivalry. The essential tenets of any nobleman, that kept him on his proper course.'

Hal watches as the needle tracks a stuttering circle, driven by some unknown force. He is at once unnerved by it, and oddly compelled.

The silence now has a different quality. Hal realizes now that a kind of magic has been performed. The Contessa has drawn them together in the telling of it, salvaging the supper by introducing this new, strange element. As conversation resumes around the table she turns to Hal, her smile one of triumph. Her gaze falls to the compass, which he is still turning, almost mindlessly, in his hands.

'You may borrow it for a while if you wish,' she says, 'to study it further.'

He feels he should demur: there is something about the needle that unnerves him. But he finds himself thanking her, slipping the thing into his pocket, where its weight pulls at the fabric. He will hand it back first thing in the morning, he decides.

In his cot, back in his cabin, he is tired but cannot sleep. The gentle rolling movement of the yacht on its anchor should be restful, but it only echoes his own restlessness. Each time he shuts his eyes he can see it like a retinal imprint: the sweep of sea, the figure in the water. And it is too quiet. He is used to the sounds of night in the city, the sirens and voices and the muffled late-night arguments of his neighbours. The few sounds that did make it across the water from the shore – the blare of a car horn, the faint jangle of music – are silenced now by the lateness of the hour. The quiet here becomes, when one listens to it, perversely loud. His ears strain for any sound beyond the slap and whisper of the water – but there is none.

He pulls back the curtain to the porthole. The sea is revealed to him bright as silver, reflecting the moon. The surface is puckered by submarine disturbances; the movements of fish and secret currents. Strange to think of that great weight of water, held back by so little. And beneath him all manner of creatures of whose existence he can only guess. Now his cabin is lit with moonlight too. The objects it finds glow rather than shine. The face of his watch, laid out next to the berth, his shoes, which he polished before the trip. The white pot, concealing within that strange broken device. Is the needle still tracking now? He reaches for it and finds that it is. Something about it unnerves him, though he could never say exactly why. He slides it into the drawer next to his cot.

Still, sleep does not come. He hasn't slept properly for years – not counting that night in Rome, with her beside him. The last place he remembers sleeping well was a hammock slung in a crowded mess deck, with the swell of the Atlantic beneath. Then, after the death of Morris, lying a few metres away from the place where his friend would have slept himself, it had become a hell. He noticed the other men glancing there, and then quickly away, as though the place were a bad omen.

How many men were sent to their fate by *Lionheart*? Somewhere in the thousands. Too great a number to comprehend, though he, like all the men on board, had been an author of all those deaths. But only one death clings to him. Has threatened, at times, to destroy him. Because it was his fault. Only he knows this, of course. Perhaps that is what gives it such power. If others knew, the weight of the secret might be lifted a little. But it is too shameful to share.

He will try and do something useful with this wakefulness, he thinks. He has brought the Underwood with him – he could type up the events of the first day. Except that his thoughts keep being drawn back toward things that won't be of any interest to the readership, who will come to it hungry for the taste of celebrity. A man in a pale linen suit whose elegance seems to bely a kind of concentrated violence somewhere just beneath the surface. A woman who, for all her composure, and for all the winking gems at wrist and throat, seems a little lost. Seems profoundly sad.

8

Her

I can't sleep. My mind is too full. The evening was such a strange ordeal. Him in particular, sitting so near to me with his questions, and his judgement. Oh, I know that he judges me, beneath his nice, British manners. I see how he looks at me, now that he knows who I am. What I am. I find myself wishing that I had the chance to explain my actions to him – though I don't know exactly what excuse I would give. And then I remind myself that he is nobody: that I don't care what he makes of me. After this, I need never see or think of him again.

And the film. I wish that I could have been prepared for what it made me feel. All I could think, as they sailed towards the new world at the end, was of her, of what she might have left behind in the way of family, of history. But perhaps there was nothing to leave.

November 1936

The radio has been on all night in my father's study: I kept waking and hearing the murmur of it through the wall. And he has been in there all night, too – I can hear him now, moving restlessly about. Eventually, I go in, to see what it all means.

He is very pale.

'What is it?' I ask, because it is clear to me that something is happening, that some change has occurred in him.

He touches the back of his head, which he always does when he is agitated. There is a thinning patch there, which reminds me of a bear that passed from me to Tino, the fur rubbed away by our embraces.

'Madrid. I have had news from Salvador. They're attacking through the Casa del Campo.'

It is a park, at the outskirts of the city. Aunt Aída took us there once when we were staying with them. I remember pine trees, undulating green, a stream near which we had almost stumbled over a courting couple. A place of peace. The idea of war – or death – occurring there is an impossible one.

'If Madrid falls,' Papa says, 'everything will be lost. All the progress the government has made. These men, they want to plunge us back into the Dark Ages. They want to turn good men and women, people who have begun to hope for something more, back into starving peasants. Do you understand?'

'I—'

'Estrella,' he says. 'I have to go and help.'

'No,' I say, 'no, Papa – we need you here.'

'They're using my words on the radio,' he says, with an unmistakable note of pride. They are, I've heard them, too.

"A time will come when ordinary Spanish men and women will have to fight to protect their freedom. Because the oppressor will fight to destroy it. At this time, there can be no distinction between the ordinary man and the soldier. We must all be soldiers."

'They're using words that I meant when I wrote them, that I should stand by. And yet I sit here, doing nothing.' He looks at me. He is waiting for me, I think, to give him my permission. But I can't. This isn't like his other trips, the ones made in peacetime.

'What about us?' I ask. 'We could come with you, to Madrid. We could stay with Tío Salvador and Tía Aída.'

'No.' He shakes his head. 'It wouldn't be safe.'

'If it isn't safe,' I realize that I am close to tears, 'if it isn't safe, then you mustn't go.' My father is many things, but he is no soldier. At one time, as many children do of their fathers, I believed him invincible. But now, as I think of those soldiers they have spoken of on the radio – men trained from my own age in war, men out for blood – he appears diminished to me, vulnerable.

'Please,' I say. 'We need you here, Papa. Tino needs you.'

'You're seventeen now, Estrella. I trust you to take care of him while I'm gone.'

I am sixteen, in fact, but there seems little point in mentioning this: it won't change anything in his mind.

'I am doing this for you, Estrella. For you and Tino. Do you understand?'

'I don't want you to go.' I hate the way I sound, like a child. But I feel like a child. I am afraid. I don't want to be left alone.

*

I wake. I'm not lying down, as I should be. I'm crouched over. Beneath me not a mattress, but something hard and unyielding.

It takes me several seconds to realize that I am not in my father's study, nor bleeding in the dirt by the side of a road outside Madrid, but kneeling on the deck of the yacht in my nightdress. I remind myself. It is 1953. I am Stella Truss – not Estrella, the girl I left in Spain. I stand, my limbs stiff with cold, shivering in my thin nightgown. Thank goodness, no one else appears to be about.

This is my own fault. I have pills I could take, to prevent the sleepwalking, but I stopped taking them because I began to feel they were making me stupid when I was awake.

It has been happening more and more of late. The dreams have been more vivid, too. There are memories that will react to suppression by finding any and every fissure to flow through. If one is not careful, they have the power to drown.

9

Hal's eyes are sore with lost sleep. If he has slept at all, it can only have been an hour or so. At some point in the early hours of the morning he was certain that he heard movement on the deck above him: a kind of shuffling tread. Roberto, probably. But there is something almost otherworldly about it. Perhaps it is simply the way in which, away from the land, everything takes on a slightly changed quality. He had forgotten this. It had been that way on *Lionheart*. He remembers lying like this at the beginning, listening to the foreign sounds of the ship. Small creaks amplified into almost human groans. Wind trapped and fractured and funnelled, producing strange distortions. When the cruiser was right up near the Norwegian coast, on patrol, a superstition went about that they were being haunted by the ghost of a Viking warlord. You could hear him at night, they said, howling about the quarterdeck. You could hear something, too, though probably due only to a shift in the wind. But one night the men on watch claimed that they had seen him, green as the aurora borealis. And Hal had written a short story about him. He was a captain, he wrote, mourning his sunken ship. Any craft that passed over his watery grave would carry him with them, for a while. Morris had read it, and declared it quite brilliant.

He met Morris in the first week, while looking for a place to sling his hammock. He had quickly learned that there was a hierarchy – not of the official kind, but of the sort he recalled from school: one imposed purely by the ratings themselves. All of the best spots were taken by the men who had served for the longest. Then the next longest and so forth. He had wandered the maze of compartments, finding suspended forms filling every space like huge chrysalises – and not a spare square metre anywhere. He would have to leave the main deck completely.

'Anyone know of a spot elsewhere?'

No answer: many of the men were already asleep, or disinclined to help, now that they were comfortably tucked up.

'Over here, lad.'

A figure was emerging from one of the far-most hammocks like a giant spider – one of the longest pairs of legs Hal had ever seen. Finally the man stood there, tall and lanky, a largish nose, amiable face.

'You can have this spot for the first week – I'll go sleep in the Capstan flat. No one wants to be on his tod for the first few days.'

Hal had seen the space the man meant: cluttered with cable-winding machinery, as frigid as a refrigerator.

'Are you sure?'

'Don't ask me again – I might change my mind. But I could do with a spell without Bennett's snoring, anyway. And I don't mind the cold.'

He would think, later, of the horrible irony of Morris saying this. It would have been the cold that killed him first.

He had thought Morris was little more than a big-hearted joker at first: a man who was always being ribbed by the other men for something – his nose, his constant talk about his new wife, Flora, or his seasickness (he suffered dreadfully, almost constantly). But then Hal learned, from another rating, that Morris wrote stories of his own, and asked to read one. It had made the hairs stand up on his arms. It had made him envious. He had always wanted to be able to write like that, with that concision, and had never managed it. Every time he tried it had come out like a spoof. But Morris' style was absolutely his own. Here was this rare talent, hidden inside this clumsy vessel. He had books, too: a veritable lending library. Some of the men thought him a bit soft, at first, because of it. But when the long, uneventful days came and sunk them in boredom, they began to ask, somewhat sheepishly, what Morris might recommend.

Back at home, Morris was a postman. You saw all sorts, he said, on the round. In London in particular: where there was such a density of life, in which rich and poor, old and young lived so near to one another. By the end of the day he would have ten, twenty stories clamouring to be told – it was a question of which one you chose. He would scribble the ideas down and then, later, he would work over them on his solitary day off. It would be more difficult when Flora had the baby, certainly. But that was life for you, getting in the way, wonderful chaos.

Hal had been humbled by it.

*

It is still early, the light through the porthole thin and grey. He washes, dresses. Up on deck he finds Roberto, smoking morosely at the bow.

'Very bad weather,' he says, as soon as he sees Hal – as though he has been waiting for hours to impart this news.

The sea is still as glass. 'It looks all right now,' Hal says.

'Ah, not now. Coming. I have lived in Liguria for my whole life: I know when a storm is on its way. The Contessa, she do not believe me – but I know.'

At this hour, Portovenere appears painted in watercolour. It seems deserted, too, save for one waterfront café where a man is putting out chairs. Suddenly hungry, Hal ambles over and takes a seat. The man spots him, smiles. 'Ah,' he says, in almost faultless English, when he sees Hal. 'You are from the big yacht, yes? Signor Gaspari's boat?'

Hal nods – lacking the energy to correct him.

'She is a beauty,' the man says, reverentially. 'And he is a great man, Gaspari.'

'Yes. He makes wonderful films.'

The man nods, vigorously. 'I thought he died, during the war. Many people thought it.'

'Why?'

'He . . .' the man makes a flitting motion with his hand, '. . . disappeared. Before the war, he used to come here in the summers, with a friend. They kept to themselves, you know, but everyone knew who he was. But then they stopped coming.'

'Well, I suppose that's not so strange. People don't live in the same way in wartime.'

The man shakes his head, adamant, 'No, it was more than that. No one heard anything of him for a long time. His name vanished, completely. Nothing in the papers, when before there had been so much. And then he appeared again, a few years ago, and made that beautiful film. It made me weep.' He remembers himself. '*Vuole qualcosa da mangiare? You want something?*'

Hal orders an espresso and some pastries to go with it. When the man comes back with his breakfast, he asks, 'Does anyone know what happened to him, Signor Gaspari?'

The man shrugs. 'No. It happened, you know, in the days of Mussolini. *Capisci?*'

Hal nods. As a child he had not properly understood his mother's distress as she watched the metamorphosis of her homeland into a dictator state. Now he does. A nonconformist to her core, and one who wore her national identity about her like one of her brightly coloured scarves, she must have felt it as a personal affront. And she must have felt powerless, too, watching from afar – feeling, perhaps, like a deserter. She tells Hal often that she had been brave, once upon a time. She had been helping her own father, a surgeon, when Mr Jacobs had come in as a wounded soldier, and left with her as his betrothed.

There is sudden noise and movement in the harbour: the fishermen are returning with the first catch of the day, unloading their cargo and their catch onto the quay. Some are shirtless, some wear full waterproofed overalls. There are men of every age but all have a common, sinewy strength about them, their skin tanned dark by wind and sun. They look done-in, Hal thinks, seeing the purple shadows beneath eyes, the set jaws. Bone-weary. He wonders: have they chosen this life, or has it been handed down to them, with no possibility of escape? But then one of the younger men, for a joke, hits his fellow across the face with a sardine and all descends into chaos and laughter. More fish are brandished, water is thrown. And suddenly the group is transformed, becoming vital, joyful.

He finishes his breakfast, wanting to explore the rest of the place while he still has it to himself. He starts with the steps that lead from the waterfront up towards the castle. The place is less eerie – and less enthralling – in the stark light of morning. There is no enchantment here, he realizes, only so many lifeless stones. Weeds thrust their way among them, reclaiming the land that was theirs before man built here. Seagulls wheel and caw and land to stalk along the ramparts – untroubled by his nearness as he passes, black eyes watchful, beaks violent-looking.

Led by an aimless curiosity, he makes for the great church below the fort. Inside it is dark and several degrees cooler than without. The air has a musty quality: faint notes of mould and incense. He feels a clumsy intruder, his feet echoing loudly upon the stones. Any second, someone will find him here, discover him to be a fraud. He will be asked to leave. Yet no one comes – in fact, he seems to be alone. He steps more confidently, giving greater rein to his curiosity. He has made it halfway up the aisle when he stops. There is someone else after all. At the front, head bowed so low between the pews that they had been almost invisible.

The figure turns, and he sees that it is Signor Gaspari. He blinks at Hal like a sleeper wakened. There are tears in his eyes.

He stops, begins to retreat. 'I'm sorry – I'd thought there was no one here. I've disturbed you . . .'

'No,' Gaspari says. 'Please, don't apologize.' He grimaces. 'I'm not a man of religion. Someone I knew was. So, I suppose it has now become something of a habit of mine.' He points to a small, framed picture on the wall. 'And I wanted to see her, too.' From afar it appears unimpressive, but as Hal moves closer to make it out he sees that it is a small, exquisitely rendered image of the Virgin and Child, the faces flat Byzantine ovals, the details embossed in gold.

'The White Madonna,' Gaspari says, softly. 'Isn't she something? She was carried here on the waves, in a plank of wood. There are a number of theories, I believe. Perhaps a merchant ship, attacked by pirates. Or a band of Crusaders, knowing they were doomed to die on a Moslem battlefield, and feeling it important that their treasure should be salvaged.'

'It's a good story.' But it is only as credible, Hal thinks, as all such myths are. He remembers studying such things in history lessons; tales of medieval relics. The teeth or bones of a saint that, when examined properly, turned out to be those of some animal.

He catches Gaspari watching him. 'You don't believe me,' the man says, 'do you?'

Hal looks at him in surprise. 'I assumed it was a myth.'

Gaspari raises an eyebrow, and beckons. 'Come.' He leads Hal towards the entrance of the church and points to a long beam of wood, dark-hued, ancient-looking, a hollow carved into its belly.

'There,' Gaspari says. 'This was her ship, if you like. Of course you can claim that this too is a fraud. But I prefer to believe in it. Not so much for any religious reason, but for the fact that such things speak of a certain magic at work in the world. That I can have faith in. It is the thing upon which I base my work.'

Afterwards they step, blinking, into the sunshine. Gaspari walks away, and Hal sees that he has gone to collect his dog, tethered outside. Sleeping in a patch of shade, she had been invisible to him on his way in. Now she wakes as the director nears her, sitting up on her haunches and yipping in delight.

'Have you seen the other church?' Gaspari asks, when he returns.

'No.'

'Ah. Also a thing of a beauty. If you like, we shall go there now.'

The second church is a smaller, sparser place than the first, but its magnificence derives from its position, extending into the sea on a finger of rock. On one side is the Atlantic proper, the water seething and foaming; on the other is the calm of the harbour. Gaspari leads Hal up onto the portion of ramparts above the church, where the views along the coast in either direction are unrivalled. With this new perspective afforded to them the town itself looks small and vulnerable. The yacht is a child's toy, dwarfed by the landscape that surrounds her.

The wind whines around them, and Nina barks and scurries after it, as though it is a thing that might be chased. Looking over the stone lip at the surf far below Hal is filled with a strange urge to jump, as though the water is pulling him towards it. He steps back, alarmed by the force of the impulse. He sees that Gaspari too is standing right at the edge of the parapet, facing the breeze with his eyes closed against it. Hal feels now that he is witnessing some intensely private moment. He turns away.

As they make their way back down to the quayside, Gaspari says, 'What did you make of the film? Forgive me, but you are one of the first to see it, and I think you are a man of taste.'

'It's a masterpiece.'

'Oh,' Gaspari looks at the ground, as though he doesn't quite know how to respond to this. 'Thank you.'

'How did you come up with the narrative for the film? I heard you wrote the screenplay – it sounds as though only the bare bones are known of the real story.'

'Ah, no. There is a little more to it than that.'

'What do you mean?'

Gaspari lowers his voice, as though concerned they might be overheard. 'There is a journal. Written by the Contessa's ancestor.'

Hal's interest is immediately piqued. 'A captain's log?'

'A little . . . more personal than a log. Like a diary. I do not think that it was intended for other eyes.'

'Why didn't the Contessa mention it last night?'

'I think, perhaps, because the film doesn't exactly stick to the facts. I used my artistic licence.'

'In what sense?'

'The film ends happily. The journal ends . . . well, not so happily.'

'Where is it?' And then, seeing Gaspari's face, 'You have it with you? On board the yacht?'

Gaspari looks uneasy. 'I do not think it would be a good idea for me to share it with you. The Contessa wouldn't like it.'

'Why?'

'Because you are a journalist.'

'Well,' Hal says, 'it would make a nice angle to the piece . . .'

'That is the problem, I think. The Contessa would rather that people believe in the happier version of the tale. If they knew it was not so, it might change how they see the film in some way.'

'All right. Then how about if I promise not to breathe or write a word of it to anyone else?'

'You want to read it for your own interest only?'

Hal nods. 'Absolutely.'

Gaspari's mouth quirks. 'You are like me. Once a thing is in your mind you will not let it rest. You want to understand things more deeply, more so than is perhaps good for you. I am starting to see that I should not have mentioned it.'

'But you will let me see it?'

Gaspari gives an almost imperceptible nod.

As they climb up from the tender, Truss and Stella are there on deck, both reading. His hand is on her knee. She is soignée in pastel yellow, legs crossed neatly at the ankle: the picture of self-possession. Except that her knuckles show white through the skin, as though the magazine she is reading is the only thing keeping her tethered in place. As Hal passes, though he takes care not to look directly at her, he sees her face turn up toward him then quickly away.

Later in the day the weather shifts. On the side of the promontory protected by the tight mouth of the harbour, the water is still calm. But on the other the sea is wild and dark, capped with foam like the froth on a madman's lips. Not yet a storm though, Hal thinks. Roberto will be disappointed.

Hal wanders down to the pathway that leads between the rocks on the rough side and sees that he is not alone: evidently Aubrey Boyd has decided it will be the perfect place for windswept photographs of Giulietta and Earl Morgan. Giulietta wears a long white dress that is already flecked with seaspray and her hair sticks wetly to her forehead. She shows surprising fortitude, Hal thinks, in the face of adversity. He would have expected her to complain – quite rightly – at the dangerous slickness of the rock beneath their feet, at the chill breeze wicking in across the sea, but she remains resolutely silent.

A crowd has gathered to watch, ranged along the lip of stone above them. It could easily be the entire population of Portovenere, judging by the number. They are a strangely silent audience, more like observers at a wake than fans. Gradually, as the wind picks up – and perhaps understanding that the spectacle is not going to change in any dramatic way – they drift away. When a few fat drops of rain begin to fall, Aubrey finally calls a halt. The few remaining onlookers cluster in, presenting photographs and autograph books for a soggy signature.

That evening, an awning is pulled out over the dining area to protect them from the rain, and with the candles lit along the table the space becomes a luminous cocoon. After supper, the Contessa has Roberto set up a gramophone on the deck. It is a huge old machine, rather than one of the smaller modern ones, with a great brass funnel. The needle is lifted on the first record: '*Perduto Amore (In cerca di te)*'. It sends a shock through Hal. The first time he heard it was when it had first come out, in 1945. He had danced to it with Suze in the Hammersmith Palais – the band there had covered it, to certain mutterings about bad taste, because it was in the language of the so-recent enemy. The words had stayed with him: the singer searching the city for their lost lover:

Ogni viso guardo, non sei tu
Ogni voce ascolto, non sei tu.
Every face I see, it isn't you
Every voice I hear, it isn't you.

And then it comes to him that he has heard it somewhere else. He turns to Gaspari:

'This was the soundtrack, for *Elegy.*'

Gaspari nods.

'No,' the Contessa says, striding over to Roberto. 'This is too melancholy. Play us . . .' she claps her hands, 'some rock and roll.' Her pronunciation turns it into a single Italianate word: '*rockarolle*'. Hal is impressed. Roberto finds an Italian cover of 'Rock the Joint': rather off-key, but with the same infectious rhythm. For a few moments, no one moves. Then Giulietta springs up, takes the hand of one of the watching deckhands, who seems almost ready to combust with joy at his good fortune. The two of them begin to spin and kick: she dragging him impatiently around after her.

'Come come,' the Contessa says, rather like an overzealous sports mistress, Hal thinks, hurrying them all to their feet. All except for Truss, who politely declines with a wave of one hand, and Earl Morgan who, at this point in the evening, cannot be expected to stand up. She takes Hal as her partner and he dances with her conservatively for a moment, until she tells him not to treat her like an antique. Over her shoulder he can see Aubrey doing an awkward little impro-visation on his own, and Gaspari dancing with Stella, Nina scurrying about their feet. For the first time, Stella seems to be enjoying herself – and he feels an unexpected regret that he isn't the one to make her smile.

The next record is played: a thirties waltz, with a slower

tempo. As they dance nearer to Gaspari and Stella the Contessa says, 'Let's swap. I wish to dance with my old friend.'

Hal sees Stella's face, and there is a moment when he thinks she is about to excuse herself. But the opportunity to do so seems to slide past, to the point where it would look odd for her to walk away. He finds, as he did on the rooftop in Rome, that her hand is surprisingly warm in his. Perhaps it is that impression of serene coolness she projects: one might also expect her touch to be cold. He rests his hand so lightly on her waist that he is hardly touching it, but he can feel warmth there, too, beneath his palm.

She does not look at him, as they begin to move, but at some point beyond his shoulder. He has never been a particularly adept dancer. Suze used to chide him for his lack of rhythm. But for a few minutes his clumsiness appears to desert him. He moves – they move – with something approaching grace.

Suddenly the melody stutters, and loops round on itself. Roberto, manning the machine, curses, and stops the thing, lifts it off to inspect the surface. Stella seizes her opportunity. 'I think that's enough for me,' she says, with a polite nod, extracting herself. He watches her go.

'Mrs Truss is an excellent dancer, no?'

Hal turns to find Gaspari a couple of feet away.

'Oh. Yes, she is.'

'Though,' Gaspari says thoughtfully, 'I think she danced best with you.'

Hal looks at him sharply, wondering what, exactly, he means by this. But the man's expression is inscrutable.

Back in his cabin he is certain that he can still feel it, the warmth of her waist beneath his palm. He catches himself.

What a pathetic figure he is in this moment: a single man thinking of another's wife. He closes his eyes, wills sleep. But he finds that an image is imprinted there, the same one that drove him from the film screening like someone pursued by a demon.

10

It was one of their favourite games, Hal and Morris. It was a way of keeping warm on deck – imagining themselves somewhere far away, in peacetime.

'What are you going to do with yourself, after the war?'

'Get married, try and write.'

'The novel, is it?'

'Yes. And you?'

'Play with my little boy. Make love to my wife.'

'How old is he now? Your boy?'

'Three.' Suddenly morose. 'I worry, you know, that he won't know me. Flora says she talks of me to him all the time, but I still think—'

'He will, Morris.'

'I hope so, Harry.' He was the only one that called Hal this. And then he'd said: 'There's something else I'd like to do, too.'

'What?'

Morris had outlined it for him. A little magazine – collecting really good work together. Stories, thought pieces. Wouldn't *make any money, probably, but that wouldn't be the point of it. Perhaps Hal would help him out? He'd know people, Morris imagined, from university – maybe people who could help them with advice about how to start. Morris didn't know anyone like that.*

Yes, Hal had said, he'd love to do it. And it became the thing that their friendship grew around, this future plan. They'd discuss what they'd call it – something to do with the sea, maybe – how they'd use a different theme for each edition. Sometimes it felt little more than a pipe dream. But it was a cure for the tedium. A way of invoking the future, too, a time beyond war – making it feel real. It had been one of the refreshing things about Morris. Some of the men spoke as though they were all doomed to a watery death: it was only a question of when and how, not if. Morris, by contrast, had an absolute conviction in the fact that he was going home.

He wakes drenched in sweat, his heartbeat in his ears. Something to do with his dream, though as he tries to grasp for it, it slips from reach. Beyond the porthole is the liquid slap of the water. The glass runs with rain. He checks his watch: almost two a.m. At least tonight he has managed a few hours' sleep.

He gropes for his jotting pad, deciding that he might as well do some more work. If he leaves it, he knows that details will begin to desert him, until he is left with only the shell of events. That would be no use to him at all. All the interest of a piece like this, as the *Tempo* editor had said, will be in the details. Exactly what they are served at supper, the watermelon hue of Giulietta's nail polish, the cocktail Earl Morgan drinks at sundown.

As he extracts the pad, though, he dislodges something on top of it. It falls to the floor with a soft thud. He looks at the thing, confused. It is a small, dirty book, and he has no idea where it can have come from. He picks it up. Now he can see that it is not so much dirty as extremely old, the pages between the leather covers warped and friable. Then he understands. It is the journal. Gaspari must have left it here for him. This fits with his impression of the man – everything done quietly, without undue ceremony.

All thought of the article forgotten, Hal opens it up, but finds the hand so small that his tired eyes strain to make it out in the weak lamplight. He has another idea: he will go up on deck, and read by the light of the moon, which will no doubt be brighter than this.

As he walks the passageway toward the ladder onto the deck he imagines that he can feel the sleeping presence of the others about him. Someone is snoring. And a low groan – so loud that he freezes for a second, like a burglar – before he realizes that it is a subconscious, atavistic sound, made by someone in the deepest realm of sleep.

He takes the steps up to the deck and finds it empty. A happy surprise, because he had somehow imagined that there might be at least one member of the crew awake to keep watch.

Portovenere, in the distance, is almost entirely shrouded in darkness. A solitary light, somewhere up near the castle, burns a fiery point in the black. The deck is washed with water, but the rain has finally stopped. He goes to one of the beds at the bow, sluices the water off it.

Then he opens the journal, and begins to read. It is slow going at first. The first few paragraphs are all bombast, as though the captain had, initially, intended it to be read.

*We are returning from Lepanto bruised, but victorious:
our number diminished, but not our spirit. The spread
of the Ottoman hordes westward is stemmed. Finally,
we are following our great leader Doria homeward.*

It is like something written by a sixteenth-century propagandist,
and the Italian is archaic, straining his powers of comprehension. Hal feels his interest begin to wane, his eye skimming
the close press of text. Until a line catches his attention.

*An arrow, taken straight through the eye. In one moment,
a man's life extinguished.*

He reads on.

*He had been only an arm's length from me. Nothing to
choose between us, except luck. Some would say Fate,
or Providence, but I find it more and more difficult to
believe . . .*
 *I have killed forty-nine. As commander of the ship, I
have been responsible for many more: though the ones
that stay with me are the ones committed by my own
hand. I have seen them die only an arm's length from
me, watched as the soul departs. As men who once lived
and breathed and loved become nothing, merely so much
cloth and inanimate flesh. I know this is not the proper
way to look upon such things. These men, these Turks,
are godless creatures whose influence must be curbed.
Lepanto has been a magnificent victory for Christendom.
And yet good Christian knights and Ottoman infidels
die in much the same way. I cannot help but remark it.
In dying, there is nothing to choose between them. The*

soul, of course, is the thing. But does it truly endure,
after death? Sometimes I find it hard to believe. When
I return to Genoa I will go and talk to the priest. I must
confess these thoughts, because I know they are danger-
ously near to heresy.

This speaks to Hal. Now, for the first time, he can imagine
a real man sitting down to write, trying to make some order
out of the jumble of his thoughts. He recognizes the impulse.
He had kept a diary himself, on board *Lionheart*. He had
tried to get it all down: the mundane and the extraordinary.
How the ship had smelt – a mixture of canned food and
disinfectant; the hours of boredom sailing through still waters
and then the sudden nighttime violence of an engagement;
the cacophony of the guns, which they could hardly load
fast enough. Watching that first enemy ship, the German
destroyer – which everyone begrudgingly agreed had fought
valiantly, even when the game was up – go down with every
member of her crew. Drowned before any could be rescued
as POWs.

After the thing that had happened, he had tried to put it
down on paper: what he had done, how he felt. And found
that he couldn't. To write it out, even if it were for his eyes
only, was too shameful. He reads on.

A strange occurrence this evening, nearing dusk. So
strange that I find it hard to put into language: but I
must try, in order to make sense of it within my own
mind. We found a woman in the water, a mile from
shore. It was an experience in no small way affecting.
I have not seen a woman in a long while. Nor have
many of the men. I must keep her from them, protect

*her from their lechery. I will watch over her until we
reach Genoa, and then . . .*

The handwriting trails away. The captain, apparently having
lost his train of thought, goes on to describe her instead:

> *. . . her hair like the black ink of a squid* [nero di
> seppia], *her eyes too. A mark on her white cheek, tiny,
> like a drop of the same ink. Her skin with a sheen to
> it like the inside of a shell. She seems a creature of water,
> as though it runs inside her veins instead of blood.*

Now the writing has life to it. A kind of desperation too. Over
the next few pages it becomes less rational, more a meandering
stream of consciousness. And yet somehow it makes for easier
reading: perhaps because Hal finds himself constructing a
narrative from it. The strange thing is that it seems almost to
come as much from somewhere inside himself as from the
page in front of him.

A LARGE SHIP. The men on board are tired and homesick,
some of them nursing injuries or sicknesses, some of them
mourning fellows slain. The only man not showing the signs
of strain – he hides them well – is their commander. A young man,
but a powerful one, scion of one of the Republic's foremost families.

They are on the homeward straight now. The men can almost
taste the cooking of their mothers, see the faces of their beloveds.
From here, the rest should be plain sailing. The familiar coast is
almost in sight: that fertile rich dark green. It is nearing dusk, and
the ship is preparing to drop anchor only a few miles from Genoese

waters. The captain finishes his supper, and decides, on a whim, to head up on deck, to look upon his homeland. It has always looked its best to him at this time. That beloved dark line, the same mountains he could see from his bedchamber as a child.

But now something else catches his eye: something nearer to hand, on the surface of the water. He peers through the gloaming, squints to bring the object into view. When he does, he does not want to believe it – but he is certain of what he sees. It is a man's head, bobbing in the water. For a few seconds, full of the horrors that he has witnessed, the young man believes that he is looking at a head that has been severed from a body. Not here, he thinks, not so close to home. But as he watches, an arm breaks the surface. He suddenly understands that he is looking not at the remains of some terrible mutilation, but a living human: swimming. What can they be doing here, so far from the coast, in such deep waters?

He calls to his second- and third-in-command, who come up on deck. He points to the figure. One man's eyesight is so poor that he cannot make anything out, but the other's is keener than his own.

'He's swimming, sire,' the man calls, 'but he's tiring. Keeps slipping beneath the waves. He won't be afloat for much longer.'

'We'll go for him.' If he is Genoese, it is their duty to save him. If he is a Pisan, they can make him their captive, and plunder useful information from him about their near neighbours.

The captain orders a tender made up with all possible speed, and boards it with two of his men.

'Pray that we get to him in time.'

Luckily, with the relative calm of the sea, it is easy to keep the figure in sight, and with the wind behind them the little craft moves swiftly.

It is only when they are a few arm's lengths away, beginning to reach hands out towards the water, that the men see what had not been apparent to them before. The figure is nude. And then they see the other thing. Not a man, but a woman. The men's hands drop – they are unsure of what they should do. None of them have seen a woman in weeks – and a woman like this? Perhaps never. The captain is not so easily defeated as his men, however. He reaches over and grabs the girl beneath her armpits, hauls her – even as she flails against him, almost threatening to pull him over with her – into the craft. She lies there, breathing in great gasps, sounds that might be made by some dying animal. The captain struggles not to look at the slender, nude white body, at the dark hair that seems to bleed onto the wood like black squid's ink.

'That's not a woman,' one of the men whispers, almost to himself. 'It's a mer-creature.'

The captain scolds him for his whimsy, but he can understand the fellow's meaning. The woman's beauty is unearthly, and the extreme whiteness of her skin seems suited to some submarine lair.

He shrugs off his cloak and wraps it about her, taking care not to touch the soft white flesh. The woman is barely sensible now: her eyes are closed, and the breath rasps out of her. But at least, the captain thinks, it shows that she is breathing. He leans in close. 'Can you hear me?' he asks her. His voice surprises him by betraying a quaver, almost as though he were afraid. Strange, because he prides himself on never showing fear.

Her eyes open, and she looks at him but there is no answer, and he does not try again. Her black gaze has silenced him.

'I don't like it,' one of the men says. 'I don't think we should bring her onto the boat. There's something odd about it.'

'What do you suggest I do?' the captain asks. 'Pitch her back in?' The fellow shrugs, but his expression suggests he thinks it might be preferable.

'The men, sir,' the other man says, 'there will be a riot. They haven't seen a woman in months.'

And neither have I, thinks the captain to himself. And perhaps I have never seen a woman quite like this: so beautiful and strange. But aloud he says, 'We're close to home now. I will keep her in my quarters. She will be protected from them there.'

When they return the captain sees that men have lined the deck, curious to discover what has caused their commander to leave his ship. He has wrapped the woman in his cloak so that as much of her as possible is hidden from view. Only the blue-pale legs are visible, and when she is hoisted up on deck they hang limply down, not unlike the limbs of a corpse. As she is carried to the captain's cabin the men stare, wordlessly, at the strange spectacle. For all they know their captain is carrying a body – not a living person. He will have to find some way of explaining it to them. The men mutter and whisper among themselves, but he hears several perplexing references to 'the ankles'. It is only when the woman is placed in the chamber outside his cabin that he realizes why. Around her ankles is a thick rope of bruises, as though something had been tied viciously tight about them.

A bed is made up for the woman in the captain's quarters, and when he goes to his own bed he finds that sleep eludes him. He cannot stop thinking about the woman in the next room. Despite the heavy drapes that divide the two cabins, he is certain that he can hear the gentle exhalations of her breath. Eventually, unable to bear it any longer, he goes through to her, simply – he tells himself – to have a quick look, to check that her condition has not deteriorated.

It is a full moon and he can see her almost as clearly as in the day: though the cold light makes her appear all the more other-worldly, like a creature underwater. Her black hair fans out about her head as though the strands are afloat. She is so still that he places a palm above her nose and mouth, to check that she is really alive. The breath comes as a shock, a surprising warmth against his skin.

Alone and unobserved he looks at her greedily, noticing all that he had not had the leisure to see before. The black eyebrows, two perfect curves, as though etched with the compasses he uses on his charts. The nose: too strong to be conventionally feminine, but somehow well suited to her face. The pale pillow of her lips. His gaze lingers there longest of all. He tears his attention away and looks, instead, at those bruises on her ankles. They are dark, purplish: evidently of recent creation. And he realizes, suddenly, that they are matched by similar patterns about her wrists. He cannot believe that he did not notice them before: was he so obtuse as to have been distracted from them by her naked body? What was she? A prisoner of some sort? But what monster would imprison such a woman? Though, of course, no crime is too heinous for the Pisans.

Eventually, having satisfied his need to look, he turns to make his way back to his cabin. But as he does he has an awareness of being watched, a sensation so powerful that he can feel it prickle down his back. He turns, and just stops himself from starting with alarm. Silently, she has raised herself from the bench so that she is sitting up, and her eyes are open. She is watching him. Quickly, he recovers himself, though he is certain that his first expression must have betrayed his shock.

'Hello,' he says, slowly, not sure she will understand him. 'I hope you are feeling recovered.'

There is a long pause. He is uncomfortable beneath her gaze, but he steels himself not to look away – that much would be a sign of weakness. Just as he has decided that she clearly does not understand him, she speaks.

'Yes, thank you.' She speaks in Italian, though her accent is strange.

'You were such a long way out,' he says. 'How did you come to be in the water, so far from shore?'

She frowns, and takes a long time to answer. Eventually, she says, 'I don't remember.'

He isn't sure that he believes her. How could someone forget something like that? Her gaze on him is unwavering. It gives him a certain thrill, to have so much of her attention focused upon him. It unnerves him too.

'Where are you from?' he asks her.

'Oh, nowhere you will know, sire. My background is a humble one.'

He waits for her to say more, but she does not. He senses a reluctance in her to reveal her origins to him. It only intrigues him further. He wants to find out more about her, and is about to ask another question, when she says, gently. 'If you do not mind, sire, I am very tired.'

'Oh.' He steps back. 'But of course. Forgive me for disturbing you.'

Just as he is about to draw back the drapes, she calls to him. 'Thank you, sire. Without your assistance I would perhaps have perished.'

There is no perhaps about it, he thinks, but does not say it. He did save her life. 'You are welcome, signora.'

The storm appears out of nowhere the next morning, bruise-dark, the hue of the marks on the girl's legs. The clouds gather themselves astonishingly fast, and there is barely time to reef the sails before the first gusts come upon them, whooping against the fabric, shivering over the deck. The thunder feels extremely close and loud, almost personal. And then there is lightning, following only a moment behind. It forks into strands of fire, a phenomenon the captain has never seen at this time of year. The wind, too, is strange. He can't work it out. Any Genoan knows the eight winds as well as he knows the names of his own wife and children. They are like a litany: *Scirocco, Tramontana, il Grecale, il Ponente, Mezzogiorno, il Mare, Borrasca, Maestrale.* But this one is schizophrenic, shifting, impossible to read.

He hears the confusion and dismay of the men all about him – can almost taste their fear. Luckily they are able to make their way to relative shelter from the wind and the swell in the deep waters close to the land. But, as the captain hears one of the men say, if the lightning struck them it could split a mast in two. There is not much to do other than brace themselves and hope that they can hold out. But then, after raging with peculiar ferocity for a short time, the storm retreats, to disappear as quickly as it arrived.

And the rumours start. They are a superstitious lot, sailors. Perhaps inevitably so, considering the vast and unknowable nature of the sea. Watching for omens is another way of navigating for some: no different, really, to reading the stars. The captain has brought a woman on board ship. Every sailor, even those who don't believe in the other superstitions, knows that this is bad luck. Moreover, she is a strange, beautiful woman who was found in the middle of the deep waters, nowhere near to dry land. It looked as though she were drowning, but might that simply have been a ruse? Is she a mer-creature, then, as the captain's third-in-command had at first suggested? Well, some of the men reason, they are certainly known to be found in these parts. What is commonly agreed is that the storm was a strange one, and it followed too soon after her having been brought on board.

The men like their captain. More than that, they respect him, and many among them feel they owe their lives to him. He is bringing them home unharmed – or as little harmed as might be hoped – to their wives and families, to their beloved city. He has always seemed clear-headed. A man to be trusted. But now the rumours start to attach themselves to him too. He is glassy-eyed and listless, they notice: like a sleepwalker. He guards the entrance to his cabin jealously, as though any man would dare enter without his permission. He acts, some say, like a man in love. Or, others mutter, like a man possessed.

Hal is aware, suddenly, of footsteps behind him. Remembering Gaspari's words, he tucks the journal beneath him, out of sight. Then he turns and sees with a shock the white shape coming nearer through the gloom. There is something strange about the way she moves, but he cannot quite identify what. Her arms hang absolutely still at her sides, her feet appear to drag.

'Mrs Truss?'

No answer. Though she is saying something: one word, over and over. It is an eerie sound. He feels the hairs on his arms prickle to attention. It is a name, he is certain: though not one he can decipher.

'Stella?' He stands, and takes a step toward her. She wears a nightdress that falls to mid-thigh but her legs, her long pale legs, are bare. Her hair is mussed, sticking up at the front from her forehead in disarray. And only now does he see why she doesn't answer him. Her eyes are open, but filmy-looking, unseeing as a blind person's.

What should he do? He has heard somewhere that you should not wake a sleepwalker. But it feels wrong to be watching her without her knowledge. It makes him a voyeur. He tries her name once more, softly. Finally, he sees the tremor of a response, and watches as the glazed look clears. She stares about herself in confusion.

She sees Hal. 'What—'

'You were asleep.'

'Oh no.' She moves her head, as if trying to shake the sleep from it. 'Not here.'

'It happens a lot?'

'Sometimes. I have pills, that I'm meant to take, to help me sleep more deeply. I must have forgotten . . .'

'I didn't know whether to wake you.'

But she isn't listening. She is looking down at her naked legs and feet below the hem of her nightgown. It takes some effort of will for him not to follow her gaze. He keeps it fixed, resolutely, above her shoulders.

Now she is looking back towards the steps, probably deciding how quickly she can get back to them. He thinks of how she must have climbed them with her eyes closed. She could have broken her neck.

'Stay.' He doesn't know what makes him say it, and the urgency of it embarrasses him. To cover himself he says, quickly, 'You should probably sit down for a couple of minutes, wake yourself up properly.'

She wavers. He moves across on the seat, to give her room. But she chooses the other sunbed, several feet away.

And to his surprise, she says, 'Yes, please. I do feel a little strange.'

They sit for a while in silence. He can't think of anything to say to her.

'You couldn't sleep?' she asks him.

'No. It's too quiet.'

'Yes. I don't think it's ever quiet in New York – not even in the middle of the night. What time is it now?'

'Two a.m.'

'Oh. So late – I didn't realize.'

He can feel her unease at being here alone with him. It is in the way she holds herself, absolutely upright, shoulders rigid, bent legs drawn as far from him as they will go.

When he sees her wrap her arms about herself he offers her his sweater. 'Please. You must be freezing.' He shrugs it off and leans forward, thrusts it toward her. She flinches away from him, as though his nearness might scorch her, and shakes her head. 'I'm fine.' And then, in an afterthought, she takes it.

She does not leave. She could, but she chooses not to. He wonders if it would be worth broaching the unspoken thing: that night in Rome. Let her know that it didn't mean anything to him – that he understands it was the same for her. She must be thinking the same thing. 'I don't know why I did it,' she says, as though he has asked the question, 'I wasn't myself, that night. I didn't think . . .' she trails off.

'I wondered whether you did it because you thought we'd never see each other again.'

For the first time, she looks directly at him. He feels her answer, though she doesn't say it aloud. *Yes.*

'Well,' he says, 'it was a surprise for me, to see you again. It must have been an unwelcome one for you.'

She swallows.

'I think, if he found out—' She stops herself, suddenly. 'I don't know what he would do.'

'You don't think he knows anything?'

'No,' she says, as though reassuring herself. 'There's no way that he could.' Watching her, he thinks he sees a small convulsion of fear. It gives him pause.

'I didn't mean anything by it,' he says. 'I felt he was almost too pleased to make my acquaintance. I wondered if it meant anything.'

She relaxes, ever so slightly. 'He's like that with everyone. My husband is . . . well, he's a very charming man.'

It is precisely the word, Hal thinks: charming. It expresses perfectly the superficiality of the man's manner.

'I wish I could explain,' she says, suddenly, 'why I did it.'

'You don't need to,' he says. 'I think I understand it. Your husband was away.' He knows that he is being cruel, but can't seem to help himself. He sees her make an effort not to mind.

'It wasn't like that,' she says. 'I really was a little mad, I think. I had just learned something . . .'

'About what?'

'About myself, I suppose.'

He waits.

'I was in an odd frame of mind. And then you appeared, and you were different, not part of that world . . .' She looks at him. 'I haven't explained it, have I?'

'No,' he says, 'but I understand. We've all made a mistake.' It feels unpleasant to say that word: mistake. It is his pride, of course.

'I didn't mean—'

'Quite clearly,' he says, 'it was a mistake. But that's all right. You don't need to say any more. If you don't mind, I'm tired. I'm going to go back to bed. Goodnight, Mrs Truss.'

'Goodnight.'

Probably, he should guide her back to her cabin, make sure that she gets down the ladder safely. It would be the gentlemanly thing to do. But it is, somehow, beyond him. There is only so much injury to his pride that he can take.

There is only so much, too, of sleep-mussed hair, of pale bare skin.

When he glances back, she is still sitting there. She is looking not towards Portovenere, but out to sea, into blackness. She seems, suddenly, to be somewhere else entirely.

11

Her

In the distance, we can hear the war, growing nearer; a constant barrage of artillery. Sometimes it sounds as though it is almost upon us. Tino wakes in the night, crying. I go to his room, and sit with him and Señor Bombón long into the small hours. I read to him with his hot form pressed against my side and the cat stretched across our knees, sometimes until dawn shows pale on the horizon. Sometimes I sing to him, snippets of song heard on the radio, lullabies remembered from my mother.

He has a new preoccupation now; a fear that has supplanted all the others. I wish that I could tell him, as I have in other times, that it is all only in his mind – that there is no threat. But I can't quite bring myself to tell him a lie.

'What will we do,' he asks, 'when they come here?'

'If they do, Tino,' I say, 'they won't hurt us.'

'Why?'

'Because we're children.' I try to make it sound as though I believe it myself. There is talk on the radio of what they are doing to people: to children younger than him, to young women like me. Though if you trusted everything you heard, you would go mad.

'And Señor Bombón?'

'He'll be fine too.'

'What about Papa?'

'He's in Madrid, with Uncle Salvador and Aunt Aída.'

'When will he come back for us?'

'Soon, Tino.'

It has been a month since my father left us. Every day, I walk into the town to see if there is a message from him at the telegraph station. He promised that he would try and send word. But each time, there is nothing for me. I remind myself that this does not mean anything in particular. Papa has never been exactly reliable at keeping these sort of promises. And it may simply be too difficult: perhaps he is not allowed to. I know nothing of such things. I know nothing of war, other than what I can hear of it, and what I learn on the radio – none of which is without bias.

The woman in charge of the station, Señora Alvarado, is a dour, matronly type with thick spectacles and prominent whiskers that Tino pointed out, once, before I could stop him. She transcribes the messages into blocky pencil capitals, which lends them a certain harshness, as though the words are being shouted. I remember Papa saying that a message of love would lose any romance when transmitted through this hand, read beneath her stern gaze.

Except that I have seen less of this sternness, of late. The first couple of times, when I asked if there were any messages, she shook her head at me impatiently. But now, when I ask, I sense something else. I think it is pity. One time, she asked me about 'the poor little boy' – evidently forgetting Tino's comment about the whiskers. I felt a flare of anger – though I know she only asked out of kindness. Yet I felt that I had been called remiss in some way. As though I don't spend most of the day worrying about how to keep him safe.

I have inherited Papa's preoccupation with the radio. I listen whenever Tino is out of hearing range, trying to hear through all the bombast and propaganda the truth of what is going on in Madrid. It hasn't fallen: that much is clear. If not from the government's announcements, dubiously optimistic, then from the fact that there are no triumphant broadcasts from the rebels to tell us that they have taken the capital.

I wonder what he is doing now, where he is. I have an idea that if I can conjure an image of him clearly enough, I might be able to convince myself that he is safe. I try to imagine him as a soldier, with a weapon, and find that I can't. I have only ever seen him in one of his loose shirts, worn thin and soft with age. In his old peasant's trousers, held up by a finely wrought leather belt: a contrast that exemplifies my father, in all his contradictions. Does he even know how to fire a rifle? Could he kill a man? Because for all his talk of the 'great fight', Papa is a gentle man at heart.

It has come at last. A telegram, for me.

And then suddenly I wish it hadn't. I don't want to read it. Because, when it is passed to me, Señora Alvarado whispers: '*Lo siento.*'

It isn't from my father – it is from Uncle Salvador. And

there, in Señora Alvarado's laboured handwriting, I read that my father is dead.

I have no memory of the walk home: I know only that I seem to arrive back at the farmhouse too quickly. I haven't had time to prepare myself for what I have to do.

When I reach him he is drawing in his sketchbook, humming something under his breath, his eyes half-closed against the bright light. He looks so content that for a second I hesitate. What if I could somehow delay his pain by not telling him yet? But that is a dangerous way to think. For a moment, I think he hasn't heard me. He looks up at me, squinting, still with that half-smile on his face. But then: understanding. I see the change happening, moving across his face, across the whole of him. It is like watching something slowly freezing.

12

Cinque Terre

The next morning the sky is clear once more and huge above them: the clouds strung into thin contortions. On one side the coast masses steel grey and dark green, shearing out of the waves.

Riomaggiore, the first of the five towns, reveals itself in this mythic landscape like a practical joke, a sudden exclamation of colour.

They are like sisters, Hal thinks, the towns. Each has her own personality, but they are linked by a definite familial likeness. Manarola – the great beauty, Corniglia, in her clifftop eyrie, Vernazza, with the protective arm of rock shielding her from view, and finally blowsy Monterosso al Mare. They are good-time girls, carnivalesque.

'You know the reason for the different colours?'

Hal turns, to find the Contessa by his side. He shakes his head.

'So that every fisherman could know which was his own house when he looked back to shore. And, if he had good eyesight, see that his wife was at home behaving herself.'

They gaze at the spectacle together for a few moments.

'They're in the film, aren't they?'

'Yes.'

'Did they exist back then?' They appear at once new – the vibrancy of the hues, perhaps – and timeless, as though they might have grown across the stone like brightly coloured lichen.

'Oh yes. Though they were perhaps not in *such* good repair as you see now. The inhabitants would have been poor country people, you know. But then the Victorians started coming and they got, you might say, a little rouge and powder.'

'You know, that is what I would like to do, with this film. When the English think of Italy, I suspect some still think of words like *Monte Cassino, Mussolini*. No?' Without waiting for Hal to speak, she continues. 'Or perhaps they think of poverty and defeat. I want them to think again of this beauty, this land of fable and romance. Somewhere in which love flourishes. How could it not, in a place like this?'

Monte Cassino. They are rebuilding the monastery there, Hal read, exactly as before, the one that was bombed almost out of existence. 'Where it was, and as it was,' the Abbott had said. If only the same could be done with a person.

They stop in Vernazza for lunch at a restaurant. When the waiter comes to take their orders, Hal sees Truss lean across Stella. '*La bistecca*,' he says, in a rather elegant accent, perusing the menu carefully. He indicates his wife. '*E le cozze per mia moglie.*'

Hal looks away.

He is seated next to Giulietta again. She has covered half her face with huge round sunglasses, but these have the effect of drawing attention to her, rather than the opposite. He is determined, this time, to draw her out.

'Miss Castiglione.'

She turns to him.

'I wonder if I might interview you, about the film.'

She frowns. 'Now?'

'If you wouldn't mind.'

Suddenly, capriciously, she grins: showing a slight gap in her white front teeth. The effect of the smile that of a lamp being turned on. 'All right. Why not?'

'Would you prefer Italian?'

'No, English is fine.'

'So, tell me. What is it like being called "Italy's finest export"?'

She shrugs. 'It makes me sound like a tomato.' A toss of her head.

'Still, what an incredible thing, to become so famous so quickly. Has it all been a great surprise?'

'No. I knew it would happen.'

'You did? Well that's . . . you must have a remarkable drive, to have made sure that it did.'

'I don't know what that means. Drive. *Come una macchina?*'

'Well, no . . . *ambizione, istinto sfrenato.*'

She shrugs again. 'Perhaps.'

It is already quite possibly the most tiresome interview Hal has yet attempted. Even the Roman politicians, with all their slipperiness, have proved easier subjects than this.

'All right. Next question. What was it like working with Earl Morgan? You two make a wonderful onscreen couple.'

She wrinkles her nose. 'He is a – oh, how you say. It begin with an "i"?'

'Say it in Italian, perhaps.'

She shakes her head, stubbornly. 'I will think. It will come to me.' She drums a manicured hand on the table.

'Icon?'

At the same time she shouts, in triumph, 'Imbecile!'

The conversation about the table stutters to a halt. Hal feels the eyes of the party upon them. With the exception, thankfully, of Earl Morgan, who has drunk a bottle of *vino rosato* and slipped into unconsciousness.

'Ah.' Hal says, quietly, reasonably, 'I'm not sure that will look so good. Perhaps something about how talented he is . . .'

'So.' She narrows her eyes at him. 'So. I think I understand it. You want me simply to say exactly what you tell me?'

'Well, no, but . . .'

'Write exactly as you like,' she says, suddenly. Like a sudden shift in the wind her mood has changed. The smile is gone. 'That's what you want, I think.' She puts down her fork and stands. 'I'm tired of this now.'

'Please,' Hal says, 'Miss Castiglione, that's not at all—'

But his words have fallen on deaf ears, because she has already stalked away to pose for the photographers loitering inevitably just beyond the entrance, arranging herself with feline haughtiness. Hal looks down at his pad. Nothing there that will make an interesting sentence, let alone a paragraph. She is a child, he thinks, a spoiled child. Yet on screen, she had had so much complexity and maturity. He rips out the page in disgust.

*

After Vernazza, they sail along the coast until they reach the bay of Levanto. If one is to continue with the metaphor, she is the mother: serious and stately, her beauty faded, but arguably the more charming for it. Along the distant quay fishermen are waiting for an evening catch.

After dinner, Hal sits with Gaspari at the bow. The little dog is asleep at the director's feet. Every so often she will let out a small, subconscious whine, and her paws will twitch with some movement carried over from her dream.

'I've been meaning to thank you,' Hal says.

'For what?'

'Leaving the journal in my room.'

'Ah. Yes.'

'It makes for interesting reading.'

'I thought you might think so.'

'I'm intrigued by her – the woman.'

Gaspari nods. 'Oh yes,' he says. 'She was the reason I took it on. I felt, reading his words, that she had the ability to arouse feelings of great passion and devotion in men, but also hatred and fear. This is something that happens in cinema, I think – in the way we see our female stars.'

'What do you mean?'

'Take an actress like Grace Kelly. People like to think of her as some Diana, a virgin goddess: golden and pure. Then, when she is reported as having a love affair, as beautiful young people are wont to do, people feel that she has deceived them in some way.'

Hal nods. For some reason he is put in mind not of Giulietta – the only film actress he has ever met – but of Stella.

'That was something I noticed about *Elegy*,' he says now. 'There was no female lead.'

Gaspari nods.

'What was it really about? You promised to tell me at the party.'

It is a while before Gaspari speaks. And then, with a little nod of his head as though urging himself on, he says, 'Once upon a time I was in love.' He smiles. 'Hard to imagine, I suppose, of one so old and ugly as I.'

'Not at all.' But in a way it is, Hal thinks. He is such a solitary, self-contained man.

'You are kind.' Gaspari inclines his head. 'Well, the film was about that love. An impossible love.'

'Impossible how?'

There is a long silence, before Gaspari says, 'I will tell you a story, my friend. Imagine a man who believes that his chance for love has left him, along with his youth. And then imagine that this love comes, unexpectedly, in later age. His lover is young and beautiful in a way that he has never been himself.'

He takes a sip of his wine.

'When they met he had not been looking for anything. He had been almost content in his loneliness, had assumed that life had offered up to him all that it would in the way of romantic attachments. And then this astonishing thing happens, coming like a summer storm out of a clear sky. It sweeps him away from everything he thought he knew.

'He has always taken Rome for granted, this man, has never truly loved the city before. But now it has been transformed for him. Before he only had time to see the bad, the dirt and decay. People talked to him about the wonder of the city and he thought they must be seeing something that had become invisible to him in all his years of living in it. But now that it is the place that has brought them together, that has formed the backdrop for their entire affair, he sees beauty in everything.

In the ruins erupting through the concrete, in the cloud pines in the small park near his apartment – even in the prostitutes who appear at night to line the Appian Way.'

Hal knows this version of the city.

'He knows that life cannot be easy for them, because, as I told you, theirs is an impossible love. And yet, in those green surrounds of the Borghese gardens, where they go to walk together, it is easy to forget all troubles for a while.

'Only for a while though. It is not easy to ignore the new presence of the men at the gates who wait and watch. At one time he liked to laugh at them, with their sombre expressions, their clownish trousers, their tight boots. They were ridiculous to him, hardly more threatening than boys playing at war games. And yet, somehow, they have got a hold and have multiplied like lice . . . no, like bright black fleas.'

This is the city Hal has never known – the one that people do not talk of. But here Gaspari is, speaking of it.

Gaspari suddenly looks very tired, and old – the deep hollows beneath his eyes and cheekbones appear all the more dramatic in the rudimentary light. He takes a sip of his cognac, and sighs. 'We have known each other such a short time, you and I. And you a journalist. And yet you seem, somehow, a man with integrity. I think I can trust you.' He looks at Hal. 'Can I?'

'Yes,' Hal says, 'of course.'

Gaspari nods. 'Well you see, Hal, the person I was in love with was a young man.'

'Oh.' Hal is, in spite of himself, surprised. That Gaspari has felt able to make this confidence to him, a relative stranger, is something extraordinary. The bravery of it, sharing something that in the wrong hands could be so dangerous.

As though understanding this, Gaspari says, 'I suppose you

are wondering why I am telling you. It is because, in this way, I can continue to defy them. They tried to pretend that we did not exist, those like myself. They tried to hide us from view, to claim that we were not proper men.'

Hal suddenly understands. 'That was why you made the film.'

'Yes. Of course, there could be nothing explicit in it. But I would know what it would mean. It would be my biggest defiance. And it was made at Cinecittà, which was created by them.'

He smiles, but there is nothing of real mirth in it. And Hal thinks now that he has guessed the reason for Gaspari's permanent state of melancholy.

'The person you were in love with,' he says, immediately feeling a prude for not saying 'man'. 'Is he . . . ?'

Gaspari nods. 'It wasn't them. Or at least, not directly. It was worse than that. It was my fault, too.'

'How?'

'I got carried away. I wanted to cast him in a film. I had been struck by his beauty and his talent at the very beginning, but I did not have enough of a name for myself then to risk an unknown. Now I wanted him as the star. I knew he would do it brilliantly. I should have seen that there would be jealousy. I should have realized that people knew – or guessed – about us. It is too small an industry to keep such things hidden. Besides, I am sure that I must have given myself away every time I looked at him.'

It is hard to imagine this solemn, reserved man, giving much away with a look.

'Someone informed on us. I have my ideas about who it might have been, but it is poisonous to look too closely into that sort of thing. It does no good, in the end. And so – I'm sure you can imagine how it goes . . .'

Hal shakes his head.

'They come to your house, they take you to their car. They aren't exactly – how to put it – gentle, either with their actions or their words.' Gaspari pauses. 'It would have been better, I think, if he had been with me at the time, if they had found us together. Then I could have protected him.'

'But wouldn't that have given them proof?'

Gaspari laughs, an odd, hoarse sound. 'They didn't need proof – that was not a concern for them. No, I mean that if they had found us together it would not have been so terrible for him. It would have been more discreet.' He sighs. 'Rafe came from an important Sicilian family. Rather aristocratic, and traditional – but more than all of that, extremely pious. For them, Rafe's actions were not merely a crime but a sin. And perhaps the worst he could have committed. I believe they might have preferred it if he had killed a man. At least that, in his father's view, would have been a masculine act.

'I tried to convince him that, no matter what society might make of what we were, he should not be ashamed. But he was, always – his upbringing had made him that way. Sometimes he would tell me he could not see me any more, and several painful weeks would follow. He would claim that he was going to join the army – or the church. Something that might help him "cure" himself. But he was always back, apologizing – and I would always forgive him, because I loved him. And I think he loved me too, despite his doubts about the morality of what we had together. I had no family, you understand. It was easier for me.

'He had hoped, I think, that he might have been able to keep his true nature a secret from them always. Though how exactly he planned to do that was never clear, especially considering his mother's matchmaking had begun to reach a fever pitch.' Gaspari smiles his downturned smile. 'We used to laugh about it. She was constantly throwing soirees, dances, presenting some suitable, willing daughter of an acquaintance. And they were *always* willing, you understand. Because he was so clever, and beautiful.'

Gaspari's face grows solemn once more. 'He was quite terrified of his parents finding out. He knew they loved him, but he didn't believe that their love for him was unconditional. If they knew the truth, he wasn't certain that they would be able to forgive him. His father, as I have said, had always made his views on such matters very clear. Such a thing, in his eyes was unmanly – even inhuman.

'When those men came to get him, I am sure that they would have used some of the same words that were shouted at me. Perhaps they would have been slightly more respectful, because his parents were well known. But I have no doubt his family would have found out that night what it was he had been trying to keep from them. I don't know for certain – but that is my guess.'

'Why don't you know?'

'Because,' Gaspari says, 'he hung himself that night, in his cell.'

Hal wishes there was something he could say that would be adequate. Unable to think of anything, he remains silent.

'They came to tell me, the next morning. He had been in the same prison as me and I had not even known it. One of them, I remember, seemed particularly pleased. But one was . . . almost kind. I think he could see how distressed I was and, later, he came alone to tell me that he was sorry for my loss.' He stops. 'I wish that he had not been so afraid – and so alone – when he died. I find myself wondering if there was something that I could have said to him that would have helped him to cope with it better. At the time I was even angry with him, because my love had not been enough.'

Hal cannot think of anything to say. He is grateful for the fact that the light has worsened to the point where he can hardly make out Gaspari's face. He knows that the expression there would be one of great pain. Now he understands why the man wears sadness about him like a cloak. The long silence that follows is finally broken by Gaspari's dog, who wakes and gives a little whimper. The director bends and picks her up, buries his face in her side. Hal is suddenly struck by Gaspari's mention of his lack of relatives. This small creature, perhaps, is all the family he has.

Finally, Gaspari speaks. 'You know, my friend, I have found that the best way to come to terms with one's past is like this, through talk. It is painful, but, little by little, it helps to diffuse its power.'

Hal looks up, to find the director watching him, expectantly, as though waiting for him to speak. But there is nothing to say.

13

Late afternoon, and the light has assumed an unusual golden hue, like that of a pale white wine. Beyond the coast, the mountains are a steep, purplish shadow. To Hal they are surreal and ungraspable, like something read about in a child's storybook.

They are running under motor now and the yacht cuts through the still waters effortlessly. The engine purrs.

Hal sits with Aubrey Boyd, playing gin rummy. Aubrey is surprisingly competitive, and a deft player. His gains are made all the more quickly for the fact that Hal isn't able to concentrate properly on the game.

'What did you mean,' he asks, 'when you said that we're little projects for the Contessa?'

'Well,' Aubrey raises an eyebrow. 'I mean, you only have to look at us all. Apart from Giulietta, perhaps. We're quite a ragtag bunch. She collects hopeless cases. You have Gaspari, with his melancholy, Morgan, with his drinking. Me, well, look at me for goodness' sake. And you, with whatever it is you're carrying about.'

'Excuse me?'

'The thing you're carrying about. The thing that makes you act like the walking wounded. Aha! Big gin! That's thirty-one points, I think.' He sits back, happily.

'What *thing*?'

'You tell me.' Aubrey glances up. 'Oh, don't look so offended. I'd have a go at it myself, if I knew it would make me half such a poetic figure as you.' He nods his head in the Trusses' direction. 'Them, though. Can't work out which one it is.'

'What do you mean?'

'You know, which one of them is the project. Perhaps neither, after all. Perhaps both.'

Hal can see Stella on the sunbed at the bow, a large sunhat obscuring her head and shoulders. He can't imagine her needing the Contessa's help. A woman like that, surely, has attained everything she has sought from life. He watches her, turning the pages of her book, rationalizing her into ordinariness. She is not so beautiful. Next to Giulietta Castiglione, not at all. The effect is that of a small wildflower – a forget-me-not – beside a damask rose. And then there is the fact that she is nothing more interesting than a rich man's wife. Women like her grace every other page in *Life*. In her pastel-coloured outfits, with her neat blonde hair, she is as two-dimensional as the illustration in an advert for a washing powder, or department store. He had thought that night in Rome that her reticence concealed something, and he had been intrigued by it. And last night, on the deck, she had seemed different, less false. But now he wonders if he was mistaken.

14

Portofino

Suddenly, there is a cry of excitement, and Hal forces his gaze from her to follow Aubrey's pointing finger. Before them is Portofino, gleaming expensively in the sun. The breeze, laden as ever with salt and pine, now carries the unmistakable scent of petrol.

Portofino is a place of self-conscious restraint. But Hal, with the keenly honed instinct of one who hasn't got much to call his own, sees wealth everywhere: in the waterfront villas half-hidden in the trees, in the quietly spectacular speedboats tethered in the turquoise harbour. Even the colours of the façades along the waterfront have a richness and sobriety to them. Much of this will be foreign wealth, some of it new. Though some of those grand residences may still stand empty, waiting for owners yet to – or never to – return.

Above them all towers a majestic castle, wreathed in trees.

The *Pygmalion*, sleekly elegant, is in her natural habitat. She makes the huge vessel anchored next to them, an ex-military frigate done up with white paint and gold fittings, look like a poorly dressed gatecrasher.

Their arrival has been anticipated, of course. The inevitable Armada of small boats approaches, the first flashbulb exploding with a pop and burst of light, the others following like a chain reaction.

'Excuse me, sir?' one of the men from the boat calls up to Hal, in thickly accented English, 'But who are you, please?'

'I'm a journalist,' he calls back. 'My name is Hal Jacobs.'

'Ah. Well, sir,' the man shouts, in a reasonable way, 'would you mind moving out of the way for a few minutes? So that we may have a picture of the beautiful Giulietta only?'

The furore continues as they disembark from the tender onto dry land. There is a frenzy of activity about Gaspari and the two stars. Truss has disappeared to make a call, and Stella is nowhere to be seen. Hal is quite evidently a spare part. He suddenly knows what he will do, with this opportunity for solitude. He goes to his cabin and retrieves the journal.

Where to read it? He wants to read in solitude. Not, then, the waterfront cafés, where people gather. He wanders across the piazza, finds a plaque that reads: 'Spare a flower, a thought for those who died.' Here, then, in this place of apparent serenity, are mothers still mourning their dead sons.

He walks away from the main drag. Here, tucked slightly out of sight, the less picturesque, more workaday crafts are moored: mainly small fishing boats with peeling hulls. In a patch of sun, three women are spreading nets to dry. The scent of the sea that emanates from them is so strong it seems to thicken the air. The women, he notices, don't even glance at the photographers and stars some hundred feet away. They are absolutely intent on their task. There is something rather refreshing in this.

He finds himself drawn towards the castle that overlooks the bay, climbing through the fragrant terraced gardens that lead up to it. There is a good spot near to a cloud pine, the mass of foliage throwing a blue shadow below it. He sits, and realizes that across the ramparts he can see the curve of the coast along which they have already sailed, stretching away through the haze. But his mind feels glutted with beauty, and he looks upon it with something like complacency. He turns from it, and begins to read. At a glance, he can see how one preoccupation peppers the pages, appearing in almost every sentence. *La donna.* No mention now of Ottoman hordes, of Genoese glory. Only this mysterious new passenger.

Some superstition has been got about among the men that she is bad luck for us. There was a storm, which is normal for this time of year – but they are convinced that it is due to the woman. The problem with sailors is that they are born superstitious: difficult to convince them with a rational explanation if they have decided on some malevolence at work. Before I felt the need to guard her from their lust; now it is from their fear.

I cannot sleep for thought of her so little distance away. I feel that I am aflame, and would quench myself in her coolness. But I cannot read her. Sometimes, when she looks at me with those black eyes, I think I see some answer to my longing there. Then I decide that I am imagining it . . .

It is an absurdity, this thing that has taken control of

*me. It is like a fever of the mind and body. I am trying
to scorch it from myself.*

*And yet, perhaps if I could make her mine, this thing
would leave me free . . .*

THE CAPTAIN'S LIEUTENANTS are worried about him. They have never seen him so distracted. They discuss in secret what is to be done. The bravest among them offers to go and speak with him.

The man finds his captain, as expected, jealously guarding the closed curtains that conceal the place where the woman resides. When the lieutenant asks if they may go somewhere else on the galleon – somewhere where she will not be able to overhear – he refuses. So the lieutenant is forced to whisper, hoping that the woman cannot hear him. It is not precisely that he believes she has dark powers, as some of the men do. But it would not do to throw caution to the wind entirely.

'It's the woman,' he murmurs, nodding towards the drapes. 'The men don't like it, Captain.' He lowers his voice further. 'They are scared of her.'

'Of her? That helpless creature? Don't make me laugh.'

'They don't think she is helpless, though. They think . . .'

'What?'

'They think she is responsible for the storm.'

The captain scoffs. 'These are grown men, and yet they are acting like children, worse – old women, with their superstitions. It's so ridiculous that I cannot credit it. And what has convinced them of this?'

The lieutenant shrugs. 'Well, sir, some of the men . . .'

'Yes?'

'Some of the men have noticed the marks around her ankles.

They say – I'm not sure this is true, I don't know about such things – but they say that one who had been meant for burning would bear such marks. They have decided that she is a witch.'

'The Genoese do not engage in such practices.'

'No, sire,' says the lieutenant slowly, 'but we are not in Genoese waters yet.'

'And do you believe any of this?'

A pause.

'Well?'

The man sighs. 'It has to be said that a few strange things have happened since she came on board. I have never seen a storm simply appear in the way that one did. It was . . . unnatural. And where we found her, so far out to sea. A normal person – especially not a woman – wouldn't have swum so far and survived.'

The captain shakes his head. 'And so you condemn her, for being brave? What sort of barbaric notion is that? We live in a modern, enlightened society. The Pisans or the Venetians might believe such nonsense, but never us.'

The lieutenant tries again. 'And she wasn't—' he coughs, 'wearing any clothing. That, surely, cannot be normal in a woman of decency.'

But herein lies his mistake. He watches as his captain's eyes glaze over at the memory of that pale nude flesh, and his gaze travels, inevitably, towards the curtains once more.

The lieutenant knows there is one more thing he might try. 'Sire,' he says, carefully. 'There is also the matter of your fiancée.'

It was the wrong thing to say. The captain explodes. 'How *dare* you speak to me in that way?' He rises to his full – and not inconsiderable – height. 'How dare you insinuate that I am in some way lax in my duty to her? My care for this helpless woman in no way affects my deep and long-lasting love in that regard.'

The lieutenant takes his leave, apologizing all the way.

When Hal looks up from the page the light has assumed the bluish quality of early evening. The trees about him are ink impressions, the air is cooler. He is also certain that he is not alone. He looks about, and then sees her emerging from the shadowy gardens below. She looks otherworldly in the strange light: her skin paler, her hair brighter.

She has not seen him yet, he realizes: he is hidden in shadow. He moves forward.

She stops. 'Oh.'

'Hello.'

'I didn't realize you had come up here.'

No, he thinks – undoubtedly if she had she would not be here.

'I wanted to find a quiet spot.'

She nods. 'So did I. And I wanted to see what the view was like.' They look together in silence, and he sees that lights are beginning to come on along the darkening stretch of coast. Then she glances at the journal in his lap. 'What were you doing? Reading?'

'Yes.'

Hal can tell she is curious, in spite of herself.

'What is it?'

'Oh,' he says, 'just an old book.'

He sees that she is frustrated by his reticence, that she wants to know more.

'Can I take a look?'

'I'm afraid not,' he says. 'It was given to me in confidence.'

'Oh.' He sees that she is stung, a little embarrassed. For a second, this knowledge gives him a kind of cruel pleasure. And then he takes pity on her. 'It's a journal,' he says.

'Whose?'

'Someone long dead.'

'Your friend?'

He stares at her. 'What?'

'You told me about him, in Rome. You told me he wrote.'

Did he? He must have done so. Yes: now he remembers. It was when he felt at liberty to share it with her, because he assumed he would never see her again. 'Yes,' he says, 'this isn't his, though.'

'What was his name?'

'His name was Morris.'

'How did he die?'

'I don't want to talk about it.' It comes out more harshly than he had quite intended. 'I'm sorry,' he says. 'There isn't any point in speaking of it now. It happened so long ago.'

She nods. 'Except, you aren't writing. You told me that you'd stopped, after he died.'

Her tenacity is a surprise. Only this morning he was thinking how weak she seemed, how flimsy and yielding. Perhaps this is his comeuppance.

'Yes,' he says, 'that's right.' And then *he* remembers something from that night, something he can use, as a way of throwing it back to her. 'Your father was a writer.'

'Yes,' she says. Now she is the one who appears wary.

'You never told me his name.'

'I don't think you'll know it. He wasn't famous outside Spain.'

'You're Spanish?' He looks at her. With the blonde hair, somehow, he would never have guessed. And yet it would explain the accent, with that foreign element beneath.

'I was.'

It is an odd thing to say. 'You aren't now?'

She is wrong-footed. 'Yes – but I mean that I'm an

American, now. That is how I think of myself.' She glances up at the sky. 'It's getting dark. I think we should go back to the yacht.'

He almost smiles. She is just as good at this game of obfuscation as he, perhaps better.

When he stands, she takes a quick step back. And then, as though feeling this might reveal too much, she steps forward again. It is too late, though, because suddenly the thing quickens into life between them, strong as it had been in Rome. Stronger, perhaps, because before there was no knowledge of how her skin would feel against his. It is a relief when she turns away.

He follows her back down through the dusk-laden garden. She wears a very simple linen dress, but with the reverse cut away to reveal the expanse of her back, the stippled line of her spine. He knows suddenly that he wants to put his hand there, to feel the soft warmth of her back. At one point she looks over her shoulder to check that he is following, and he nearly stumbles, caught out.

The scent of the flowers is stronger now, as though the dark has kindled it. 'What is that?' he asks, and it comes out as a hoarse whisper, as though the perfume is another secret between them. 'That smell?'

'Star jasmine,' she says, as though she has had the answer ready for him.

Forever after, he thinks, his memories of this spring will be steeped in the scent.

*

'Tonight,' the Contessa announces, after supper, 'I thought we would play charades. I will divide you into teams, and give you each your challenge. You will be playing famous characters from the real or imagined past – and we must all guess who they are. The way I play it is that the teams must confer, and whichever team presents the winning answer is spared. The others must drink a glass of *anis*.'

She is already setting out the tiny crystal cups, pouring measures of the syrupy liquid into them. There is no time for dissent before she has paired them all off. Earl Morgan and Gaspari, Truss and Giulietta, Aubrey Boyd and Roberto – who tries to protest, to no avail. And then, with a strange kind of inevitability: Stella and Hal. She passes him a slip of paper.

He reads it, and then shows it to Stella, so that only she can see.

Lancelot and Guinevere. When he glances up toward the others, he catches Truss watching him. He feels pinioned by the man's gaze. Truss smiles, revealing that row of white teeth, and Hal smiles back, but it is a physical effort: the muscles in his face are taut as rubber bands.

Earl Morgan and Gaspari are first. Interestingly, Hal thinks, all the subtlety of the performance is Gaspari's. Morgan's performance is strained melodrama, and without the benefit of his rich voice it all feels rather thin. Hal finds himself wondering how many takes it requires to portray him at his scene-stealing best. When Morgan plunges an imaginary blade into Gaspari's back, and Gaspari turns with a look of agonized betrayal, Aubrey leaps from his seat. 'Julius Caesar,' he shouts, in delight. 'Caesar and Brutus.'

The little glasses are passed round to the losers. While the others grimace Hal savours his, enjoying the warming liquorice taste.

Aubrey Boyd is Titania, smoothing imaginary gossamer skirts over his lap for his lover to lay his head in, and Roberto

– clumsy, scowling – is unintentionally hilarious as Bottom. Then Truss and Giulietta make an interesting pairing as Samson and Delilah. As on screen, Giulietta is magnetic: by turns seductive, devious, righteous. It is as though the character has been poured into her, filling the empty spaces. Truss merely suffers the performance, as though he is indulging the game of small children, but there is something between them, a tension, that makes it interesting.

Their turn will be next. Hal turns to tell Stella how he thinks they should do it, but she has risen from her seat. 'I'm sorry to break up the game,' she says, 'but I'm very tired. Please—' as the Contessa makes to stand too, 'don't worry about me. I'm going to go to bed.'

Her

I am anything but tired, as I make my way below deck to the cabin. I feel that I have come very close to danger. As soon as our names were called together, I had to extricate myself. Perhaps it is irrational, but I felt that had we had done it, acted out our parts, everything would have been visible. That night in Rome. The thing that is between us now, that made itself known in the garden this evening – though neither of us would acknowledge it. But I saw his face when I turned back to him.

I have taught myself better than this. People are lazy. They see, usually, only the thing that you choose to show them. And I have learned that the more they think you say, the less you can get away with revealing. This has suited me well – I have become adept.

Yet with him it is different. It isn't just that I think he sees through this performance – which I am beginning to suspect he does. It is that I find myself wanting to tell him more. I haven't spoken of my father in more than ten years. I haven't even alluded to that former life. Yet this evening, when the two of us were alone, with the quiet of the garden all around, it was all I could do to remain silent. I wanted to keep talking.

That night, Hal has a strange dream. He wakes disorientated and aroused. Gradually, fragments of it come back to him. It was her, Stella. That night in Rome. His sleeping self remembers, no matter how hard he has worked to forget it.

He sits on the side of the bed. At least it makes a change from the other dream. But he needs to get a hold of himself. A married woman. It could have no future. He had his chance for that sort of happiness with Suze, and he ruined it. And there could be no happiness in this. But then perhaps this is why he is drawn to her, because he knows there is no future in it. Later, he will remember these attempts at rationalizing the irrational, and he will smile at them. But later still than that, they will hold no humour for him.

Unable to get back to sleep – and half worried that if he does he will dream again of her – he sits on the bed, groggy, and tries to bleach his mind of thought. Eventually, to distract himself, he picks up the journal and begins to read.

THE NEXT TROUBLE to befall the ship is the pestilence. Several of the men, overnight, are overtaken with a terrible illness: bouts of vomiting and delirium. Men – brave men who have fought many a bloody battle – lie on their backs wishing aloud that they might die and be spared the horrors of the sickness. There have been various contagions before that have spread quickly among the men: the sharing of quarters, food and space are no help in such cases. And yet none have spread with such ferocity as this disease. And none of the men, this time, are left in any doubt as to the cause.

The lieutenants meet again. 'We must find some way of getting her removed from the ship. Without the captain discovering how, of course.'

And so a plan is hatched. The captain's evening meal will contain several teaspoons of a powerful morphiate from the medical supplies. Then the men will take the woman back to shore in the tender – and leave her there. They will be kind, they decide, they will send her on her way with food, and water, and the clothes on her back. It is a brave plan, because none on board are in any doubt now about the scope of her power. But so long as they treat her well – or at least not ill – they hope to be spared.

It works well. The captain lies in his berth in a drugged stupor. They will tell him, when he wakes, that he must simply have been exhausted. He will, no doubt, be too embarrassed to investigate the matter further.

Under cover of darkness the tender leaves the ship at anchor, makes the short journey to the shore and back again. The woman was surprisingly acquiescent when they explained what they must do: she merely nodded her head and gathered her cloak about her. She looked particularly young then, and – if the men didn't know otherwise – rather harmless. If they didn't know that she was something other than what she seems, they might have known something like guilt for leaving a young woman on her own on a deserted shore, vulnerable to men, beasts and nature itself. But none among them allows himself to feel this. And none of them turn to look at the small figure left upon the beach. She is no more to them now than a problem solved.

Only one difficulty remains. How to explain the matter of her disappearance to the captain. They will simply have to pretend that they, too, slept the sleep of the dead and woke to find that she had left. Swum away, perhaps.

But the captain's reaction, when he wakes and hears that she is gone, is something for which none of them had been prepared. He is like a mad man – or as one lieutenant privately decides, less human than that – more like a wild animal. His eyes shine with a strange, crazed brightness. He stalks the length of the ship, searching everywhere for her, in impossible places: under men's bedrolls, inside the foodstores, within the arsenal. When one of the lieutenants bravely goes to him and tries reasoning with him, he shrugs the man off with such violence that he is thrown to the floor. It is a sad and terrible thing to watch: that such a great man should be brought to such a low place by mere sexual infatuation.

For a day, they observe him like this, wondering what – if anything – they can do about it. Eventually, it is decided that it would be best to let him sleep on it, in the hope that some vestige of reason will have returned to him in the morning. But when the day dawns, calm and bright, they discover that he has played them at their own game. The tender is gone, and their captain has deserted his ship.

An odd thing seems to have happened. Somehow the remnants of Hal's dream must have become tangled with the words on the page. Because, as he was reading, the figure of the woman in his mind began to change. Became someone he recognized. Became *her*.

15

San Fruttuoso

The next day's destination is San Fruttuoso, a tenth-century abbey set in its own bay.

'You have seen it in the scene in which the captain goes to pray,' the Contessa says, 'to ask advice from God. And several of my ancestors' remains are interred in the crypt there – though whether any of them are his is unknown.'

Hal makes a quick note of this. It would be an interesting detail for the piece: a nice foil to the modern glamour. Even though, no doubt, it will then be edited out.

'So he might not have made it to the Americas?' Aubrey asks.

'Well,' the Contessa says, carefully, 'it isn't absolutely known. Certainly all mention of his name disappears after a point, from the records kept at the time. So . . .' she looks to Gaspari, 'we thought that it would be an interesting ending to the story.'

'Ah, and there is a hike that one can do,' she says. Hal

has the distinct impression that she is suddenly eager to move on from the subject of her ancestor. 'It begins here in Portofino, and goes up over the top. Spectacular views. Is anyone brave enough to do it with me?'

Hal and Aubrey Boyd offer to at once. Aubrey's eagerness is a surprise, because he always appears so indolent.

The Contessa is pleased. 'Anyone else?'

'I'd like to do it,' Stella says, suddenly.

Truss turns to her. 'And do you plan to walk it in your high heels, my dear?' he says, lightly. 'Or perhaps in your bare feet? I don't imagine there's anything in your wardrobe that would be appropriate for a hike.'

'I have some plimsolls with me.'

'Where did you get those?'

'I bought them.'

Truss looks momentarily bemused. 'Well, if you're sure, Kitten.'

'I am.'

She does a good job of keeping herself in check, Hal thinks. But if one is watching at exactly the right time, he has noticed, it is possible to see the electric flare of emotion beneath the surface. A flicker of unease, a silent, tiny spark of anger. She is like this with her husband. When he insists on her doing this, or not doing that, or eating exactly the thing he has selected for her. There is an instantaneous rebellion, immediately quashed.

The first part of the climb is straight up out of the town. The air is thick with the pungent scent of wild garlic. Hal's calves burn, and his shirt sticks to his back. He has always thought of himself as fit, but it is more challenging than he would have expected.

Aubrey Boyd is appalled by the ascent.

'I thought you said,' he gasps to the Contessa, 'that this was a walk? This isn't a walk – it's a prolonged heart-attack.'

The Contessa turns back to him with a smile, barely out of breath herself. 'It will be good for you. And think of the view from the top.'

Aubrey's enthusiasm for the expedition, Hal learns, is his expectation of some photographic opportunities. 'I have a vision of you,' he tells Hal as they begin climbing, 'standing atop a rockface like a Greek god, king of all you survey. And perhaps you could be, well, shirtless too.'

'I don't think so,' Hal says. 'I'm the journalist – what will you do with the photograph? It can't go in the story.'

'It could,' Aubrey says, a little petulantly.

'Not if I had anything to do with it.'

'Fine. But I'm going to keep pestering you. You're too good a photographic opportunity to pass up.'

'I'd rather be – as you might put it – on the other side of the lens.'

'I can see that, I think. You like to be alone. Your own man.'

'I suppose so.'

Aubrey nods. 'Me too. I don't like all that mess.'

'Mess?'

'Well, you know. The *heart*.'

'Ah.' Hal can't imagine Aubrey with a woman – he is fairly certain that isn't the way the man would be inclined. And yet he can't quite see him with anyone.

'How long have you lived in Rome?' Aubrey asks.

'Five years or so.'

'And your parents?'

'Back in England. How about yours?'

'England, too. Oxfordshire. Hardly ever see them, though. We don't get along.' He sighs. 'My father has always thought what I do is quite ridiculous. I could make pots and pots of money from it, and he would look on it as ill-gotten gains.'

'Why?'

'Oh, he doesn't think it's a proper vocation for a man. If I photographed conflict, say – well, that would be another matter. Though, come to think of it, that would probably still be a little *artistic* for his liking. Much better if I had a job in finance, or the civil service. Goodness, he'd probably prefer it if I emptied dustbins for a living.'

It is said with humour, but the archness doesn't quite ring true. For the first time, Hal realizes that there may be more to it than mere affectation. He remembers certain men on board, always ready with some flippancy, who sobbed with terror when the cruiser came under fire.

'Does anyone's father approve of them?' he says. 'I know mine doesn't.'

'What's your crime?'

'Mainly that I enlisted with the navy, in the war. He's army: a brigadier. I think he believes it was some act of rebellion on my part.'

'Was it?'

'No – or at least, not consciously. I enlisted as a rating – which I suppose was something of a revolt, as I knew he would have wanted to pull strings to get me an officer rank. But mainly because I'd always felt at home on the sea. I sailed a lot as a boy. I thought I might be better at it.'

'Were you?'

'Is anyone good at war?'

'Not sure. I'm a pacifist.'

'Ah. Well, it wasn't quite like sailing dinghies in the Solent, that's for certain.'

He thinks now that if he had joined the army, his way of seeing the sea would not have changed dramatically. Now, he sees death in it: death lurking beneath the surface, ready to blow him to pieces; death, readying to swallow men down into the dark. And then, suddenly, the shift will occur and he will see his hand, but smaller, a boy's hand, skimming the surface as he leans over the edge of his boat. The water fracturing over his fingers into dancing beads of light.

'Oh,' Aubrey says, 'thank goodness. We're nearly at the top.'

The steps are indeed growing shallower, then petering out. The Contessa has got there first, and has found a great stone slab to sit on. Hal and Aubrey join her. Stella, who stopped to look at something at the edge of the path, is gaining on them now, moving with a weightless agility. Beneath her arms and at her neckline there are patches faintly darkened by sweat, her cheeks flushed dark red. It is a marked departure from her usually immaculate appearance, and Hal finds something fascinating in the transformation.

She stops a few feet away, and he moves along the rock. 'You want to sit?'

'Oh no,' she says, quickly, 'I'm fine standing.' She turns to take in the view, and he looks with her. He is gratified to see how high they have climbed. The fishing boats are like specks of lint in the harbour and even the *Pygmalion*, which has not yet set sail, looks dwarfed.

Stella turns back to them with a smile. She seems briefly unfettered.

'What were you looking at?' the Contessa asks. 'By the path?'

'Oh.' She points nearby, to a white bloom that looks like a child's drawing of a flower. 'This – I think it's called cistus. I haven't seen them for a long time; since my childhood. They're all along the path here.'

'Bring some with you if you like,' the Contessa says. 'I'm sure we have a vase on the yacht.'

'Oh no,' Stella says, 'it's all right. I like seeing them like this, growing.'

Once they have all recovered their breath they continue, picking their way along the path, which is wider in places, then narrowing to a foot across in others. Hal is just behind Stella now. He likes watching her quick plimsoll-clad feet. There is no hesitation in her movements when they come to a steep drop, a thin and knotty piece of path.

It is only when he hears Aubrey call his name from some way off that Hal becomes aware of the gap they have opened between themselves and the other two. He turns and sees them some thirty feet away.

'What is it?'

'An injury,' Aubrey calls. Hal sees that they are on one of the thinnest parts of the path. He can't see the Contessa, and for a horrible second he imagines that she has fallen. But as he jogs back towards them he sees her, sitting on the verge.

'What is it?'

'Oh,' she says, quite cheerfully, 'I stepped badly and turned my foot.'

'I'm afraid I didn't see,' Aubrey says, sheepishly. 'I was taking a photograph.'

'Shall I take a look?' Hal is no expert, but has played enough sport to know the signs of a sprain.

The Contessa manoeuvres herself onto a nearby rock, and pulls up her trouser leg a little. The ankle beneath, Hal notices, shows no sign of swelling compared to its twin. But the Contessa is elderly, and no doubt frailer than she appears.

'We should get you back down,' Hal says. 'I don't think you can carry on like this.'

'Ah, no no.' She waves a hand impatiently. 'I will be fine in a few minutes.' They continue, at a much slower pace than before. Yet only a few minutes into the next leg of their journey she shakes her head. 'It is a great shame, but I cannot continue.'

Hal turns back. 'We'll all go—'

'No,' she says, quickly. 'I can go alone. Or . . . Aubrey, you will help me, yes?'

'Of course.'

The Contessa gestures to Hal and Stella. 'You two must continue.'

Both begin to object simultaneously.

'Please,' the Contessa says, firmly. 'I will be upset if you do not. Someone must do the walk.' She sighs. 'I have to accept that I am so feeble now that I may never do it again. So, please, do it in my stead?'

'Fine.' Hal holds up his hands. 'I give in.' Stella nods, with evident reluctance.

The Contessa smiles. 'Thank you.'

Aubrey has the Contessa brace an arm around his thin shoulders, and they begin their slow return back towards the town. Stella and Hal watch them until they are out of reach. For a few moments, a strange new quiet descends. Then Stella says, 'Do you think they'll be all right? Just the two of them?'

'I hope so. Either way, we weren't exactly left with much choice in the matter. There isn't any disobeying our leader.'

'No.' And then, to his surprise, she laughs.

*

The wildflowers are incredible. As they pass these clouds of colour Hal asks Stella if she can name them. She lists them for him, pointing out each variety as they pass. Wild garlic, more white bursts of cistus, pale yellow dandelions. The occasional bright flag of a poppy.

'Where did you learn all this?'

'It interests me. We had a garden when I was young.'

'You don't have one now?' Hal asks. He finds it hard to believe that a man as wealthy as Truss would not.

'Oh, that's different. It's managed by a tribe of gardeners. If I had the chance to plant my own it wouldn't be like that. I would not want that rigidity, that show. I would want it to look as though it had simply flowered from nature.'

He is confused by the fact that she talks about her own garden as though it didn't belong to her. 'Could you not recreate that yourself? Explain to the gardeners how you would want it?'

She hesitates. 'No.'

Hal looks at her now with her hair in disarray, her face bare and gleaming. He thinks of the other version of her: pristine, finished. He thinks he can guess which of these is to her husband's taste.

'Tell me about your garden – the one you had before.'

'There were orange trees,' she says, tentatively, 'below my bedroom window. In the spring I would wake up to the scent of their blossom. And there was the vegetable patch, close to the house. A vegetable patch and a fig, and at the bottom of the garden—' She stops, abruptly. 'I've forgotten.'

He is certain that she hasn't. 'Was this in Spain?'

'Yes.'

Beneath them the ground falls away sharply on one side for a stretch, so that it feels they are a grass stalk's breadth from plummeting into the blue below. Hal feels again that strange, almost irresistible pull towards the void. It is hard to believe that one would be dashed to death at the bottom in a place so serene as this. Surely one would merely soar, like the gulls he can see circling, scanning the waves for their prey. He hears Stella catch her breath. She appears to be leaning towards it – so much so that for a second he considers reaching out and catching hold of her, to prevent her from falling forward.

'I think this is how I imagined it,' she says. 'How the sea would look, when we saw it.' He waits for her to explain, particularly that use of 'we', but she seems to have retreated to some private place, far from him.

As they continue to walk the breeze dies away and the heat begins to build – though, unlike the mugginess of a warm day in the city it is a clean heat, and without the ferocity of a summer sun behind it.

Suddenly she says, in a kind of rush, 'There were beehives, at the bottom of the garden.'

'Oh?'

'My little brother looked after them. He taught himself, from a book. The honey they made was . . .' she pauses, and he turns to see that she has shut her eyes, as though invoking the memory, 'I haven't tasted anything like it since. I suppose it was because it came from particular herbs, flowers.'

There is such longing in the way she says this that he wishes he could find some of it for her, this impossible, lost-to-time taste.

'Of course,' she says, 'it's hard to know whether you remember things as better, or more special, than they actually were. Do you think that could be it?'

'Perhaps.' He remembers now a particular cake his mother makes: a bright yellow sponge, made with polenta and lemons. It is an Italian recipe – and he has had it, since, in Rome. But never have any of these versions, however expertly baked, tasted quite the same. 'I think there's something about the person behind it, too,' he says. 'If it's someone you love.'

Immediately he is embarrassed. He feels he has revealed too much feeling, too much of himself, in this.

'Yes,' she says. 'I think you're right.'

Then, as if some vault of memory has been thrown open, she tells him, too, of sleeping under the stars with the sounds of frogs and the light of fireflies; of a life lived barefoot beneath a warm sun, a town of red-tiled roofs and green fountains, of olive trees stretching in their marching lines as far as the eye could see. And looking at her as she is now, with her sweat-damp brow and her flushed cheeks, he can suddenly see the girl she might have been then.

'It sounds like a heaven.'

'Yes.'

'Why did you leave?'

'Because I had to.'

'Your father?'

'He died, at the beginning of the war. He insisted on going, to fight for the Republic.'

'Is that why you don't go back? Because—'

'There isn't anything to go back for.'

'Tell me.'

16

Her

December 1936

'Can we take the bees?'

'We can't take the bees, Tino.' And before he can protest, 'I'm sorry – but they'll be all right on their own. You've always told me that they are good at taking care of themselves.'

I can see him make an effort to be brave. And then he asks: 'Señor Bombón? Can we take him?'

'Well . . .' I think. 'I suppose there's no reason not to.'

'And Aunt Aída will be pleased to see him.'

'Yes. I'm sure she will.'

We have to leave. The war is coming here. We can hear it, only a few miles away. At times it can be seen, too: a whitening on the horizon like false lightning. The planes see us now. We have become a target. Two days ago a bomb fell near the centre of the town, killing a young woman not much older than myself, and an elderly man too far gone in years to have anything to do with war. Even if Tino wanted to run outside to watch them, I would not let him – the thought is unthinkable now. He does not, though. In a few months, he has become a different little boy. His face has altered. I am not feeding him enough, I know – there is not enough food – but I do not think it is just that. It is the change that this war, and Papa's death, has wrought in him.

I am convinced that if we stay we will wake one morning and find it here, on our own doorstep. I have explained as much to Tino as is necessary.

'But I thought you said that they wouldn't harm us, because we're children?'

'No.' There is talk on the radio of the bombing of school-houses. 'But it doesn't hurt to be sure. And Aunt Aída and Uncle Salvador are waiting for us, in Madrid.'

This isn't quite true. I have sent them a telegram. No reply – and no time to wait for one. No way of telling if it has even reached them. In his telegram, the one in which he told me that Papa had been killed, my uncle told me to stay put. Madrid *no es seguro*. But it is not safe here any more, either. And the truth is, I'm not sure that I can protect Tino properly. Not on my own. I'm not sure that I want to try.

In our cases: clothes, a little food, and supplies for Señor Bombón, put together at great pains by Tino. Also several colouring books for Tino, and a collection of various books about pirates: his latest obsession, perhaps because we have never seen the sea. When all of this is over, I think I will take him there.

It is very cold when we leave the house, and a freezing mist hangs low over the ground. We walk for an hour, as far as the main road to Madrid. As we reach it, a fine rain begins to fall and then, gradually, worsens, sweeping over us in curtains. Through the hush of its falling comes the occasional staccato of gunfire, somewhere in the west, somewhere near. Every so often, there is a yowl from Señor Bombón's cage, and Tino crouches down to whisper words of encouragement to him.

'Be brave,' he says, 'be brave.'

We wait for an hour, trying to shelter beneath the branches of an old olive, which seems to have wandered out of the marching lines of its compatriots to stand here beside the road. I am beginning to wonder if I have made the right decision. There is nothing going towards the capital – though we have seen several trucks pass in the opposite direction, carrying soldiers.

We are waiting on the main route from Valencia to Madrid – I had thought it would be easy. But this is the first time I have left the town and its surrounds since the beginning of the war. The scope of my own ignorance frightens me.

Finally, just as I am starting to calculate the journey home, and whether Tino will make it – or if I will have to carry him and Señor Bombón – there is the sound of an engine. Several engines, in fact. In the distance a black mass grows larger. They are going in the right direction. We crouch behind the olive, and watch, until I see the flag. Only then do I step out into the road, raising my arm. The first truck graunches to a halt: there are three others behind.

The driver leans from his cabin and shouts: 'What are you doing? I could have hit you!'

'Please,' I walk towards him. 'We need to get to Madrid.'

He frowns, wipes sweat from his brow. 'Why, child? Others are leaving fast as they can.'

'I know. We have nowhere else to go. We have family there.'

He looks from me to Tino, shakes his head. '*Vale*. Fine, OK. You can climb in.'

I lift Tino into the driver's cabin next to him, our small bag, Señor Bombón – protesting furiously – in his cage. I scramble up beside them.

We have joined a convoy of supplies to Madrid. In our truck, foodstuffs. In the two behind, weapons.

'Better stuff now,' the man – Luis – tells us. 'From the Russians. Up until recently, our lot have been fighting with guns twenty years old.'

'Why?'

'England and France sold us down the river. So the government will buy anything: second-rate planes with the faults plastered over, rifles that backfire, or don't fire at all – that haven't been used since the eighteen hundreds. All sold to them at the highest possible price, by charlatans, because they know that we're desperate. Straight into the pockets of criminals.'

I think of my father, who had to my knowledge never fired a gun, trying to use one of these useless weapons against a trained soldier. Was that how he went?

In the thick air inside the truck the smell of the supplies form a powerful, not entirely pleasant fug: a petroleum tang combined with the distinctive sweetish hum of meat that has spent too long in the warm. I pull Tino close to me, and press my nose to the top of his head. Normally, he might wriggle away from me: he feels he is getting too old for such embraces, I know. But since Papa's death he has been different. He remains where he is, in my arms. Gradually, lulled by the heat and the sway of the truck, I let my eyes close.

I come groggily awake. Then I hear the thing that has woken me. I know this sound: I have heard them pass over, high above. I don't understand the other sound, though. A high-pitched scream. Not human: the shriek of a machine.

As an idea surfaces – the possibility of what it might be – I am being hurled through space, and all behind me is white heat.

I am lying on my back. A hot bubble of silence surrounds me. I feel detached from myself, thrown loose. For a moment I wonder if this is dying. No, I realize, it is merely that I have come within touching distance of that veil that separates life from death.

'Oh,' Stella says, stopping on the track.

'What?'

'I think we're nearly there.'

There, in front of them, San Fruttuoso has appeared through a brief gap in the trees. There is the pale expanse of beach far below, the façade of the abbey gleaming like bone. The yacht is visible too, moored a hundred feet or so from the shore. The change that comes over her now is marked. The words are stopped up, the sadness and the energy . . . all seem to dissipate. She is combing her hair with her fingers and smoothing it behind her ears, drying the film of sweat from her brow. Before his eyes she is diminishing to a negative of the woman she was a moment before. His opportunity to comfort, to empathize, has passed.

As they pick their way down through the trees she stumbles, once, and he catches her arm to stop her fall. She thanks him, shortly, but these are the only words that pass between them.

When they are nearly at the beach, he tries. 'Stella,' he says, and then stops. He wants to show her how it has affected him, what she has told him of her past. He wants her to continue. But the words he finds are inadequate.

Gesture might be better. He could reach out, to touch her shoulder. But it would be imprudent. Since the night when they danced together he has avoided touching her at all costs. Especially now, since the dream of the night before. He lets his hand fall to his side, and feels his failure.

17

They discover the party in a restaurant beside one of the encircling arms of rock, perched above the water. The beach is surprisingly crowded: Italians lie or sit chatting and smoking on beds spread out across the sand, the women in brightly coloured swimming costumes and caps. A couple of children run shrieking in and out of the shallows, splashing one another. Behind all, rising solemn and pale, a *memento mori*, is the ancient façade of the abbey. He wonders what it has seen in all the centuries it has stood here.

Stella sits next to her husband once more. The transformation is complete: she wears a sunhat, a silk scarf. Her face is obscured by the brim of the hat. She might as well have put on a mask, Hal thinks.

At the head of their table, the Contessa is cooling her injured ankle in a wine bucket of iced water. But when she goes to stand, Hal sees to his surprise that there is no apparent pain as the foot takes her weight.

'Strange,' Gaspari says, 'to see it again like this – without the film crews here. You know, we got here, and discovered the whole place covered with seaweed – there had been a storm. It took four hours, perhaps more, to clear it all. And when the sun came out it stank.'

'Lucky that you can't transmit an odour through the screen – yet.'

Gaspari smiles. 'Sometimes I worry we do too much of this in film: show the sanitized version of a place, a person. Whether we should be showing things as they really are, in all their ugliness and complexity.'

Hal looks surreptitiously at Earl Morgan and thinks of how he looks in the film. Compares that now to the ruin before him. The truth would make a depressing spectacle indeed.

'To a lot of people,' he says, 'I think that's what film is about – escaping the ugliness for a couple of hours.'

'For you?'

Hal sees Stella's head turn slightly. He shrugs, eager to deflect attention from himself. 'I think, in art, it is as noble a thing to try to make people happy, to help them escape, as it is to make them think. And perhaps more difficult.'

After lunch, there is a move to the sand. Hal and Aubrey Boyd sit against the sun-warmed bank of rocks that flanks the shingled beach on one side. The shadow from the rocks bisects the ground between them: Hal on the sunny side, Aubrey on the other, in what might be the only patch of shade on the whole beach. He has somehow got very sunburned: his skin is a terrible, raw pink and there are painful-looking blisters along his hairline.

'I'm not built for this climate,' he tells Hal, forlornly. 'Mine is a Nordic complexion, suited only for temperate weather, not this barbaric heat. I have delicate skin.'

Hal has fared better than Aubrey: his skin has merely begun to tan. Only the crevices between his fingers bear evidence of his former, paler self.

Ahead of them, Giulietta Castiglione frolics in the surf in a bikini that displays her formidable curves to their best possible effect, laughing for the few photographers that have, of course, materialized among the crowd. Hal is beginning to recognize familiar faces among them: a couple have appeared at every stop. They click away delightedly as Giulietta splashes the water, tosses her hair, and is that carefree child–woman once more – quite different to the shrewd, often morose person that Hal has glimpsed in private moments.

'She's a little bitch,' Aubrey says, 'as far as I can tell. But she photographs extremely well. And one has to admit she's divine to look at.'

'She is.' It is inarguable fact.

'I've always loved beautiful things,' Aubrey says. 'Ever since I was a boy. There was very little beauty at the school I was sent away to. Grisly place, terrible interiors.' The glib tone has a brittleness to it. It can't have been easy, Hal thinks, for someone like Aubrey at a boys' boarding school.

'If it was anything like mine, I can imagine.'

'Of course, it makes one appreciate one's home all the more.'

'Where did you grow up?'

'Kent. Not much more than a cottage,' Aubrey says, 'but a big garden, which was the walled kind, you know – with climbing roses, and beds of lavender, and apple trees. In the summer, I wanted to spend my every waking moment there. And there was Feely . . .'

'Feely?'

'My older sister. Ophelia. When she came out into the garden she was the most beautiful thing in it. She'd let me dress her up in shawls and paste jewels – as an empress, or a fairy queen, and paint her in watercolours.'

Hal looks at Aubrey, and realizes that a change has occurred. In his voice, his gestures, there is a new softness, where before there was all haughtiness, arch sarcasm.

'Cigarette?' Aubrey asks.

'If you're having one.'

Aubrey passes him one, and lights it. When Hal inhales he coughs at the peculiar taste.

'Sorry,' Aubrey says. 'Should have warned you. They're Turkish: perfumed. I won't be offended if you hate it.'

Hal sniffs it, dubiously. 'Perhaps they take some getting used to.'

Aubrey takes a long drag on his, and gives a little sigh of pleasure. 'I discovered these on a job in Istanbul. Never looked back – the normal stuff tastes ever so boring now.' He waves away the cloud of smoke between them. 'Where was I?'

'Your sister – the garden.'

But now Aubrey is distracted, looking towards the water. 'Oh look. Mrs Truss is going for a swim.'

They watch as Stella wades through the shallows, with only a momentary hesitation at the shock of the cold, and then begins a steady crawl directly away from the beach. His thoughts return inevitably to the walk. How different she had briefly been, before the inevitable retreat into herself. He wonders how he could have thought her two-dimensional. And remembering her on the path, quick and nimble, watching her now, swimming steadily, he wonders how he could have thought her weak.

He looks up and finds Aubrey watching him, curiously, realizes that he is vaguely aware of him having said something. 'What?'

'I said you're rather pensive. Penny for them?'

'Oh,' he says quickly, 'I'm a little tired, from the hike.'

'Goodness, I can imagine.' Aubrey takes a drag of his cigarette. '*She* doesn't appear to be tired, though. One might almost think she were attempting to swim to Corsica.'

Hal follows his gaze. Stella is a long way out now, and still swimming hard. He can see the occasional flash of her limbs, her golden head.

'Perhaps she is.'

'Can it be safe out there?' Aubrey says. 'It looks rather choppy. Oh look – he's wondering the same thing.'

Truss is standing at the edge of the beach now, almost in the shallows, one palm shading his eyes. He makes what appears to be a beckoning motion with one hand – but Stella would be too far away to see it, even if she were not facing in the opposite direction. He might do better to try shouting, but Hal is certain that he will not. He knows enough of the man now to understand that Truss would consider this a sign of weakness: a lapse of control.

Hal watches as he walks across to the beach lifeguards, and says something. He turns to Aubrey, who is watching too. 'Did you hear that?'

Aubrey is frowning, confused. 'It's odd, but I thought that I heard him say . . . no, but then why would he?'

'What is it?'

'Well . . . I thought I heard him tell the man that Mrs Truss was in trouble . . . that he thought she might be struggling to stay afloat.'

'She looks all right to me,' Hal says.

They watch as Stella's arm rises, just as surely as before, to propel her through the water.

'Well,' Aubrey says, 'perhaps he can see something that we cannot.' Hal remembers the riptide that had so surprised him in the Gulf of the Poets. It is possible – but then Stella isn't making any sort of attempt to swim back to shore: rather the opposite.

The lifeguards, finally, seem convinced, and have snapped into action. They are pushing a small motorboat down the shingle, into the shallows. Truss follows them and, at the last minute, steps into the boat too. The craft takes off across the water with an oily gurgle, listing wildly before levelling.

Hal stands, to get a closer look. They are almost upon Stella now – her distance from the shore is only significant in swimming terms. They are slowing, drawing nearer. Truss is leaning over, gesturing to her, and some sort of discussion appears to be taking place. Then one of the men – and Truss – lean over the side and hoist Stella into the boat. There appears to be a brief struggle. She falls into the craft with an audible thump.

Aubrey winces. 'Gracious.'

The boat makes a swift U-turn, and returns to the beach, one of the men leaping out to guide it towards the shore. Truss steps down with a single, elegant stride. Then he turns and lifts Stella out of the boat, as though she were a child. She has a towel wrapped around her, and her face is expressionless. She does not appear grateful, or relieved. And Hal is certain that what they have just witnessed was not a show of husbandly concern so much as a demonstration of power.

They moor for the evening in the bay. Stella has not left her cabin – and does not appear for supper.

'My wife would like me to pass on her apologies,' Truss tells the assembled party. 'She is not well, this evening.'

'I suppose it must be the shock,' Aubrey says. 'Of getting in trouble like that, on her swim.'

Truss turns to Aubrey, and smiles. 'Indeed,' he says, languidly. 'I believe you could be right. And there was the exertion of the walk, too. My wife is a delicate creature.'

Hal thinks of her stepping nimbly in front of him along the path, of the strength and speed with which she had cut through the water, and thinks it is almost as though they are talking of different women.

Later, Hal remains on deck with Aubrey, watching as the last of the light dissolves into the water.

'What do you think happened?' Hal asks.

'What?'

'About—' He finds that he is about to say Stella, and stops himself. 'About Mrs Truss.'

'Well,' Aubrey says. 'It looked as though she had got a little further out than was perhaps safe. And Mr Truss, I presume, was concerned for her safety—'

Hal interrupts, losing his struggle with himself. 'Did it honestly look like that to you?'

Aubrey looks flustered. 'Well, I don't know . . .'

'I thought,' says Hal, in an undertone, 'that she looked like she was fine, and that he decided, for whatever reason of his own, that he wanted her back on the beach.'

'I say,' Aubrey says, 'I don't—' And he stops abruptly, looking beyond Hal, his face frozen.

'Hello, chaps,' Truss says. 'Can I get either of you a drink?' He indicates the bar. His smile is broad.

They accept, dumbly, and watch as he makes them – shooing

away the offer of one of the staff to help. They sit in uneasy silence until he carries the drinks over, placing each down with a deft flourish.

'Would you like to join us?' Aubrey asks, in a strangled voice.

'Ah.' Truss shakes his head. 'Thank you, but no. I shall go back and see to my wife.' He smiles at each of them in turn, meeting Hal's gaze last. 'Good evening.'

'Oh,' says Aubrey, sitting back in his chair. His hand, as he lifts the drink to his lips, is trembling so violently that a little of it spills on to his sleeve. 'My nerves . . . I can't bear it.'

'Sorry,' Hal says. Did Truss hear him? Impossible to say. He must have approached them as silently as a cat. He sees now how pale Aubrey has gone, and thinks quickly of a way to placate him. 'Tell me about your work. I'm ashamed to say I haven't seen it before.'

'Oh.' Aubrey makes a dismissive motion with his hand, but seems rather pleased. He sits up a little in his chair, appears to recover some of his poise. He reaches for his drink again and gives it a stir with the silver stick, his tremor noticeably better.

'Do you have anything with you?'

'Well,' Aubrey says, hesitantly pleased, 'as a matter of fact I do.'

'Will you show me?'

Aubrey disappears, and returns to the desk with a large, leather-bound portfolio. Hal takes it from him. He had been prepared to be underwhelmed. Photography of Aubrey's speciality – personages and fashion models – has never interested him. And yet, sifting through the pages, he finds images of great beauty. More than this, he discovers images that disturb and move him. There is a dark-haired woman standing on a station platform, her arm raised toward the train in greeting or, possibly, farewell. No doubt her pose and the setting are intended to display the silver fur coat to its best advantage, but nevertheless it speaks to Hal. The next image shows another brunette woman, her face framed by the shoulder of the man with whom she is dancing. Her eyes are cast down. The image makes a convenient frame for the jewels at her ears, the rings that glitter on the hand that grips her partner's back – but Hal sees in it something more than that. It is a melancholy image. To him she appears trapped. Impossible to tell whether that is the intention, or his own projection. All the women have a particular look: pale skin, dark hair, fine bones. They are not the same model – though at a glance they could be mistaken as such.

'Aubrey,' he says, and looks up to find the photographer watching him intently.

'Yes?'

'These are wonderful. They're . . . they're really something.' It feels inadequate, but it seems to be enough. There is something rather touching about Aubrey's expression of delight. He is a celebrated artist, and must be used to receiving his fair share of compliments. And yet Hal's clumsy praise has evidently found its mark.

'And,' Hal says, 'I wanted you to ask you something. The subjects . . . they all share similar features. I thought they *were* the same woman, at first. I suppose I was wondering if there was some reason for it.'

'My sister,' Aubrey says.

'Ophelia?'

Aubrey nods. 'They all look like her. I don't always manage to pick my model, of course – and sometimes a brunette is not right for the image. Take Mrs Truss, her blondness so perfect next to your darkness in that image with the yacht. But I only keep the images like this in my portfolio.'

'Your sister must be a beautiful woman.'

'She was, yes.'

'Oh,' Hal says, wrong-footed. 'I'm sorry—'

'She's alive,' Aubrey says. He sighs. 'It's a rather strange, sad story, I'm afraid.' He grimaces.

'And you don't have to tell it to me, if you don't wish to.'

'No. Perhaps I had better not.' He sips his drink. 'To the very journalist writing an article about us all.'

'It's not that sort of article – as I'm sure you know.' He recalls the *Tempo* editor's words. 'It's about what Giulietta has for breakfast – what Earl Morgan has for a nightcap. Though' – lowering his voice – 'that will involve some artistic licence. More importantly, I'm not that sort of journalist.'

'But what is "that sort" exactly? Would any journalist admit to being it – even the lowest hack? People are ever so good at deceiving themselves into believing that they are somehow superior, set apart. I'm as guilty of it as anyone – it's probably why I make such a fuss about those parasites following us about with their flashbulbs.'

'Well,' Hal says, 'perhaps. But I can assure you, I have too many secrets of my own to risk revealing anyone else's.'

'That,' Aubrey says, raising one long finger, 'is logic I *do* understand.' He peers at Hal. 'What is it about you? You're good at asking questions, but you aren't so good at answering them yourself.'

'I'm not sure you've asked me any.'

'No, perhaps that's right. I am ferociously self-interested.' Hal wonders if this is absolutely true. He witnessed the care with which Aubrey had supported the Contessa as they began the descent.

There is a long pause, and Hal realizes Aubrey has closed his eyes. At first, it almost looks as though he has fallen asleep. But then, in a tone that has lost all of its archness, he says: 'I told you, earlier, that my sister was a great beauty.'

'Yes.'

'I don't mean,' he opens his eyes and looks up at Hal with surprising fierceness, as though challenged, 'I don't mean in the usual sense, you understand – not in the way in which prettiness is sometimes described as beauty. She was beautiful in a way that shocked people, that caused strangers in the street to turn and stare.'

Hal nods, because some response is apparently expected of him.

'She was like that from childhood. Though many children are lovely to look at, even those who turn out to be terribly plain adults, so it only became properly noticeable when she was a young woman.'

Hal studies Aubrey, and thinks that he could only ever have been an odd-looking child, just as he is an odd-looking adult. But there is perhaps something to that sad brown gaze that, in another manifestation, could become something like beautiful.

As if he has guessed at Hal's thought, Aubrey says, 'Don't imagine that we resembled each other, of course. Nobody knows where my looks came from. My mother used to despair over me.

'My mother was obsessed with my sister's looks. She had once been called a beauty herself, but she was first to admit that she hadn't been anywhere in the register of Ophelia's looks. I think that was probably where the trouble started.

Ophelia wasn't allowed in the sun, or at least not until any exposed area of skin had been covered. She couldn't ride, or play tennis, in case she had an accident and bruised or – worse still – scarred herself. So she was extremely sheltered. We didn't have pots of money, but what we did have was spent on Ophelia.' He says it, thinks Hal, without rancour. 'Then my sister had her coming out as a debutante. It's an idea as old as time, of course, but my mother was convinced that she would be the one to restore the family's coffers. It might have worked. My parents went to a great deal of expense over it: because it was an investment, in some respects. And one young man in particular was quite taken with her. But it all went rather wrong.'

'How?'

'The thing about Feely,' Aubrey said, 'was that she was too nice to people. She was too sheltered. It was the third visit of this particular young man to our house, and he'd been asking about the history of the place: very interested. She'd been telling him about the escape route, for priests, that led from our house to the nearby chapel. She *was* sheltered, but perhaps she had some romantic idea of their having a chance to be alone together – without my mother watching their every move. Anyway, she offered to show him the priest hole. And—' Aubrey closes his eyes. 'He attacked her.'

'Oh, God.'

'It turned out he'd had some trauma, in the First War. Had been in the tunnels – had some horrible experience of small spaces. He must have got confused, suddenly, frightened. He picked . . .' Aubrey clears his throat. 'Excuse me. I haven't spoken about this in a while. It was ever such a long time ago, but—'

'That doesn't mean anything,' Hal says.

'Thank you.' Aubrey nods. 'He found a bit of brick, somewhere, and hit her with it. I got there too late. I mean – too late to stop him from hurting her. I mean, it was lucky, really – he could have killed her . . .' He trails off. 'It's why I'm a pacifist. That war could do that to a young man who in all other respects might have been a kind and perfectly normal chap . . .

'The problem with Feely is that she had been taught that her looks were everything, the only currency she had. And there was some dreadful scarring.' He reaches for his drink, drains it completely. 'She's not in desperately good health, now. Physically, she's fine, except a little frail. The funny thing . . .' He stops, and shakes his head. 'The funny thing is, she is one of the cleverest people I know – and the most talented. She's a tremendous painter. I sometimes think that if only she'd been born ugly, or even just a little less beautiful, she might have had a chance to be happy.'

He looks across at Hal, and gives a funny smile. 'There. Now tell me if that isn't at once the most absurd and tragic tale you've heard for a while.'

'It is tragic, certainly.'

'So now,' Boyd goes on, almost as though Hal hasn't spoken, 'all the women I choose to photograph – the ones I pick myself – seem to have some essence of her. The same look, you know – dark, exquisite bones, rather haunted-looking. I suppose I have this idea . . .' he pauses, 'this idea that through my photographs she is living the life she could have had. Does that make any sort of sense?'

Hal looks down at the book. On the current page, the model sits by a swimming pool reading a novel, a cigarette dangling from her hand. She looks like a woman with a story to tell, someone who lives a large life. 'Yes,' he says, 'I think it does.'

18

Her

I lie awake. My thoughts move back and forth: between the humiliation of the afternoon, and the walk before it. Both a strange relief and a new burden, telling Hal about Spain. Relief, because I haven't spoken of it in so long. But in doing so I have created a new tie between us, a bridge of knowing, when I had sought to do the opposite.

I hear my husband come into the cabin. I am turned away from him. I will pretend to be asleep.

'Stella,' he says, softly. 'Kitten?'

I don't answer.

'You understand, don't you? I was worried for you – you were so far out. I was concerned that you would put yourself in danger without realizing it.'

I can't make myself breathe normally, as I would if I were asleep. The air seems to catch inside me and burn in my chest.

'Goodnight, Stella.' He places his hand on my hip and I flinch involuntarily. It is not the reaction of a sleeping person. But it is a tiny movement. He doesn't mention it – perhaps he doesn't notice, after all.

I don't know exactly what happened. I started out with no real sense of purpose. Then, at the point at which I might usually have turned around, I found I wanted to continue. I felt that I could have continued forever, in fact, outswimming all that has been resurfacing around me. When I told him, I saw it again, all that could not be unseen – and how it had altered me. It was more than just a loss, you see. It was a realignment; a sea change.

February 1937

I am lying on my back on the tarmac of the road. Above me the sky rushes, but I seem to be fixed in place. It is too silent. I wait for the one sound that is important: the sound of Tino's voice.

There are things scattered about me: things that I recognize, out of place here in their domesticity. The brightly coloured pages of a children's book, a wicker basket: Tino's things, relatively unscathed.

But where the cabin of the truck used to be is a catastrophe of blackened metal, twisted by incredible force, shattered glass. Somehow, I have landed clear of it.

I understand, as I look about me, that Tino has not. He is in there, still.

I try to stand, but my body won't obey me. I begin to crawl, instead, through the littered glass, keeping my eyes upon the horror in front of me, waiting for any sign of movement. I have never felt fear like this.

There is something beneath that ruin of metal: a colour that I recognize. Something that insists itself, but that I cannot allow myself to believe. Even as I refuse to do so, and even before I reach him and try to free him, to take him in my arms, I know.

Since I first held him I have done everything in my power to keep him safe. It has not been enough.

Light, pressing pale red through my eyelids. There is pain in my hand, a hot concentration of it, and I hold to it, to distract me from that other pain.

I am in Madrid. I have lost two fingers from my right hand and have a slight concussion. Some of the sounds come to me as though through water. Otherwise, I am unharmed. I was miraculously lucky. The convoy was targeted by a fleet of Heinkel bombers. The driver of the final truck, uninjured himself, had found me beside the wreckage.

'There wasn't . . .' I sit up. 'He didn't see . . .' I don't know why I am asking. I know. I saw. But it is almost still possible to believe in it as a terrible waking dream. Until the nurse stops me and says, 'There was no one else, *querida*.'

They need to discharge me: there are others with injuries far worse. They wear their strain heavy about them, these men and women. These are people stretched to their limit. I wonder what they have seen – and then try not to think. Do I have anywhere to go? They ask it, but without the requirement of an answer. Either way, my bed is required – I must be on my way.

'Your cat,' the nurse comes to me, holding what appears

to be a brown bundle. When she sees my face she says, 'It isn't yours? We thought . . .'

I look into the hoary old face of Señor Bombón and feel a sudden, brief loathing for the animal, who has somehow managed to live when my little brother has died.

'No,' I hold out my left hand, the one without the dressing. 'He's mine.'

I am not myself. Madrid, too, is at once the same and strangely altered – like somewhere in a nightmare. I have known it as a place visited for Christmas, holidays, special occasions. Sometimes, when Papa did not want to be disturbed from his work, Tino and I would come here to stay with my aunt and uncle. They would take us for trips into the city, and I understood then what it might be like to have a parent who had a little more time to give.

There are landmarks I remember from those trips: the House of the Seven Chimneys, the parlour my aunt once took us to for an ice cream, now boarded closed, the Metrópolis building on the Calle de Alcalá, with its winged seraph, the pet shop on Calle de Cervantes where Uncle Salvador once helped Tino pick a toy for Señor Bombón: also shut. Actually, the sign has been painted over with an Anarchist slogan: I don't think it has sold budgerigars in a long time. But in between these are scenes of frozen violence: metal ripped and twisted, stone pockmarked with holes, façades that have been torn asunder, leaving interiors gaping like toothless mouths. As I pass an apartment block I can see straight through to the rooms inside. I understand this new Madrid, as I look upon it. I am like this city. At a first glance, perhaps, relatively intact. But I too have been shattered, warped. I will never be the same.

When I turn into the street, with its row of acacia trees, the elegant houses in shades of pistachio and umber, it is as though nothing has changed. I remember this from childhood, I remember coming here on a searingly hot day. But some twenty yards away is a new impossibility. The houses on both sides are torn down to their foundations. This new horror. This new unimaginable thing. Where their house once stood is a blank; a sad mess of mortar and brick. It is all too familiar. As I move closer I see furniture broken into matchsticks, I see dust-covered rags that once might have been curtains. A rug like a red wound, a piano sagging drunkenly in the middle, keys scattered on the floorboards. Closer still: broken china, glass. Closer still: a small object . . . a woman's leather glove. And then I stop. I won't continue, not this time. There is no need to get any nearer. No one could have survived this.

I sit on the stoop of one of the houses opposite, and shut my eyes. I am so tired, and very cold: Señor Bombón is the one warm spot, curled on my lap.

When I next open them the light has changed. I must have fallen asleep: the stone is hard against my back. My feet are so cold I can no longer feel them. In the rubble that was the house there is sudden movement. It is an impossible sight in the midst of the destruction, like a resurrection. I watch as a woman emerges from the mess, her arms full: cans of food. She is young, but holds herself crouched over like an old woman, braced against the sky. Yet she moves like a cat, careful, light-footed. She doesn't see me until she is very near and then she stops dead. 'Why are you loitering there? Are you trying to get yourself killed?'

I don't answer, but I do wonder if it is, in fact, what I am trying for.

'It isn't stealing,' she says, clasping her bounty of cans to her chest. 'They won't need these where they're gone.'

Still I don't answer.

'Come on,' she says. 'Do I have to carry you? I will leave you here.'

I sit up. And I realize, as I do, that my lap is no longer warm. Señor Bombón is gone. I find my voice. 'Have you seen a cat?'

She looks at me as though I am mad. 'No, no cat.'

He was a hateful creature, really. He bit and scratched Papa and me. The only one he liked was Tino. And yet I discover that I am weeping.

'Ah,' she says, raising her eyebrows '*¡Qué lío!*' What a mess.

An underground station. A dark press of bodies: the occasional flicker of a lighter, bursts of laughter, talk, the wail of a baby. People are living here. They have come prepared, with blankets, with miniature stoves, with books and toys.

The woman – Maria is her name – persuades a group – a family, I think – to make space for two more. She has a blanket, which she unrolls carefully. She does not offer to share it: it is obvious that it would not be large enough for both of us. I have my father's jacket, anyway. It begins quickly, inevitably: the drone of engines somewhere far above, then the terrible sounds that follow: that high scream. And then the impact, so near that at times the platform vibrates beneath my head, as if for an incoming train.

'That house,' Maria says. 'Was it yours?'

'It belonged to my aunt and uncle.'

She doesn't ask me if they lived. Perhaps that part is obvious. She doesn't apologize, either, for looting the remains. 'You do what you have to do,' she says, '*sabes*? To stay alive.

You do . . . things you would never have dreamed of doing, in normal life.'

In the morning, Maria is gone. She has disappeared into the city. Perhaps she doesn't stay in one place for too long; perhaps she has been killed. She might have saved my life, yesterday. I'm not sure whether to be grateful.

There is something shameful in it, this need to survive. It is beyond thought. Papa, Tino are gone – I have nothing left. Yet this will to live is as strong as an undertow, it sweeps me with it. When I hear the sirens I cower and run like any other. In the days, I venture into the city to find the things I need – food, mainly. I have no money. I would work, if I could, but there is nothing; the usual patterns of life disrupted. Shops open for only a couple of hours – if at all. The whole city has shut down by 8p.m.

I become shameless. I stand in line and then, when it comes to my turn, I put out my hands and beg. Often the grocer or one of the men or women in the queue will take pity on me, and I will walk away with something: a heel of bread, say, or chickpeas, which I will tip into my mouth straight from the tin. I have no qualms now about clambering into broken houses to relieve them of their contents. Usually, though, others have got there first. The thing is to get there first, the morning after the destruction.

There are things that I see.

I will try not to think of them.

I pretend that my eyes are the lens of a camera. That behind them is nothing but the mechanism of a machine, blinking, viewing, but not processing.

At night I return to the metro station like a rat to its hole. The dim platform is a microcosm of life above ground. There is fear, but here is something I've learned: fear is an exhausting thing, and life goes on around it. There are men playing cards, a woman darning something, a boy about my own age colouring in a book.

It is the families I find difficult. They huddle in tight groups. They press together to keep warm. I can remember the compact heat of Tino's body beside mine as I read to him, his thin arm threaded through mine. How he clung to me, particularly in those final months. Assuming comfort, protection, in which I failed him, in the end.

I can still summon him to me, but never whole – only in the details. The sight of him amidst the green at the end of the garden, the sudden pale oval of his face turning back to look. The intensity of him, bent over one of his strange, beautiful diagrams. And the colour of his hair, darkened slightly from its old, infant blond. He was in a state of transformation, his lines growing sharper in the last year, losing the last softnesses of early childhood. I had seen this at the time as something to mourn; as the end of something. Now I would give anything to see those changes continue. I cannot believe that he will not continue to transform. The boy he could have become, the adult. These possibilities have been extinguished, forever. Most of all, I cannot believe I will never see him again.

So I watch them jealously, the families. These are people who have been bombed out of their homes, who think, perhaps, that they have lost everything. I wonder if they will come to realize that what they have here is everything that matters.

Outside, it is as though two Madrids – the wartime and the peacetime city – are layered over one another. Certain streets have been left almost unblemished. Certain people, too. I glimpse a woman hanging out her washing on a roof terrace, as bombs fall less than half a mile away. I see children playing in the street metres from the spot where a team of soldiers are using picks to dig an unexploded shell from the tarmac. I watch an elderly couple share a pigskin of wine, sitting on the blanket they have spread on the pavement.

But for some the fear has swallowed everything. One night in the metro there is a woman who has been driven mad by the bombing. She shrieks in the darkness, wails, grinds her teeth. People try to persuade her to be quiet – perhaps out of the superstitious idea that she will somehow draw the bombers' attention upon us. And partly, I think, because the sounds she makes are like an articulation of their own terror. I wonder if they are thinking the same thing as me: that it would be so easy to become like her. To loose the few remaining threads keeping sanity and dignity in check.

There is less and less food. People are less pitying now, less inclined to share their own supplies. Sometimes I queue and come away with nothing. I catch myself worrying for Tino – how I will keep him healthy, strong – and I remember that it is only me now. For a few moments it can be an odd sort of relief. I have nothing to care for, any longer, nothing to protect. Really, I have nothing to live for, now. But it is something beyond my control, this will to survive.

At dusk one evening, on my way back to the station, I see the woman, Maria. I am drawing closer to make sure that it is her, ready to greet her, when I see a man approaching from the other direction. I hear her call out to him. She shifts herself and then I see the white flash of thigh as she draws up her skirt. I turn and walk quickly away.

*

I hear a rumour that people with any claim at all to British heritage, or French, are throwing themselves on the charity of those embassies. They say they have better supplies there. I go to the British Embassy, but am turned away by a young Englishman who seems frightened of me. As though I, a sixteen-year-old girl, could do anything to him. But I have seen this hunger, my own hunger, reflected in the gaze of others, and it *is* a frightening thing. At one time, it was love that defined me: for Papa, for Tino. Now it is hunger. Something worrying: day by day those memories that I summon are losing their immediacy and clarity. It is a second loss. With it, I lose a little more of myself.

In the hotels, where the foreign correspondents stay, they say they dine on sardines and fresh bread and fruit. On my stone bed, with the dark shuddering around me as the bombs fall, I dream of those sardines, my mouth wet with longing.

A day without food. The city has been picked clean of it. At first, hunger sharpened everything: thoughts became extremely clear. Now, they are fracturing into incoherence. Daily I am growing weaker. Perhaps this will be how it ends.

I return to the metro station. Sometimes, someone has shared something with me there – though it hasn't happened of late. At the very least, I can lie down in the dark and sleep, and for a few hours postpone the struggle to keep myself alive.

On the way, I pass an entrance to one of the great hotels on the Gran Vía. It is the hotel bar: the smell of the food hits me like an assault. I do not think – I follow it, like a starving dog. The people in here are cleaner, their faces fuller:

hunger hasn't reshaped them yet. There are eyes on me. I am an outrage, among them. But I am almost beyond shame.

The barman is a thin, wiry man with skin like tanned hide, and an abundant dark moustache – compensation, perhaps, for the sparseness of the hair on his pate. He meets me halfway across the room. 'You can't come in here.'

I see how he looks at me, and what he thinks I am. I think of Maria. In this moment, there is very little I wouldn't do for a meal. I have only the haziest idea of things, but can it be so bad, really? It is just a body, after all.

'I'm not one of them,' I say. 'I came to see if I could get any food.'

'You can have some food if you can pay for it.'

'Please,' I say, 'I'll work.'

He shakes his head.

I turn from him, half deliberating as I do whether I can reach out and snatch a bread roll, a fistful of something from a plate. I could be eating it before the barman had time to chase me out. And as I cast about myself, deciding upon my target, I realize that I am being watched.

A man in a pale suit. I can feel his gaze as tangibly as if he has brushed my face with the palm of his hand. I wonder if I should be afraid. He is just on my right – I can make out the blurred shape of him at the corner of my eye. I turn. I look. In doing so I make the connection. I have allowed him in.

19

Early morning, and Hal hopes to have the deck to himself. Perhaps he will lie in the newly risen sun for a while, then go for a swim. There is something exhausting about spending every moment in such close proximity to others, especially for one who has spent the last five years living alone. But when he reaches the top of the steps he sees that he is not the first up.

'Mr Jacobs.' Truss is sitting at the dining table, Gaspari opposite him, a chessboard between them.

'Yes?'

'I've been meaning to thank you. I realize I didn't get a chance yesterday.' There is a strange law of diminishing returns, Hal thinks. The more cordial the man is, the less he likes him. He mistrusts his manner entirely. Because even when Truss smiles – especially when – his eyes remain watchful.

'For what?'

'Escorting my wife, yesterday, on the hike.'

'Oh,' Hal says. 'Well, I didn't exactly . . .'

'She can be very determined about things,' Truss says, 'but, as I'm sure you have by now seen, she is also quite frail.'

'She didn't seem to be having any difficulty to me,' Hal says. 'If anything, I had to keep up with her.'

'Well,' Truss says, patient, 'it might not be obvious to a stranger, but she gets very tired.'

There is something distasteful in his speaking of her as though she were an invalid. Hal doesn't want to hear any more of it. He nods to the chessboard.

'Who's winning?'

'Oh, we've only just started.'

'And yet,' Gaspari says, 'I do not – what is it they say – fancy my chances.'

'It's a fine set,' Hal says, looking closer.

Truss smiles again. 'Thank you. It's mine – a travelling one.' He picks up the white queen and passes her over. Hal studies it. A tiny nude, small enough to fit in the centre of the palm.

'It's very fine.'

Truss smiles. 'Evidently we share the same tastes, you and I. I was there, you know, when they killed the elephant. I have a few other pieces made from the same ivory – but she is my favourite.'

Hal hands the piece back to him.

'I rather like the idea that this little thing, so pale and refined, has come from some great beast – hulking, shitting, crashing through the forest. You should have seen the blood, too, when we slew it. Rivers of it – very dark, almost black.'

'Yes,' Hal says. The piece has suddenly become abhorrent to him: an object of barbarism. He looks at Truss, who is studying the piece minutely, as though he has never seen it before. He has time to observe in more detail the sleek head, the hair combed precisely back from the brow. The short, manicured fingernails, the long elegant fingers. Hal cannot imagine him on a game drive, his clothes covered in dust from the road, sweating in the heat. He does not look like he sweats. But then Hal thinks of the ivory: the violence polished into something benign.

20

Genoa

Genoa is a barnacled, salt-sprayed place. A city of astonishing contrasts, of sublime beauty and of profound ugliness. In the harbour handmade sailing boats jostle with beasts of maritime industry, and the sea – the very same sea that laps at the feet of Portofino – carries a surface scum of oil, debris and what on closer inspection might turn out to be fish guts.

The contrasts continue within the city itself. Here is a gorgeous palace, appearing in all its decadent finery: the *trompe l'oeil* façade, the intricately carved gargoyles and seraphim. They recall Genoa as it was portrayed in the film: the gilded capital of a Renaissance state at the height of its power – a fitting rival to Venice, or Florence. But as soon as one glances down from these wonders, there in the midst of the street is a heap of refuse, the odour ripening in the heat, or a scrofulous cat stretching its thin body across a doorstep.

An excited crowd has gathered around them, hooting and

cheering, pushing at one another to get to the front, brandishing autograph books. For Genoa is not like Rome, in which film stars mingle daily with the city's populace. There is no Via Veneto here, where one may merely go and observe them like animals in a zoo, sitting at coffee tables and looking for all the world almost like ordinary people – only not quite.

'Please, excuse,' a young man touches Hal's arm. 'I was in the film.'

Hal turns to him. 'Really?'

'Yes.' The man smiles, revealing a gap where his right incisor should be. 'I was a sailor, on one of the ships in the battle, at the beginning.'

'Ah, yes. An important scene.'

'You've seen it?' The man peers at him.

'Yes.'

'Did you see me?'

Hal doesn't quite know what to say. How to explain to the man that the battle sequence is only a minute long and that, in the onscreen chaos, it would be impossible to recognize one's own brother?

'Yes,' he says. 'Do you know . . . I think I might have done. Yes – I'm almost certain.'

'Ah!' The man beams, and Hal is suddenly sure that he has said the right thing. 'I won't see it. Too expensive. I have a family, you understand. But it is good to know.' He claps Hal on the shoulder, and disappears back into the throng.

Hal turns away. As he does, he catches Stella's gaze. She smiles.

'This palazzo used to be in my family,' the Contessa tells them, as they step inside one of the wedding-cake constructions on the Via Cairoli. 'It was rumoured that one of my ancestor's courtesans was housed here, for a time.'

This woman could have been the one from the journal, Hal thinks, with a secret thrill. Now he knows why the street's name sounded familiar. He has read it there.

The place is typical of Genoa: the umber paint of the façade faded and stained in places, but with the beauty of the place all the more visible for these flaws, for it is a gorgeous edifice in spite of them. Inside is more finery: *trompe l'oeil* painted ceilings and walls, a conspicuous demonstration of once great wealth.

Gaspari leans over. 'We filmed some of the interior scenes here at first,' he says. 'It is the right period.' He grimaces. 'But one of the frescoes got damaged by the lighting team. After that we had a replica made up for the studios.'

While a photocall takes place for the stars in a silk-lined salon, Hal is free to explore. Wandering along one of the corridors, he discovers a series of gilt-framed paintings. They are Renaissance oils, with that peculiar effect of being lit from within, the faces appearing to glow out of the darkness. He gropes for the word. *Chiaroscuro.* They are by different artists, Hal sees – superficially similar, but the effect in some noticeably more deft than in others. And yet none hold Hal's attention for long: he has never had much interest in this era of art. It is caught up with religious concerns, too sombre: the women depicted as versions of the Madonna, the men after classical gods and Old Testament heroes. He passes quickly. But as he reaches the end of the corridor, something halts him in his tracks. He has an uneasy feeling; as though from the corner of his eye he has just glimpsed something terrible or impossible. And when he turns the thing he sees is indeed an impossibility. Staring down at him is the woman from his imagining, the woman he has read of in the captain's journal. He cannot take his eyes from her.

'She is beautiful, is she not?'

He turns, and finds the Contessa standing at the end of the corridor.

'Who is she?' His voice is hoarse.

'No one is quite certain where she came from.'

'The woman in the water.'

The Contessa nods. 'That is one theory, yes. How interesting, though, that you should make the connection. What made you think it might be her?'

He speaks without thinking. 'The mole, beneath her eye, there.'

She spins on her heel, and looks at him, and he realizes his mistake. 'You've read the journal, haven't you?'

He doesn't answer.

'How did you get it?' Then, to his surprise, she throws her head back and laughs. When she has recovered, she says, 'I tell him not to show anyone, and he gives it to the journalist.'

'I promised not to mention anything of it.'

'I suppose that he trusts you. I do not blame him for that – I do, too.'

'Thank you.'

'And it is a rare talent, yours.'

'What do you mean?'

'You invite . . .' she searches for the word, '*rivelazione* – how do I translate that?'

'Revelations, I suppose. Or, confidences.'

'Precisely. It is your quietness, the fact that you do not demand them of people in the way that many do – and certainly the way those of your profession do. You are . . .

discreet. And because of this, people feel encouraged to make confidences of their own accord.'

'I'm not sure that's true.' He thinks of the terrible interview with Giulietta Castiglione.

'Ah. But I am. That is the other thing about you. You are modest.' She smiles. 'Would you like to see him? My ancestor? He is here too, you know. The same artist, in fact.'

'Please.'

She leads him back to the end of the corridor. He had passed the painting without seeing it – dismissing the bearded figure as another John the Baptist. But now he stares. He has not had a clear idea in his mind of how the captain would look – other than Earl Morgan's brawny portrayal – but now this seems exactly right. A young man verging upon gaunt, all the bones in his face very prominent. The painter has been accurate to the point of cruelty in depicting the sallowness of the man's complexion, the haunted gaze.

'He does not look well,' the Contessa says.

'No.'

They look at the painting for a time in silence. Then the Contessa leaves, telling him she is going to check in on the photocall. But Hal remains for a while longer, unable to drag his eyes away.

Afterwards he wanders into the city. Some of the medieval passageways that thread their way through the heart of the city are so slender, and the buildings that flank them so tall, that the light barely penetrates the lower reaches, even in the brightest part of the day. A few feet remain permanently steeped in blue shadow. He is reminded of the lower reaches of the ocean, those cold hidden parts of the seabed that remain in constant darkness. Here, he thinks, is history, layer upon layer of it, in all its glory and grime and intrigue.

He wanders without paying much attention to the direction in which he is walking, his mind turning over the matter of the portraits.

'Hal?'

He glances up, and spots her through the throng. Stella. It is the first time he has seen her properly since his dream. And their conversation of yesterday has caused a shift, too. Something between them has been removed; something else has taken its place.

She is walking fast, and as she nears him, he finds himself taking a step back, surprised by her look of panic. She speaks quickly, her hand worrying the silk scarf at her throat. 'I was walking Nina – Gaspari asked me to. He said that it would be fine to let her off the lead, because she normally stays close by – but she's gone.'

'We'll find her.'

'I can't bear the thought of it. If he lost her . . .' Her eyes are wild. He understands the worry, but her anxiety seems out of all proportion. In her, usually so collected, it is all the more marked. He finds himself wondering what else might be behind it: what fragment of memory suddenly dislodged.

'We'll find her,' he says again, soothingly, 'she can't have gone far.'

She doesn't appear to have heard him. 'I don't understand it. She was there, and I got distracted by some people pushing past. And then, when I looked down, she was gone. You don't suppose—'

'What?'

'Well, that someone might have taken her? Hal, if she's gone, I don't know what I'd do . . .'

'No,' he says, gently, 'I'm sure that's not it. She's probably followed an interesting scent.'

They begin their search, threading their way through the streets, trying to remember landmarks that will help them to find their way back to the start, should Nina return there: a shrine inlaid into the cornerstone of a house, a faded façade, a grocers' display that fills the air with the wet-earth scent of overripe tomatoes. He has to hurry to keep up with Stella at times – she seems propelled by her anxiety.

At some point the streets grow even thinner, and their surroundings less picturesque. This is a poorer, dirtier part of the city. Washing, strung across the gap above, flutters like bunting in the breeze.

A group of similarly scantily dressed women shift in the shadows like a shoal of exotic fish, murmuring and beckoning. One of them, sitting on a doorstep in little more than a stained pink *pegnoir*, face so lacquered with make-up that it is difficult to tell her age, leans forward and calls to Hal: 'Your wife is beautiful, signor, but I can show you things of which she would never dream.'

Amused, he glances at Stella, and sees that she is looking at the woman oddly, almost fearfully.

They call Nina's name, and the sounds ricochet about them before being absorbed into the stone. In these gloomier passageways the light has taken on a shifting, changeable quality, like dusk. Several times Hal thinks he sees something move in the shadows – only to look again and realize that it was a trick of the eye.

Suddenly, Stella stops.

'What is it?'

'I've just thought,' she says. 'I've stopped paying attention to the way we've come.'

'So have I. We'll ask someone.'

Around the next corner the street opens suddenly, like an exhalation, into a small courtyard, with a stone basin spouting a plume of water. The sudden space is a relief – but it is also a dead end. He is about to suggest they turn back when he hears something. He listens, concentrating on the tiny sound.

'Do you hear that?'

She listens, intent. 'Yes, I think so—'

A whimpering, coming from a dark corner of the courtyard. As they look, one of the shadows consolidates and becomes the little dog. She makes as though to run to them, but falters in her step. Stella rushes to her and lifts her into her arms, oblivious to the grimy paw-prints appearing on her shirt. Her relief is palpable. Hal watches as she examines the animal with exquisite care. 'Her paw,' she says, showing Hal.

It is a small cut, but smeared with grime. Hal picks her up and tucks her under one arm, and together they wash the wound in the fountain, the dog looking up at them pitifully. Then Stella unfastens the scarf from around her neck to tie about it.

Hal goes to stop her. 'You don't need to do that. We'll find a napkin somewhere.'

'No,' Stella says. 'I don't like it much.'

He looks at the scarf wrapped about the animal's paw and sees the word printed in the corner: Hermès. He thinks of the diamond bracelet around her wrist the first time they met, the pale fur about her shoulders. How different their worlds are, he thinks. And how far she has come from that teenager she described, walking barefoot in the dirt with her chickens, foraging for herbs. But then he remembers her catlike agility on the path yesterday, her knowledge of all the wildflowers. Perhaps that girl is there, still, if one is to look for her. And perhaps in the very act of sacrificing a silk scarf for a dog's dirty paw, she is making herself known.

They leave the courtyard and begin trying to retrace their route, without much success. It is almost as though the city is determined to resist and frustrate their attempts to navigate it, presenting junctions where they had not noticed them before.

They wander into a street with a bar and a couple of trattorias.

'We didn't come here,' she says. 'I don't recognize this at all.'

'We'll ask someone – see if they can point us in the right direction.'

But the owner of the trattoria frowns and shakes his head when Hal describes the palazzo.

'You could stay,' he says, hopefully, 'and have a drink here first?'

Hal suspects that the man's lack of geography is nothing more than good business sense. But perhaps it would make sense.

'We could stop here for a bit,' he tells Stella. 'Recover our bearings. If we carry on walking we may find ourselves getting more lost.'

He watches her deciding. Finally, she nods.

He orders them a bottle of cold, straw-coloured wine. It costs far more than he would ever normally spend, and yet he thinks that it is probably one of the cheapest wines she will have tried in a while. Nina, who the bartender treats with the same care and deference as an infant child, is given her own dog bed and a bowl of water. She lies on her sheepskin like a reclining queen. Stella and Hal, meanwhile, are crammed in around a small table, their knees close, occasionally touching. This contact of skin troubles him. He wonders if it is the same for her too: he sees how her hand trembles as she raises it to her lips.

She laughs, nervously. 'Have you noticed how we keep seeming to end up alone together? It is almost as though someone is conspiring for it to happen.'

He toys briefly with the idea of telling her that the Contessa's sprained ankle no longer appears to be giving her any trouble whatsoever. But he decides not to. It is only a suspicion. Instead, he says: 'How are you? I heard that you were exhausted, after your swim.'

She takes another sip of her wine. 'I'm perfectly all right, thank you.'

'I saw the boat go after you,' he says. 'The funny thing was, you seemed to be all right then, too.'

Her eyes meet his for a second. Then she looks quickly away. 'Please,' she says. 'Don't.'

'What?'

'Please don't pity me. I can take anything else, but not that. I don't need it. And certainly not from you.'

He wonders what she means by this. Probably that he himself is the one to be pitied. She has seen the way he lives, after all. Perhaps she has a point.

'I don't pity you,' he says. He sees her relax, a little. But then some rogue urge, some need to provoke, makes him say, 'I don't pity you, because I understand that you've made some sort of choice, to be with a man like that.'

Her face has flushed red, with anger, he thinks, or humiliation. 'You don't understand.'

'Explain it to me, then.'

21

Madrid, March 1937

'Hello.'

In spite of myself, I am intrigued.

'Hello,' I say. The man smiles. He is younger than I thought: though not young, still twice my age, perhaps. He isn't Spanish. His clothes are foreign, English or American, I think: a fine jacket, a waistcoat, matching, spotlessly clean trousers. I wonder how he manages it, in the midst of a war.

He introduces himself: he is an American. He has a way about him in fact, an air of ease, that is even more of a rarity in this place than clean clothes.

And he is attractive, I notice – in a way that only becomes apparent when you keep looking. An elegance, perhaps, rather than a handsomeness.

'Thank you.'

'You shouldn't be here,' he says. 'It isn't safe for someone like you.'

Where has he been, that he thinks this warm bar is a place of relative danger? 'It's better than anywhere else.'

'Well,' he says, studying me, 'are you old enough to drink?'

'I'd prefer food.'

'In that case,' he says, 'you shall have some.'

The food comes. His eyes are on me. I am eating like an animal, I know: but I do not seem to be able to stop. Not the dreamed-of sardines but a dish of broken eggs, just as good. I slow only when I realize that if I carry on at this speed I will be sick, and it will be for nothing. I have decided what I will do: I will eat, and then I will excuse myself and leave.

But there is wine too, which I am not accustomed to even in normal circumstances. It loosens something in me. I begin to talk. I can't speak about the circumstances, but I tell him of Papa and Tino, how the loss of them has changed everything, that without them, I don't know myself. All the time he watches my face, as though he finds something fascinating there.

It is only at the end of the evening that I realize that while I have laid myself bare before him, I don't know anything about him beyond his name and his nationality. Is this due to rudeness on my part, my preoccupation with my grief? Or some reluctance to tell on his?

'Come tomorrow,' he says. 'I'd like to buy you supper again.'

The meal has worked its effect upon me already. I feel stronger, steadier in my thoughts. If I can eat again tomorrow as I have done this evening, it won't matter if I can't find food during the day. It doesn't ever occur to me to refuse. Why would I?

*

The next evening I am determined to ask him about himself. This time I notice a definite resistance to my probing. It is subtle, but it is there. He begins to turn everything towards me again, but I have already talked enough; feel hollowed out with it. So I persevere.

'Why are you here, in Spain?'

He takes a sip of his whisky, savours it. 'Have you heard of the International Brigades?'

'Yes.'

'What do you know of them?'

I tell him. They are men who have come from around the world, American, Englishmen, French – even German and Italian – to fight against Fascism. They say that their bravery is unparalleled. There is talk of how, last month, they met the rebels in the Jarama Valley and fought them off with suicidal valour.

He nods.

'You're one of them?'

'Yes. In a way, I am.'

Suddenly I am seeing him in a new light. His reticence becomes something heroic. 'Why are you here, in Madrid?' What I really mean is: why isn't he in uniform, as his compatriots are? Why is he staying in a hotel, drinking wine with me, rather than on a battlefield somewhere?

'Ah,' he smiles, and seems to understand my meaning. 'My work is unusual. It's . . . somewhat clandestine. That's about all I can tell you, I'm afraid.'

I nod. I want him to know that he can trust me not to press him for information. That his secret is safe in my keeping. I think how much my father would have liked him, this man who is here, in a country not his own, out of a sense of moral duty.

I notice details that fascinate and disturb me: the triangle of pale chest revealed by the open neck of his shirt. The coppery hairs that scatter the skin there. The largeness and elegance of his hands, the way he fills his clothes – indeed his own skin – with such confidence and grace. He is not a tall man. But there is such a sense of conviction about him, of condensed energy, that he gives the impression of height.

In the mirror in the powder room I find myself (how can I be thinking of such things at a time like this?) combing my hair back from my face, holding it up, to see if it might make me look older, more sophisticated. I rinse my face. I pinch my cheeks and watch them fill with colour. But all that I can see is a grubby girl. I think of the female journalist I have seen in the bar, cutting through the room like a blade through silk: tall, effortlessly elegant, in military-issue clothes that fit her so well they might as well have been couture. By comparison, the reflection I see in the mirror is that of a shabby, unfinished person. A not-quite woman.

'Where are you staying?' he asks me, on our third meeting.

I tell him.

'Oh,' he says, shocked. 'That's not good. You should move here.'

I'm not exactly sure what he means by this. He must know that I can't afford it. I feel a little stupid, from the wine. 'With you?'

He smiles his charming, impossible-to-read smile. 'In a room near to mine, if you'd like. I'm on the best side. It's funny, the rooms that were the most expensive – the rooms at the front, are those that nobody wants now, because they're in the line of fire. I have one of the smaller rooms at the back of the hotel – which are the most sought-after. I could have you set up in one of those.'

'No, thank you.'

'Come, it can't be a difficult choice, surely? You know,' he says, 'in this hotel we have running water. Hot and cold. They say it is the last supply in the whole city.'

I am encrusted, now, in a thick layer of the city's grime. It hasn't troubled me at all, before this moment – but suddenly the idea of being able to sluice it from myself is almost as enticing as the food. But it won't come for free: I'm sure of that. I'm not like Maria, I'm not one of them. Not yet, not quite. And yet, like the madwoman in the Gran Vía metro, it does not seem such a long fall. Does it matter much, anyway?

'No, thank you.' I stand.

'I've offended you,' he says.

'No.'

He reaches across the table to me, and lets his hand fall a few centimetres from my own. 'Just a bath,' he says. 'I offer it because I can, and I would like to do something to help you. Not because I expect anything in return.'

I sit in the bathtub and take in my surroundings. A gilt mirror, elaborately wrought. I catch sight of myself in it: a pale face, eyes that look darker than they are. The protuberance of my spine.

The walls are painted a very pale green. Seafoam, I think this hue is called. Is the sea ever this colour? I wonder if I will live to see the real thing, to compare it with. A fresco of fat cherubs on the ceiling, rosy flesh. What a strange, sickly creature they must think me. This bathroom speaks of plenty, of permanence. Impossible to imagine it rendered into so much mortar and dust by a bomb. Except, looking closer, I find a long crack running from one corner of the ceiling to the centre. It is, I am sure, a fresh destruction. It severs the shoulder of the sixth cherub from his neck. Here is another victim of this war.

'How is the water?'

He sounds so near that for a second I think he is in the bathroom with me. I cover myself. No, he is outside the door: but he must be right next to it.

'It's good,' I say, 'thank you.' Suddenly, to linger any longer seems too much like an invitation. I step from the bath, find the towel. I dress, quickly, as though there are eyes on me.

When I open the door he is sitting in the armchair, in his immaculate suit. 'It can't have been so very wonderful,' he says, 'if you got out so quickly.'

'Oh, I—'

'Well,' he says, 'you can have another. I've got you the room next door.'

*

She stops, to take a sip of her wine. Hal imagines her as the young girl she was then. She would have been a rare thing indeed: a point of bright light. And then he imagines Truss, watching, wanting to make that light his own. The idea sickens him.

'Ah,' they hear a familiar voice from the doorway. 'There you are.'

'Oh,' Stella says, shooting quickly up from her seat as though it has burned her. She is standing, smoothing herself down.

'We lost our bearings,' Hal explains.

'Of course.' Aubrey smiles, looks between them. If he sees anything odd in the two of them having been sitting together like this, his expression doesn't betray it. 'I had to ask some ladies of the night if they'd seen you. They were quite helpful, actually, especially after I promised to send them the photograph I'd taken of them.'

'Are we late?' Stella asks.

'Oh no, not particularly. The Contessa just wanted everyone to start gathering back on the yacht. And you aren't the last – we've lost Morgan to some other drinking hole.'

'My husband,' Stella asks, 'was he looking for me?'

'I don't imagine so,' Aubrey says. 'He's spent the whole afternoon shut up somewhere making a call – business in Milan, he said.'

She visibly relaxes, and her reaction depresses Hal. It seems horrible to him that a man like that should have so much influence over her.

Her

Shortly after the beginning of my new life, my husband began to address me as 'Stella', removing, with a few letters, the foreignness of my name. At first I found it odd. But gradually it started to make sense to me. It was part of the necessary detachment of my old self from my new. Estrella could not be anything but foreign. Stella could be from anywhere, or nowhere. Now I have been Stella for so long. Impossible to talk of my old life with our acquaintances in New York. They understand me only in the context of my husband, our wealth, the city. They would not understand. Until quite recently – until my discovery, that is – this suited me absolutely. In fact, I feared not being seen as one of them, of being exposed as something different. I worked to extinguish every trace of my old accent, every vestige of the girl I had once been.

With him, it is different. That night in Rome – we knew nothing of each other. We were absolute strangers. The liberation of that. And when he talks to me, now, I feel that perhaps he sees something more than Stella, the rich man's wife – and that, too, is freeing. It isn't just that I find myself wanting to talk of that time – I seem to be unable not to do so. And yet there is a reason I haven't returned to that time for more than a decade. To go back there is to leave myself vulnerable. It is liberating – but also dangerous.

When we are gathered back in the harbour once more, my husband takes me to one side to tell me that he must travel to Milan for a few days.

'Would you like to come with me – or would you prefer to stay?'

For some reason I feel under special scrutiny. It would be safer to go with him. I would escape the particular kind of danger here. But I don't seem able to help myself.

'I think,' I say, 'that I would prefer to stay. It would be rude, otherwise, to desert the Contessa, the other guests.'

He inclines his head slightly, as though he had expected the answer already. Then he takes my chin in his hand. I feel the grip of his fingers, for a second, and then he tilts my face up toward him and kisses me.

PART THREE

22

'But it's such a shame,' the Contessa says. They have not yet left the Genoese harbour, and Truss has announced that he must travel to Milan for a few days for business. 'You really must go?'

Truss nods. 'I'm afraid so. I should be back in time for the screening, though.'

'Not both of you?'

'I would love Stella to come with me, naturally.' He smiles at her. 'But we both feel that it is much better if she stays. She will have a happier time here.'

They set sail from Genoa a couple of hours after Truss has left them. The air has an odd stillness to it: the ever-persistent breeze briefly absent. The heat gathers in the lull. It is something to do with the bank of cloud that has massed during the afternoon, keeping the warmth trapped.

That evening, after supper, they play a game, which involves marking anyone who gets a rhyme wrong with a blackened stub of cork. By the end, the marks on Morgan's face have nearly joined together, the Contessa has only one, Hal thinks, and Stella has three. The one on her forehead is smudged into her hairline, and she is flushed with laughter, and perhaps a little from the wine. Hal looks at her and wonders how he could ever have imagined her ordinary, or two-dimensional. But then she is a different woman, tonight, to the one who looked like she might have sprung, fully formed, from an advert in a magazine.

Afterwards, they play a game of forfeits. Anyone with the lowest hand in any given round, the Contessa explains, must display a talent. Aubrey is first – and chooses to do impressions. His first is a mimicry of the dowager duchess he was summoned to photograph in Biarritz – 'If you allow me to appear with more than one chin, young man, I'm not paying.' Hal sees Stella throw back her head and laugh. Next, he chooses Hal. 'You have to imagine me a great deal more handsome,' he says, pretending to gaze sombrely into the middle distance, and then to scribble on an imaginary page. For a second, Hal wonders how Aubrey could possibly *know*. Then he realizes that, of course, Aubrey is imagining a journalist's pad, nothing else. Finally, he chooses Stella. He smoothes his hair behind his ears, and props an imaginary magazine in front of himself. His face changes, becomes a tight, anxious mask. Hal sees immediately that Aubrey has misjudged. It is unmistakably her, but it is the wrong side of cruel. Knowing what he now does of Aubrey, he is prepared to forgive him. But when he glances at Stella, he sees that the smile has left her face.

The Contessa claps her hands, loudly. 'Aubrey, well done. You have great talent. But let us begin the next round.'

The lowest score is Hal's, and it is a relief. Here is his chance to distract them all from Aubrey's unwitting cruelty. Without stopping to think, he leaps up, and launches himself across the deck and into space. He somersaults, twice, and enters the water sharp as a blade. The sea rushes in a cold shock around him, and he surfaces gasping. Blinking up at the yacht, he can see that a row of heads has appeared over the side.

'You're a madman!' Aubrey shouts.

And from Gaspari: 'Bravo, *ragazzo*, bravo!'

Even Giulietta, when he climbs aboard, appears less bored than usual, is even looking at him with something like approval.

He doesn't look at Stella. Probably she thinks him a fool, an exhibitionist. Little does she know that he did it for her. That he hasn't dived like that since the Navy training pool at Southampton, in 1942, and never thought to do so again.

A couple more rounds follow. Hal sitting wrapped in a towel brought by one of the stewards – though he insisted he could get one himself. Earl Morgan's chosen talent, opening his gullet and downing a bottle of red wine, is met with a stunned silence. Then Giulietta gets up and performs a folk dance in bare feet, her skirt foaming up over her knees, her black hair lashing about her shoulders. The Contessa recites a sonnet by Dante:

'*Io mi senti' svegliar dentro a lo core*,' she begins, '*un spirito amoroso che dormia . . .*'

I felt in the deep chamber of my heart, a passionate spirit out of slumber move . . .

Then it is Stella. She looks about herself uneasily for a taut moment, and Hal is certain she is about to decline. He sees Giulietta's look of contempt, Aubrey's frown. He wills her not to. But then, a little awkwardly, she pushes back her chair and gets to her feet. She clears her throat. Silence. And then she begins to sing.

There is nothing finessed or tutored about her voice, but this is its power. It is raw, and pure. It is at once a pain in the centre of the chest and a balm. It is yearning and fulfilment. At first Hal is so disabled by the sound of it, and all that it makes him feel, that he doesn't realize she is singing in Spanish.

When she stops, a profound silence follows. The listeners look at one another across the table, unspeaking. Gaspari fumbles in his pocket and retrieves a handkerchief. Earl Morgan has covered his face with his hands. Giulietta, however, looks absolutely furious. Though there was never any form of competition, she must understand that she has been outdone.

Later, in his cabin he lies awake. The oppressive heat isn't helping. He goes to the washstand and splashes his face with cold water, and then fills the bowl and submerges half his head in it trying to block out thought.

For some reason he thinks now of the paintings. He can see the captain, the haunted aspect of him, as clearly as if the thing were hanging here in front of him. What drives a man to look that way? He thinks he is beginning to understand.

They have stolen her from me. I must find her.
But it will mean leaving my ship, my men . . .
It would be a disgrace . . . I would be shunned.
So be it.

I would forsake a hundred ships for her. I would forswear my reputation. I would forget my name.

THE CAPTAIN MOORS in the first small town. He is certain that this is where they will have left her – they would not have risked going ashore in Pisan territory, no matter their urgency.

Dusk is falling, and the lanterns are already lit. There are a couple of fishermen tending to their nets, and he goes to them, asks them if they have seen a young woman, oddly dressed. He describes her long black hair, the extraordinary pallor of her skin. They watch him curiously as he talks, and he realizes how strange he must look to them – a frantic, disarrayed nobleman.

'There was a girl like that,' one man mumbles. 'She were dropped off here by a boat. She were taken to the whorehouse, I believe.'

'The whorehouse?' The captain stares. 'But why?'

The other man shrugs. 'She looked like a whore, is why.'

'She is *not* a whore.' The men react to the sharpness of his tone, their expressions become hostile, wary.

'All women are whores,' the first man says, 'when you get them with the lights off.' His companion chuckles.

The captain sees that he is beginning to lose their interest. Besides, he knows where the establishment they refer to is. In what seems now like another life, he once visited it himself. He throws them a couple of small coins – it always helps to make a friend in such a place – and is on his way.

She is more beautiful than he remembered. And, though it should appal him, seeing her done up like the other women, it excites him.

The rouged lips and cheeks, the flimsy, revealing gown. He would be half-tempted to merely ask her to lead him to one of the rooms . . . But no. He stops these thoughts before they even begin. He has nobler aims than that.

She seems . . . not precisely delighted to see him, but no matter. He would not expect her to be in her proper humour. She has had an ordeal. Not, thankfully, the ordeal that he had feared. He has promises from the Madam that she has not yet been visited by any other man. The woman extracts an eye-watering price from him, too, before she allows him to take the girl: two solid gold *genovini*. It is only fair, she says, taking into account future lost earnings. He has made the novice haggler's mistake, he knows, in letting her see how much he desires the purchase. But no matter. She is his again.

When he wakes the next morning he is convinced that he is still upon the ship, and is thrown into confusion by the unfamiliarity of his new surroundings. Then it comes to him. He has left the ship, *his* ship. Is he mad? What can he have been thinking? But then he remembers *her*, and everything falls into place.

Before, there had not been time to think. He had lost his head over her entirely. Now, though, he begins to plan. When he left the ship the night before he felt prepared to give up everything, if only he could find her. Now, he realizes that this may not be necessary. He may return to Genoa without recrimination. His lieutenants will not defame him, or give him away: his uncle is one of the most powerful men in the city. He will simply say that he was needfully detained by business. Before, he might have been prepared to marry her. But now he realizes that he would be a fool to throw away the opportunity afforded him by his engagement to tie his lot in with one of Genoa's richest families. He will marry Beatrix, but he will not need to give up— He stops. He *still* has not found out her name. Well. No matter, there will be

time for all that. He will not need to give her up, that is the
important thing. Many great and revered men have acted as he
will do.

Gently, he explains his plan to her. They will go first to his
house near Portofino, and rest there for a couple of days. There
she will become his mistress. He will send out for fine clothes and
jewellery – the things that are due to the mistress of one of such
high standing as himself. Then they will return to Genoa, where
he will set her up with a fine house. There is a long silence, and he
wonders if she has not understood him.

'Well,' he asks finally, softly, 'what do you think of that?'

'No,' she says. 'I would prefer not.' There is another long silence.
He asks her what she means.

'I would prefer to leave, and be on my way. Thank you, though,
for your kind offer.'

He is absolutely perplexed. He thinks of how they had found
her: half-dead, with those bruises about her ankles. 'But you would
want for nothing. You would live like an empress. Do you understand? Do you understand who I am?'

Slowly, she nods. 'I understand,' she says, 'that you are a kind
man. That you helped me when I was in need.'

'But where would you go?'

A silence.

'Do you have family?' He is already certain that she does not.
She shakes her head.

'Do you realize how vulnerable that makes you? Do you wish
to find yourself back in the whorehouse?'

He sees her considering, turning it over in her mind. Struck by
inspiration, he says, 'I was hasty. You don't have to make any . . .
commitment to me in that regard yet. I won't touch you, if you
do not wish it. But let me ensure that you are safe, at least for the
next few weeks.'

Finally, she seems to agree. They sail to Portofino, and there he outfits her, as promised, in gowns of the finest cloth. Still, she will not tell him her name. In frustration, he chooses one for her, one that he feels suits her. 'I shall call you Luna,' he says, 'for your beauty.' The captain is a learned man, proud of his grasp of the classics. He takes her silence as her acceptance of this new moniker. It suits her, and her beauty, far better than any other name would, he decides.

They spend two weeks in his villa in Portofino, just the two of them – and the small army of servants he keeps there. Gradually she begins to unfurl. He draws her story from her. She tells him that her parents are dead, and that from infancy she was brought up by an elderly woman who was not her relative. This woman was a healer, she explains, who taught her everything she knew. But she, too, is no longer alive.

What he really wants to know is how she ended up half-drowned, so far from land. But on this point she is reticent. Every time he alludes to it, she steers the conversation from the subject. Which only intrigues him further. Intrigues and – if he were to be absolutely honest – slightly unnerves him. For she is *strange*. Her manner, her way of speaking. Her beauty: hair so dark it looks hardly natural, and her pallor. Paleness in a woman is highly desirable, of course, and yet sometimes he finds it hard to believe that blood really beats somewhere beneath the surface.

Twice now, he has found her roaming the corridors in a sleep-state, moving with her eyes closed but her feet carrying her as surely as if they were open. He has not dared to wake her – has watched instead in dumb horror as she makes her slow but purposeful circuit of the palazzo.

There are further terrible storms, too, battering their way along the coast, howling through the bay. One evening, having gone to check if she is frightened by the racket, he finds her watching the spectacle through the great window, her face lit by excitement. He cannot help but remember the suspicions of some of the men when the first storm had arrived from nowhere. He remembers, too, the word his lieutenant had used. He forces it from his mind.

23

At some point, Hal must have fallen asleep. He wakes to find himself slumped over the desk, his cheek stuck to the open page of the journal. The air is oppressively warm and close, as thick as honey. He has no idea of the time – but it feels late. He reaches for his watch and finds instead that the thing he has picked up is the compass. He squints at the face. Is it his imagination, or is the needle tracking faster than before? Not for the first time he has the unnerving conviction that its motion is transmitting some code for which he lacks the correct cipher.

His skin feels feverishly hot. He reaches for the catch to open the porthole just as light explodes through the room, illuminating the whole cabin. He sits back on the bed, disorientated. Seconds later the thunder follows: a great roar of noise, fire and dynamite. The silence that follows the commotion is textured, unlike the quiet that preceded it. He waits, tensed, for the next assault. It comes sooner than expected, with greater ferocity.

He goes back to the window to try and see anything, but all is dark, and the only thing he can make out is the black gleam of the water. No rain yet. The air crackles. And now there is wind, beginning to rustle and then moan about the boat, whistling in the rigging.

A cry – a human cry, he thinks, but high as an animal's. Then, following on its tail, another catastrophe of light. A terrible splintering, wrenching, tearing sound – then the sigh of something falling: a crash that reverberates through the whole space.

Now there are shouts, footsteps running. The yacht seems filled with hundreds of men, ten times the number that are actually aboard. Hal, finally, is properly awake. He runs to the door and flings it open. Outside in the corridor is a scene of panic. Roberto and another member of staff thunder past. Someone is sobbing wretchedly.

He follows the men up to the deck, where he finds a scene of devastation. Where the main mast once stood is a smoking stump. Scattered about it are the remains of the rest of it: flakes of ash, smouldering chunks like the remnants left in the grate after a fire. The rain, now, has finally begun, and it drenches everything, leaving a sorry, black mess.

The men, ready to act but unable to do anything to help the situation, pick listlessly through the charred remains.

Hal remembers the cry. He goes to Roberto, who is surveying the damage, looking perhaps the happiest Hal has ever seen him.

'Was anyone hurt?'

'No,' Roberto says, with something unmistakably like regret.

'I heard a scream, I thought someone . . .'

'Ah, yes – one of the signoras, she took a great fright at the flash. She saw it all happen. She is inside, very upset.'

He points to the stern of the boat, and Hal sees that the weeper, surprisingly, is Giulietta Castiglione.

'I hate storms,' she says, furiously, when Hal approaches, dabbing at her blotched face. For the first time since Hal has met her, she looks less than groomed: her nightdress crumpled, her hair static. Her face without make-up is vulnerable-looking, like a superhero divested of his mask. Stella and Gaspari sit with her, muttering words of calm. Earl Morgan sits in one of the chairs, rubbing his eyes and looking about groggily.

The only person who does not emerge until the last possible moment is Aubrey Boyd. His silvery head appears at the top of the stairs, followed by the rest of him, clad in a pair of maroon silk pyjamas and a *chinoiserie* robe. He peers about himself in bemusement.

'What is this all in aid of?' He sounds vaguely peevish, as though the gathering is a party to which he has not been invited.

'The storm . . .' Hal begins, and then stops, because surely it is obvious.

'Storm?' Aubrey blinks at him. 'Wasn't aware of any storm.' Now he sees the stump of the mast. 'Good Lord.'

'Yes,' Hal says. 'We were hit.'

'With what? Thor's hammer?'

'Lightning.'

'Well.' A pause. 'How *thrilling*.'

The Contessa returns from where she has been talking with Roberto. She makes a little twist of her mouth.

'It does not look good, my friends. The second mast will have to be mended before we can sail all the way to San Remo. But, as with all things in life, there is a positive. We are not far away from my husband, who is staying at our tower near Cervo. We can limp our way there, Roberto tells me, and wait while the yacht is mended.'

24

The castle sits high on a sward of land that plunges into the water below. When the lifeboat draws closer the slope separates into different iterations of green, and as they lurch towards shore in the little tender, Gaspari turns to Hal. 'This is all quite an adventure, no? Something for you to write about.'

'I suppose it is.' Hal lowers his voice. 'What is the Conte like?'

'Ah,' Gaspari whispers, glancing at their hostess, who is turned away from them, toward the shore. 'Quite as unique as our wonderful Contessa – they are an excellent match.' And then he smiles. This time it is not that downward smile Hal has become accustomed to, but a real smile – one that transforms his face. He would never be considered a handsome man, Hal thinks, but it lends his features their own unusual charm.

They unload their bags onto a stone jetty. Above them a flight of steps ascends some fifty feet toward the castle. Hal makes a move towards Stella's bag but she grabs it instead. 'It's fine. I can do it.'

He goes to pick up Gaspari's bag instead, knowing that the director is too frail to manage the climb with the burden.

'Don't,' Gaspari says, seeing what he is doing. Hal mistakes it for pride, at first, but then he says, 'The Contessa will call them. I've seen this before.' He points at the stone wall of the cliff. Partially hidden beneath the trailing fronds of ivy is a brass telephone. The Contessa goes to it, lifts the receiver and waits. All watch and listen. Now the tinny rattle of an answering voice can be heard through it. The Contessa speaks into it, rapidly, then she turns to the group and gives a thumbs up – a gesture that, from her, somehow appears wonderfully incongruous.

'What happens now?' Hal asks.

'We wait.'

And in a minute, a man and a youth of about sixteen appear at the top of the steps, and hurry down towards them.

'They are the gardeners,' Gaspari says. 'I have met the older one – Gino – before.'

Sure enough, when the man reaches the jetty he greets Gaspari like a long-lost friend. He looks over the others, and whispers something to the director, who shakes his head. Then, with a little smile, he asks something else. Gaspari shakes his head.

The bags are swept up – Hal manages to keep hold of his own. He is still not comfortable with the idea of someone else carrying them while his own hands are free.

'What did he say to you?' he asks Gaspari, as they begin to climb, the two of them bringing up the rear.

'Gino? He wanted to know if he would have a chance to

meet Giulietta – he asked if I was making a film with her. I said not yet.'

'And what was the other thing he asked?'

'The other?'

'Yes.'

'Oh . . . he, ah, wanted to know about Mrs Truss. I explained that she is a married woman.'

Hal had guessed it when he saw the man's gaze run over her. The cheek of it. He thinks he has managed to keep his expression neutral, but he gradually becomes aware that the director is watching him curiously. He looks away.

At the top of the stairs stands an elderly man, extremely tall and thin, clad in a safari suit and deerstalker hat. He observes their progress up towards him through a pair of impressive binoculars. When they reach the top the Contessa goes to him, and they embrace.

Gaspari turns back to Hal. 'The Conte.'

Hal considers the elderly couple. How well suited they are to one another, both hewn into interesting shapes by life. They live lives almost independent from one another, evidently. And yet Hal sees the Contessa's fingers interlace with his, her gaze caress the raw-boned face. And the old man stoops from his great height to kiss the crown of her head.

The room he is shown to is dark and cool, echoing in the same important way as the church in Portovenere. The warmth of the day outside quickly fades from memory – the floor has a particular chill to it that Hal decides must be peculiar to ancient stone; the cold of centuries. At first glance, everything in the room looks as though it might have remained there since the era of the castle's inception: from the faded pastoral scenes frescoed upon the walls to the four-poster bed with its threadbare but beautiful damask coverlet. Gradually, though, other elements reveal themselves: pieces that speak of exotic travels. Three wooden African masks hung on one wall, a Moorish patterned rug on the floor, the curved scimitar sword in its embellished scabbard.

Aubrey Boyd is in the room beside Hal's, Giulietta on the other side. Stella, Earl Morgan and Gaspari are in rooms on the next floor.

Now he can hear voices upstairs. He pushes his door open to make them out more clearly.

'This room,' Giulietta is saying, in her most imperious tone, 'is far bigger than mine. I would prefer to sleep here.'

The Contessa, of course, proves a worthy match. 'But I am afraid it is not your room,' she says, pleasantly, 'it is the one I have given to Mrs Truss.'

Now Stella speaks. 'It's all right,' she says, wearily. 'I don't mind swapping.'

The Contessa tries to dissuade her.

'No,' Stella says, firmly. 'I don't need a large room.'

Hal closes the door. Fame, he thinks, has a great deal to answer for. It rewards behaviour that should otherwise be stamped out long before adulthood. He will find some way of making sure that some trace of this infiltrates his piece.

Supper is served in the courtyard outside the castle, which sits above a sheer drop down to where the sea froths against the rocks beneath. Behind them the wall of the castle is almost completely obscured by an ancient growth of wisteria with blossoms from which tiny purple petals, dislodged by the breeze, take to the air and land all around. Several cats of every imaginable size and colour have appeared and they circle the guests curiously, the bolder among them threading their way between table legs and ankles. Nina watches them warily, letting off the occasional warning bark, but the animals are unperturbed by her presence.

'We used a cat for one scene in the film,' Gaspari says.

'I remember it,' Hal says, 'the one that leads the man through the streets to the shrine.'

'Yes. That's it.' Gaspari nods, pleased. 'We trialled several different animals before we found the one that would do what we wanted, and only then because we bribed it with little pieces of chicken tied out of sight. It would refuse to do anything – *anything* – unless there was chicken involved. And people think that the film world is a glamorous place. Auditioning cats – imagine!'

The Conte sits on Hal's other side. Hal is pleased by the novelty of having someone to talk to who hasn't also been on the *Pygmalion*. And the Conte makes an excellent dinner companion. For all his bizarreness of appearance – he arrives at dinner in a purple Chinese silk tunic and matching trousers – and his great age, he is lucid as the grappa that is handed around after the meal. He regales Hal with his tales of the Syrian desert, where he and the Contessa once spent a whole six months living with a Bedou tribe. He tells Hal of the storms of sand, in which the fine particles in part assumed the characteristics of water. A sea that seethed and stormed, enveloping all.

'You have to keep moving – so that you do not become like *un sarcofago*. It happens in seconds, otherwise. I almost lost my wife like that. She was trying to take a photograph of it . . . imagine.'

He describes to Hal the Bedou tribes' strong sense of

honour and hospitality, and of their customs: the poetry they would recite in the evening, their great piousness.

'There is a purity to a desert existence, to living according to its laws. But there is also a strength of mind and body required for that life. I was too weak.' He gestures, 'I missed the sea, I missed the green. But sometimes, now, the Contessa and I find we miss the desert, too. It is something that gets into the blood, a most rare and powerful drug. Who knows, maybe one day, we will return there, my wife and I. Our bodies are weaker but our minds, perhaps, have acquired the necessary resilience.'

When they have finished eating he takes Hal to the tent they have brought back with them and erected at one end of the courtyard. It is a long, low shape, a thick coarse cloth made from woven goat hair. Hal climbs inside the dark space and smells woodsmoke and incense and something else, too – something indefinable. A residue, perhaps, of the intense heat of the desert sun which has by some magic permeated into the fabric itself.

'You have the best night's sleep of your life in these,' he tells Hal.

He used to be a keen aviator, too, but the war put paid to that. 'I used to dream about building aeroplanes. When I was a boy it was my passion; all I could think about. I spent my days designing them. And then as a young man I gave up the engineering part – I had not the mathematical brain that was needed – and instead became rather good at flying the things. But to see my hobby become something that could kill . . . it destroyed my passion for it completely.'

Hal thinks of the fact that he hasn't set foot in a sailing dinghy since 1938. 'Will you ever fly again?'

'Perhaps. But my eyesight is not how it was. I have other interests now: my garden, my fishing.'

The Conte and Contessa spent the war years in Switzerland, wanting, as the Conte explains, to distance themselves as far as possible from the disgrace of the country under Fascism.

'From the mid-thirties we were exiles. We stayed with friends, we lived in one of the spa hotels for several years. For a while I thought we might not recognize the country when – if – we returned. And it is changed. We are all changed. But luckily there is enough of the old place, and of ourselves, left to recognize.'

He rises from his seat now and pours another round of grappa for everyone.

'To new friends.' He salutes Hal, Giulietta, Aubrey, Stella. 'And to old.' This last with a fond smile for Gaspari. 'To the sea.' He sweeps a hand across the blue. 'To Italy.' He has almost put down his glass when he remembers something. 'And to love, of course. To the older kind,' he toasts the Contessa and then, unmistakably, he raises his glass to Hal and then to Stella, 'and to young.'

There is a strained silence.

'*Caro*,' the Contessa says, with a quick smile. 'I explained it to you. Mrs Truss' husband has had to travel to Milan. Hal is the journalist.'

'Oh.' He frowns.

'I think you have had too much grappa, *carissimo*. You cannot drink as much as you used to.'

'Ah yes,' the Conte says, as though finally remembering his lines, and giving them all a winning smile. 'Forgive an old man his confusion.' He taps his forehead. 'It is nothing but so much spider's yarn up here.'

*

Later, when most of the guests have retreated to their own rooms, Hal finds the Contessa sitting out on the terrace alone, a glass of grappa in her hand. 'Look at them,' she says, and points.

At first he cannot see what it is she means. And then they begin to appear like retinal scratches: tiny filaments of light appearing from and dissolving into the dark.

'Fireflies.' This is the first time in his life he has seen them.

'Sit with me,' she says. 'And have some more grappa.' She pours a little into a second glass and passes it to him. They watch the strange show for several minutes in silence.

'They are early this year – it has been warm. But soon,' she sweeps a hand, 'they will fill all of this. They will almost vanquish the dark.'

'I'd like to see that.'

'Perhaps one day you will return, join us here for a longer time.'

'I'd like that.'

'Tell me,' she says. 'You are Italian, are you not?'

'My mother is.'

'I knew it. You speak the language too beautifully for it to be otherwise. And that was why you chose Rome for your escape?'

'Escape?'

'That was what you told me at my party. The reason you gave.'

He remembers. 'Yes, I suppose so.'

'But what is a young man like you doing all alone? Aubrey I think I understand – he seems, well, if not content, then certainly resigned to his aloneness. But I don't think it is the same with you.'

From anyone else this questioning would be prying,

impertinent. But from the Contessa it is curiously inoffensive. Perhaps, Hal thinks, it is the authority lent by age.

'I was going to be married – in England.'

She raises her eyebrows.

'It didn't work. We met before the war; I was studying in London, she worked there, as a clerk. I was twenty when I proposed: I'd hardly lived at all. And then, after the war . . . I suppose we weren't the same people that we had been before it.'

Not *quite* true. Suze had been very much the same. He was the one who had changed out of all recognition. It wasn't that he hadn't tried to return to the man he had been: he had. But it was as though the cells of him had undergone an irreversible change. There was no way back.

He remembers that final, terrible reckoning in a Kensington teashop near Suze's flat. He had never seen her cry before that, not even during the war. And yet however terrible it had felt to know that he had been the cause of this pain, there had also been a secret, queasy sense of relief that it was done, that it was over. Because in the end it had come down to his fear of disappointing her, of not being the person she thought she was marrying. And his realization that, though he cared for her, he did not love her enough to spend his whole life trying to be that person.

'You know,' the Contessa says, after a long silence, 'I wasn't always married to the Conte.'

Hal turns to look at her, in surprise.

'No,' she says, slowly, 'before him, I was married to another. I was unfortunate enough not to realize my mistake until after my wedding. He wasn't a pleasant man. The Conte was my salvation.' She gestures down at herself. 'You see now someone who is not afraid to be the person she truly is – who will wear the colours she wants to, who will let herself grow old without mourning the loss of her beauty. Because I am free to do as I choose, be exactly how I want to be. He made me see that it could be like that. And that is what love is, I think. But my former marriage – you would not have recognized me then.'

'What happened?'

'We were stationed in Eritrea, my husband was posted there a couple of years before the First War. He started having affairs almost instantly – he was a handsome man, a charming one when he wanted to be – and when he came home he would describe to me my shortcomings in comparison: the smallness of my breasts, the size of my nose, the thickness of my waist. The fact that I did not know how to seduce a man, how to please him. I was not then the woman I am now. I began to believe in my own deficiencies.'

Hal is stunned by the cruelty of it.

'Then I met the Conte, at an expatriate drinks out there. I thought he was a buffoon: bald, far too tall, badly dressed. Obsessed with his plane. But he showed me how to be free. In a way, I wish that I could have learned it on my own – but sometimes we need another to show us our own bravery.' After a pause, she says, 'I had a little boy, once.'

'With the Conte?'

She shakes her head. 'With my first husband. He got malaria. Oh, it was such a long time ago now – almost a lifetime. But it is strange how often he is in my thoughts, even now, in my old age. Perhaps it is because he was my only one.

'He had dark hair, and blue, blue eyes. It is a Ligurian trait, this combination. You know, it was what I first thought when

I saw you – that you looked as though you could have been born here. And my second thought was that you reminded me of him, my son. I can't explain it. But I would hope that, had he grown to be a man, he would be something like you.'

He finds, suddenly, that he has to look away.

An hour later, all have excused themselves. Alone in his room, Hal finds himself returning inevitably to that other world.

HE HAS SET her up in a house in Genoa. There are whispers about the mysterious woman living on the Via Cairoli. She has been seen, and noted, by a number of the Genoese quality. This perturbs the captain, because he has specifically told her to leave the house as little as possible. As expected, his departure from the ship has not become the scandal it could have done. His uncle is not impressed with him, he can tell, but will not risk opening the thing up to gossip.

Still she has not allowed him into her bed. But he can be patient. It is only a matter of time. She is kind to him, after all. Once, when he had complained of a congestion in his head she had asked the cook to make him up a remedy of her own invention – a poultice of pungent herbs that he could hold to his face and inhale. And it had, incredibly, worked. He had been grateful and also – though he would hardly admit it to himself – unnerved.

'All that you need,' he tells her on his next visit, as they sit drinking their tea in the salon he has had decorated for her, 'you have here. You should have no reason to leave the building.'

He is right, of course. There is a good-sized garden with the most fashionable features available: an artificial grotto, and a mosaic tricked out with delicately coloured corals and glass.

There is a bathroom with its own private bath: a rare luxury. There is even a miniature chapel, which he learns from the housekeeper she never uses. He has cakes brought to her from the finest *pasticceria*, wines from his own store. Rare fruits, purchased at great expense from the best merchants. She has, in short, everything.

'So why,' he asks her, 'would you want to leave?'

'To see the sea.'

'You can see it from the upstairs windows.'

'I don't want to see it like that. I want to see it up close. And to walk in the fresh air.'

'You have your garden.'

'It is not the same.'

'And to see other people.'

This last fills him with horror. '*See* people. Who, tell me, would you want to see? You see me, often. I visit whenever I can.'

'I don't mean anyone specifically. I just mean real people, in the streets.'

'But this is a dangerous city. You shouldn't be travelling about on your own.'

'I'm not. I have Bear with me.'

Bear is the stray she found in the alleyway beside the house, a dog that looks half-wolf half-hound. A beautiful, dangerous animal – with eyes that almost match her own – and obedient only to her, apparently. He rather regrets having let her keep the creature now. She lavishes so much attention upon the animal that there does not seem to be any left for him.

And the idea of the dog as her protection is not enough to placate him. For it is not just concern for her safety that he finds troubling: it is the thought of having to share the sight of her with the rest of the world – with the paupers and grocers and fishermen who flock into the streets. But it isn't that, he thinks. He is worried for her safety. He will meet her halfway, he decides.

'I will throw you a ball.'

'A ball?'

'Yes. Though I will make sure that there is no . . . unseemly connection between us. I will explain that you are my ward – the daughter of a Corsican family, who is in need of my protection. That will explain the accent, too.' He knows that this is nonsense. Those that care will already have made their assumptions about the sort of relationship that exists between them – the sort of relationship, in all honesty, that he would wish them to have. But he does not want to offend her.

'In that way,' he says, warming to the idea, 'you may meet people, and be safe.' And he rather does like the thought of showing her off to the envy of all others, in a controlled situation, of his choosing. Beatrix is no concern: she is a practical, unromantic sort. He knows that she harbours no illusions about their relationship. Though perhaps he would not be *quite* so bold if she were not safely tucked away at her father's estate in the countryside.

The ball is a success. *She* is a success, in a silk gown embroidered with silver and gold thread. It is an outfit that would give the *magistrato delle pompe* forty fits, because such levels of ostentation on a single garment are forbidden.

'I would like to paint her.' He overhears this, and turns to find the speaker. It is the Flemish painter – a young man, but already renowned for his great skill. At first he is unsure about the idea. To have an image made seems to him merely another way in which he would be forced to share her with other people. But as he thinks on it, he realizes that it need not be a portrait for public viewing. It could hang in his own house – in his own bedchamber, even. Then he would be able to feast on her beauty always. In fact, it may be the best idea he has had for a long time.

He approaches the painter, imperiously. 'I would like to commission you, to make her portrait.'

The man is delighted.

'How much?'

'Well,' the artist says, earnestly, 'to have such a subject would be payment in itself.'

The captain is the scion of merchants – he understands an excellent bargain when it is offered. But for some reason that he cannot identify, he does not like the idea of it. 'No,' he says, firmly, 'I would pay the fair price for such a work.'

If the man is surprised he does not betray it. 'Certainly.' He names his price, and it is exorbitant. Yet suddenly he desires this image of her more than anything. The man could ask for the moon itself and he would find some way of fishing it from the sky.

Hal puts the journal down. Something has happened. Around him the castle sleeps. Except, in the midst of the silence he hears something. A sound of pain, low and animal.

25

Her

I have seen the plane coming for us. I have seen it this time: I know, somehow, that it is coming for us. I reach out to Tino.

'Tino,' I say, 'we have to jump now.'

I think for a moment that he is coming, too – that we will both escape. And then I see him hesitate. I see him turn back into the dark space in the truck's interior. I never manage to get him out of the truck.

There is a sudden violence between us, a white blast. But I am still reaching for him, clawing the air.

*

A sudden cry, splitting the silence. He walks to the corridor, puts his head outside. Bars of blue moonlight slit the dark, illuminating dusty lengths of stone. Stella's door, he cannot help noticing, is slightly ajar. The silence is absolute once more. It is a nearly full moon – particularly low and large, as though buoyant upon the water at the horizon. It seems to Hal that the light of it is forming a path for him: along the corridor, and out into the garden. And so he follows it.

Outside the air is quite cool, with only the faintest breath of the earlier heat in it. As he descends through the terraced gardens he is aware of an odd sound, low and guttural, fracturing into a multitude of separate sounds as he nears it. Not the sound he heard – in fact, it is like nothing he has heard before. As he passes the stone well it grows louder, and he realizes that it is coming from within. Frog music. He peers down into the dark mouth of the well and the noise wavers, then stops completely. He imagines the creatures looking back up at him, but can see nothing beyond a black gleam of wetness at the bottom. As he moves away the noise resumes, hesitantly at first, and gradually building to the pitch of before. Now that he understands it, it makes him smile.

He continues down the steps beyond the courtyard, where there is a second paved level that he hasn't yet explored. As he moves away from the uproar of the frogs there is another sound, a liquid sound, coming from the direction of the swimming pool. Curious, he moves towards it. And then he sees her. A white shape in the blackness, entering the water. He begins to run.

'Stella,' he calls to her, stumbling, tripping down the path. 'Stella, stop!'

She is in up to her waist. The fabric of her nightdress foams about her like a pale sea creature.

Without thinking he plunges into the water. He reaches for her and finds her arm and then her waist, through the floating skeins of material. He pulls her toward him.

At first she is limp in his arms, still lost to sleep. But then her hands are gripping him. She is blinking, gasping with the shock of the cold – which must be what has woken her. 'Hal,' she says, staring at him. 'How—'

'You were sleepwalking,' he says.

She shuts her eyes. 'I thought I was there,' she says. 'I had almost got him free.' Her teeth are beginning to chatter. For the first time, he becomes aware of the cold, and of the warmth of her against him.

'Come on,' he says, helping her to climb out.

She is silent on the journey back up through the garden – embarrassed, perhaps a little in shock. But when they split to go to their separate rooms, she lays a hand on his arm. The warmth of her palm sears him through the wet material.

'Hal,' she says, 'thank you.'

There is something in her face, a new openness, he thinks. Something has changed.

He returns to his room and towels himself dry, changes into dry clothes. He can hear her moving about in her room too, no doubt going through the same ritual: the opening of drawers, her feet on the flagstones. And then, after a few minutes, he hears the groan of her door opening. He listens, intent. She is outside, he is certain.

He goes to the door. He cannot hear anything, but he can sense her presence on the other side, as tangibly as if he could see her. What is she doing? Is she deliberating whether to knock? He imagines her hand, lifted, wavering. Well, he thinks, he will decide for her. He turns the handle. It is stiff, slow to move, and he has learned now that he has to put his whole weight against the door to get it open. When it finally does, he is greeted by darkness on the other side, the blank dark of the empty hallway.

It is for the best.

He climbs back into bed, and reaches for the journal, which is increasingly becoming a means of silencing the clamour of thought.

THE PROCESS BEGINS. The painter visits the house on the Via Cairoli every day, and the captain waits eagerly for the great unveiling. He asks, on a number of occasions, whether he may see the portrait in its unfinished state, but the young artist assures him that it would ruin the effect of the final piece for him. So over the weeks that follow he tries not to become too impatient, reminding himself constantly of the great prize that awaits.

When he visits Luna she seems happier than before. She is friendlier with him when he visits, too. The housekeeper tells him that she no longer leaves the palazzo as often, which is a pleasing result – though the restless sleep wandering does continue, to the perturbation of the whole household.

On one visit, encouraged by her smiles, he attempts to embrace her. It is the first time he has made such a move toward her – he feels that the moment has come. But as he reaches for her, a fearsome growl comes from the corner of the room. He draws back, confused. The dog is crouched low, its teeth bared in a snarl. It looks as though it is readying itself to leap: at him. He takes a step away from the girl, and the animal relaxes slightly. He glances at Luna, seeking some sort of explanation, but she merely looks back at him steadily, as though nothing is amiss.

Again, he moves towards her. Again, the dog growls. It is a terrible sound. This time the creature is stalking towards him. Feeling foolish, and not a little afraid, he makes his excuses and begins to retreat slowly from the room, all the while keeping the animal in his sights, making sure that it is not about to pounce on him.

There is nothing for it, he thinks furiously, back in the safety of his own palazzo. The beast must go. It will not be easy explaining this to her – there is such a bond between girl and dog that he suspects she will be upset. There is another thought, too, one that he tries to avoid entertaining. But it keeps coming to him, try as he might to push it away. There is something they say about women who share a peculiar bond with a particular creature. It is meant to be a sign of something . . . But no, it is mere superstition. He is a modern, intelligent man who can allow no time for such ideas. And she is good, and innocent. He is certain of it.

Hal feels a shiver of recognition. The painting, in Genoa. One and the same, surely, as the piece mentioned here. And there was something in it, wasn't there? A sense of complicity that felt like some secret, shared, between subject and viewer. Or subject and painter.

26

The next day dawns warm and gorgeous: there is summer in it. Hal has come down to the stone jetty with the intention of going for a swim. The cold water hits his skin like a slap – memories of the previous night surfacing – but he becomes accustomed to it. He turns onto his back, sculling away from the shore. This sea supports him, seems almost to cherish him. Above him the land rises high as a cathedral into the blue.

As he turns to make for shore, blinking the sting of the salt from his eyes, he sees a figure on the jetty. It is Stella, sitting on the jetty, watching him.

'Hello,' she calls.

'Hello.'

He hoists himself up onto the stone, and as he stoops to pick up his towel he can feel her eyes upon him, on the naked skin of his chest and stomach. He enjoys it. And when he turns to look at her, and catches her watching, she looks quickly away.

When he has towelled himself dry he sits down beside her. In her sundress and her white plimsolls, with her hair tied back, she looks very proper – like a country club tennis star. So different to his vision of her last night, with her wet hair across her forehead, her nightdress sodden.

She has her handbag beside her. 'Are you going some-where?'

'I was going to walk to Cervo,' she tells him. 'The little town? The Contessa tells me it's worth a visit.' A beat. 'Do you want to join me?'

He gestures down at himself. Once again he feels rather than sees the warmth of her gaze upon his skin. 'I'll have to get dressed.'

She inclines her head. 'I can wait.'

He dresses with a kind of frenzy. He had thought, after the strangeness of the night before, that she might be guarded with him. But the opposite seems to be true. He can feel her eyes on him, still.

Her

I don't know what makes me ask him. But I'm not sure why I've done many things over the last few days. I don't feel completely in control. Last night, for example. Waking to find myself in the dark water, with him wading in after me. This is exactly why my husband insists I should be taking the pills: the sleepwalking is dangerous, he says.

After I returned to my room I found myself opening my door, stepping outside. I stood in the corridor beside his door with my hand raised, ready to knock, before I realized what I was doing. But I was very much awake then.

This is not the woman who thinks out every sentence before

she utters it, who is measured, self-possessed, never unexpected or controversial. But then neither was I her the other night on the yacht when I opened my mouth and sang. These are the actions of someone who meets a stranger at a party and asks him to take her with him into the nighttime city.

27

Cervo

A red-roofed, pastel-coloured town – little more than a hamlet – perched above the blue sweep of the Mediterranean. On the flat rocks that extend into the sea several dozen bronzed bodies are visible, lying prone in the warm wash of the sunlight. A place where one might live like a king on very little. He could be happier in a place like this, Hal thinks, than if he were to stay in the best hotel in Portofino.

The cobbled walkway up to the town is fringed by an embarrassment of flowers: reds and pinks, yellow and purple and white: colours that might never be put together by design. But nature, who knows nothing of convention, has the audacity of a genius.

In the medieval streets at the heart of the place the buildings seem to lean towards one another, pressing inwards. Stella moves in front of him like a pale flag against the shadows, looking about herself. He wants to know exactly what it is that draws her attention there, at the apex of two buildings, or there, in that dark corner. But there is almost absolute silence around them, and to speak into it would be to break the spell. Perhaps the entire population of the town is on the beach, because it seems they are the only ones here.

Suddenly they are launched into sunlight: a bright square above the sweep of the sea revealed on one side. Now the heat of the day is upon them again: a vivid, pressing warmth. Before them is a majestic church decorated in marine colours – seafoam, coral, palest sand – looking almost as though it were once something dredged from the sea.

'Do you want to go in?' he asks Stella.

'You go,' she says. 'I'll sit there—' gesturing to an ironwork table and chairs set up in one corner of the square.

He knows what she will do: sit, and gaze out at the sea. It holds a particular fascination for her, as though she never grows tired of looking at it. He thinks he understands. For one who grew up with it, as he did, it was – until recently – something like an old friend. For her, it is still a mesmerizing stranger.

'All right.'

The colours used inside are the same, but in the shadows they gain depth, majesty. There are a couple of bowed white heads in the pews: indistinguishable from Hal's position as men or women, their stillness absolute. They could have been sitting here for hours – days. He never inherited his mother's religion – agnosticism is one of the only things on which he and his father agree. And yet he has always been fascinated by her faith, her absolute trust in a higher power. He has wished at times, since the war, that he shared it. That belief in a higher plan in particular, the conviction that everything that happens – even the terrible things – happens for some reason too complex and mysterious for understanding. And the act, too, of confessing – and through that confession, to have some hope of finding absolution. The funny thing is, he often finds himself in the role of confessor, like some sort of a secular priest. It has always been this way: at school, friends had confided in him their various misdeeds, their shameful secrets. And on *Lionheart*, too. But since he has had something of his own to confess he seems to have met only with resistance. Suze brushing his words away as though they might soil her. Or his own suppressions, his own shame.

He steps outside a few minutes later. Stella, he sees, has been joined by an elderly woman, and both sit deep in conversation. It takes him a moment to recognize the language they are speaking in as Spanish.

As he approaches they both glance up, and the old woman springs to her feet with surprising agility. She is quite incredibly small: not much taller standing than Stella sitting, and Hal wonders whether she has always been that height, or whether it is the press of age. They have been drinking coffee. The woman now is gesturing to the cups, hurrying inside a door behind them that he had not noticed before.

'She's going to bring you one,' Stella tells him. 'She has a café here.'

Hal looks at the solitary table, and thinks that it is possibly the smallest café in existence. 'You were speaking Spanish?'

'Oh,' Stella says. 'Yes. Her parents were Spanish – the family moved here before the turn of the century. We got talking about the town, and I asked her how long she had lived here.' She takes a sip of her coffee, frowns. 'I'm not sure how it happened. Suddenly, I was no longer speaking English . . . and it was so easy. I thought I had forgotten it. I hoped that I had.'

'But it came back?'

'Yes. Surprisingly well.'

'She wanted to know why I knew it.'

'What did you tell her?'

'That I'd spent some time in Mexico. I'm not sure she believes me . . . my pronunciation is too different. But I didn't want to get into a long discussion—' Stella breaks off, looking up as the woman appears with a cup for Hal, and a metal pot, from which she pours a thick dark stream of coffee. Then she disappears inside and returns with a plate of little cakes, which she places proudly between them.

'Please,' Hal says, gesturing to the remaining chair. 'Sit with us.'

'Ah, no, *grazie*, no.' She looks between them and grins, broadly. Then she leaves them. They sip their coffee in silence for several minutes, and eat their cakes, which are delicious. Almost immediately tiny birds appear to search out the crumbs, scurrying about on feet as fragile as leaf skeletons.

For the first time since they started out for Cervo, Hal finds himself properly aware of their aloneness together.

'When was the last time you spoke Spanish?' he asks.

'A long time ago – 1937.'

'That was when you left Spain?'

'Yes.'

'Tell me about it.'

Her

New York, June 1937

In New York, I discover that he is rich. It feels less a part of the metropolis, the area in which he lives, than it does some exclusive settlement. There are manicured box hedges, ivy wending its way up old stone. Of all the grand buildings on the street his apartment is grandest of all, a gothic tower spearing the sky, the lights glittering like so many precious stones.

I left Madrid with him, when he made his offer, because I had no other choice. If I had stayed I might have become another Maria, but I knew that I had nothing of her strength, at least not any more. Here was an opportunity for a new life – if one could look at it in that way. Really it was more like dying. It was a relinquishing of the struggle to survive, the shedding of a self. Though my grief crossed the ocean with me. It was the one thing I brought with me from my old existence to this new.

In the second week, I find myself left for a couple of hours in the apartment. His home is so different from everything I have known. The two guiding principles are wealth, and order, neither of which had any place in the farmhouse. Hard, gleaming, geometric. Metal and glass. It feels like being caught inside a vast lantern. Every so often I catch a glimpse of myself in one of the many reflective surfaces, and see a small pale being: a moth who has flown in by accident.

It is in good taste – even with no knowledge of such things, I can tell that much. But then I already knew that my husband was a man of taste: it is evident in the elegance of his person. What I want now is to discover new, as yet unknown aspects of him, to educate myself about this man who fascinates and frightens me. Furtively, I find myself looking for things that might reveal these. The home is where one learns such things about a person, isn't it? The private self, of which they only expose choice glimpses to the world.

Papa claimed that a person's bookshelf revealed most about them, so I go to these first. I don't quite know what to make of what I find. There are a great many volumes, but they are anonymous in their ubiquity. The complete works of Shakespeare. Boxed collections of Dickens, of Thackeray, of Austen. Sets of encyclopaedias, the histories of the Romans, Ancient Greeks, the Americas. They are beautiful editions. But where are those idiosyncrasies of appetite? The odd preoccupations, the dog-eared indulgences? Our house had more than most, perhaps, but everyone must have them.

I look for photographs. I have a sudden need to find a picture of my husband at another stage of his life – in a more fragile, unformed phase, perhaps as a fat baby, or in adolescence. Best yet, a family member – to lend context to who he was before, his history. I begin to look in drawers, to open cupboards.

'What are you doing?' His tone is one of curious amusement. I am pleased that he isn't angry – the idea of him angry is horrible. But I am also humiliated, aware of how ridiculous I must look, caught red-handed like this.

He repeats his question.

'Oh,' I say, improvising. 'I'm looking for a pen.'

'A pen? Why would you want a pen?'

'I—' I try to think, but my mind is a blank. 'I wanted to write a note.'

'What sort of note?'

'To . . . to thank you. For everything you've done for me.'

'Ah. But you aren't going anywhere – are you?'

'No.'

He smiles, kindly. 'You don't need to write me a note, then. You can simply tell me.'

'Of course. Thank you.'

In the morning, a wrapped parcel is left outside my room. I lift the layers of tissue to reveal a dark-blue fountain pen, exquisitely made.

For the first few weeks, I see the city through the windows of the sitting room, which look out onto a wide thorough-fare of shops and traffic. He does not want me to go out alone, at least for now. He is worried I might get lost, or picked up by the police. I could be deported. I am aware that my status in this new country is hazy. He arranged all of it: the passage out of Spain and into France, the flight from there. I have seen nothing of my new country other than the airport and a blur of streets, filled with people, on the drive to the apartment.

Then, one day, he tells me that we are going shopping. He wants me to have everything new, he says, as I am draped by the shop assistants in silk and chiffon, cashmere and tweed. He wants me to be transformed.

Looking in the mirror, back at the apartment, I am filled with wonder and a kind of horror. The person before me is not someone I recognize. I look several years older, several degrees more beautiful. I have never been beautiful before. I have never worn make-up before, and am fascinated by its transformations. The red lipstick, in particular, that has made my mouth into a symbol. And there is the French *eau de parfum* that leaves its voluptuous impressions upon my clothes, in my hair.

I move differently in my new clothes. Or, rather, I move less: they are cut tight about the body, in fabrics quick to stain or crease. These are garments for one who lives a rare-fied indoor life: my new existence. My old clothes withstood many daily abuses. These clothes are a beautiful forbiddance.

And there is the lingerie too. He left the boxes on the dressing table of my room: wisps of silk and lace held together by boning and ribbon that bite more fiercely than one might expect, stockings as fine as cobweb. They weigh almost nothing, and yet I am more aware of them than of any other aspect of my dress.

Does he think about me wearing them, these items that he has selected?

He hasn't touched me, yet. I'm not sure why, because certainly he looks. Though sometimes I cannot help thinking that there is something in his look that is less like appreciation than a qualified sort of appraisal. He will make remarks – always with the greatest possible tact: do I really want to wear this scarf with this blouse? Don't I feel that it would be better to wear my hair swept back, my hemline longer? Perhaps drink the wine a little more slowly, with my hand held just so? *Ah, no* – always patient – *that's not quite it. Like this, yes, exactly.*

I am becoming someone new – no longer an almost-woman, but a definite person. And yet who that person is, exactly . . . of that I am unsure.

'Sometimes I think about it,' she says. 'If I had stayed, in Madrid. I had no home, no money, no family. I think I would have ended up selling myself – if I was lucky.'

'If you were lucky?'

'Or I might have ended up dead. After, when Madrid fell. If they had found out who I was, who my father was.' She sees his expression. 'You don't believe me.'

'I think you would have found a way of surviving – without any of those things having to happen.'

'I think you have more faith in me than I do in myself.'

'Perhaps,' he says. 'But it doesn't mean I'm wrong.'

She seems about to say something, but stops herself. As they look at one another, the silence between them shifts. It becomes like the silence of the night before, when he had waited for her to knock on his door. It becomes like the silence of that night in Rome, when she had shrugged out of her clothes, her eyes on his.

The woman appears to collect their coffee cups. As soon as she sees them, she stops, and begins to retreat – apologizing as profusely as if she had caught them in a state of undress. So, Hal thinks, it is not only in the imagination then, this thing that is happening between them. It is visible to a stranger.

The last part of the walk is along a coastal path, close to the water's edge. The sea is more agitated now, and every minute or so there is a wave powerful enough to send spray foaming up into the air, speckling them with seawater. On one occasion Hal hears a curse behind him, and turns to see Stella has been got by a wave, her hair drenched. They stare at one another for several seconds, and then they begin to laugh. The laughter is a surprise, like the sudden hit of some euphoric drug.

He has a light pullover with him, and he unties it from about his waist, so that she can dry herself. He is about to hand it to her when she inclines her head toward him. Her eyes are on his. He doesn't know what it means, so he focuses instead on the task. Slowly, he begins to dry her hair for her with the gentlest movements possible. There is a peculiar intimacy to the act. He notices at this proximity the soft, downy hair at her temples, paler than the rest, and the way her freckles cluster in the skin nearest to her hairline. He notices the white creases in the corners of her eyes, the blonde at the tips of her eyelashes like a fine gold dust. Her mouth is slightly open. He could kiss her. Or rather, he could try – and he thinks she might not prevent him. The thought goes through him like a dart. He hasn't wanted anything like this, not for as long as he can remember. His desire in Rome was uncomplicated, little more than instinct. It was the simple excitement of the unknown. This is something altogether more complex. For this reason, he steps away.

28

He sits on the terrace before supper, smoking a cigarette. The Conte, perhaps seeing something of his agitation, has given him a bottle of wine and a glass – telling him that a sunset should always be toasted with a little alcohol. In an attempt to dull his thoughts, Hal has poured himself several glasses.

Not to do it had felt against nature.

He fishes his tin of cigarettes from his pocket and lights one. His hand is clumsy as he does it, his fingers won't work properly.

He had taken a step back, and, in this one action, the possibility of it had been extinguished. Her expression had been inscrutable, before she looked away.

It was the only thing to do.

He had his chance with Suze. She was everything he once thought he would have wanted. She was phenomenally clever – far more so than he – and beautiful, and great fun. But he had found himself cancelling plans they had made, or worse, simply not turning up.

In a gentler time, it might have been safer. But in this violent, bloody century, when death rained from the sky or rose up from the sea to meet you, with the spectre of a bomb that could flatten cities overshadowing everything . . . Love, in a century like this, was too dangerous to contemplate.

'For God's sake, Hal,' she had said, after he failed to make her birthday party, 'anyone would think you were going out of your way to destroy things for us.'

Was he?

He did know that whenever he felt happiest with her – when they had taken a bottle of wine and a picnic blanket down to the riverbank, and kissed one another with the drone of summer insects all around, or when she had emerged from the bathroom in the hotel room they had booked (Suze was very much emancipated) looking like all his boyhood fantasies combined in one being – he would think of Morris' wife, when he had gone to see her. Little Flora Eggers in her bedsit, crying quietly, politely. And then he would want to ruin everything.

That last, dreadful meeting, in a café near her flat in Kensington. He had never seen her cry before. And now, suddenly, she was crying so much he could hardly make out the words.

'I don't understand,' he had said, taking hold of her hand. 'What are you trying to say?'

'Oh, Hal,' she had shaken her head, pulled her hand away. With the other she had brushed at her blotched face, trying to stem the flow of tears. 'Don't. I've tried so hard. But it's enough now. It's enough. Nothing's happened yet, but . . .'

'*But what?*'

'*I've met someone else. He isn't you, Hal. But you aren't you, any more.*'

He had waited, on the walk back to his flat, to feel the hurt of it. That was the worst thing of all, though – it never came. He only felt numb.

'Hello.'

It is a woman's voice, and he turns, thinking that it is her. But, to his surprise, it is Giulietta Castiglione, carrying a glass of spumante.

'Hello,' he says.

'May I sit here?' It is rather amazing, Hal thinks, that she has bothered to ask at all. It doesn't seem to be in her usual way.

'Of course.'

She takes the seat next to him, then gestures to his tin of cigarettes. 'Can I?'

He lights one up for her, and she puts it to her lips with a little sigh of pleasure. He watches her, thinking that of all the strange occurrences that have taken place on this trip so far, this is perhaps the most surreal of all. The most lusted after film actress in Italy – some might even argue the world – is sitting next to him in her sundress, smoking one of his cigarettes. Many would pay thousands of dollars for this opportunity. And yet, though he is aware of the charisma that emanates from her like perfume, and though her beauty is an unarguable fact, she leaves him almost unaffected.

She opens her eyes now and looks directly at him. He had not realized before, but her eyes are not black, as he had believed, but a dark blue.

'I think we have not talked properly before,' she says, 'you and I.'

'No,' he says, 'I think you're right.' He remembers the short-lived interview.

'And I think,' she says, squinting slightly, 'that you do not like me much.'

'That's not true,' he says.

But Giulietta ignores him. 'I know what you believe I am.'

'What?'

'A . . .' she searches for the word, 'a bimbo.' Her accent draws it out: *beem-bo*.

He shakes his head. 'No, that's not true.' He wonders, too, why she would care.

'Really?' She surveys him. 'That is what most people think. Why should you be any different?'

'I have spoken to Signor Gaspari about you. He told me that he believes you are one of the most intelligent actresses he has ever worked with.'

She squints at him, as though trying to decide whether to believe him. He can see that she is pleased, in spite of herself. But she is not finished. 'Tell me then,' she says, challengingly. 'What you *do* think of me.'

'I think you are very talented. I remember thinking it when I saw your first picture, *A Holiday of Sorts*.'

'Oh that,' she says, rather dismissively, 'that was not my best work. It was a Hollywood picture. I was typewritten.'

'Typecast.'

'Yes, yes.' She waves a hand, to show that it doesn't signify either way.

Hal has remembered the incident with the bedrooms. Here, out of context, she seems no longer a lofty movie star and more like any young, arrogant nineteen-year-old. And he finds that the alcohol has loosened his tongue. 'I do think that you are spoiled, though.'

'Excuse me?' But she has heard him. Something flashes across her expression – but it is not outrage, as might be expected, but something else, almost like excitement.

'You think that I am *spoiled*.' She speaks slowly, as though trying the words out for size. 'You know . . . no one ever say that to me before.'

'They probably didn't dare to.'

She considers this. 'No, perhaps that is true. I find it . . . I find it amusing.'

'Why's that?'

'Do you know how hard I have worked to get here?'

'No doubt extremely hard.'

But she is not finished. 'Yes, but that is only something you are saying, to placate me. I do not think you understand the whole thing. I am not like . . .' she gestures, dismissively, 'oh, your Signora Truss, married to a rich husband who will provide for her. I could have that – but I do not need it . . . or want it. When I might have needed it, there was no chance. Shall I tell you a story?'

He seems to have little choice in the matter. 'All right.'

She takes a delicate sip of her spumante. And then she begins.

'There were ten children in my family. My mother was a shell of a woman: old before her time. You have never seen such an ancient-looking thirty-year-old. But that is what it does to you, that sort of life: to have a new baby every year and to care for the others at the same time. My father left her, in the end, because she grew so tired and ugly. She was like . . . an old husk of wheat, when the goodness has been removed and left is the dry part – not good for nothing. Once upon a time she was beautiful, I think – maybe almost as beautiful as me . . . though her figure was never so good, and her nose was not such a good shape as mine.

'The war nearly was the end of her. We were put in a camp – where my littlest brother died . . . though he was always sickly, so perhaps he would have died anyway.' She says it almost matter-of-factly, as though she is talking of someone she hardly knew.

'Why were you put there?'

'We were Romani. I *am* Romani – it is where I get this face.' She lifts her chin. 'Romani women are the most beautiful. But they don't like me to talk of my background. It is bad for my image.

'Once the war ended it was better – we could make our living once more. And the tourists began to return. We lived near the city of Firenze, a beautiful place – but to us that didn't mean very much. It was simply where we worked, in the shadow of the Duomo – you know it? – helping my mother.

'When we grew old enough, you see, we could be useful to her. We stop being like little maggots, hanging off her, asking for feeding. We were a team: my three older brothers, my sister and I. When the piazza was full of people it was easy to move amongst them and take things from them: wallets, bags, cameras, watches. We did this so we could eat, not because we were greedy.' She gives a quick, sly grin. 'But I kept a pretty thing for myself sometimes: a watch, a bracelet.

'My mother felt badly about letting us do it. She went to her grave feeling badly about it. But she have no choice.

'Then I grow older, and I turn from being a little toothpick into someone who men stop and stare at. It was even easier, then. I, you know . . . open my blouse a little, bat my eyes like this . . . and while they were looking, looking,' she gives a slack-jawed impression, 'one of my brothers would sneak up behind him like a monkey and fish everything from his pockets.

'One day, there was a man who *kept* looking. Normally, they would stop – they'd get embarrassed, or their wives would appear. But this one . . . he would not stop. I begin to have fear, because I thought that he could be a policeman – something like that – trying to catch me out. And then he start walking over to me. I panic, and turn to walk away. He follow me, up towards the *mercato* and when I went faster he come after me faster, too. By the time I got to the market I was nearly running, but my shoes were poor and in the end he caught me.

'I could tell that he was an American, but he spoke Italian all right. "I've let your brother – your boyfriend, your pimp – whoever he is . . . take my wallet, my camera and God knows what else. The only thing he hasn't taken is my goddamned watch – do you know why?" I said that I didn't. "Because I don't wear one." Then he said that the least I could do, after his trouble, was to come and have a drink with him.'

She looks at Hal, frankly, and says – without any apparent embarrassment, 'I decide that I will at least go with him, and see what sort of hotel it was. I wanted to know how much money a man like that might have. And I was curious . . . I had only ever seen hotels from the outside, you know. I wanted to see what one might be like inside.'

'And what was it like?'

'To me then it was a palace. Now, of course, I know that it was not of the best sort. But I had nothing to compare it with, you know?'

Hal nods.

'He tell me that he wants to take my photograph. He thinks I have a certain "look", he says . . . the quint . . . the quinta-something.'

'Quintessential?'

'Yes . . . yes, the quintosensual Italian goddess. I do not tell him then – or ever – that I am Roma. I think that might spoil his idea of me. Anyway, he tell me that he work for a new business, exporting olive oil to the United States, and they need a "face". He can't promise anything, but he will take some photos and send them off, and we will see what happen.'

'So you let him take the photos?'

Giulietta raises her eyebrows, as though she cannot believe the stupidity of the question. 'Yes – of course. I was a little rat, running around stealing crumbs in the Piazza del Duomo. Anything would have been better than that.'

'What were they like?'

'Terrible. I do not want to talk about that part – it is too ugly. But I think of it now as like . . . you know how some monks wear shirts of hair, or starve themselves, in order to become holy? I think of it like that. That man, who probably like to think he "made me". He want to marry me, you know. I laughed in his face. I left him far far below me, looking for his next prey.'

She flicks the ash from her cigarette, and Hal has to quickly slide a foot out of the way to avoid it falling on his shoe. She takes a long, pensive drag upon it and as she does, lost – apparently – in the memory of the inauspicious start to her career, Hal studies her face. Some of her features, on their own, taken out of context, veer towards ugliness. The nose is a little too long, the eyebrows thick and dark – almost mannish.

And yet there is something magnificent in these peculiarities, in their audacity. If one had the talent, Hal thinks, it is the sort of face that could be drawn with a thick stub of charcoal in a few seconds, and the essential character of it would be immediately recognizable.

Giulietta looks up at him, catches him watching her, and blows a thin stream of smoke into his face. He coughs and looks away. The same sort of reckoning could be applied to her personality too, he thinks: she is at once repugnant and strangely alluring.

'Well,' she says. 'You see now why I laugh at you when you call me spoiled?'

'I suppose so.'

She draws on her cigarette, eyes narrowed. 'You remember, when you asked me, how it feel, to be called "Italy's finest export"?'

'Yes.'

'I will tell you truly. I feel pleased, and angry, all at the same time. But most of all, I feel triumphant. And you know why?'

'Why?'

'Because at one time, they told my family: "In this country, you don't belong. You are less than us, you are low-down beings." And now, when they say to me, "Oh, signora, you are perfect, you are all that is good about this country," I want to celebrate, and punch the air, and sometimes . . . sometimes, I want to spit in their faces.'

So war is in her story too. And while the rest of us, thinks Hal, are doing a passable job of simply surviving, she has forged something from it, has made it a part of her success. This is not to be scorned.

After letting this sink in, she says, 'You understand why I

don't like you telling me what to say, for your article? It is because I am not *una burratina* – a puppet – you know? But Mrs Truss, she is such a puppet.'

'No,' Hal says, quickly, almost instinctively. 'She isn't. You don't know anything of it.'

There is something cruel in her smile now. 'You try to protect her.' She bites her lip. 'A little like,' she pauses, as though searching for the perfect word, '. . . a son.'

'She is only a few years older—' he says, and then stops himself.

'Only a few years?' she raises her eyebrows. 'I would have thought more.'

For a few moments they sit in silence. And then Hal feels a warm pressure on the bare skin of his ankle. He glances down and sees her small, tanned foot caressing him. The toenails are painted a dark, glossy red. His first reaction is involuntary – a leap of uncomplicated desire. But almost as quickly it is quashed by the sense that he is committing some betrayal. He knows that it is absurd but the feeling remains, all the same. He extricates his leg.

'You should come to my room,' she says, in murmured Italian now, 'after supper. I'd like to practise my English further with you.'

It is a terrible line, but perhaps such an approach to seduction is effective if one is a goddess of the silver screen.

'Ah,' he says. 'Thank you, but no.'

She frowns – not so much with annoyance, more as though his response makes no sense to her.

What is wrong with him? One of the 'most desirable women in the world today' – according to *Life* magazine – is making herself available to him, and yet he wants nothing of it. He is a single man, with no tie to another soul.

Giulietta flings her cigarette into the shrubbery, where it smokes ominously for a few seconds before dying out. She stands, and, with a toss of her dark head that says she refuses to waste another second on such a hopeless case, she takes her leave of him. Hal pours the remainder of the bottle into his glass, and, like a man taking his medicine, knocks it back in a single gulp.

29

Her

The peculiar intimacy of that night in Rome. For a year, I have not let myself think about it. And the tenderness. I had not known it could be like that, not with a stranger. No, it was something more than that. I had not known it could be like that with anyone.

1939

My husband has a house in a place called Southampton, and a yacht moored there. I have never properly looked at the sea before. In Spain, we lived in the heart of the country, surrounded by dry land for miles around. And I saw it on our journey to America, of course, but only as a uniform blue void, miles below. Now, the broad sweep of the Atlantic Ocean terrifies and fascinates me. All I can see is blue – and it emphasizes how far I have come from my old country, from my previous life.

I decide that if I learn to swim my fear of it might be managed. I will have some measure of control over it. He doesn't like the idea of it, exactly – I can tell. He tells me that there are dangerous currents. But I persuade him. I tell him that the prospect of going sailing on his yacht – which he wants me to do – will terrify me until I know I could save myself if I fall in.

I teach myself. He offered to find me a tutor – as he has for language and elocution – but I want to do it on my own. I want it to be something that is mine alone. After a few weeks I can manage a clumsy crawl. Soon I am addicted. When I am in the water I feel powerful. And if I force my muscles to work hard enough I discover I can almost empty my mind of the grief and the guilt that remain still tied to me like my own shadow. Perhaps, one day, I will be able to outswim them.

My husband is proud of his yacht. I know nothing about boats, but even I know that she is beautiful. I suppose that I should say 'our' yacht, but that wouldn't feel right. I don't yet know that anything here quite belongs to me, not even the lace underwear I wear.

The first time he takes me out on her, he tells me the story of how she came to be his. 'I bought her in 1930. You could say rescued her, to be more accurate. She was ready for the seabed when I first saw her.'

'Why?' I ask.

'Well, it's a funny story. Her previous owner had her built in 1927. Absolutely no expense spared, you understand – his only stipulation was that she would be the most beautiful boat in any harbour she might grace with her presence. She was his pride and joy.'

'I can imagine,' I say.

'Only this fellow made some unwise decisions, bad moves – whatever you'd like to call it. Anyhow, he ended up losing everything in the Crash, like so many others. Even his wife, by all accounts. She went and married some other fellow. So he rigged up this boat and sailed out to sea. No one else on board. It isn't, I'm sure you can appreciate, the sort of yacht one man alone can handle.'

'No.'

'So he would have come to a sticky pass, in the end, as it was. But he shot himself, first, once he'd got a way out. And then it all went to hell, of course. The boat ended up wrecked a little way down the coast. She was almost unsalvageable, and I think many thought I was mad when I said I wanted to buy her. I rather liked the thought of it – the poetic justice of it, if you like. He lost everything as I was making my fortune.'

He wasn't always wealthy. I know a little about what it is that he does. His work is, he tells me, in seeing opportunities where no one else would think to look.

Whichever side loses the war that has begun in Europe, he says, there will be opportunity. One of his specialisms is in buying ruins – concerns that have failed, or been run into the ground – and transforming them into something new. A little like his yacht, I suppose.

Not long ago, I had an unpleasant experience at a gala with a man who had had far too much to drink. I was coming back from the powder room, looking for my husband in the crowd.

'Tell me,' the man said, sliding himself in front of me, and looking me up and down. His breath smelt of alcohol. 'How does he do it?'

'Excuse me?'

'He gets everything, doesn't he? How does a nobody like him end up with so much?'

'I don't know what you mean.'

'Ha! Oh, you don't, do you? I suppose you'll be telling me you know nothing about Spain, either.'

It caught me off guard. 'What?'

'Well, we all know he'd made a good haul before then – picking over the scraps of '29, when every decent fellow was losing all he had. While my father was losing most of my inheritance. But he came back from Spain rich as Croesus.'

'My husband,' I said, with the tremor of my anger in my voice, 'was in Spain to fight for a cause he believed in.'

'Fight for a cause . . .' he drew the words out, making them ridiculous. 'Well, that's a new way of putting it. I suppose it fits, in a way.' He shook his head at me, almost pityingly. 'But you don't know anything, do you?'

I think he wanted me to ask him what he meant by this. I refused to give him that pleasure. Besides, I did not – do not – want to know.

I never mentioned it to my husband. I convinced myself that it was too absurd to be worth repeating. And yet, really, it was that it had stirred up in me some unnamed fear, which I carry with me still. It is a thread I don't want to risk pulling.

There is a couple who come out on the yacht with us sometimes, and often to supper. Randolph and Gloria Standish. I'm not sure about the husband. But I like her. She seems more straightforward than any of the other wives I have met, unafraid to speak her mind.

One evening, when we have all had too much to drink,

and whilst the men are down on the jetty smoking cigars, Gloria tells me about her husband's infidelity.

'Can I be absolutely honest?'

'Of course.'

'Part of me prefers it when he has some other piece on the side. He bothers me less. I certainly get a great deal more beauty sleep. Men, and their appetites.'

I am a little taken back by her confession, but also encouraged by it to make one of my own. 'My husband doesn't touch me.'

'Lucky you.'

'No,' I say. 'I mean never. He never has.'

Her eyebrows go up. 'Oh.'

'I was wondering . . . well— I wondered if he might be,' I lower my voice, aware this is something more scandalous than anything we have discussed so far, and also something about which I know little, 'not interested, in that regard.'

But she is shaking her head, and looking at me, I think, almost pityingly. 'Oh my dear, no, that isn't right at all.'

'I know I shouldn't say it, but—'

'No, I mean it *really* isn't right. If you must know, he and I had a fling – aeons ago, long before he met you. And I can tell you that he isn't one of those.'

I plan a confrontation of sorts. A seduction might be a more appropriate word, but I have so little idea of what I am doing that it hardly merits the word. He has been away on business for several days upstate. On the afternoon he is due to return, I take a long bath in the scented oil, which I never normally use, finding its scent too much. I dress myself in the cobweb-fine lace and silks. I look in the mirror. Do I have it, that elusive, specific appeal that Gloria Standish undoubtedly does? I'm not sure.

I try to arrange myself in a way that I presume is seductive, but I am flustered, my heartbeat thudding through me. I do not know why I am so afraid. Perhaps it is the fact that for the first time in a long while, I am attempting something that hasn't been suggested for me. I listen to him opening doors, no doubt wondering where I am. He says my name, and then again, a little louder. He would never shout, my husband – it would be too undignified. I could call to him but it would ruin the surprise, so I remain quiet, hardly breathing. Finally, the bedroom door opens, and he stands in the frame, looking in. I watch his face.

'What are you doing?'

Suddenly I feel cold. I could reach for the blanket at the end of the bed, but this would involve exposing myself further.

'I thought . . .' I say, 'I thought I would surprise you.'

He steps closer to the bed, but I realize his eyes are cast away from me now, as though he can't bear the sight of me like this.

He cuts me off. 'Please, get up. Go and put some clothes on. This,' he gestures in my direction, 'is not who you are.'

Only now do I begin to understand. This is not the part he has scripted for me. I am his picturesque companion at dinners and social functions, outfitted in the latest fashions. I am virginal, pure.

I slink from the room like a criminal.

But later, he comes to my room. He doesn't turn on the light. The cover is pulled back, and immediately he is pushing up the silk of my nightgown. I do not know what to expect, but I have always assumed that there must be pleasure in it.

Otherwise why would the Standishes go about conducting their various affairs? But apparently there isn't time for that. And all the time, while I press my face into the pillow, he hisses words in my ear – words I thought men only used for women they detested.

Afterwards, he speaks into my hair, his voice gentle. 'I'm sorry,' he says. 'Forgive me. You are so good, and so young. I don't know what came over me.'

In the morning, it is as though it never happened. He is if anything more attentive. Over breakfast, he suggests we take a trip together. Where would I like to go? Have I ever been skiing? No? He will take me skiing then: we could go to the Colorado mountains. I will love it.

I eat my eggs, and sip my coffee. This is the bargain that I have made. I understand now.

30

In the hall outside, an old clock strikes one o'clock. Hal is lying in bed, turning the compass over in his palm. He has become used to the particular weight and feel of it in his hand. Of late, he has even begun to carry it with him in the pocket of his trousers. Even as it unsettles him, he feels now a connection with it that he wouldn't be able, even if he tried, to put into words. At some point, he will have to give it back to the Contessa. The idea fills him with a powerful regret.

As for the journal . . . he is aware that there are only a few pages of writing left. He is reading these last few more slowly. He can't decide if this is because he wishes to eke them out, because then this peculiar journey will be finished, or because he is apprehensive of what they will contain.

 A MONTH HAS passed, and the painting is still not finished. He is beginning to grow impatient. There is a particular expanse of wall that he knows will be perfect for it. The Flemish artist suggests that if he were to come and work on it every day – rather than a couple of times a week – the wait could be shortened. The captain agrees. Often, when he comes to visit Luna, he finds the painter just leaving – having spent a long morning at work on the piece. He has the chaotic look peculiar to men of his ilk, the captain thinks: his hair and clothes in disarray, his face flushed with the exertion of his craft.

Several times, he has asked to see the painting. But the painter refuses. 'It might affect the rest of the work,' he says. 'I must be allowed to create without the weight of another's opinion informing me of how to proceed.'

The captain would like to say that, as he is the one paying for the painting, it perhaps shouldn't matter if his opinion informs it. But he knows little of the artistic process, and doesn't want to jeopardize it. He must continue, instead, to be content with looking at the subject herself in the snatched time permitted between sittings for the portrait and the hours she spends resting in her chamber.

Finally, the artist informs the captain, the unveiling is ready to occur. The painting is finished. The captain is almost beside himself with excitement. He has already instructed a master framer to get ready a gilt frame for the dimensions of the canvas: it will be on his wall in a matter of days. He enters the salon where the painter and Luna wait for him.

He waits with breath held as the artist draws back the curtain of material shielding the image from view. The scent of the oil – rich, resinous – reaches him before the painting is exposed, and he closes his eyes to better appreciate it.

When he opens his eyes, it is before him. There she is in all her loveliness – as lovely, if not more so, as the woman who sits beside the canvas. It is a work of brilliance: some source of light appearing to shine from within it, illuminating the bones of the face, the whites of the eyes, casting the shadow of long dark lashes upon her cheeks.

But something is wrong. He cannot understand it at first. It is not the image itself, so much as the *feeling* that emanates from it. Confused, he glances back at the painter and the girl, just in time to see a look, quick as a shift of the light, pass between them. And in that look is all the answer he needs.

He lunges for the girl. '*Puttana!*' His hands find her upper arms, he drags her from the seat onto the floor.

The painter grapples with him, but the man is slight, small-boned, and shaken off easily.

'Is it true?' he shouts at the girl. 'You would let him seduce you, and not me?'

She will not answer him, even as his fingers dig into the flesh of her upper arms.

There is a growl, and then the beast of a dog is hurtling toward him, teeth bared. The weight of it knocks him to his feet, and its claws rip quickly through the silk of his shirt, scouring the tender skin beneath. The creature's breath, hot and foul, is in his nostrils. The thing will consume him, he thinks – and he shrieks in fear and pain. There is a pause, long enough for the dog to reveal its rows of crooked teeth. And then it is clambering off him, with evident reluctance, and trotting to its mistress' heels. She has called it off.

He has never known such humiliation, and such rage. She has betrayed him, utterly. She needs to be taught a lesson that she will not forget. There is only one place he can think of going.

'Father,' he tells the priest. 'I have been bewitched. I am ashamed to say it, but I have allowed myself to be seduced by one who follows the way of Diana.'

The whole story is told. The first encounter, the storms, the remedies – her strange bond with the dog.

The priest listens, intent. And then he speaks. 'My son. We live now in a more enlightened age. At least in the Republic of Genoa. We are no longer in the practice of rounding such women up and murdering them. Of course, there are people who choose to take matters into their own hands. And I would not necessarily judge them. There are villages where whole crops have failed because of the work of such women, where all the infants have sickened and died. But the Church cannot sanction such extreme measures. My advice would be to distance yourself as far from her as possible.'

'I can't.'

'Excuse me?' The priest frowns. 'She is keeping you imprisoned in some way? But you are free to visit me here.'

'I mean that I can't leave her. This is what I mean when I say that she has bewitched me.'

'Ah,' the priest says, with something almost like a smile. 'But this sort of attachment can occur without the work of witchcraft. We call it, then, an infatuation.'

'Father. I can't sleep. I can't think of anything else.'

The priest steeples his hands. 'My advice, my son, would be to take yourself away from the problem. Your mother's family has lodgings near the hamlet of Cervo, I think?'

The captain nods.

'Go there. Eat good food, drink wine, feel the sun on your face, swim in the sea. I know the priest there. I will send a letter with you, so that he may understand your predicament, and guide you.'

The captain leaves strict instructions with the housekeeper not to allow the girl to go anywhere unchaperoned. As an afterthought, he goes, too, to the studio of the painter.

'I want you to make my likeness too.' He names a sum.

'Of course. Shall I come to your house tomorrow, to begin?'

'No. You are to come with me to my residence near Cervo.'

He sees the man's hesitation: and in this is all the proof he would need, if he did not have it already. For a poor painter to be reluctant to take such a lucrative commission shows the tie upon the man must be strong indeed. But, in the end, the money is enough: the man accedes.

The weather is fine in Cervo. But the captain can no longer appreciate the warmth of the sun on his skin: he feels cold, all the time. His nights are sleepless, and his appetite does not return. His days are spent sitting for the painter, and visiting the priest in his coral church, praying only half-heartedly for freedom from her. For this is perhaps the most insidious effect of the sickness: he does not truly want to be rid of it.

As the painter works, the captain looks at him, trying to decide what it is that has drawn her affection while he himself has failed. He is hardly a majestic example of manliness, after all. His limbs are thin, his features somewhat crooked. His manner is weak, the captain thinks, scornfully, almost timid. It is ridiculous. He would want his rival to be a worthy match for himself, at least. One day, he can stand it no longer.

'What is it,' he asks the man, through his teeth, 'what is it that a puny, womanly creature such as yourself can offer a woman? Explain it to me.'

The painter looks at him, stunned. 'I don't understand your meaning, sire.'

'Oh, I think that you understand me well enough.'

'I'm sorry, sire, but —'

'I mean that I am trying to understand why that whore would pick a rodent like you over me.'

Perhaps it is his use of 'whore' that does it. A change comes over the other man. He looks, suddenly, a little taller, and his eyes gleam. All of a sudden he seems to have forgotten that he is in the captain's pay. 'Because,' he says, 'you don't understand anything of her. Because you have tried to own her, and you can't own another human being – least of all a woman like her. You can only love her.'

Cervo. The name, when he sees it on the page, gives a thrill. Hal is certain that the town had not been on the Contessa's original itinerary. And yet, by chance, he happened to visit the place today. He recognizes the description of the coral-hued church. He has spent the day, quite literally, in the other man's footsteps. Ridiculous, to suppose it anything other than coincidence. And yet would it be such a step to imagine that he is being in some way influenced? He has already accepted another impossible thing: the fact that a compass, five centuries old, is moving as though driven by some internal mechanism.

He puts it down. He needs fresh air. Another walk outside. And . . . yes, he will go down to the swimming pool again, to make sure.

When he steps outside the strange song of the frogs fills the air again. He climbs the steps leading down towards the pool, so that he can just make out the dark rectangle of water.

The water looks silver from this angle; like liquid mercury. To swim in it, it seems, would transform one. He finds himself beginning to shrug off his clothes, stripping down to his briefs. He is tempted to take off even these; but the possibility of someone else being awake too stops him. The cool night air surrounds him. Now he begins to climb down into the colder embrace of the water, exhaling quickly as it reaches his thighs, his waistband, his chest. He turns onto his back, and pushes away from the edge, the breath tight in his chest. When he glances down at himself his submerged limbs appear pale and unfamiliar, as though they do not quite belong to him. Finally, with an effort of will, he dunks his head and surfaces filled with a strange euphoria. He swims several lengths, up and down. He is beginning to enjoy himself: there is something transgressive about it, this swimming through silver darkness while the rest of the world sleeps.

He briefly thinks that he hears his name called. But then he decides that it must be the strange musical effect of the water in his ears. He ploughs on, making swimmer's turns at the ends, tucking his body around itself – movements not performed since school, and yet sewn forever into the fabric of him. He is cutting through the water now rather than tussling with it. His body is a graceful, efficient machine. The breath is singing through him. Again, he thinks he hears his name. Again, he decides it is some strange distortion of the wind and water. He swims on. Finally, he surfaces for air. And recoils in surprise when he sees the figure at the end of the pool. He blinks furiously. It is her.

She is definitely awake. They watch each other like two animals, wary, alert. Neither of them speak. Keeping her eyes on his she takes the hem of her nightshirt and in one fluid motion lifts it over her head. He stares. He never saw her like this on that night in Rome: it had been too hot, close, fast. Still, she keeps her gaze fixed on him. She makes no effort to cover herself – and this is the bravery of her, he thinks, her ability to overcome her natural reserve. She is far braver than him. She descends into the water. He moves toward her, and holds out his arms. She steps into them.

Now, suddenly, it is hot, close, fast – far more so than before. More of everything than before. She is biting the skin of his shoulder, her legs are wrapped about his back, and at the centre of everything a pleasure so intense that it is almost agony.

Afterwards, they remain together for several minutes at the corner of the pool. Neither of them speaks. He is amazed by what has occurred. He strokes her wet hair with his hand, feels her ribcage rise and fall against him with her breathing. His mouth is against her neck beneath her ear, where the pulse beats fast beneath the skin.

Later, they lie in his bed, the sheets tangled about them. This time it is slower, more controlled. Until she pushes him over, gently, so that she can move on top of him, her legs tight about him. Both of them, then, make more noise than they should.

Afterwards, in a kind of wonder, he says without thinking: 'Where did you learn to do that?' And then the horror of it grips him. He feels repelled by the spectre he has allowed into the room.

31

Her

I have impeccable taste, as our acquaintances say. I know which white burgundy to serve with a lobster dish, which is the best table at Le Pavillon, what to order there. We host dinners at the apartment in New York, at the house in Southampton. Every so often, I will catch sight of myself reflected in the mirror at some event and I will think: she looks like one of them.

Because there are two women. There is Stella and there is Estrella. I am aware of how this sounds: a little like madness. I am not mad. We all have different selves, I think, that we become, or promote, depending on the company. The difference with me is that in *all* company – and especially with my husband – I am Stella now. Stella, who wears designs by Balmain and Jacques Fath, who has learned to smoke cigarettes from a silver holder, and to drink champagne with the glass cradled just so. Who has almost all but covered up her history with fluency in this new life. I enjoy being her. It is only when I am alone that I remember Estrella, the child–woman who tried, and failed, to be a mother to Papa and Tino, to keep them safe. Estrella, who had to make decisions, who chose wrong. I am only her when I sleep. I return to that time when I lost everything – when I lost myself, too, and I wake breathing hard, cold with sweat.

At other times I lie in bed awake, and worries that in the day are manageable become looming fears. I don't know my husband at all, I think. Worse, still, I don't know myself. I think: Estrella is slipping from me, gradually – but Stella is merely a shell, all surface. Love, once, made me strong. Without it, I am weak. Once, my responsibility was to care for another human being, to make choices that might – that did – mean the difference between life and death. Now my sole responsibility is to present myself well. I don't even know which are my opinions any more, and which are ventriloquized from those about me. It would be better, I think, to be eking out a penniless existence in Madrid, than to be living this false one. It would be better to be one of those women I glimpsed in the hotel bar.

In the morning, I am always better able to reason. Back in Madrid, I remind myself, poverty would have been the best possible outcome. As Papa's daughter, I might by now be imprisoned, or dead. Spain could not be a home for me. And the whole of Europe is ablaze with war.

Of course I know my husband. I certainly know him as well as – if not better than – the wives of my acquaintance know theirs. I know his thoughts on opera (Wagner, not

Verdi), on the way Southampton society is changing (not for the better). I know what champagne he likes (Tattinger). I know his thoughts on Harry Truman. I know, yes – *say it* – what he likes in bed. Anyway, how well can anyone know another person, even the one they live with? He is attentive, he is generous – extravagantly so. Though it is perhaps shameful to admit it, I like being looked after. I like being treated like something precious. Wouldn't you?

Is this not enough? Even if it were not – or at least not enough for happiness – I have no other option. I find that I must always return to that. I don't think I could get back to Estrella now, even if I knew for certain that I wanted to. Too much has happened in between. Sharp edges have been worn into yielding softness. I am pliable as clay. This life is, on the whole, extremely easy: as easy, as reading from a script. Being her was a constant struggle. It meant caring too much.

Sometimes, for this reason, I think it is for the best that we don't have children, though I know that this is a source of disappointment for him. He arranged for me to see a doctor about it, but the results came back normal. He doesn't mention it again for some time after that.

But a few months after the visit to the specialist there is an incident. I know then that he has not stopped thinking about it. We have been intimate, and I am back in my bathroom, getting ready for bed.

'Spit it out.' He has appeared, suddenly, behind me in the mirror.

I am so surprised that the opposite happens: I swallow it. He moves towards me. I have seen the look on his face before, in relation to other people – staff, business associates who cross him. Never with me, though.

And suddenly, he has me by the throat, and I feel myself being bent over the sink.

'Spit it out,' he says, again.

I try to speak, but his hand is so tight about my throat that I can't do it. And then he has released me, and I am retching into the basin.

'What was it?' he says. 'What did you just take?'

I pick up the glass bottle, and show him the label. 'The doctor prescribed them – your doctor – to help me sleep. To stop the sleepwalking.'

His face changes. And then he has dropped to the ground and put his hands around my waist, like a supplicant.

'Forgive me,' he says. 'I shouldn't have doubted you. I know you wouldn't deceive me.'

I find myself on the stretch of Fourth Avenue between Astor Place and Union Square that they call 'Book Row'. I believe that any volume that you might care to find could be sourced here, if you looked hard enough. My husband can't understand why I don't buy books new. I think it is the idea of the lives they have lived before coming into my hands. The pages smell of these past lives. The covers are creased, soft as skin. Sometimes I find the mark of a pencil – occasionally a name – and there is a strange excitement in it.

Usually I only shop at the front of the store, among the English-language novels. I'm not sure what's different, today, but I find myself drifting to the other end of the shop where there are several untidy shelves of books I have never really looked at before. If you look carefully, the bookseller – an elderly man who I have never heard speak a single word (perhaps he can't) – has inscribed markers in the wood of the shelves. These are the foreign language books. A surprising number of languages are represented here: evidence of the number of nationalities crowded together onto this small island. I move along the shelves. French. German. Spanish. I stop. I am suddenly aware of my heart beating in my chest. It seems so loud in this quiet space that I'm certain the elderly man must be able to hear it. I'm not sure why I'm looking here, or what for. No: that isn't quite true.

I find various editions of Cervantes' plays. A collection of poetry by Lorca. And suddenly, there it is: his name. Papa. My own name: the one lost when I married. My hand trembles as I ease it from the grip of the other volumes. Then I see something odd. The title is wrong. His book is called *La Lucha – The Struggle*. This is *La Pelea – The Fight*. A small but definite difference. I pick it up, looking behind me guiltily, to see if I am being observed. I am not. I find the description of its contents, and discover the thing I suspected, but did not believe until I see it here, in print.

It is my father's second book; the one that was never published. The war, and his death, came before it could even be sent to the publishers.

My mind races through several impossible conclusions. And then, rifling through the pages at the front, I see: *Foreword by Salvador Ruiz.*

'My brother,' I read, 'was a great mind taken from us far too early. He had given a copy of the book to me just before he died in the struggle he wrote of, the fight of a liberal man against Fascism. I was fortunate enough to be able to escape Madrid following the bombing of my house there – though I left with a heavy heart. My exile, however, away from the suppression of free speech that still exists in Spain, has allowed me to ensure that this great work finds a readership at last.'

It is dated: 1945. University of Lausanne Press. There is a little about him, too. He has retired to a village in the Swiss Alps, where he is writing a book of his own.

I make my way back to the apartment with the book pressed to my chest. Uncle Salvador is alive. I even know where he lives. I could write to him at the university.

But back in the apartment, I find that every attempt feels wrong. I find myself asking why he deserted me, and Tino. But this is the wrong tone to take, too hectoring, destructive. Perhaps I should describe what happened to me. But it all begins with Tino. I cannot write about him. I can't find the words, or even commit his name to paper. Then I find myself trying to explain the person I am now, the life I live now and realize I am ashamed. My uncle, like my father, was a man who shunned ostentation, or superficiality. He would not recognize the woman I have become. I can't do it. I have gone too far, changed too much. He is a part of my former existence. I crush the paper into a ball.

I tell Hal of my discovery.

'He doesn't know that you're alive?'

'No. He left me in Spain. He didn't wait to find out if we were alive then.' I see his expression. 'You think I should have contacted him.'

'I don't know,' he says, carefully, 'I just think that he might have spent his life feeling guilty about having left, before he could make sure that you were safe. He might have made the decision in a moment of fear, and spent the rest of his life regretting it.'

'It isn't the only reason, though. He wouldn't recognize her – the person I was – in who I am now.'

He reaches for her, with the hesitancy, the strange shyness, that comes to them both in the moments where they aren't driven by desire. 'I didn't know you, then,' he says, 'but I recognize her.'

32

At breakfast the next morning the weather seems to have forgotten itself, and launched into summer. Already, it is too hot to be sitting in full sun. Aubrey has covered himself with lotion that has made him paler than ever, and has found the deepest possible patch of shade, beneath a parasol. Against the colour that surrounds him, he looks as though he has been rendered in negative.

Hal glances at Stella as little as possible. Merely to look for too long, he senses, would be to give all away. She must be playing the same game, for throughout the meal her face is turned resolutely seawards.

'Well,' the Contessa says, 'I think we must find a way to cool down. This is a day to be out on the water.' As Hal is wondering if she intends them all to clamber into the tiny, unstable tender of the yacht, she turns to the Conte. 'What do you think? Time to give the old lady an outing?'

*

This old lady is a speedboat. Despite her great age she is as beautiful, perhaps more so, than the day she was handmade from caramel-coloured teak. On her boards: a pair of matching water-skis shaped like butter-knives.

'Have you ever done it?' The Contessa turns to Hal.

'No,' he says. 'I'm not sure I fancy my chances. Though I have skied before – badly. Will you try?'

'Alas no, my surgeon has forbidden me. I used to be very, very good,' she says, 'I am not embarrassed to say so. I could balance on the one ski only. Those days are gone now. But it gives me almost as much pleasure to see others do it.'

And Hal can see her, almost, as she would have been: sapling-lithe, cutting a swathe.

They move out toward the horizon at an astonishing speed. Hal grips the rail and feels his teeth clatter together as they crest a wave, leaping unexpectedly into space. Earl Morgan lets out a whoop of exhilaration, and when Hal looks at him his eyes seem, momentarily, to have lost their dazed look. The breeze created by their movement is instantly cooling, and Hal feels the skin beneath his shirt prickle. Every so often, the contact with a larger wave sends a fine spray arching over them.

They reach a distance from the shore that the Contessa is happy with, and the Conte idles the engine. Immediately the warmth returns. The shoreline shimmers in the heat, suddenly remote.

'Well,' the Contessa turns to them. 'Who will go first?'

There is a nervous silence. Then Stella says, 'I will.' She stands, and shrugs off her shirt and shorts to reveal her black bathing suit. It is the one she wore on that first day, when he spotted her on the jetty. He tries harder than ever not to look. The memories of the previous evening crowd in upon him now, demanding attention.

The Contessa helps her fit her feet into the rubber. Then she is sliding into the water, gripping the tow rope. Slowly, the Conte manoeuvres the boat away from her until the tow rope has fully unfurled. Now Hal looks. And suddenly she appears very small, with the vastness of the ocean surrounding her. It is too familiar. The tightening of fear in his chest is involuntary. He ignores it.

Stella raises her thumb to the Contessa's shouted enquiry. Then the engine thrums, and the line tugs taut. There is no way that Hal can look away now. He feels that if he did so, even for a second, she might disappear from view. He is gripping the metal rail of the boat so tightly he is surprised it doesn't come away in his hand. On the first few tries her balance falters almost instantly, and she collapses back into the water. Hal finds himself hoping that she will call it a day. But every time, she nods her head: yes, she wants to go again. Finally, the miracle happens. She lifts out of the water and stands, and remains standing, the muscles in her legs taut, her arms straight out in front.

'Bravo,' the Contessa shouts, delighted.

Hal is no longer watching her in fear, but awe. She is magnificent to him. How could he ever have thought her weak? She doesn't fall again. Eventually, when they have made several circuits and figures of eight with her following, poised as a ballet dancer, she makes the sign for them to stop, and drops gracefully back into the water. When they pull her in, she is laughing, and Hal feels again that tightness in his lungs, looking at her, though it has a different cause this time.

'Well,' Aubrey says, 'that's done it for the rest of us. How can we have a hope after that?'

*

Back at the castle, the rest of the day stretches before him. Will it be the same? They seem to have moved further apart than before any of it happened. It is hard to believe now in the intimacy of the night, in the confidences she made to him.

But later, in bed, it is simple again. They might have known one another for centuries. When they are together like this they fit so perfectly that their two bodies might be the archetypes from which all others are but imperfect iterations.

It is only afterwards, with the clumsiness and misunderstanding of speech, that the distance grows once more. He feels a kind of hopelessness. They are too polite, too cautious, feinting towards one another. Until she turns onto her side, and says, 'Tell me about your writing.'

'I don't know . . .'

'I've told you everything. And I know almost nothing about you, in return. You told me you stopped after your friend died.'

'Yes.'

'Why?'

He knows that he doesn't have to tell her; that he has a choice. It is the thing that he could not tell Suze, the thing that she refused to hear. He could choose not to tell Stella now, and continue just the same. Not quite the same, perhaps, because the unspoken thing would force yet more distance between them.

He has to tell, he understands this. She has to know. 'It was my fault.'

She makes no answer. It is a relief: if she were to interrupt him now he might never find the courage to keep talking.

'We were up in the Arctic, above Norway. The ship was covered in ice. I'd been tasked with clearing some of it off the main deck – me, and a few other men. Morris was one of them.

'I saw it coming before anyone else. This wave was huge,

much bigger than the ones before it. Something had happened to my brain. I can't explain it, but it was so cold. It was as though my thoughts were slowed down. I didn't say anything until it was too late. Morris and I – we were right next to the rail. It swept us off our feet and over the side.'

The confusion of seeing only water where before there had been solid metal. How it had seized the breath from him. Unbelievable cold – though it didn't feel like cold so much as the opposite, like a searing heat. He couldn't get his breath back, no matter how hard his mouth and lungs worked. The ship, suddenly, seemed an Everest of steel, sheering unscalable out of the water. A row of tiny heads had appeared above the rail. Probably they were shouting, but he couldn't hear anything except for the wheeze of his own tortured breathing.

He had heard a shout – or not so much a shout, more a cry, like that of an animal in pain. He turned and saw Morris, some ten yards or so further away, fighting to stay afloat. Really struggling.

He managed to pant out the words. 'Are-you-all-right?'

And the answer had come back in agonized gasps: 'I-think-my-leg's-bro-ken.'

The ship wouldn't turn, he knew this. They couldn't: they were in convoy. Such things went to the highest level; a misstep could endanger the entire fleet. They were the last ship in the formation, too. There was nothing coming for them.

It came to him. They would die here, surrounded by miles of frozen emptiness. Not by the hands of the enemy, but by random bad luck. His mind became oddly clear and calm then, even his breath seemed to come more easily. Let it be quick, then.

And then a miracle: a tiny object against that pale polar sky, growing gradually larger. A black hoop. He had seen it in its snug compartment on deck; but never thought much about it. It had always looked more ceremonial than functional, with the name of the ship embossed in gold lettering. Now, it was everything. It was life itself.

It fell a little ahead of him.

Morris behind him, the lifebelt in front. He could swim to Morris, and then try and get them both to the lifebelt. But already it was moving further away from him; there would be another wave – and soon, he could feel the tow as it gathered itself. He might have only a few seconds' opportunity to get to it.

No: he couldn't not try to save his friend. He began to try to swim towards Morris. But he was dragged back by the terrible sodden weight of his clothes, his boots. He tried to shrug himself out of them, but he was so weak, suddenly, his efforts rendered ineffectual. The cold had drained his energy, eaten it from him. Morris was reaching for him, but he seemed even further away. And suddenly he understood. He wouldn't make it. Not to Morris and then back to the lifebelt. It was one or the other.

By the time he was hauled aboard, his friend had drowned. One of the men had seen him go under. He hadn't resurfaced. And then the next wave had come, and put an end to any doubt.

He hasn't told anyone this – not the whole of it, anyway. The men told him there was nothing he could have done. He couldn't blame himself.

But he did. If he had tried a little harder, if he had been brave enough to risk everything, he might have done it.

Morris' wife, Flora. When she had asked: 'Did you see him, at the end?' Did she, somehow, know? She couldn't, could she? She was only asking in the way that a wife would, of the man who had seen her loved one's last moments. Yet all the way back from her flat, on the bus, his hands had shaken.

He finds he can't look at Stella as he speaks. He knows that she is watching him. But he doesn't want to see her face, to see a judgement there.

'Sometimes,' he says, 'I imagine that he said something to me, that he gave me permission. You know, that he understood.' He laughs, without humour. 'But he didn't. He wanted to live – he was fighting for it with everything he had left. He wanted me to save him. And I might have done it. If I had only been less of a coward.'

He covers his face with his hand. It is done now, at least, his shame laid bare. He tries to tell himself that this is something. Whatever she may think of him now, however she may despise him, he has relieved himself of the burden.

'We do what we have to,' she says, carefully, 'in the moment, to survive. It is easy in hindsight to think you might have done more, that you might have tried harder.'

From anyone else, this might sound like a mere platitude. But from her, with what he now knows of her, it is something different.

He shuts his eyes. 'There's more, though.' Might as well tell it all, now. How, after the war, he had gone to see Morris' wife Flora. She had sat and wept quietly, politely, as though she was embarrassed by her show of emotion in front of this stranger. It should have been him. He didn't have anyone relying on him to come home. Not to the same degree, anyhow. His parents – his mother, certainly – would have been devastated, but they had one another, and they had money. Looking at little Flora Eggers, in her flat that rattled with the movement of the passing trains, looking at the mismatched furniture and her cheap haircut, he had become very aware that Morris must have been everything to her and the boy, Fred, too solemn for such a small child. This was what love did to you, he thought, watching her.

He had gone back, a few months later. He had remembered some anecdotes that he wanted to share with her – Morris at his best. He had some idea that it would help. He had bought a tin of biscuits from the Woolworth's next to the station, but then, looking at them as he waited for her to answer the bell, they became inadequate. He wished then that he had had the foresight to go to Fortnum's, get her some of the really good sort.

A middle-aged woman had answered the door, and he had stepped back in surprise. Flora's mother, perhaps.

She had frowned at him, then at the biscuits. 'Sorry, dear,' she said. 'If I want to buy them, I can go and get them myself. Don't like being sold to on my doorstep.'

'Oh, no – I'm not selling.'

'What are you after then?'

'I was wondering if Flora was at home?'

'Who?'

'Mrs Eggers. Flora Eggers.'

Her demeanour had changed absolutely. 'Oh,' she had said. 'Oh, my dear . . . you haven't heard. And that poor little boy.'

She had gone out one morning, only a short walk to the track. Leapt into space.

There is a long silence.

'Hal.' She takes his hand, again with that tentativeness

strange in two who are lovers. 'Every day, since Tino died
. . . it is what I go back to in sleep – every time a little
different, but always with the same outcome. I'm too stupid,
or too slow. I think of who he might have become. He was
so bright, so interested in everything. He could have been a
scientist, or an artist. He would have done a better job of
living than I have. But,' she grasps his hand with a new
urgency, 'hearing you talk of your friend has made me wonder
something.'

'What?'

'Whether we blame ourselves because in a way it makes
things easier to understand if they have a reason, a fault,
behind them.' She looks at him. 'Do you think that could be
part of it?'

For the first time he meets her gaze, and he finds no judgement there – only a surprising tenderness.

Later, it is his turn.

'That night in Rome,' he speaks into her hair, 'why did
you ask to come back to my apartment?'

'I told you—'

'No, you didn't. All you said was that you had gone a
little mad.'

'I think I said, before, that I recently found out something
about him. When I met him, I thought he was an
International Brigadier, a man who had come to fight out
of his sense of duty. They were everywhere in Madrid, at
the time: every nationality, men who had come to stand
up against Fascism. He let me believe it. I found out the
truth a year ago, in Rome.'

*

Her

1950

It starts one day when my husband is away. He has business in Italy, now. The war, he tells me, has left it 'wide open' for investment.

I am in New York, at home in the apartment. There is a call from the concierge.

'Excuse me, Mrs Truss? There's a man here who has asked to speak to you. I think he's from the press.'

I have been approached before by women's magazines: will I speak to them about my decorative style, my wardrobe choices? My husband doesn't want me to talk to them, though – he thinks it 'tawdry'.

'Please,' I say, 'tell them I'm not interested.'

'All right, ma'am. That's what I said to him before – though he's persistent. He says he has something he wants *you* to hear, not the other way around.'

'Oh.' This is new. And for some reason, I feel a small trepidation. It is like catching the trace of something rotten on the breeze. 'No,' I say, feeling more sure than ever now, 'I don't want to talk to him.'

By the afternoon the apartment, despite its size, has become oppressive. I will go for a walk in the park, I decide. In the green surrounds I move quickly, not processing my surroundings, but pleased to be doing something that may take my mind off the thing that is troubling me. It is the idea of what the man wants to tell me. It looms large in my imagination. Perhaps, after all, I should hear him out. Knowing might be better than not.

But I am afraid. Of what? Nothing. Everything.

After my walk I go to a little café that I have discovered. It is one of my secrets. I suppose it sounds ridiculous: to have a secret as benign as a place serving coffee and cake. I know he would not like the thought of me coming here. The crockery is a little worn, and not of the best sort; the cakes are served in large, inelegant slabs. They serve doughnuts, too, fat hoops crusted with thick rinds of sugar. It is all, in short, not in the best taste.

I order my doughnut and eat it quickly, furtively, licking the sugar from my fingers. I reach for the book I have brought with me, open it to read, begin to relax.

'Excuse me, Mrs Truss?'

I look up, and know that it is him, the man who came for me at the apartment. He must have been following me. For how long? Did he wait for me until I left the building, tail me in the park?

'It's about your husband,' he says, in a rush. He is quite young, I realize, and he doesn't look unkind. But that doesn't mean anything.

'Please,' I say, 'leave me alone.' I stand, and try to get past him. He doesn't move at first so I have to push my way out.

'Please, Mrs Truss. I want you to hear it from me first. It's about your husband,' he repeats. 'What he was doing in Spain.'

When I hear that, I begin to run. I know that whatever it is, I don't want to hear it.

When my husband returns, I tell him about it. 'A man tried to speak to me, twice. He said it was about you.'

'Oh?'

'About Spain.'

'He came after you?'

'Yes. He followed me in . . . in the park.'

His face is frightening, though I know his anger is on my behalf. 'Did you find out where he worked? What newspaper?'

'No— I just tried to get away from him.'

This is the last time we speak of it. A few days later, my husband asks if I want to go with him this time, back to Italy.

'Why do you need to go back so soon?'

'Everything is being set up – it's a delicate time. But I thought it would be pleasant to get away together, anyway. We can go to Rome.'

'I haven't been to Europe since I left.'

'Even more of a reason, then. It's time you did.'

We spend two days together in Rome, being driven around the city's sights by a chauffeur: the Pantheon, the Colosseum. The roads are frenetic, screeching chaos, and it feels sometimes that we are being assaulted on all sides by traffic. Our driver swears, gesticulates. I feel queasy in the back seat, seeing the city slide by behind glass. I suggest to my husband that perhaps we might walk for a day instead, but he tells me that it is a dirty place – I would ruin my shoes – and full of pickpockets and worse.

On the third day, in the Bulgari showroom, he has the shop girl fasten various necklaces around my neck. The one he chooses for me – emerald – is beautiful. It is also the heaviest, and I have to make an effort to keep my head lifted.

'You know what people will understand,' he says, 'when they see you wearing this?'

'What?'

'They will know you are loved.'

'Thank you.'

We are invited to drinks at the American ambassador's house. My husband suggests that I might wear my new necklace.

I dread the thought of having its weight about my neck for the whole evening. 'Oh,' I say, 'I wanted to save that for something truly special.'

'I'd like to see you wearing it. You don't like it? It was the best piece in the shop.'

'I love it.'

He smiles. 'Then wear it. For me.'

I expected the drinks to be a turgid affair. Tired from the change in time zones, I have been dreading it. But I meet an interesting woman there.

'I've been admiring your emeralds,' she says, when we are introduced.

'Thank you.'

'Though, I couldn't help wondering – are they a pain to wear?'

'It's not so bad.'

She nods, smiles. She introduces herself: she is Italian, quite elderly. An air of energy, of slight eccentricity.

She begins to tell me about her new project: a small film studio that she had saved from bankruptcy. 'We are looking to produce the first picture,' she says. 'But we need funding for it.'

The director she has attached to it is a good friend. I ask her his name.

'Giacomo Gaspari.'

'I saw his film, *Elegy*.' There is a European picture house

I go to sometimes, to pass the slow hours in the middle of the day. 'I loved it.' I did. What I don't mention is that I had to leave halfway, because the bombed city had suddenly become Madrid, and the grief had become my own.

My husband approaches, introductions are made. I mention the Contessa's film, and excuse myself to the powder room. I know that the idea will appeal to him: it will be an opportunity to display his good taste on a larger scale.

The next morning, at breakfast, he tells me: 'I must go to Milan. But there is the Contessa's party: I thought you should go – I'm thinking of investing in her film. We can arrange a car to take you this evening. I'll be back tomorrow evening.'

For a few hours, I sit outside in the hotel garden. Beyond the walls I can hear the city: at once foreign and familiar. I try to concentrate on the plot of the novel and then, when that fails, on the images in my magazine. But somehow the city begins to seep in about me. I keep thinking of the little cafés, full of life, that I glimpsed from the car window. There is nothing stopping me from going in search of one, I realize.

'I'm going out for an hour,' I tell the concierge – as I would tell the man at the front desk in our building in New York. He gives me an odd look, and it occurs to me that I needn't have said anything to him; that I needn't say anything to anyone at all. In the street I feel a vertiginous sense of freedom. Everything is unknown. I could go anywhere, walk the city for miles. But then I realize that I could get lost, might not be able to find my way back. I decide to stop at the first café I happen across. I order myself a coffee.

'Anything else, signora? Something to read, perhaps?'

'Yes, please.'

The man disappears and returns with my coffee and a sheaf of newspapers: *La Repubblica* and, surprisingly, the *New York Times*.

'A few days old,' he says, apologetically.

'Thank you.' I begin to leaf through it, mindlessly. I am more interested in observing the crowd around me. There is a mother with her fat toddler; a young couple who seem fused together, oblivious to anything else. A couple of dark-haired men drinking espressos; one of whom is intent on a trio of beautiful girls. The pages pass through my hands largely unread. Until I see something. My name is there: incongruous in that foreign, sunlit square.

Mrs Stella Truss was unavailable for comment . . .

I want to put the paper down; I want to run back to the hotel. But this thing I have seen cannot be unseen. I force myself to read the rest.

Originally, like a number of other profiteers, Mr Truss had been helping to arrange the supply of armaments to the Fascist rebels in Spain. Then, when Germany and Italy pledged their support and effectively put them out of business, many of these men switched sides, taking advantage of the non-interventionist policies of Britain and France. The Republican government, desperate, were plundering the coffers of the Bank of Spain; prepared to pay well over the odds for ancient – and often faulty – weaponry.

The journalist explained that he been contacted by an anonymous source who had known of my husband in Spain.

Some of those providing arms to the Republican army did so for ideological reasons – or they claim they did. But Frank Truss: he was out, pure and simple, to make a quick buck.

The war that had killed my brother and father had made him rich. The worst part? I had suspected. Or, rather, I had known that there were aspects that hadn't fitted. The immaculate suits, the lack of a uniform, the way he was able to get hold of anything he needed – anything at all – in the midst of a war-torn city. The simple fact that he avoided any specific detail about where he had been fighting. And then there had been that drunkard at the party, with his questions and his scorn. The man I have married is a liar; but so am I: perhaps a worse one than he, because I have managed to deceive myself.

Back in the hotel, I sit on the bed, a suitcase half-packed beside me. What will I do? Where will I go? I have no money, no roots anywhere. I'm not sure I even know how to survive on my own any longer.

The telephone rings. For a moment I think it might be him, that he has somehow found out about my discovery. I lift the receiver.

'Signora,' the man says, 'I am calling to tell you that your car is waiting.'

The party, which I have forgotten all about. Somehow, it is already evening. I will go. Away from here there may be space to think, to decide what I will do. I dress like one in a dream, travel through the twilight city in the same stupor.

The Contessa tries, admirably, to draw me into conversation with my fellow guests, but I find myself unable to follow the thread of any conversation. I drift through the crowd, avoiding the gaze of others, avoiding the attempts made by other guests to speak to me. At the end of the room is an open doorway, and I find myself drawn towards it, out into the night.

A roof garden, above the city. To my relief it seems I am the only one to have found it. Finally, here is space and relative quiet.

I have two options, as far as I can tell. I can remain or I can run away.

But then, looking out across the black void that is the city, another way presents itself. The idea has its own strange appeal. I take a cigarette from my bag. I will smoke it for courage. Though I wouldn't need nearly as much courage to do that as I would if I am to run. I will finish it, and then I will decide.

Before I can find my matches, I hear movement on the metal ladder. I watch a man emerge, look about himself. I can see him because of the way the moonlight catches him – though I am certain he can't see me. I know instantly that he isn't one of them. The other guests are all people like my husband; but he lacks that same patina of wealth – the ease of it.

He has come so near to me now that I have to say something, or risk him stumble across me.

'Hello,' I say.

I see him start, turn to face me. It is the first time I have had a proper look at his face. And something in his expression catches at me. There is something in it that I recognize, something that makes me realize I don't want to choose oblivion; not quite yet.

*

I wake before dawn the next morning.

He is here next to me, the stranger, his arm thrown behind his head. The underside of his arm is pale: blue-white, soft skin. There is a vulnerability to his face in sleep that I thought he must go to great pains to disguise in his waking hours.

Last night, I was brave, or mad, or something between the two; blown towards him by the force of my despair. I sought another kind of oblivion through him. The woman of the evening before was a completely different creature to myself now. Part of me wishes I still had her courage. I know that I am a coward again, I can feel it. I am a coward, and I will go back to my husband, because the other options available to me are too frightening in the light of day. I run from the apartment like a thief.

On our flight back to New York, I am aware of an ache in my chest, almost like grief. I suppose it is the knowledge that I really have said goodbye to her this time – that girl that I was.

She moves in his arms so she can look at his face. 'So you see, I tried to leave him, and I wasn't brave enough to do it. And when we returned to New York everything went back to how it had been. I had thought it would be hard, pretending I didn't know. It was easy. So much easier than I would have thought.'

'You should leave him. If not for how he lied, then for how he treats you, now. He diminishes you.'

A long silence. Then she says, 'I know. But I thought all of that before, and then I realized that I wouldn't know where to begin. You get used to living in a certain way. I've left it too late. Starting a new life at sixteen is one thing, but now . . .'

'You don't have any ties. You don't have any children, even.'

'No,' she says, quietly. 'I don't. But I do have a home, a life.'

'Even if those are a sham?' But he stops himself from saying more. Who is he to convince her to give these up, he who has neither?

There is a long silence. Then she says, 'I keep wondering—'

'What?'

'If the reason I feel free, now, is precisely because this' – she gestures to the bed, the room – 'isn't real life. It's make-believe. It is a fantasy.'

'Is that what you think?'

'Don't you?'

He had, at first. Right at the beginning, he had wondered if the very reason he was drawn to her was because she was beyond his reach. But he doesn't believe it any longer. He tries to put it into words. 'I think,' he says, 'actually, that this might be the one real thing that has happened to me in a long time.' For once, he is articulate. In saying it he realizes the truth of it. How, suddenly, the future is all possibility.

He turns to her. 'Do you know what I mean?'

She won't look at him. 'It's impossible, Hal. I have had . . . a wonderful couple of days.' He sees her wince a little at the triteness of it. 'But something like this, it can't last.'

'What if it did, though?'

'What do you mean?'

'I don't know.' Never has he felt so inarticulate: never has he so keenly felt the need for the right words.

She shakes her head, half-smiles. 'You and I don't know one another well enough to discover the things we will hate about each other yet. That's all it is.'

He looks at her, wonders if she can mean it. Reminds himself of all her talk of playing a part. No doubt she has become very adept indeed. Besides, she is right. They hardly know one another. It is the thing that, sometimes, is too easy to forget. Especially now that she has become the keeper of his secret, too.

The intimacy between them has disintegrated. She excuses herself, returns to her room, and all the strange magic of the last hour goes with her. But he has told her, that thing he hadn't until now even been able to put on paper. Already, it has changed him. That, at least, is real.

33

That afternoon, Hal sits with Gaspari on the stone jetty. The director has been swimming, and Hal realizes it is the first time he has seen him less than immaculately turned out. His wet hair is plastered to his head, the thin patches showing the whiteness of his pate. He looks frailer still without his clothes, the hunch of his shoulders appears more pronounced, and his skin in the sun's glare is parchment-coloured.

Hal watches as he closes his eyes against the light, and stretches himself back on his towel. 'It is always a pleasure,' he says, 'coming here. A funny thing, that being struck by lightning could turn out so well.'

Hal nods. If Gaspari knew the whole story, he thinks. In the couple of days here, everything has changed.

'It is them,' Gaspari says. He nods toward the Conte and Contessa, who are some way out, swimming strongly. From here, one might almost believe they were two youths. 'There are days when I assume it is over for me. Love, real happiness . . . I decide that these things belong to youth. I decide that it is the way of someone like me: to be alone, to be melancholy. And then I spend a few days with them, these people who found one another a little later in life, and I begin to have hope.'

'Would you choose it again, even knowing the pain it could bring?'

Gaspari nods. 'When you find something that rare, *amico*, it is seldom a matter of choice. If you find it, you must hold to it, fast.'

He goes for a walk, alone, along the sea path. All afternoon, the idea has been insinuating itself to him. Each time, he tries to stifle it. He imagines himself tramping it down under his feet with each step. And yet . . . several hours later, it is still there on the edge of thought. At supper, they sit on opposite sides of the table. Coiffed, immaculate, she is unnervingly the other version of herself once more. Until those occasions when her gaze meets his and then ricochets quickly away.

His plan to leave Rome, to leave Europe for somewhere wilder, more remote. He had assumed he would go alone. But what if they went together? If they were to do so, it would be a constructive act. They could make a new life somewhere. The thing that had stopped her, she said, had been her own cowardice, her fear of starting again on her own. This would be different.

It could be madness, to even consider sharing the sacred thing that is his plan for the future with someone who is still so nearly a stranger. It would be a gamble. The thing that he comes back to, though, is that the alternative will be to lose her, for good. When considered like this the other thing is not so significant a risk. And a risk in contrast to what? His solitary life in Rome, the unlovely apartment? The key is to convince her: she who has more to lose.

As it is, the moment is forced.

'I have had word from your husband,' the Contessa tells Stella, at supper. 'The yacht is mended, and he will travel with Roberto from Genoa.'

Hal watches Stella, and thinks: the time is now, is tonight. He would wish for longer. Everything between them is still so new. But he knows that as soon as Truss returns she will retreat until her braver self is all but suffocated.

When he is certain that the others are sleeping, he goes to her room, and knocks quietly on the door. He puts his case to her with all the certainty and composure of a lawyer. When he has finished she puts her hand to her forehead, as though she has a headache.

'Oh,' she says. 'I suddenly feel very old. Old and tired. We don't—'

'I know,' he says, 'I know. But we could get to know each other. And, if it didn't work . . . well, I would let you go.'

He watches her, thinking it through.

She looks up at him. 'Hal, he would go mad. I'm sure he would know how to find me.'

Hal can believe it, too. Truss seems the sort of man who would be ruthless in tracking down the whereabouts of something he had lost.

'We would disappear. We'd go somewhere no one could find us. That would be the whole point. We could change our names, we could become different people completely. I've heard of men in Rome who will make up a passport in any nationality or identity you like so long as you pay their fee.'

'You've thought about it.'

'Yes,' he says. 'I have. It may be that we hardly know each other. I agree, it would be a great risk. But you are the only person with whom I have shared that part of myself. And I think it's the same for you.'

She nods.

'That has to be important.'

For the first time, she appears to properly consider it. He can see the shift as she turns it over. 'Hal,' she says, 'no. It's madness.'

'Fine.' He is humiliated: she has made him look needy. He wants to tell her that it has cost him to get to this point, how he worked to convince himself, too – how he is certain of it, now. But there is no use in it: he has put his case, and she has rejected it.

He leaves the room.

Her

After he has gone, I sit for a long time on the bed, thinking. It would be an act of madness, exactly as I told him. But I wonder if he saw how I was pulled towards it, this idea of his. I am, even now. It would mean starting again, rewriting myself. The prospect excites as much as it terrifies. It is what I did in Madrid. That, though, was an act of survival. The necessary thing. But the last time I did it, I was so young. I was still a child. I had even less to lose. I had nothing, in fact – except myself.

*

Hal sleeps badly. He tries telling himself that it is for the best, that it would only have caused complications. This way will be cleaner. The problem is that the future, without her in it, appears less complete. If none of this had happened, he might have been content – or as near to it as possible.

And then he sees the door opening.

'Explain it to me again,' she says, coming towards him, 'how it would work.'

PART FOUR

34

It is the Contessa who sees her first. '*Ah, la mia barca!*'

All turn to see. And there she is: the distinctive shape of the sails, gleaming like silver in the morning light, the twin masts good as new.

She gains upon them all too quickly, growing from a speck to a toy yacht to the real thing, and Hal watches in trepidation, as one might the approach of an advancing enemy. This only increases when the yacht is close enough for him to see the figures on deck. Truss is talking to Roberto at the stern.

'Ah,' the Contessa says. 'But of course. Roberto must have picked him up in Genoa. How sensible.' Yet she does not seem overly pleased at the sight of him.

Hal glances at Stella, and finds her looking at him, her expression unreadable. Is she slipping a little away from him? Is her resolve already becoming muddied? He will have to trust her: there is nothing else. Out of sight, below the wall, he brushes his hand against hers. He feels her fingers thread through his, and grip them, briefly, before she moves them away.

A couple of hours later, sitting on the deck of the *Pygmalion* once more, with the castle lost to view, the events of the last couple of days become yet more unreal. Hal cannot help but notice that both Stella and Truss have disappeared. He tries not to pay it any attention, not to let those thoughts take root in his mind. In only a few days' time they will be alone together once more. Now they cannot risk suspicion. Naturally, for the time being, she must play her part.

They will leave when they reach France – during Cannes. Of course there are doubts. The important thing, he thinks, is that none of them are powerful enough to change his mind.

35

San Remo

A place of blowsy splendour: sea-front phalanxes of tall palms, orange trees laden with ripe fruit, the wedding-cake grandeur of the Casino and the Russian Orthodox church.

'It is a little vulgar,' the Contessa says to Hal, joining him at the bow. 'But that is the French influence, naturally.'

'Of course. God forbid the Italians are ever ostentatious on their own.'

She laughs. And then, suddenly, she grows serious. He hasn't seen her like this yet.

'What is it?' he asks.

'Be careful, Hal.'

'What do you mean?' he asks, carefully.

'I know it is easy to believe that we elderly ones see less, because our eyesight may not be as clear as it once was. Or that we feel less; that the passion is withered up in us. But we have seen more of everything, because we have lived longer. Because of it, we are perhaps better able to read certain signs. Do you understand what I'm saying?'

'I'm not sure.'

She frowns. 'Will you make me say it out loud?'

'No,' he says, too quickly, suddenly fearful. 'No, don't do that.'

'So it is true.' She smiles. 'I am pleased for you, Hal. You deserve that happiness.' She lowers her voice. 'As does she. That is why I am telling you to be careful.'

There is a moment of pure pantomime outside the Casino. Giulietta, garbed in gold shantung silk, ascends the steps like a queen. Earl Morgan acts as her escort – and there is a delicious moment when, not recognizing him, one of the waiting photographers calls for him to stand aside. Flashbulbs explode about her. The Casino's president rushes down the steps and, at a loss in the face of such a spectacle, bends at the waist in a deep bow. Giulietta acknowledges him with a regal nod.

Inside they are each presented, ceremoniously, with a bag of chips. Hal looks about him and sees, to all intents and purposes, a palace – or perhaps a temple to some ancient god. The light from the chandeliers spills upon gilt and stone, red velvet and chrome.

Truss, he sees, is not given a bag of chips. Aubrey Boyd asks him why.

'Oh,' he says, with a smile. 'I don't gamble.'

'Ah – you are afraid you'll lose?'

'I prefer to choose not to leave anything to chance. There is such a thing as making one's own luck.' He turns to Hal, and says, 'And yet I think I can see *you* as a gambling man, Mr Jacobs. Would that be a fair assessment?'

'No,' Hal says, keeping his tone light. 'On my salary it wouldn't be a wise hobby to adopt.' He is aware of the man's eyes on him. Does Truss mean something specific by it, or is it merely another attempt to diminish him? It is impossible to tell.

After a turn at the roulette table and several rounds of blackjack, Hal's chips are nearly gone. The colour and noise of the place has become oppressive to him: his head aches. Stella is nowhere to be seen. The evening, visible through a sliver of open door, calls to him. He cashes in his chips and leaves, telling Aubrey that he will meet them back at the yacht.

The air outside is velvet-soft, and he breathes it in with relief. The sky, not yet quite dark, is an odd colour, a pale but profound grey with a quality of opalescence to it. The black shapes of the palm trees are stamped against it like cut-outs. Music – the groan of a saxophone, the soft wail of a clarinet – threads its way up from the centre of the town. He follows it, as though in a trance.

In the main street, men and women cluster outside bars. Eventually he finds the source of the music. The band are set up outside one of the bars. A saxophonist, a clarinettist, a double bass. And then the singer appears. She wears midnight blue silk against her dark skin: a floor-length sheath. There is a strip of silver ribbon tied about her cropped head, and she wears it like a diadem. She is magnificent, but when she begins to sing her voice is even more so: deep and roughly beautiful. There is strength in it, and great sadness.

A woman comes toward him, a young woman, and asks him if he wishes to dance. Together they move to the music. She is shorter than Stella; and her perfume is sweet, little-girlish.

At one point she looks up at him. 'Where are you?' she says.
'Excuse me?'

'I am thinking: you're dancing with me, but you are not here. You are somewhere else.'

'Sorry.'

At the end of the piece she pushes away from him with a small, slightly wistful smile. 'It's enough, I think. I'll find a man who really wants to dance with me.'

He makes his way toward the bar. And something catches his eye: a sheen of gold. Stella. She sits at one of the pavement tables with a man, right in the middle of the listening crowd.

He cranes forward and sees to his relief that her companion is Gaspari. He makes his way to them through the throng. Gaspari glances up and, seeing Hal, smiles and raises his glass in a toast. Stella turns and looks at him and smiles cautiously, politely.

He takes a seat from the next table along and joins them.

'You too were bored of the casino?' Gaspari asks.

'I lost all my chips,' Hal admits. 'And it wasn't my idea of fun.'

Gaspari nods, approvingly. 'Horrible places,' he says. 'Full of falseness and gaudiness. This is real life, here.' He gestures to the crowd, the music. 'I asked Mrs Truss if she would escape with me.'

They listen for several moments in silence as the voice floods over them, almost terrible in its beauty.

'It feels like something more than real life to me,' says Hal, thinking what the phrase means for him: long hours in the bureau, the too-small apartment, the heat and grime of summer in the city.

'What did you say?' Stella turns to him.

He coughs. 'Like something more than real life. Do you know what I mean?' It is how our new life will be, he thinks. Braver, truer.

She nods. He sees that her eyes are shining with tears.

'Mrs Truss,' Gaspari asks, 'are you OK?'

'Yes, I'm fine.' Then, after several minutes of silence, she says, 'It's the music, isn't it? It does something to you.'

'I think we should all have another drink.' Gaspari calls over one of the waiters.

The music shifts into a different key, and the singer produces a tambourine to tap against her leg as she sings. Gradually, some of the couples get up from the tables to dance.

'Mrs Truss,' Gaspari says to Stella, 'why don't you dance with Hal here?'

'Would you like to?' Hal turns to her.

She hesitates for a second. He can see her asking herself the same question: would it give away more to accept, or decline? She nods. 'All right.'

They stand, and move together, but only just. He can feel the pressure of her fingertips upon his waist and shoulder and he, likewise, holds her as though she were made of the finest, frailest porcelain that might fracture with too much handling. But he can feel the warmth of her skin beneath his palms, feel her breath upon his collarbone: all of these things that remind him irresistibly of the fact that she is not china, is anything but frail.

At one point he glances back towards the table, and finds the old man watching them, curiously. Afterwards, when they sit back down at the table and have another drink, he can feel the director's gaze moving between them. Making, perhaps, surmises . . . connections. He looks at Gaspari frankly, half-challenging him to make some comment. But Gaspari merely raises an eyebrow, and looks back down at his drink. He wears a small, secret smile.

Now a man comes and offers a hand to Stella. Hal is about to step in and prevent it, when he catches himself. She glides away with her new partner without a backward glance. It is the act, he reminds himself – all part of the act.

'She is a good dancer, Mrs Truss,' Gaspari says, watching Stella and her partner. And then he looks at Hal, 'But I said it before. I thinks she dances best of all with you.'

Hal looks at him.

'I do.'

Hal wishes that he could talk to him – share the wonder and the fear of it with this man who he feels would understand absolutely. Gaspari would keep their secret, he is certain. But they cannot take any further risks. Not until they have taken that final, all-important risk.

As they make their way back toward the yacht, leaving the centre of town for the quieter streets that lead to the marina, they see an odd triptych of figures before them, stumbling in the same direction. Cast in darkness, their appearance is sinister, but as Hal, Stella and Gaspari draw closer they reveal themselves in the weak light of a streetlamp. It is, Hal sees, Earl Morgan – supporting or perhaps supported by two women, his arms about their shoulders, his head hanging down in front. His companions have that peculiar synthetic beauty common to women of a certain trade, or at least to those that prosper from it. Tight, glittery gowns and high shoes. From an angle, if one squinted slightly, they could be film stars or fashion models. But there is a hardness to them that speaks of rougher experience.

One of the girls, hearing the approaching footfalls behind them, starts and turns about. When she sees them she gives a little exclamation. Morgan and the other girl follow her lead. Morgan blinks at them, stupidly. Then recognition dawns and he smiles widely, slurring a greeting to them. 'What are you doing here?' he asks, sounding genuinely bemused.

'We're going back to the boat.' Hal tells him, stepping forward. 'Same as you, I'm sure.'

'Oh no,' Morgan shakes his head, grins. 'No, no. I'm going to a party with my friends here. You could come if you'd like.'

'No thank you.'

'Suit yourself.' Morgan shrugs. 'But let me introduce you. This is . . .' He gestures to the first woman, stops, and giggles. 'I've forgotten.'

'Federica,' she supplies.

'And . . .' He turns to the other.

'Bianca.'

'We met in the Casino,' Morgan says earnestly. 'Lemme tell you, these ladies know a bit about baccarat.' He slings an arm around the one called Federica, who insinuates herself against him. Then the other girl makes a little pantomime of being left out, and with a laugh he wraps his other arm about her.

'Hal,' Stella says quietly, turning to him.

'Yes?'

'I think that we should try to get him back to the boat. Without any fuss.'

'Indeed,' Gaspari murmurs. 'If a photographer gets hold of this it will be a great scandal.' He looks behind them at the dark, empty street. 'Thank goodness this is not Cannes – that is one thing to be grateful for. But it won't take them long.'

'All right.' Hal walks up to the trio. The girls eye him.

'Who is he?' the one called Bianca asks. 'He is a famous actor, too?'

'I'm nobody,' he tells her, baldly. 'I'm poor.'

'Oh.' Her gaze slides away, disinterested.

'If you wouldn't mind,' Hal says to them both, 'I'd like to have a quick word with my friend here, in private.'

A lopsided grin from Morgan. And then in a childlike, wheedling tone, he says: 'But right now? We're having a good time, you see . . .'

'Please,' Hal says, with a smile. 'It's about something important. I—' he improvises. 'I need to ask your advice on something.'

'Oh.' He can see that Morgan, despite his stupefaction, is flattered by this appeal to his wisdom. 'Well, all right . . . but for a few seconds. I don't want to let these two get away.'

They aren't going anywhere, Hal thinks. And that is part of the problem.

He draws Morgan to one side. The man smells terrible: stale sweat and alcohol, very possibly sex. Hal takes an involuntary step back.

'Well,' Morgan says, impatiently, 'what is it then?'

'I'd like some advice . . .' Hal thinks, quickly. 'About . . . acting.'

'Acting?' Morgan looks bemused. 'I thought you were . . .' he appears to search through the fug of alcohol for anything he knows about Hal. 'A writer, something like that.'

'Well, yes . . . but that's only because I haven't been able to make it as an actor yet.'

'Ah.' Morgan nods sagely. 'It's hard for me, though . . .'

'Why?'

'I've always been famous – since I was a boy. Almost sixty

films.' As he speaks, Hal glances over and sees that Gaspari is talking to the two girls. There is a bit of gesturing, something that looks like an intense negotiation, and then, with a reluctant look back at their drunken date, the girls sidle away.

'Did you hear me?'

Hal turns quickly back to Morgan. 'Oh, I'm sorry – no.'

'I was saying that Crawford robbed me of the Oscar, in 1950. Everyone thinks it was some sort of fix.'

'Oh,' Hal says. And then, unable to resist. 'I didn't realize you were nominated.'

Morgan frowns. 'No – I wasn't. But that was a fix too, of course.'

'Of course,' Hal says, quickly, soothingly. Stella and Gaspari have approached, without the two girls, and he turns to them. 'Shall we go back to the yacht?'

For the first time, Morgan realizes that the girls have disappeared. 'Where have they gone?' he asks, forlornly. 'My friends?'

'Oh,' Gaspari says. 'Unfortunately they were called to another engagement.'

Morgan looks genuinely bereft. He makes such a pathetic figure that Hal feels, momentarily, rather sorry for him. 'We were going to have a good time.'

'Yes.' Gaspari nods. 'They send their regrets.'

Now Stella steps into the breach. 'Tell me, Mr Morgan. You were talking about the Oscars, I think . . . ?' She draws him a little way away, as though in confidence. Something about the earnestness of her expression – as though she were talking soberly to a guest at a dinner party – makes Hal smile.

'How did you do it?' he whispers to Gaspari.

The director looks pained. 'I'm not proud of it. I made sure it was worth their while to leave . . .'

'You paid them?'

'Yes – what they would have made from him. I think they understood it was in their best interest. That way they got their money without having to deal with a drunken American actor – or an unconscious one, or worse.'

'Ah.'

'Still, there's nothing stopping them from making some trouble if they want to – telling some grubbing journalist about it. But with no proof, it won't carry much weight. We are lucky that we are not in Rome. There, there is always a man following with a camera.'

Suddenly there is a cry behind them. Hal turns to see Morgan pawing at Stella, his great hand upon her waist while she tries to extricate herself from his grasp. It is such an unexpected sight that both he and Gaspari are frozen on the spot for several seconds.

'*Per amor di Dio . . .*' Gaspari mutters.

Without pausing to think, Hal launches himself at Morgan.

'Hal,' he hears Stella say, 'don't . . .'

In Morgan's state, all his brawn is useless, and he yields instantly to the force of Hal's shove. Hal finds himself sprawling upon the ground with Morgan's face – wearing an expression of slack-jawed surprise – beneath his own. If he had his wits about him, he would stop, now. But he finds himself pulling his arm back and catching Morgan a hard blow across the face. He is ready to go again when he realizes that he can't get his arm free, that he is being restrained.

'My friend. 'That is enough.'

He turns and sees Gaspari, gripping his forearm with both bony hands. Only when he is satisfied that Hal has calmed sufficiently does he let go.

'I think,' the director says, in an undertone, 'we will not speak of any of this again.'

'No.' And Hal understands that by this he means to encompass everything – the last part most of all. He glances across at Stella and sees her face. He has to look away. Her disappointment nearly floors him.

He wakes, and then wonders why he has done so: it is still dark. Then he realizes that there is a knocking – soft, but insistent, at his door. He opens it to find Stella standing there in the shirt she sleeps in. Instantly, he is filled with longing. He wants to gather her to him – but as he goes towards her she shakes her head.

'No, Hal. I have to go back in a few seconds. I told him I was going to get a glass of water.'

He quashes the surge of irritation and jealousy this provokes in him. A matter of days, and she will be his.

'I don't know if we should go.'

'What do you mean?'

'It may have ruined everything.' She speaks in a whisper, but there is all the force of her anger in it. 'Don't you see how it looked? Your overreaction?'

'I couldn't let him do that.'

'Oh,' she is exasperated. 'Don't be absurd. Do you think I can't protect myself from him? He is a drunken fool.'

'Stella,' he says, 'it will be fine.'

'But what if he talks about what happened? How you reacted? Frank will guess . . .'

'That I knocked him out because he was pawing at you? It doesn't exactly paint him in the best light, does it? I don't think he will be in a hurry to tell anyone. Not when he's the hero of his own story. You're worrying too much.'

'What about Gaspari?'

'Not a chance. If he has guessed, then he is on our side.'

She runs a hand through her hair. 'It could have ruined everything.'

He nods. 'All right. I'm sorry.'

'Good.' A brief smile. And then, with a quick movement, she turns her face up and kisses him. It is almost violent, and he thinks he again tastes the salt of tears on her lips. But before he can look at her properly, she pulls away.

'Goodnight, Hal.'

'Goodnight, Stella.'

36

He is sitting on deck, looking across at San Remo, the sorbet colours paled by the morning light. They set sail soon for Cannes. It will be the first time he has left Italy in several years.

In his mind he is threading the stages of their journey together. In Cannes, he will do some reconnaissance the morning before the screening, and find somewhere disreputable-looking enough to make them new documents without any risk of it getting back to the police. He'll use his old photograph, but Stella doesn't have her passport. Truss has it. It is too much of a risk to try and take it from him, and chance him noticing. Hal feels certain, though, that they will work something out. He feels certain about all of it – about the rightness of it – more than he has about anything in as long as he can remember. He feels as though he has reconnected with life. He wants to wrest things from it. Incredible to think that such a short time ago he was quite content to drift through it.

With their new documents they will board a ferry to

Tangiers. It will all happen during the screening. He won't enter the cinema at all: in the chaos, he won't be missed. Then Stella, halfway through, will excuse herself to go to the bathroom, and never return. Hal has studied a map of the city in the library room. The ferry port is within running distance: he'll be waiting with their tickets.

In making these plans, it has become real. The disaster of yesterday evening feels like something that happened in a dream. The future is before them, in all its captivating uncertainty.

'Morning.'

He turns. Earl Morgan looks terrible. The bruise is in the first, purple stage: the eye swollen, almost half-closed. In strange empathy, Hal's knuckles smart with the memory of the blow. Hal wonders if the Contessa or Gaspari have seen him yet. Their leading man looks like he has been in a bar brawl – which isn't altogether so far from the truth.

'Good morning.'

'Look, old man,' Morgan says, 'I came to say I'm sorry.'

'You're sorry?' Hal wonders if the actor was so drunk that he has forgotten how it all played out.

Morgan indicates the other seat. 'All right if I sit there?'

'Of course.'

He collapses into it. 'Here's how it is. I'm a mess, I know it.' Hal can't think of any way to refute it without sounding disingenuous, and remains silent. 'I think I got lost somewhere along the way.'

When Hal doesn't answer, he says, 'Can I tell you a story?' And then, showing a surprising level of awareness, 'It can't go in that piece you're writing, of course.'

Hal almost laughs. 'Of course,' he says. 'It won't go in.'

'The problem,' Morgan says, 'is that I'm not who people think I am.'

'Are any of us?'

'You are. You've got it together, I can tell.'

'I'm flattered,' Hal says, 'but it's not true. And besides, you're an actor. Surely it comes with the territory, pretending to be someone else?'

Morgan covers his face with his hand, and then drags it down until his features are distorted in a grotesque mask. 'But that's the thing,' he says. 'In the movies, I'm the hero. I'm running around saving the good folk, killing baddies, winning the broad.'

'Like in *POW*.' Hal remembers it well. He and Suze had gone to watch it at the Lumiere. If only it had all been like that, he had thought at the time: light and dark, good and evil. Enemies who were never vulnerable, or afraid, or simply like men also caught up in a catastrophe not of their own choosing. The enemies in the film had made no secret of their desire to kill innocents, to enact evil. They had exploded in conflagrations, fallen riddled with bullets, snarling until the end. And around him in the picture house, the audience had roared their approval: many of them schoolboys still in short trousers. In the midst of all of it had been Morgan: the affable, handsome, all-American hero. Morgan without, yet, the yellowish cast to the whites of his eyes.

Morgan groans. 'That's the worst of all.'

'What do you mean?'

'In real life, I'm a goddamned coward. All of that war hero stuff in the movie – it's a joke.'

'Ah,' Hal says. 'I was in the war. I don't think anyone was as heroic as they make out in the movies. You aren't alone.'

'But I wimped out.'

Desertion, Hal thinks. Still a word never spoken aloud. He didn't come across it much – mainly because of the practical difficulties of escaping a ship at sea. But there were tales of men never returning to base after leave: and of the retribution that could follow.

'I got out of the draft, on a medical.'

'Oh,' Hal says. 'Well, you can't blame yourself for that.'

'A false medical.'

'How?'

'The studio head. He got some quack to sign whatever he told him on the form, so long as it kept me out of service. Told me that what he paid the guy would put one of his kids through college. Blood pressure problems, that was what went on the form. Though I'd always been healthy as an ox. Sure I've got those problems now – probably a whole heap of other ones besides.

'But the studio head, he told me that I could do more good for my country by staying home and making movies. Morale. I knew it was bull. But it worked for me: I didn't want to go fight in Europe, in some other people's war, maybe get killed. So I agreed.'

'You know,' Hal says, carefully, 'there are many men who, if they'd been given that chance, would have taken it.'

'My little brother, though,' Morgan says.

'What do you mean?'

'He didn't have a studio head, or a paid-up doc. He worked our pa's old farm – would never take anything I offered him. He was shipped off to the Philippines.'

'He was . . . killed?'

Morgan shakes his head. 'Had his legs destroyed. He's a cripple now.'

'I'm so sorry.'

'You know what my ma said, when I went to visit?'

'What?'

'"It should have been you." She come up to me, and she
said, quiet and calm, "It should have been you. Never set
foot in this house again."'

'That's—'

'She was right.'

'You believe that if you'd been out there too, you would
have been able to protect him? They might have sent you
two to different continents.'

'I don't know,' Morgan says, wretchedly. 'Might have been
that we'd have been – you know – exchanged.'

'Exchanged? Fate, you mean?'

Morgan nods. 'What do you think?'

'I think,' Hal says, 'that I know a lot of men who believed
in Fate, almost above all else, and who did all they could to
appease it – and it did nothing for them. The same for God,
for luck – for any sort of superstition.

'There's something I've learned, recently,' he says. 'Something
someone told me.'

'What's that?'

'Things happen. And they happen whether or not we're
there to influence them. And we can either let them eat away
at us, and destroy us. Or we can go on living. Sometimes
that is braver.'

He watches Morgan. He can't be certain that he has got
through to the man. So difficult to tell, with someone who
makes a living through pretence. A funny thing has happened,
though. As he was saying it, he began to believe it himself.

37

Cannes

They arrive late that afternoon. Cannes itself is almost entirely obscured from view by the shoal of boats in its harbour. There are crafts of all sizes: other sailing yachts, hulking motor boats, tenders, even the odd dinghy dwarfed by the larger crafts. Hal sees the passengers of other crafts turn to look at the yacht as it passes, their speed now slowed to a crawl to navigate the throng. It remains, despite the array of competition, still the most beautiful of all. As they draw nearer to the shore he can make out a phalanx of beach umbrellas along the Croisette, and the vast, shifting crowds of people who mill among them. It is a heartening sight. Among such chaos one might easily disappear.

He retreats below deck. Passing through the bar he stumbles upon Aubrey, smoking furiously on a cigarette.

'They're still there?' he asks Hal, squinting up at him. 'The idiot photographers?'

'Yes – I'm afraid there are more, in fact. Another boat arrived as I was coming down here.'

'Oh for goodness' sake. I mean . . . how ridiculous. I had to remove myself – they make me too angry to look at.' Then he looks up at Hal, a little slyly.

'Tell me – what happened last night, exactly?'

'Oh,' says Hal, evasive. 'Morgan got himself in some trouble.'

'There will be some talk at the Contessa's party,' Aubrey says. 'Personally, I think it is an improvement.'

Hal spends the next hour in his cabin, typing up the remainder of his article from his various notes. It is a much more pedestrian affair than he might have wished to write, but according to the brief, it is perfect. It has the qualities the readers will be looking for: the pseudo-salacious detail, the whiff of glamour, of larger-than-life personality. He will wire it across to the editor at *Tempo* when he goes ashore. When he thinks of what he might have put into it. The real history behind the film – which he has only allowed himself to allude to in the most benign way. The darkness veiled by light.

The one good thing about this inane sort of writing is that he has been able to keep all of the secret truths, told to him in confidence, out of the piece. He has written much, yet told little. It is a skill, in its own way.

Afterwards he begins to write a letter to his parents – an attempt to explain everything. It is one thing his living abroad in Rome, never coming to visit. It is another thing to disappear entirely.

Please don't let on to anyone that you've got this. I've had to go away for a while . . .

He stops. He can't send it, he knows. But the act of writing his thoughts down is cathartic in itself. He writes things that he would never dream of sharing with his parents: of his feelings for Stella, of how they have changed him. It is an altogether more eloquent piece than the one he has written for the *Tiber*.

There is a knock on his cabin door. He balls the letter and shoves it into his suitcase.

'Come in?'

It is Aubrey Boyd, dressed, Hal sees, in white tie – and yet somehow looking almost exactly the same as he does in his 'casual' uniform of linen trousers and shirt.

'I thought I'd come and give you a heads up, old chap. Things are starting soon, so you might want to get dressed into—' he gestures worriedly at Hal's crumpled outfit, 'something else.'

Hal sits up. 'I'll wear my suit.'

Aubrey looks pained. 'Is it the one you wore last night? At the Casino?'

'Yes, why?'

'Look – I don't want to offend, but there might be something else I could lend you.'

So Hal finds himself dressing in Aubrey Boyd's black tie which, other than being a little too tight in the chest, fits him surprisingly well. He glances in the mirror and experiences a strange moment of dislocation. The character staring back is unfamiliar to him, like an eerily accurate impersonator.

*

There is another knock on the door. Aubrey, coming to see how the suit fits.

He opens the door. 'Thanks—'

It isn't Aubrey.

It seems to happen in a fraction of a moment – a span of time far too short for movement. And yet the second before, Truss was several feet away, framed by the doorway. Now, suddenly – unbelievably – his hands are about Hal's neck. For another distinct moment, Hal is too transfixed by shock to move. And then he begins to struggle. He tries to shout, but his windpipe is being crushed closed: the only sound he can make is a low growl; like an animal in pain. The pressure is incredible, intolerable. And Truss' face, close to his own, betrays little of the immense effort it must be costing him to exert such pressure. Hal's hands are on Truss' wrists: grasping, pulling, scratching – anything to try and tear them away. He should be the stronger of the two – he is taller, broader. Yet there is some magic to Truss' grip. He cannot break it.

His vision now is clouded with silver fish, with blooms of red. His thoughts feel confused, washing tantalizingly close, and then ebbing away. There is something that he needs to do . . . but he cannot think what it is. The pain is still terrible, but it is something remote now, almost as though it were happening to someone else.

And then, suddenly, the agony, the awareness, come screeching back in. He is on the floor on his knees, retching, clawing at his neck. The deadly pressure has gone and yet his flesh remembers the fingers, strong as iron bands, pressing into the soft tissue.

He looks up at Truss, who stands over him. He has never been bested in a fight. Truss merely had the element of surprise. If he wanted to – when he gets his breath back – he could knock him to the ground. He could kill him.

'You may have been wondering,' Truss says – and there is no strain, Hal realizes, no breathlessness, in his voice – 'if I have noticed.' He smiles. 'Well. I have noticed.'

38

His first thought is that he needs to find her. They shouldn't wait, he thinks, not now. They should go this evening. He staggers to his feet and hurries from the cabin. She is nowhere to be found below deck. He climbs up the ladder, and sees that the bow of the yacht has been transformed. A bar has been set up, and one of the crew is pouring glasses of champagne with a commendably steady hand, considering that the boat is listing slightly on its anchor. Lanterns have been lit around the perimeter of the deck, and in place of the sunbeds, right in the centre of the bow, is a grand piano.

But no sign of Stella.

He finds Roberto. 'Have you seen Mrs Truss?'

'No, Signor Jacobs,' the man says, giving Hal an odd look. 'I imagine that she and Mr Truss are getting ready for the party.' He continues to look, so curiously that Hal begins to wonder if he has something on his face.

Sitting down at the piano, a man in a tuxedo begins to

warm his vocal cords. A champagne cork is discharged. The Contessa, gold-turbaned, is issuing instructions.

Hal is beginning to be worried for Stella. He is half-tempted to go to the cabin and find her, challenge Truss outright. He would have the upper hand – he will not let himself be bested again. But that would be to blow it all wide open and jeopardize their plans. There is no saying whether Truss believes it to be a one-sided infatuation or not. He will wait for half an hour, he thinks, and then he will go down. One of the waiters brings him a glass of champagne, and he drinks it down without tasting it.

Gradually, the guests begin to arrive. They come on a fleet of boats, dressed in all their finery. Here and there appear faces so familiar that they do not look quite real – or at least less so than their celluloid or newsprint form. Giulietta, however, clad in wasp-waisted Dior, is the toast of the evening: and she leaves none present in any doubt of this fact. He watches all of this like one in a dream, waiting for the only face that is important.

Aubrey, in his element, moves through the crowd with his little portable Leica. He sidles up to Hal, gesturing to the suit. 'It fits you. I wasn't sure if it might be a bit tight.'

'Thank you.' Hal cranes over his shoulder, still looking for her.

'Not at all.' Now Aubrey is looking at him more closely. 'But my God, man, what's happened to you?'

In answer, Aubrey fishes a gold compact from his pocket. 'It's not for me. I keep it for the models, naturally, so they can touch up their lipstick before I shoot.'

Hal flips it open. In the mirror he sees that the whites of both his eyes have filled with blood.

'Oh,' he says, the first thing that comes to mind, 'some sort of infection, probably.'

Aubrey takes a marked step back, and reaches for the compact. As Hal goes to hand it to him he seems to change his mind and shakes his head. 'No,' he says, faintly, cringing away, 'I have another. You may keep that one.' And then his eyes light up. 'Oh, doesn't she look divine. You know, I'm almost converted to blonde.'

Hal turns, and sees her.

She wears a black dress that stops at mid-calf. It is a simple piece, high at the front and falling away behind. And yet against the pale gold of her skin, and with her slender arms left bare, the effect is anything but mundane. No deep décolletage and no heavy carapace of jewels for her, only the two small gems winking at her lobes, and a thin, diamond-set chain about her neck. Surrounded by famed beauties of screen and stage, she is – Hal thinks – the most exquisite.

She is unharmed. He sags with relief.

How to get her attention? He watches them across the crowd – but particularly her: listening politely to one guest, her head on one side – and then to the next, nodding in understanding. He sees that Truss has his arm about her waist. Then he sees Stella reply to something Truss has said, and, quick as a flash, Truss' hand flies back up – but this time to land on her upper arm. To the casual observer, it would be a protective gesture. But Hal can see how tightly the fingers grip. He remembers the feel of them about his neck.

He moves a little closer, aware, vaguely, of someone turning to say something to him, but absolutely fixed on his goal. Now he almost has a clear view. Now, in fact, Stella's face is turned in his direction. Her arm is still caught in Truss' grasp. He wouldn't dare do anything here, Hal thinks. So long as he keeps them both in his sights . . .

And then Truss turns, and looks straight at Hal. Hal freezes where he is. And Truss smiles, and raises his glass.

For several seconds Hal is pinioned by the look. Then he lifts his own drink, and returns the toast. Finally, to his relief, Truss looks away again. Hal takes a long gulp of his drink.

'Hello.'

He turns, and sees Gaspari, moving toward him with Nina trailing at his heels.

'What are you doing,' he asks, 'over here all by yourself? What were you looking at? I watched you come over here – you were like a hound following a scent.'

And then he looks, and sees. 'Oh,' he says.

He watches Stella for as long as he is able, waiting for his opportunity to catch her alone. The crowd mills between them, and they are frequently lost to view. He tries not to let his frustration show. To be too concerned, too watchful, would be the most unhelpful thing he could do. He goes to the bar, and orders a whisky: it will help him to relax.

'Hello.' He turns. It is her – somehow she has detached herself from Truss, who is caught in conversation on the other side, his back towards them.

'Hal,' she is peering up at him, 'what's happened to you? Your face . . .'

'Stella,' he says, urgently, 'thank God. I have to tell you something. I think we should leave tonight . . .'

'Hal,' she cuts him off. 'I've already told you. We must wait . . .'

'But he knows. He did this, to my face.'

'What?'

'He knows, Stella. That's what I'm trying to tell you. We don't have time. We have to go immediately. We could get on one of the boats back to the harbour.'

'And be seen by everyone? How long do you think that would last?' And then, before he can reply, 'No, Hal, we need to play our parts for one more night. He hasn't said anything. If anything, he's being more affectionate. I think . . .'

'What?'

'Something he said . . . I think he believes that you are infatuated with me. But he doesn't know anything more, thank God. He saw you looking at me. You have to stop, Hal. I think it would be better if you went downstairs for a while. It's too obvious.'

'I'm worried for you.'

'We can't be seen talking like this. For tonight, I'm going to stay by his side, be the dutiful wife. It's all the more important that we play our parts now.

'Here,' she thrusts one of the glasses of champagne at him. 'I brought you a drink.' She passes him the glass. 'Have that, and calm down.'

He drinks it as she walks away. It tastes bitter to him – tainted, no doubt, by his unease. Truss isn't in sight, but he sees another man step in to talk to her. He is standing too close, this man, and his hand comes up briefly to touch the bare white curve of her shoulder. The audacity of it. Hal feels rage bloom, and forces himself to swallow it, to take another sip of the drink, to look away.

Darkness falls, and the evening becomes a series of increasingly surreal and distinct experiences, strung together like the bright beads of a necklace. There is the game of skittles, played with empty champagne bottles, at the bow – with either Cary Grant or a man who might as well be his double managing a full strike on almost every go. There is the wild dancing. Giulietta and Brigitte Bardot – or possibly a girl who has styled herself as her doppelgänger – compete with one another to be the most provocative. But at the epicentre of the party, the true source of its energies, is the Contessa. She seems almost to be everywhere at once, and always where the laughter is loudest.

Hal had not meant to get drunk, but somehow he is. Or not so much drunk as very tired, as though he were trying to wade through syrup. The three glasses of champagne must have affected him more than he thought – the lack of food, perhaps. At one point he stumbles over what he thinks at first is a rope, and then realizes is a man's leg, protruding from beneath a folded piece of sailcloth. There is a stifled yelp and then the top half of the man appears. It is a rather famous English actor.

'Hello, old chap,' he says, with a drowsy smile, 'having a little nap under here. Has everyone gone?'

'No – there are still plenty of people here.'

'Oh, great. I must make sure to get another dance in.' And with that he heaves himself up and lurches away in the direction of the noise.

At midnight a group of acrobats begin to perform, to gasps of fear and delight from the guests. There are men who climb the rigging with roses in their teeth, leaping and somersaulting between the masts. There is the woman who shrugs off her gown to reveal a silver bathing suit, snaps on a pair of goggles, and executes a perfect arcing dive off the bow of the yacht, spilling a silver wake of phosphorescence as she enters the dark water.

The yacht is a chaos of noise, of sensation. Some of the guests have departed on their assigned craft with the lanterns now lit at their prows, motoring back across the water toward Cannes in a moving chain of light. But by some strange trick there appear more people on board than ever. The bathing-suited woman is now seated at the piano and is playing a nimble-fingered jazz number, her goggles pushed up on her brow. One of the crew is sweeping up the remains of the champagne-bottle skittles match.

He is no longer wading through the evening, he is floating upon the very meniscus of it, never breaking the surface. The people around him blink on and off like so many fireflies.

Every so often, he catches sight of Stella. She is the only one who seems real. Her light is different, he thinks, it burns brighter. Clearly, others see this too. He catches the glances that linger, that follow, and again, and forces himself to swallow his jealousy. It is something new, this – brought on, no doubt, by all that is at stake. It is like a kind of temporary madness. Or perhaps it is the alcohol. He tries to think clearly. When they have escaped, when everything is safe and certain, then it will be different.

When she passes by, he steps toward her.

'Come,' he says, landing a hand on her wrist. His words come thickly, as though he is trying to speak through cotton wool. 'Dance with me.'

'No,' she snatches her arm back. And then, in a whisper, so that they cannot be overheard, 'Hal, you're drunk. Go and sleep it off downstairs. Or you will make things worse for both of us.'

When he sees the fear in her expression he is chastised. He is drunk. And he knows that she is right. If Truss believes the thing to be one-sided it is for the best. They are only in danger if he makes a further connection.

He retreats below deck, understanding now that to remove himself from the scene is the only way to prevent himself from making some sort of scene. He heads for the library, takes one of the armchairs, and shuts his eyes, willing himself sober. He is sober enough to realize the irony of it. All those sleepless nights and only now, now that it is important to stay alert, is sleep trying to claim him.

39

'Hal. Hal, wake up. Wake up, Hal.'

His eyes feel glued shut. He has to force them open. He is not in his cabin, he realizes, blinking around himself at his unfamiliar surroundings. He is in the library, still in the armchair. His back aches and his mind is a hot blur of pain. He must have drunk far more than he had meant to. The English actor is curled in the chair like a sleeping babe, an empty tumbler clutched against his chest.

Then Hal becomes aware of someone saying his name.

Gaspari stands before him, looking small and tired and much older, somehow. Hal can see immediately that something is the matter. He is about to ask, but Gaspari speaks first.

'Have you seen Mrs Truss? Stella?'

His instinctive reaction is guilty, defensive. 'No. Why should I have?'

Gaspari makes a helpless motion with his hands. 'No one has.'

Through the fuzz in Hal's brain comes the same, insistent message. Something is wrong.

'What do you mean,' he says, carefully, 'no one has?'

'She isn't on the boat.'

He sits up, suddenly charged with awareness. He looks down at himself, and realizes that he is still wearing Aubrey Boyd's tuxedo. But there isn't time to change, he decides. He must find Stella.

'What time is it?'

'Five. It is getting light.'

'But . . . where else could she be?'

'They thought, perhaps . . . they wondered if she might have taken one of the boats back to the shore. But no one saw her leave. The crew were manning them, and they would have recognized her. But she is not on the boat.' He coughs.

'I don't understand,' Hal says. He realizes that he is looking at Gaspari as though expecting him to provide a solution.

'None of us do,' Gaspari says. 'The police are here now, talking to Truss.'

'The police? Why the police?'

'They think,' Gaspari covers his face, muffling his voice, 'they think she went in the water.'

'Went swimming?' Hal thinks of the acrobat woman in the silver bathing costume, diving a perfect arc into the inky water; a falling star.

'No,' Gaspari says. 'Not that.'

The next few hours pass in a kind of shifting fog. In a Cannes police station Hal is interviewed by the sole police officer who speaks any English, who receives his questions from his superior, so that there is a strange time lag for every one, even the shortest and most banal of enquiries.

'What was the last time you saw Mrs Truss?' the man asks.

'Last night.'

'When would that have been?'

'Ah—' Hal thinks, hard. It is important to be certain, he realizes, it will aid the men in their work. But his thoughts are clouded by fear. In his gut is a rising nausea. 'About nine o'clock, I think.'

'Was she alone?'

'No – she was with her husband, Mr Truss.'

'Oh?'

'Yes.' Hal isn't sure he likes the man's tone.

'Because he said that he was certain he saw *you* with her, later in the evening.'

'Oh, yes. Yes, I did.' Of course – now he recalls that brief, strained conversation he had had with her – when she had pleaded with him to leave her be. How could he have forgotten? His mind doesn't seem to be working properly. Too many other thoughts are crowding in.

'When was that?'

'A little later. Perhaps – midnight. After the acrobats. Look,' he says, 'there must have been some sort of mistake. She can't simply have disappeared. What efforts are being made to find her?'

The man looks at Hal for a few seconds, as though deciding whether or not to humour him by answering. 'We have a team of divers on their way.'

'Divers?'

The man nods.

The meaning of this now forces itself on him. He had dismissed Gaspari's implication; it had been too horrible to contemplate. 'But that is presuming that she is . . .' He won't say the word, cannot entertain the possibility of it. 'She can't be . . . Is that what you think?'

'Mr Jacobs,' the man says, following a gruff prompt from his supervisor, 'I am here to ask the questions of you.' The supervisor says something, now, and he translates: 'We have been informed that you appeared to be particularly . . . shall I say, preoccupied by Mrs Truss.'

'Preoccupied?'

'That you – ah – *watched* her a great deal. Mr Truss has told us that he felt you had *inappropriate feelings* with regard to Mrs Truss – feelings that were not reciprocated. There is an implication that you had an unhealthy interest in Stella Truss. What do you say to that?'

If only they knew . . .

Hal is dimly aware that he may be in some sort of trouble. But he finds that he does not care. His only concern is to find Stella. Perhaps, he thinks, she decided she had to leave early. Perhaps Truss had threatened her – as he had that time before. She could have taken one of the boats . . .

He turns to the man. 'Are you certain that she did not leave on one of the boats?'

The man waves away his question, as though heading off an errant insect. 'We know how to do our jobs, *monsieur*.' The *monsieur* stressed, sarcastic. And then he leans forward, ready with his question. 'So. Do you have an – ah – "unhealthy interest" in Mrs Truss?'

'No.' Hal thinks . . . if he tells them the truth, might it help them in some way? Certainly, it might help to banish this pointless line of questioning. But then he would be jeopardizing all of the plans that he and Stella have made. And yet perhaps they are already – and irrevocably – jeopardized.

Hal tries to remember anything from the night before that

might be of help, but finds himself groping through a champagne-filtered fug of useless sensation and impression. Nothing solid, nothing that might absolutely be relied upon. Why did he allow himself to get so drunk? 'Look,' he sits forward. 'What makes you think that Mrs Truss has—' he stops, unable to say *drowned*, 'has come to harm?'

The two officers look toward one another, as though deciding upon something. The superior gives the other a little nod.

'There is some blood, at the back of the boat. Quite a quantity. It is being looked at by an expert now, but it looks as though there may have been some sort of struggle.'

For a moment, Hal feels as though he may vomit. He thinks of the terrible pressure of Truss' hands about his neck, the impassive expression the man had worn throughout.

'It can't be,' he whispers.

'Excuse me?' the younger officer leans closer, cupping his ear in an exaggerated gesture.

'I said . . .' Hal looks up at the men, thinking. He wouldn't *kill* her, would he? But he thinks again of that coldness, and shudders. 'Look,' he says. 'Mr Truss . . . I think he may have wanted to hurt her.' As he speaks he thinks of Truss' hand on her arm, steering her through the crowd, the visible pressure of the grip.

'There may not be much time.' Perhaps she is merely wounded, somewhere. If they can only find her . . . The men are watching him warily. He realizes that his tone is wrong, heckling. He attempts to control it. 'It is very important that you listen to me.'

Hal tells them the whole story. He knows that his only recourse now is to be honest. He tells them of the plan, of

Truss' attack of the previous evening. He pulls down his collar to show them the marks. 'This,' he says, 'is what he did to me a few hours before the party.'

They inspect his neck, with reluctant curiosity. The senior policeman says something in French. The other translates. 'My superior thinks it looks like a shaving rash,' he says, with an unmistakable smirk. 'And the redness in your eyes – that could be merely the effect of too much drink, *non?*'

Hal is thrown. He had been certain that if he were to tell them the truth, they would take him seriously.

'It is all very interesting,' the younger policeman says, after a prompt from the other. 'Your theory.'

Hal looks between them. 'You have to question him—'

The man interrupts. 'We have already spoken to Mr Truss.'

'And?'

'He has been extremely helpful. We are quite satisfied that he is in no way responsible.'

'Why?'

'He has an alibi.'

'Who?'

'We cannot reveal that.'

Hal stares at the man, trying to understand. And then he thinks he might be able to guess. He looks at the man's cheap watch, the elderly, scuffed shoes. But he cannot voice his suspicion outright: to do so would be to turn them absolutely against him.

'I think you need,' he says, carefully, 'to question him again. The last time I saw her, she was with him . . .'

'We do not feel we have any need to speak to Mr Truss again.'

'Look,' Hal says, 'I don't know what he's said to you. I don't know what he has done to . . . *persuade* you.'

He has got it wrong, he knows, the second that the words leave his mouth. The policeman's face colours ominously.

'The only thing,' the man says, slowly, dangerously, 'that will persuade me, that will convince us of anything, is *evidence*. And there is nothing to suggest that Mr Truss has anything to do with the disappearance of his wife.'

'I've shown you the evidence!' Hal realizes vaguely that he is shouting, but he is beyond trying to reason with them. He pulls the collar of his shirt down again to reveal the marks. 'I've told you that she was planning to leave – with me.'

'There is no proof of that, either,' the man says, 'only your own words.' He spreads his hands, and says, in a reasonable tone, 'Another way of seeing it, of course, would be as the work of a jealous imagination. You are lucky that you your-self have an alibi, in the form of Mr Morgan, otherwise we would be asking a different set of questions.'

Hal is standing up. 'This is ridiculous.'

'Mr Jacobs,' the man says, 'sit down.'

'No,' Hal says, 'this is absurd. I'm going to find him myself. I'm going to *make* him talk to me.' He has visions of taking Truss by the neck in retaliation: forcing the confession from him.

But the policeman is standing too. And when Hal turns, he sees that two further men have entered the room behind him.

'Mr Jacobs,' the man says, 'I'm afraid I am going to have to arrest you on suspicion of the murder of Stella Truss.'

He paces the cell. He knows the guard is watching him, and that his agitation is the reason. He is aware that the impor-tant thing is to try and stay calm: that shouting and raging won't help him get out faster; won't enable him to help her. He has to believe that he will be able to help her.

Eventually, he lies down on the hard cot, in an attempt to clear his head. Something bruises itself against his hip and he reaches into his pocket to find the journal and compass. Incredible, that they didn't take them when they had searched him. He finds himself opening the journal, as though he hopes to find some clue there.

PART FIVE

40

If he cannot have her . . . well, he will not let anyone else do so.

He comes for her in the night. The housekeeper meets him at the door, bleary-eyed. When he tells her that he has come to take the girl, she makes to protest – and stops herself. He follows her thoughts as clearly as if she had spoken them aloud. She cannot afford to forget her position.

He makes his way quickly up to Luna's chamber. She looks at him in confusion when he enters, blinking away sleep.

He tells her that he has come to take her somewhere. She is in her nightshirt, and asks if she may get dressed, but he shakes his head. 'It won't be necessary.'

He thinks he sees a faint shiver of fear pass through her at this, but then she sheds or conceals it. She climbs from the bed and walks towards him. He tries not to notice how her body is revealed by the thin fabric. She cannot have any power over him now – he cannot let his mind be turned from what he must do. She is taking her robe from her seat, and he lets her do it. It will be cold, after all. Before they pass out into the street he catches the looks that pass between her and the housekeeper. From her: entreaty. From the other woman: apology, sympathy . . . dread. He takes her arm and pulls her on, out into the waiting carriage. They move through the sleeping streets, pressed close together in the dark confines. The night outside is blue, not black. The moon is almost full, and he has planned it like this. He will need the light to guide him.

'Sire,' she says – her voice a surprise in the silence.

'Yes?'

'Where are we going?'

He doesn't answer her. He doesn't want her to become difficult.

There is silence for a little while, and then she says, 'I wanted to ask you about my dog, sire.'

He can hear her fear in her voice, hear how she is trying to keep it from quavering. He is rather impressed – for a weak creature, as all women are, she is showing a surprising fortitude. But then she is not absolutely a normal woman. If her powers are indeed as strong as he told the priest, then he may be putting himself in great danger by his actions. But no matter: he must hold firm.

She continues, 'I know that he behaved badly, sire. But that is my fault, not his – I promise to train him properly. He has been my loyal companion since I arrived, and I miss him greatly.'

She hasn't guessed, he thinks. Or perhaps she has – and is using this pretence as a way of calming herself.

The craft waiting for him in the harbour is a far smaller vessel than he is used to – but it is perfect for this: easily manoeuvred, and fast. And the wind is good: it will be behind them for most of the journey.

Only twice has he questioned this plan. The first time, when she stepped into the craft, and looked up at him, questioning. Her face then appeared so pure that he could not believe any wickedness of her. The second was when she had asked him where they were headed, and had done so with such seeming innocence that he could hardly believe his own answer to the question.

The place is a secluded bay, hidden in trees, where an ancient abbey of pale stone watches over the water. San Fruttuoso. He has decided that the proximity of such holiness will sanctify his actions. And, with the moon shining, the abbey glows with an unearthly light. He chooses to take this too as a sign that the act he is about to commit is something done with divine permission. Only when he comes to tie the rope about her legs does she begin to struggle. She makes quickly for the side of the craft – and he throws himself at her bodily, drags her back by her ankles, uses his weight to pin her down so that she cannot thrash away from him. Now he understands why she has been subdued. She was not resigned to her fate after all: she always intended to escape this way. She has already proven herself to be a strong swimmer. He cannot allow that to happen.

Now she begins to scream – a terrible, animal sound – and when he presses his palm into her mouth she bites the flesh so hard that he feels the skin break. It has become nasty, brutal: this is not how he intended. He must be quick about it. With a blow of his hand, her eyes close, her head falls back. He drags the anchor towards himself, and fastens it tight about her legs. A true man of the sea, he knows the right knot to use in any circumstance.

When it is done he looks back at the shore, suddenly convinced that he has been observed. The beach is deserted – and from that distance very little of what has occurred would be visible. And yet the windows of the abbey have become so many hollow eyes, impassively watching. He can no longer find any validation in its presence. He is struck by the sudden knowledge that he has acted alone, without any form of divine support. His whole body trembles with the horror of it. He steels himself to look down into the black water, certain that he will see her white form, far below. But there is nothing – not a ripple, not a bubble. Instead, in the moonlit surface, he sees his own face. And he looks like a man who has lost everything: his faith, his sanity, himself.

He needs to get away from this place. But he seems to have lost all sense of the way. He gropes in his cloak for his compass: his trusted companion since his first sea voyage. But something is wrong. The needle refuses to still, tracking, instead, in a continuous circle. He watches in horrified fascination until he can't bear the sight of it any longer, then tosses it to the boards. The stars, then. Any sailor knows how to navigate by the constellations. And yet when he looks heavenward, all he sees is an empty void. The moon, too, has been lost to view. What had been a clear sky has filled suddenly with clouds. The wind has stilled. But on the horizon comes a white streak, blinding in its brilliance.

He understands, now. He is nothing but a piece of jetsam, caught in the calm before the storm.

41

Essaouira, Morocco, 1955

I was only in the cell for a few hours. Several people – including Earl Morgan – could vouch for my having been seen asleep in the library during the hours under scrutiny. I think, more likely, the officers had chosen it for me as a form of punishment, for insulting their integrity.

I was released into the afternoon. The Contessa was waiting for me. She looked, suddenly, every one of her years; older. With all the energy gone from her face, her features had a wrung-out look. When she saw me she came to me, and took my arm in hers. Before I could even ask if there was any news, she shook her head.

As soon as I saw the line of the sea I broke into a run. With the Contessa's shouts in my ears and the exclamations of the crowd that straggled the shoreline, I ran down to the sand, past the beach umbrellas, shrugging off clothes. I swam straight out in a strong crawl, as though I had a specific destination in mind. At that moment, I felt that I could swim forever, for as long as it took. It was only when I reached the deeper water that I knew my own impotence, a tiny being surrounded by the vast unknowableness of the sea. I shouted her name and the breeze swallowed it almost instantly. I dived beneath the surface and saw only stinging clouds of greenish blue.

I am not stupid. I understood the futility of it. I was hours too late.

Afterward, the Contessa shepherded me into one of the cafés that thronged the Croisette, with the stares of the waiters and other customers upon us. She made me sit down, with all the care of someone looking after the frail or elderly. The irony of this was not lost on me.

'Hal,' she said, taking my hand, 'I'm so sorry.'

'Truss,' I said. 'Where is he? Have they questioned him? It's him, for God's sake.'

'Hal,' the Contessa said, gently, 'he has many people who can vouch for him from that night.'

'Whom he paid, no doubt. The police too – I'm certain of it.'

She touched my shoulder. 'They think that it was a terrible accident.'

She called the waiter over, had him pour us cups of coffee. She watched over me as I drank mine, attentive as a nursemaid. In the harbour, they were still searching. A flotilla of rescue boats trawled back and forth – a far cry from the pleasure boats of the day before. The crowd still watched, even as a fine rain began to fall, silent and solemn as mourners at a funeral.

'He drowned her.'

She looked at me sharply. 'Hal, you can't say such things. They don't think—'

'In the journal,' I fished it from my pocket. 'He drowned her, Luna, the girl in the water.'

She frowned. 'I don't understand.'

'The film is a lie.'

'Hal, you aren't making any sense.'

'Look,' I opened it, turned to the final pages, showed it to her.

She read, her brow furrowed. 'It doesn't say anything.' She passed it back to me. I read what was written there.

I need to remove her from evil influences here. I do not blame her – she is green and impressionable, and was perhaps not quite ready for Society. I am taking her away for several weeks. We will sail down the coast, back to the house in Portofino.

It finished there. 'But—'

'It is understood that there was a great storm,' the Contessa says, 'recorded only a little while after this entry. There is, too, a letter from another in the family, dated from a similar time, speaking of "our poor drowned cousin". The compass was found on the seabed, not far from San Fruttuoso. So yes, it is likely that he perished, that they both perished – but not that he drowned her. We choose to reinterpret the ending, to make it about a new life, rather than the end of one. A hope that all of us deserve.'

'I don't understand.' I began to leaf through the remaining blank pages, certain that there would be something more there. But I could find not a word – not even a mark.

'Hal,' she said then, 'I do not think you should speak of

this to anyone.' Then, when I didn't answer, she said, 'I feel some responsibility for all that has happened.'

'No,' I said. 'It's nothing to do with you.'

'It is.'

'What do you mean?'

'I saw you both, at my party in Rome. I had met her before, and saw that she was miserable. Like someone wearing a brightly painted porcelain mask. And I met you and you seemed, well, equally lost.'

I remembered Aubrey's talk of her little projects. 'And you tried – what – to bring us together?'

She shook her head. 'Nothing so crude as that. I couldn't be certain of what I had seen between you. But I thought . . . perhaps I might have the capacity to bring happiness, of the sort I have had.'

'It nearly worked,' I said.

She had suffered some sort of terrible accident. This was the conclusion that they arrived at. And the blood? It wasn't as much as they had made out, actually. It might be entirely unrelated. Or perhaps she had tried to make like the lady diver and hit her head. There was much made of the fact that she could be reckless, impulsive: that she had gone swimming off the beach at San Fruttuoso and nearly drowned.

The divers found her diamond necklace on the seabed. The clasp was broken. What force had done it? I remembered the hands about my neck.

One of the guests remembered seeing some disturbance of the water near the boat, the gleam of something. Could it have been a person? He wasn't sure. 'It could have been a fish,' he had then gone on to suggest, entirely invalidating his account, 'or one of the champagne bottles. Or . . . or I suppose that I could have imagined it completely. I had drunk a great deal by that point.'

There is a current, apparently, from near where the boat was moored – not far from the Île St Honorat – and straight out to sea. If Stella had got caught in that, she might have found herself in danger. It would also explain why they had not yet found her. A diamond necklace, if detached, would sink instantly. But a body might be carried some way by the water. But they expected to find a body in the end: that much was clear.

I knew that if Truss had her killed, he would have made sure that no one would ever find her. He would have calculated, prepared. And though I did not want to believe that she was gone, it was a better explanation than an accident of her own making. I did not recognize this 'reckless' character that they had fabricated. She was brave, and rebellious, but not reckless. And that night she was as cautious as I had seen her. The suggestions of inebriation did not convince me either. When I had spoken to her, only a few hours before she supposedly disappeared, she had been absolutely sober.

I spent a few days in Cannes, trying to persuade the police to take my suspicions seriously. But it was clear that my credibility had been damaged for them irreparably. Whether that was the disastrous interview in the station, or the work of Truss, I do not know.

I had the Contessa's cheque to live on. I didn't want to take it at first, it felt sordid, and I hadn't earned it. *Tempo* didn't want to publish the article, it felt wrong, the editor explained, after the Truss woman's death. They weren't that sort of publication.

'Please,' she had said. 'Let me do this for you, at least.

Take it for me; so that I know you can start a new life for yourself.'

I took a bus to the coast, and found a ferry terminal. Morocco, where we had planned to go together, was far enough away for a start.

I drifted through Marrakech, but found it too fractious. Eventually, I discovered Essaouira. Of all places, this liminal town, facing the broad expanse of the grey sea, best echoed my state of mind.

And something happened to me. I began to write. About her. I wrote with a kind of mad energy, as though if I could get it all out of me, I might somehow release myself from the pain. And from the dreams, too. They have not left me, though. In them I see her slipping beneath the black water. I see her struggling, and then I see her give herself over to it. I see his hands about her neck. But the worst dreams are those in which I see *my* hands about her neck; forcing her beneath the surface.

A year ago, Gaspari came to visit me. I was living hand to mouth, and I think that he was shocked by how he found me. My savings had almost petered out.

I was eking out the money by living as cheaply as I could, because I understood that when it was gone there would be no more coming. I bought stale bread. I befriended the fishermen by the quayside, and at the end of the day they would give me fish they had not sold for a sum that was nominal only. I could have sold the last things I own of value: an antique compass and a solitary emerald earring, but both held me too strongly in their thrall. I would as soon have sold my own organs as part with these reminders of that spring; of her.

I had not cut my hair for months, and I had grown a dark growth of beard. There was no decision to actively neglect my appearance. It had simply not occurred to me to pay any heed to it. It was only when I saw Gaspari's face when I met him out of the taxi, that I understood how I must have changed. When I looked in the mirror, after that, I saw a wild man. And when I led him into my rooms, I saw him take in the squalor and deprivation of the place. He said nothing. I understood that he did not want to embarrass me.

At first we talked of everything but her. I knew much of it already, from the letters the Contessa continued to send me. How Earl Morgan had renounced film to live on a farm in Oklahoma, of all things, and was very much the happier for it. That Giulietta Castiglione was much her old self: most recently seen in a café on the Via Veneto with a tame cheetah on a lead.

We talked of *The Sea Captain*. The film, not the real story – I didn't want to talk of that. The picture had been a triumph. In one of the letters the Contessa had admitted that she feared it was in part due to the scandal – it lent a spurious, tragic glamour to the whole project. I could see that it made Gaspari uneasy, and I felt for him. He deserved the success without that association.

He had brought a paper with him: a recent copy of *Le Monde*. I could not avoid news of the outside world entirely, it seemed, when it was literally brought to my doorstep. As he began to read from it, I did not listen properly at first. I was too preoccupied by noticing the changes in my friend, which I could look for now that his attention was diverted. Older, yes, greyer, but his terrible thinness was gone, his stoop less pronounced. He looked . . . cared-for.

Then I heard him say something that caught my attention.

'Say that again.'

'This is what I have come to tell you, my friend.' Gaspari cleared his throat, and repeated the sentence. '"Human remains were discovered by a honeymooning couple swimming off the Île Saint-Honorat. The remains are believed to be those of Mrs Stella Truss, who disappeared during a party on board a yacht—"' Gaspari broke off. I think he saw my face. 'I am so sorry. But I thought that it would help you to let her go.'

'Are they certain that it's her?' It could not be true, I thought. I could not let the possibility of her survival be taken from me.

'As certain as they can be,' Gaspari said. 'They do not reveal all of the details, but they say here that "they are certain of the gender, though the remains are badly decomposed—"'

'Stop,' I said, because I could not hear any more. I thought of Truss, and felt that familiar rage return. 'But this must be enough proof for them. Surely, now, they will have to bring him in.'

'Hal . . .' Gaspari says, a little desperately, 'they are saying here that the police are satisfied with their original assumption: that it was a terrible accident. Or that she took her own life—'

'She would never have killed herself.' Even as I said it I thought of the night I had met her in Rome, when she told me she had contemplated throwing herself from the rooftop. But it was different, this time. She had hope – we had had each other, we had a future.

'They say here that the circumstances of her background were tragic. That she lost her whole family in the war in Spain. She could have been depressed . . .'

'It is not true.'

'You must let it go. Hal, please, let her go. I thought that this would help you, knowing for certain that she is gone.'

It didn't help. But I wouldn't tell him that. I understood that he was trying to be kind.

Later we sat on the flat terrace above the building, with the lanterns lit, looking out over the dark sweep of sea. When the wind is up this is impossible – it is powerful enough to blow the lamps off the roof. But that evening there was only a light breeze, enough to keep us cool and quiet enough to talk over.

'This life,' Gaspari said. 'It is such a solitary one. And this place may be beautiful, but it is lonely too. Come back to Rome for a few days. You can stay with us.'

'Us?'

He smiled, and nodded.

'Who?'

'An Englishman,' he says. 'A photographer.' And then, 'He is vain, yes, and he can be disagreeable, at times. And yet he is one of the kindest men, underneath. But I think you know that.'

42

Essaouira, Morocco, 1955

Not long ago I received a strange message, from a hotel in Tangier. A guest, the telegram announced, would like to speak with me face to face. Could I travel to Tangier at once? I replied saying that I would speak with them, but they would have to come to me in Essaouira.

It wasn't possible, came the wire back. I had to come to them.

Who was this person, I asked, who needed so urgently to speak with me? They preferred not to name themselves, came the reply.

The whole situation was absurd. Essaouira to Tangier is no small journey, and the roads are bad. I knew that it would mean a day's travelling, and no inconsiderable expense. I suppose that I could have merely ignored the summons – for a summons was what it was. But curiosity had got the better of me.

There was one other mad idea. A hope, secretly cherished – but so impossible, so preposterous that I cannot even bring myself to name it here.

I had avoided Tangier. I did not want to be surrounded by expatriates and the clamour and complications they brought with them. It had sounded a frenetic place, and I had desired solitude. But it was not so different in aspect from Essaouira: the white buildings, the rough navy of the sea.

The hotel, *el Minzah*, is the best in the city, possibly in the whole of Morocco. I was shown up to the grandest of the suites, the door swept open for me by a member of staff who disappeared like smoke along the corridor.

I did not recognize the figure sitting before me at first. The linen suit was still immaculate. But the body inside was terribly changed and diminished. His face was the worst. I could hardly look at him, this simulacrum of the man he had once been.

Whenever I had imagined seeing him again it had not been like this. In my fantasies he had been strong, healthy, and I had gone at him with all the fury of an avenging spirit. It was why I had not allowed myself to try and meet with him: I had known that I might not be able to stop, that I might actually kill him. But I could see, even without having it confirmed, that he did not need my assistance in that regard.

'Hello,' he said, and his voice too was a broken thing.

Even now, I felt that he had the upper hand. My shock on seeing him like this had unnerved me, thrown me onto the back foot. I tried to remember what it was I had decided I would say to him at this point.

'Have you decided to confess?' I asked him.

He smiled at me, and his face was a grinning skull. The

charm of that smile was all gone. 'Why,' he asked, 'because I'm dying?'

Before I could decide how to answer him he said, 'I am, of course. Well on the way.' I saw the brief tremor of it then, the fear that his manner had attempted to conceal. 'I was ill then, too – though it was the early stages. The business trips I made to Milan, if you remember . . .'

I nodded.

'I was travelling over the border, to Switzerland, to a clinic there. At that time there was still a possibility – they were trying transfusions, to get rid of the bad cells in the blood. In some cases it works. I did not want her to know. I did not want my shareholders to know, either. It was convenient if it was believed that I had business in Italy.'

'Why did you come here?'

'Oh, I haven't made a special journey for you – you need not worry about that. I have come here for treatment. Conventional medicine has had no effect – but there is a man, a Sufi. He cannot cure me, but he is able to do something for the pain.'

I wouldn't pity him. 'Do you know how far I have travelled, to get here?'

'It is why I could not come to Essaouira. They tell me I am too ill to be moved. And I thought that we still had some matters to discuss, you and I.'

'There is nothing you can say to me that I am interested in hearing,' I told him, 'unless it is your confession.'

'Well,' he said, 'then I am afraid that you have travelled all that way in vain.'

He got up from his seat unsteadily, and made a few shuffling steps towards the corner of the room. His movements were those of an elderly man, cramped and painful. I watched him, trying to decide where he was headed, wondering what could merit the difficulty of it. And then I saw the drinks cabinet set up in the corner.

'I had it sent over,' he said, seeing me look at it. 'From New York.'

Only a man like Truss, I thought, would have had his cocktail cabinet shipped overseas to a Muslim city to accompany him in his dying days.

He got to work with the lemons, the spirit and sugar. I saw that his hands as he made up the drinks were surprisingly steady, betraying only the faintest tremor. I imagine that he achieved this by some great effort of will. He brought them over to the low table between the seats. I took the chair opposite him. He sat, lifted the drink to his lips, savoured it. It was difficult not to stare at his face, at the thin grey skin, the architecture of bone sharp beneath it. I still could not believe it was the same man.

'In fact, I would like to make a confession, of sorts. But not the one that you are asking for, that you feel you deserve. I know that you will never believe me, but I am innocent of that.' His voice had changed, I realized. The authority had gone from it. 'I loved her.'

'No,' I said, remembering all that she had told me, 'you loved the idea of her. In the same way that you loved that chess piece.'

He shook his head. 'It wasn't like that,' he said.

'Tell me, then, what it was like. Because I think that you took a sixteen-year-old girl, who had lost everyone she loved, and tried to force her into your idea of the ideal woman. And when she realized this, and tried to escape, you killed her.'

'No.' He was shaking his head now, his eyes closed. 'No,

that isn't right. I married her because she was brave, and good. I thought that she could make me good.' He opened his eyes, and I was unnerved to see that he was weeping. 'I know that I failed her. But I did not kill her. I wanted to kill *you*, when I realized it.'

I have to ask it. 'How did you know?'

'I suspected it, before I left Genoa. I knew it, when I returned, and saw the two of you, how you were with one another.

'I had just learned that the treatment had failed – and there you were, looking like the future come to mock me. But I could never have hurt her.'

He paused, took another long draught of his drink. 'So, there it is. My confession. I was a weak man, a liar. But I was not a murderer.'

He died three weeks later. Strange to think that he was already on that journey the first time I met him, though death had only marked him so visibly for its own in that final phase.

He had been a bully and something approaching a criminal, but perhaps not a monster. In my mind, I had made him into one. It had been easier to imagine him thus.

And the worst part of it was that, in spite of myself, I believed him. I believed that he had not done it. Which meant that I was forced to confront the idea that she had not wanted the future we had discussed together. That she had taken her own life. If she had done so, I refused to think it might be because of him, because of his bullying. Was there some part of her that had been broken all those years ago in Spain, that had not healed?

It was not the ending that I would have written for her, had I that power.

PART SIX

43

Her

Forgive me. I know it will be difficult to understand, but I have to do this on my own. For so long I have been a weak, frightened person, incapable of independent action. You have helped me rediscover whom I was before. It is important that you know it. It is how I have found the courage to do this.

We can't do it together. Firstly, because it would be more dangerous for both of us if we did. And secondly, because from this moment on, I know I can't let myself be reliant on another person again. It wouldn't work. I know that, in the end, you would come to resent me. If we meet again, it must be as equals.

I drag myself up the wet sand. I am nearly out of the reach of the water, though it feels as though the last of my strength may finally desert me before I am able to quite crawl to safety. A curiously hard thing, this saving of oneself. And it feels as though it would be easy simply to stop, to let the waves reclaim me. That last part of the swim: I could not have foreseen the difficulty of it. Unimaginably hard. All of my preparation, the hours of swimming I have put in over the last few months, had not readied me for it. In the end only the desperate animal need to survive had forced me on. My mind, in that last stretch, had begun telling me to give in.

It is the darkest time of the night, though the city is permanently lit, and many of the boats in the harbour have kept lamps alight. Impossible to tell which is the yacht from this distance. It had been quite easy to slip away, in the end.

As the party had continued at the bow of the boat I crept to the dark stern, made my way, quickly, to the ladder.

I am certain that no one saw me. Everything was exactly as I had hoped it would be, save for one exception. As I crept to the edge I trod upon a piece of broken glass. The sound had come before the pain, and to me it had sounded catastrophically loud. I remembered the champagne-bottle skittles, the man sweeping frantically for the shards. Clearly, one had made it beyond the reach of his broom.

I used the hem of my dress to mop at where I thought my blood might have stained the wood, but it was too dark to see properly. It would have to do – there wasn't time to be too diligent about it. And no doubt I was not the first on board to have sustained such an injury from the glass – it could be anyone's blood, an inevitable remainder of the evening's chaos.

The pain from my foot came only when I entered the water, and the salt bit at it. But the cold was more painful. I had not been prepared for it, and had to fight not to cry out with shock.

*

The sun umbrellas are silent sentinels.

I am very, very cold. My teeth chatter together so violently that I think they might crack. It feels as though the chill has permeated right through to the centre of me, that I may never get warm. Perhaps the cold will kill me. There would be some terrible irony in pulling oneself free of a death by drowning only to perish on the beach.

The beach is deserted, but I hallucinate movement in the shadows. If someone saw me, they would raise the alarm and everything would be ruined. I must leave this place absolutely unseen. I half-crawl along the sand, dropping low whenever I imagine the presence of some silent watcher. I am almost delirious with cold.

I am wearing only my underwear, but I swam with my dress tied about my waist like a belt. Now, crouched behind a stack of beach loungers, I pull the sodden fabric over my head. To walk through the streets like this will at least attract less attention than if I were half-naked. In the meagre glow of the street lamps, hopefully, the black fabric will not be obviously wet. As I stumble further up the beach I find, by a stroke of luck, a pair of sandals – discarded on the sand by some careless sunbather and, a little further on, a scarf. A dampish towel – I rub myself dry with this; a man's jersey – I put this on for warmth. The scarf I tie about my hair, to conceal the colour of it. Thank goodness for the film festival, which has drawn the carefree crowds, forgetful of their belongings.

I walk through the deserted streets. The sandals are a little large and my feet slip in them, which I am sure gives me an odd, shuffling gait. My wounded foot throbs dully against the sole – but it does not bleed much now. The salt water has sealed the injury into a pale, puckered fissure.

At one point I catch sight of myself in the glass of a shop window and am surprised. I do not look the eccentric figure I had guessed I would make. I look, simply, poor. In a place like this it is the best possible disguise. The poor are invisible.

I have not seen myself like this for a long time. And for the first time, I see not a suit of armour, but myself. Or, at least, someone that I recognize.

The important thing is to move quickly, and not draw attention to myself. Luckily, there is no one about at this hour, and dawn is not yet beginning to show on the horizon. I am making for what I guess to be the outskirts of town, for the poorer neighbourhoods, where I can blend in and disappear.

I take my jewellery into the least salubrious pawnshop I can find, deciding that the proprietor of a place like this will no doubt have things to hide. I know as soon as I push at the door and find the place open that I am right. No normal business would be open at this hour.

There is a small, handmade sign advertising '*passeports – tous les pays.*'

'How much?' I ask, pointing to the sign. My French feels thick, clumsy.

'What nationality?'

This gives me pause.

'Spanish,' I say, eventually.

He gives me a sum – it is surprisingly little. I wonder if an American or English passport would be more.

'How long will it take?'

'If you use one of the photographs in here,' he says, 'one hour, at maximum.' I look into the drawer that he has opened.

In it are perhaps two hundred photographs: subjects of every conceivable nationality and age. There is something uncanny about them. Where do they come from, these blank, unsmiling faces? Where are these people now?

I think. Will he talk, this man? If he hears of the disappearance of a blonde woman, and remembers the one that came into his shop, and asked to have a passport made? If so, it is already too late – the damage has been done. But I think not. I suspect he is a man who would have as little contact as possible with the authorities.

'All right,' I say. I peer into the drawer. Together we find someone with a not dissimilar likeness. She isn't my twin, but she could at a squint be my sister. Dark hair, but that is soon to be rectified. It will do.

This is what Hal had meant to do for both of us.

When I hand him the jewellery, the man looks at me as though he is trying to decide if I have stolen it. I can only imagine what his reaction would have been if I had handed over some of the finer jewels. But I was careful to wear only the simplest and most anonymous pieces. Nothing newsworthy, nothing recognizable, unless one knew exactly what one was searching for. After I've purchased the passport, I haven't got as much left over from the sale as I'd hoped. I am fairly sure that he has short-changed me, but I am not in a position to bargain with him. Besides, the necklace, which would have fetched the most, detached itself as I swam and sunk. I had tried to grasp for it but it had been lost to the black water before I could catch it. Perhaps it is for the best. Of all the pieces it would have been the most recognizable.

In a public bathroom I dye my hair black. A transformation. I look a little ghoulish – the dark colour makes my skin pale by comparison – but I also look absolutely unlike myself, which is perfect. They will be looking for a blonde.

At the train station, I will myself invisible. As I hand over my new passport my heart beats so hard in my chest that I am sure it must be audible to the man behind the glass. But – thank God – he barely glances at it, or at me. I am so confused by this that I almost volunteer my false reasons for travelling, anyway – *visiting my cousins in Geneva* – and manage to stop myself in time.

In the reflection of the train's window I am reminded of how different I appear, with the headscarf, and my face leached of make-up, wan with exertion and cold. But it is more than that: I look changeable, unfixed, like someone in a state of metamorphosis. And for the first time, I feel a certain confidence in my plan. I am already someone other than the woman my husband will be looking for.

In the quiet of the carriage there is too much space for thought. I think of Hal, of how I have deceived him.

When I thought about that night in Rome, I had convinced myself that I had been overtaken by a brief fantasy, a sudden rebellion. I had known him for an outsider as soon as I looked at him, with his beautiful face and his worn suit, and I knew that it had to be him. But it had started then – something over which I had no control. And then something that came very close to happiness.

Could it have become love? I think so, if it had been given its proper chance. I believe it could have been there, waiting for us. Handing over that jewellery in the pawnshop – understanding as I did that it represented the renouncement of my old life with all its wealth and comfort – was surprisingly

easy. Relinquishing the possibility of that new life with him
. . . that was the wrench, the thing that sits inside me now
like grief.

But I need to be someone who can survive on her own. I
don't know exactly when I decided it had to be just me.
Certainly it helped my decision, when he struck Earl Morgan,
and I realized how reckless he might be. But I think it was
even before that, when he first suggested it. I knew how I
would do it, too. I'd use the pills I was meant to take, to
help me sleep. They would knock him out for the right period
of time, prevent him from coming under suspicion.

I tried to explain it in the note I wrote him, in the back
of his notepad. But once it was done I knew I couldn't leave
it. I couldn't risk my husband finding it, and understanding
what I had done. I ripped it out and took it with me, to
dispose of in the water.

My destination is a beautiful place – the sort of village in
which one might decide to live, even if one was not running
away. The foothills of the Alps, with the highest of the peaks
still holding that faint tracery of white, a permanent reminder
of the winter. But the air is warm, and the light peculiarly
bright. It is difficult to imagine the green swards in the valley
concealed by snow.

The first shop I come across is a patisserie, and all at once
I am ravenously hungry. Until now it has been all about the
escape: but now my stomach protests. I have not eaten for
twenty-four hours. I buy a loaf of bread, which I take around
the corner to a bench and eat like an animal, ripping into it
with my teeth. When I think of what those New York
acquaintances would think, if they could see the refined Stella
Truss now, it makes me smile. When I have taken my fill, I

go back into the patisserie, and give his name – counting on it being a small enough place that the woman will know him. She looks at me curiously as she gives her directions. This is apparently not a place used to visitors. I hope she does not remember too much of this. I keep my head bowed.

I am confused, at first, by the appearance of an elderly man at the door. My first thought is that he bears a passing resemblance, but can't be the same man. Then I realize that it is him. I can't believe how he has changed. I should have been prepared for this, I know – and yet I am not. My memory has kept him preserved in time, in the same way that it has my father. Would my father be similarly aged had he stayed alive? Impossible to imagine it.

But despite the changes in my own appearance, and the more profound changes in me, he recognizes me straight away.

'Can it be you,' he says, moving towards me, 'little Estrella?' There are tears in his eyes. 'I had assumed . . . I had thought, oh, a terrible thing—' He speaks in Spanish, and the sound of his voice, unlike everything else about him, is exactly the same.

'It is me.' I wait for Aunt Aída to appear behind him, too, but the corridor remains empty.

'Where—'

'In Madrid,' he says, quietly. 'In the house. There was nothing I could do.'

'Tino,' I say, and can't say any more – but it is enough. My uncle knew him, and loved him, and seeing the shock of it hit him now makes it all new. I loved my aunt. I have come ready with questions, with accusations, ready to lay my pain before him, but now I know that there was great pain for him, too.

He holds out his arms to me and I go toward him, this

familiar stranger. And I breathe in the coffee-and-tobacco scent that is so like my father's, and find that I am crying.

After what could be minutes or hours, he ushers me in, and as we move through the chalet I see that he has filled it with memories of Spain. On the walls are photographs, old posters advertising the toreadors. And there is a photograph . . .

I look away.

'It is my favourite photograph of us,' he says, behind me. He smiles. 'Of course, sitting next to your father always made me appear fatter and balder than ever.'

I force myself to look back at it. The two men sitting together in our garden. My father, handsomer than even my memory of him. Both broadly smiling for the camera, small cups of coffee on the table between them, the overflowing ashtray suggesting a long afternoon spent in the same spot. I can almost taste that coffee: thick and black in the Turkish style. It was my father's favourite way to drink it. I remember how he laughed at me when I tried it, and told him it tasted like boiled earth.

There are other photographs. The garden, with the orange blossom in bloom. My father must have been taking the picture, because the rest of us are all there. Tino is very young here. He isn't looking at the camera. In the corner of the frame I see the thing that has no doubt caught his attention: a furred tail, disappearing out of sight.

Of all the faces in the image, only my uncle and I are left.

He is looking, with me.

'I sent a telegram,' I say. 'I came to Madrid. We came—' I pause, try to collect myself, 'We had nowhere else to go, after Papa. The farmhouse wasn't safe, any more. And I was a child . . .'

I realize that despite my efforts to remain in control, I am crying again. *My life would have been different*, I want to say, if you had been there. I know, of course, that this is a false way to think. It was my mistake alone. But I was so young.

'Little Estrella,' he says. '*Pequeña Estrella*.' So strange to hear my name like this, with his use of it tethering the two back together somehow – me to her. 'I'm so sorry. I had just lost Aída, our house. I knew a man – a Frenchman – who could get me out, but it had to be then. I had a chance, and I took it.' He puts out his hands, palms facing up, in a gesture of contrition. 'I can admit that I was afraid. I am not a brave man. I have never pretended to be anything other than a coward.'

'So you left.'

'Not before I had tried to make contact with you and your brother. I sent a telegram myself. I had a feeling that if you had survived I would hear of you. Or you would see Gregorio's book, somehow, and know . . . and come to find me.' He looks at me, hopefully. 'And you did.'

I look at him, this elderly man who is in some ways exactly as I remember him – his short-sighted squint, the uniform of the badly buttoned cardigan with the poorly matched shirt. And yet so terribly changed, at the same time: hunched and crumpled by age, and perhaps a little by his guilt, too.

I realize that what anger I have for him is slipping from me, is being replaced by something like pity. It is a feeling almost like powerlessness, this loss. But it is also the setting down of a great burden.

If I had come here with him, I think, all those years ago . . . I can see how it would have been. He would have become a father to me. I would have been safe. And then, one day,

I would have left him to start my new life. But always with the security of knowing that I could return whenever I needed to, that I was loved. The sort of security that would, by its very existence, have allowed me my independence. I would have had a different life. But this cannot matter now. I am still young, still almost whole.

EPILOGUE

I can see her, down on the sand. She has long dark hair, which she is towelling dry. It is a very dark colour – not a natural colour, I think. There is something about her that renders me transfixed. I cannot take my eyes from her. Why?

She seems to be alone. All around her there are groups of people – fishermen, elderly women talking, some local children playing with a cat. Yet she appears to be no part of any of these tribes: no recognition passes between her and any of them. She moves through them, alone. She is like a wisp of dark smoke among them: a wraith, a wanderer from another world.

I move a little closer. For some reason – I know it is madness – there are tears pricking behind my eyes. And when I lift my hand to catch them before they spill, I understand that it is too late; my cheeks are wet where they have already fallen. I had not noticed that happening. What is happening to me? Am I, finally, falling apart?

But no, I do not feel like I am coming undone. I feel the opposite, if anything: a concentration of feeling. It is something to do with her, this slender figure before me, this smoke-woman, this ghost.

It seems as though she is making straight for me. Certainly, she is moving in my direction. I realize now that I was wrong, before. She is not smoke: she is the flame: burning so brightly that I can hardly stand to look at her. But I must look at her – she has absolute command of my attention.

Why is no one else staring? I cannot be the only one beneath her power. And yet the hubbub of the beach goes on around me, loud, oblivious.

She is so near now. For the first time I see not a flame, nor a curl of smoke, but a human being. And she is . . .

But it can't be.

She is smiling, though her eyes are watchful.

'Hello, Hal,' she says.

ACKNOWLEDGMENTS

So many people have contributed to the making of this book, and worked so tirelessly on it, that their names should, by rights, be on its cover. At least I have the opportunity to show my gratitude here. Thank you to:

Cath Summerhayes: agent extraordinaire. For being such fun to work with, and such brilliant counsel.

Dorian Karchmar, Annemarie Blumenhagen, Siobhan O'Neill, Ashley Fox, Jamie Carr: thank you for your passion, your diligence and your humour! I am so lucky to work with you all.

Kim Young: for seeing what this book could be, and for your incredible editorial investment in it.

Carina Guiterman: for taking the reins with such skill and dedication.

Jennifer Lambert: for loving this book!

The team at HarperCollins UK: Charlotte Brabbin, Ann Bissell, Sarah Benton, Heike Schüssler, Charlotte Dolan, Anne O'Brien and Rhian McKay.

The team at Little, Brown US: Zea Moscone, Reagan Arthur, Julianna Lee, Terry Adams and Jayne Yaffe Kemp.

The team at HarperCollins Canada: Kelsey Marshall and Natalie Meditsky.

David Mathieson, historian, author and Spanish Civil War expert: thank you for a phenomenally interesting tour of key sites in Madrid, and for your help with innumerable small and tricksy queries afterwards. (Readers interested in the Civil War, I urge you to visit his site: spanishsites.org, and book onto one of the tours, as well as read his book: *Front-line Madrid*.)

Gregorio Salcedo, or 'Goyo': thank you for another fascinating tour, this one to the remains of the trenches at Jarama just outside Madrid, and in blistering heat! (Goyo owns a museum in nearby Morata de Tajuña: the Mesón El Cid Museo Guerra Civil, with an incredibly rare collection of artefacts from the war, collected by Goyo himself. I highly recommend visiting. Leave at least a couple of hours free to peruse.)

Laura MacDougall and Simon Chadwick: for all your linguistic help. Thank you for your speediness, patience and fluency.

To my cheerleaders within the industry who have done so much for a new author. Special mention to: Mark Lucas, Richard Charkin, Fiona Foley Croft, Daniela Schlingmann, Chloe Healy, Holly Martin, Paddy Reed, Blair Wood, Georgina Moore, Sherise Hobbs, Clare Foss, Emily Kitchin, Anna Hogarty, Holly McCulloch, Clare Gatzen, Patricia Nichol, Sarah Tyson, Anne Williams, Julie Cohen, Emylia Hall, Katherine Webb, Erika Robuck, Miranda Beverly-Whittemore, Jennifer Chiaverini, Lucinda Riley, Mary Simses, Kerri Clarke.

To all the friends who have lent their support and gone out on a limb for me. I appreciate all you have done for me in reading my books and recommending them. Special mention must go to Vee Dix, Heather Gibbons and Toby Stevens for being the best friends a girl could ask for.

To my family (and almost-family!): Foleys, Allens, Crofts, Colleys, Osterweis, Martins.

To Liz and Pete: for your encouragement...and guerrilla marketing in the North East!

To Robbie and Kate: for all your support, and for inspiring me constantly.

To my husband: still, always, my first reader. Thank you for making life such fun!